I0747374

THE DIVINER'S SCROLL

THE LOST ANCIENTS
DRAGON'S BLOOD: BOOK FOUR

MARIE ANDREAS

OTHER BOOKS BY MARIE ANDREAS

The Lost Ancients

Book One: The Glass Gargoyle
Book Two: The Obsidian Chimera
Book Three: The Emerald Dragon
Book Four: The Sapphire Manticore
Book Five: The Golden Basilisk
Book Six: The Diamond Sphinx

The Lost Ancients: Dragon's Blood

Book One: The Seeker's Chest
Book Two: The Finder's Crown
Book Three: The Hunter's Chalice
Book Four: The Diviner's Scroll

The Asarlaí Wars Trilogy

Book One: Warrior Wench
Book Two: Victorious Dead
Book Three: Defiant Ruin

The Code of the Keeper

Book One: Traitor's Folly
Book Two: Destroyer's Curse
Book Three: Keeper's Tempest

The Adventures of Smith and Jones

A Curious Invasion
The Mayhem of Mermaids
An Intrigue of Pharaohs

Broken Veil Trilogy
Book One: The Girl with the Iron Wing
Book Two: An Uncommon Truth of Dying
Book Three: Through a Veil Darkly

Books of the Cuari Trilogy
Book One: Essence of Chaos
Book Two: Division of Chaos
Book Three: Destruction of Chaos

Magic and Sorcery Chronicles Trilogy
A Touch of Magic
A Slice of Sorcery
A Dash of Devilry

DEDICATION

In memory of a wonderful woman, great friend, and steadfast Scaper, this book is for Deborah Tindall, also known as Dabee. You are sorely missed.

Acknowledgements

FIRST AND FOREMOST, A MASSIVE faery mob sized thank you to Laura Schilling for finding, creating, and naming Direidus Salvia, she's just what the faeries need!

I want to thank my editors-beta readers: Lisa Andreas, Patti Huber, and Lynne Mayfield—excellent work keeping the faeries controlled (as much as possible)! And thank you to Ilana Schoonover for excellent proofreading. Any errors or mistakes that remain are completely mine.

Thank you to Adriatica Creation for a wonderful cover!

Thank you The Killion Group for print interior formatting!

CHAPTER ONE

———

ILOOKED AROUND THE RUINS OF the castle courtyard, sighed, and sipped my tea. We'd been hiding here for a month. Even though I knew this spot was created by magic similar to the *tir cudds,* secret pockets of magical reality, this felt more peaceful than they did.

Probably because we explored the entire grounds and no monsters were waiting to attack us. Although the place was hidden magically behind the castle wall ruins, the trees overhead soothed me. Sounds from the unseen waterfall, which aided in hiding us, helped with the calm feeling.

I loved all of my friends, but I'd found when I got up early enough, I got some much-needed alone time.

"We's halps!" As Garbage and a dozen faeries ran into the courtyard, her yell signaled the end of my peaceful reprieve.

I loved the faeries like family, but it was nice to get away from them too. The brains in our group were working on finding a cure for the spell that removed the faeries' ability to fly. Because it was contagious, something I didn't think could happen, we'd sent messages to all the other faeries, including the wilds, telling them to stay away from us.

So far, no one had nailed the spell down. Between Alric, Padraig, Mathilda, and Cwin, we had some serious magic users with us. Sadly, no solution had been found yet. I think I was more upset than the faeries were. The girls simply ran everywhere. Once in a while they brought out their war cats and puppy to race around the ruins, but mostly the animals remained in their magically enhanced tiny brown and green bag.

According to the faeries, the bag the animals were in was larger than our current accommodations. Sometimes the faeries joined them there.

"What are you going to help me with, sweetie?" I was sitting in a piece of the ruins that made a comfy seat—once I added a folded blanket to it. The faeries tended to steal the spot when possible, so I wasn't certain Garbage's offer wasn't dealing with seat acquisition.

Garbage darted over to me, with the rest of her current pack roaming around the courtyard as if everything was new.

"Is times." Hands on her hips, she gave a slow nod. "Needs for boom."

It was a good thing I'd already had two cups of strong tea—clearly, it was going to be one of those days. "Time for what boom?" I used to think that boom meant an explosion of some type, but I now knew it meant a wide variety of things. Although the faeries had been using the term less as of late, it still made me nervous when they did. I doubted that I was ever going to know precisely what 'boom' was.

I ducked down as a distinctive hum warned me that Bunky and Irving, my two construct buddies, were coming in for a landing.

And were far too close to my head.

Bunky was about the size of a well-fed black cat, round, but with a goat's head and a goat-like set of tiny legs, and improbably tiny wings.

My people, the Ancients, had created chimeras to store information and protect our people. I recently found out he'd been mine when I was young and had many memories and images of my family and me in his head. Aside from discovering I had two older brothers, Elgar and Griff, I hadn't delved into them much.

When I accidentally sent all of my people into the future, myself included, the chimeras went underground to wait until we came back.

Irving was a construct replica of a relic I'd used to create my massive, life-changing mistake: the glass gargoyle. Irving was made by Siabiane, an elf friend of mine currently trying to help sort the ongoing disasters up north in Beccia with another elf friend, Lorcan. She also made two brownie constructs, Welsy and Delsy, but they returned north with her.

Garbage whistled and the other faeries in the courtyard came running. Then the ones still sleeping in the ruins came tumbling out as well. All in all, they had about sixty faeries with them. Normally the number of faeries varied. Unfortunately, these had all been with us when the contagious non-flying spell struck.

"Boom. Is times to leaves. Things. Many *things* to dos." She flapped her wings and grinned at me. "Needs fly. BOOM!"

I looked at the faeries' hopeful faces. I was the last one to sort out how to fix them. Alric, Padraig, and Mathilda were massively powerful elven mages. Cwin was a grimarian siramage, part of a group of former monks who held enough power to make my other magic-using friends impressed.

I had magic, probably far more than I currently knew how to use. When I'd flung myself twenty-five hundred years into the future and landed near Beccia over fifteen years ago, I arrived locked into my human form with no idea who or what I was.

I also had no magic. Which changed as I regained access to it. But even with the recent addition of stored memories from Bunky, I wasn't able to do what most of my magic-flinging friends could.

"I think they're still working on it." I gave Garbage my most supportive smile, which she deflected.

Crusty ran over and climbed up to my lap. "Yous. Yup. Is yous." My little blue Crusty Bucket was usually my most confused and goofy faery. However, she had been slowly changing in the past year, and the serious look in her golden eyes as she stared at me was unnerving.

"I'm going to fix you all?" I rubbed Crusty's back between her wings—it was a favorite place for most faeries and she purred in contentment. "I don't think I can. But our friends are working on it." I hoped. The fact that even with so much brain power and magic ability, we hadn't seen anything work in almost a month was worrying. Not only did we rely on the faeries and their ability to fly and pop in and out of places while doing so, but it was something they loved.

They were holding up well, but I did wonder how long it would last.

"Yous changes. Then poofs! Fix all." Garbage also ran up to my lap and spoke with great exaggeration. And lots of arm movements which almost sent her tumbling off.

"What's going on? I didn't even notice you left our room." Alric, the tall, smart, sexy elven love of my life came out of the ruins looking out of sorts. His bright blond hair stuck up in odd clumps and his normally stunning green eyes were confused and half-open.

A definite cause for concern. He never looked this muddled unless he was in disguise. He was sleeping more than usual during the past week.

Also, something unheard of.

"I was talking with the faeries. Are you okay?" It was easy to lose track of time inside this hidey hole of ours.

The sky was our only indication of time passing and heavy trees blocked a lot of it.

"Is lates." Leaf Grub joined Crusty and Garbage on my lap and nodded solemnly.

"Is something wrong here?" I was so busy enjoying my solitude I hadn't noticed it was far later than I thought until I saw more of the sky.

"Noes."

"Yes."

"Maybes." The three words came out so close together I wasn't sure which faery said what. The faery swarm nodded in agreement to some part of it from their locations on the ground.

Alric came over, rubbing his arms as if cold. It wasn't hot, but it certainly wasn't cold. "I'm not sure. But I feel like I should go back to sleep for a few days. Where's everyone else?"

"Sleeps. Noes good." Garbage put her hands on her hips. "Goes fix. Then fix us. Need leaves now." Her lower lip stuck out and her eyes narrowed. Well, one eye narrowed and the other bugged out. It was her way of being fierce.

The faeries worked on their own schedule and their own reality. They often saw or felt things no one else did—things most of us discounted. But Alric, standing there ready to collapse, reinforced Garbage's words.

I got up and moved Alric to my spot and forced him to sit. There were plenty of places to sit in the ruins, but I wanted him secure and not likely to fall if he dozed off.

"You stay here. Girls, have some of your faeries stay and watch him. The rest come with me." I kissed Alric when he tried to argue and pushed him back into the seat. "Something is wrong, I have to check on our friends. But I need you to stay here."

"What if we've been invaded? You don't even have a weapon." He wasn't wrong; my on-again off-again elven spirit sword had been gone since we first set up camp here. Rhyfel, my tricky Robukian dagger, was still on the injured list. A fight with another of his kind, before we went into hiding, had zapped him of his ability to zap. The only consolation was that the evil elf dude who took Rhyfel's power also had a Robukian dagger, and it seemed to be in the same situation after the two met.

At least his dagger hadn't been able to crackle or shock me as the elf attacked Irving and stole the canfydd crown. The one I'd almost taken over the world wearing and that my super smart friends, and Crusty, insisted couldn't be used properly without the gems Crusty had tucked away in her tiny black bag.

Questions of why *I'd* been able to use it without them were met with shrugs—Crusty—or an explanation which hovered around my unique Ancient nature— the rest of my magic using friends. Like many things, I shoved those questionable answers into the back of my mind and ignored them.

"I have my magic and I'm more awake than you. I'm sure everyone is fine; it's not like my sword popped up." The moment the words were out of my mouth, my spirit sword, sheath, belt, and all, dropped to the ground. In theory, it only appeared when there was danger around. Alric and Padraig also had spirit swords—and were able to control them. Mine popped in when it felt like it.

Alric narrowed his bright green eyes and made his spirit sword appear. "I'm not letting you go alone."

I opened my mouth to argue, then put on my sword belt instead. I loved Alric, but sometimes arguing with him was akin to arguing with the faeries.

There was simply no way to win.

Not to mention the arrival of my sword, and the lack of appearances of our friends, did increase my concern that something was seriously wrong.

We'd enjoyed a peaceful and relaxing couple of weeks here. After all we'd been through, we needed it.

I should have known it wouldn't last.

Alric did let me lead after I gave him a few glares. He was still paler than normal and I wasn't certain a strong breeze wouldn't knock him over. Bunky and Irving stayed on guard in the courtyard along with half of the faeries.

The interior of the castle ruins was quite homey. At least once some housekeeping was completed when we first arrived. The castle fell more than a thousand years ago during a battle to end all battles, but the final group of defenders used magic to create this last refuge. It wasn't clear how long they survived here or what finally happened to them, but we hadn't found any skeletons or graves.

Padraig's room was the first we came to and he was sound asleep. Which was even more disturbing than Alric's grogginess. Padraig was an old elf, but one who had been betrayed many times in his exceedingly long life and slept like a squirrel in a nest of hungry cats.

I had to shake him almost a full minute before he blinked at me. Even then he was sluggish. His long, dark hair was so twisted that it looked like a bird's nest.

"Sees? Bads." Garbage was in full general mode now as she pointed to Padraig. If she could fly, she would be flapping her wings in my face at this point.

"What? What's happened?" Padraig's spirit sword appeared next to him, but it took another moment or two for him to wake up enough to grab it. "Damn it. We've been spelled." It wasn't a question but his anger was dimmed by a massive yawn. "Where are the others?"

"We're still finding out. You were the closest." Alric was looking a little better but I still thought he, like Padraig, would lose any fight they faced.

"This isn't good." Padraig got to his feet and tried to look alert. And mostly failed. In the past few years of traveling with him, I'd never seen him look this out of sorts.

Alric scowled. "Not at all."

"We should split up; we'll check everyone faster."

I glared at Padraig for his suggestion and used a single finger to push him back a step to his bed. "No, we shouldn't. You two can barely stand. This time the faeries and I are in charge." I let my statement bounce around in my head in panic for a bit, before shrugging it off. Then I took the lead to the next bedroom.

This was a larger room and Covey was sprawled face down across her straw-filled mattress. Covey wasn't a magic user, but as a trellian, a reptilian species with a history of violence, she had amazing hearing and reflexes.

It took both Alric and me to roll her over and she still didn't wake up.

"We's halps!" Crusty yelled as she led five faeries onto the mattress to start waking Covey up by jumping on her stomach. It worked, but Crusty and the five other faeries were smacked into the wall before Covey realized who they were. The faeries laughed and ran back to her.

"What are you doing here in the middle of the night?" Covey sat up but was moving slowly for her—which meant my normal speed.

"Middle of the day, not night. Everyone was spelled except for me, the faeries, and the constructs."

"What?" Covey leaped to her feet, then slammed into Padraig, which sent them crashing to the ground.

"Yup. Although Taryn and the faeries might have

gotten an edge of it." Alric turned to me. "How long have you been out there today?"

I shrugged then sighed. "Not long enough for how late it is. And the faeries and constructs only recently arrived."

"Let's get the rest of our crew." It said a lot about how off she was feeling when, unlike Padraig, Covey didn't try to have us break up to wake the others. She realized something was horribly wrong.

CHAPTER TWO

——

I LED THE WAY WITH GARBAGE and her troop behind me and the other three following. Cwin and Mathilda had a room near the back. Like everyone else, they were both unconscious.

Mathilda was another ancient elf and looked relaxed in sleep. Cwin was a grimarian. Her usually neat gray fur was ruffled and she seemed to be trying to cast spells as she flung her arms in the air.

Unlike the other three, they wouldn't wake up. They were our most powerful magic users, which might have magnified whatever this spell was.

"I don't want to leave them like this, but we need to check on Foxy and Grillion." Neither of them was a magic user, but as we saw with Covey, this didn't seem to be a magic user-centered issue.

"I'll go with you," Covey said, pointing to Alric and Padraig. "These two stay here and wake them up."

"We's splits." Garbage apparently approved of the plan as she separated the faeries with her into two groups, said a few words in native faery to the ones staying behind, and then marched to the doorway. "Now we's goes." She scowled and waved her hands toward the final room.

"You heard her." I shrugged at Alric and Padraig. I still didn't like the idea of splitting up, but having those two watch the unconscious magic users seemed the best option.

Especially if Foxy and Grillion were similarly unable to be awoken.

Covey and I had to jog to stay ahead of Garbage and her group. The faeries were content staying behind me before, but not anymore. They sprinted toward Foxy and Grillion's large room.

Foxy, along with Covey, was among my oldest friends in Beccia. He owned my favorite pub, the Shimmering Dewdrop, which made him like family. He was an odd mix of many races and looked like a cross between a troll, a wild boar, and a neighbor's pet dog. Right now, he was a massive lump in the middle of his bed.

Covey went to the second bed, where Alric's relic thief buddy, Grillion, was curled up in a tight ball. Unlike Foxy, the tall, thin man was twitching and whimpering.

Garbage ran after Covey and climbed onto the bed, then pointed at Grillion. "This ones dids it."

"Sweetie, Grillion isn't a magic user. I'm pretty sure there was a spell involved." Grillion was many things, it seemed, but a magic user wasn't one.

"Is. The. Problems." Garbage tightly folded her arms and gave me another shot of her fierce look. She almost closed one eye completely and bugged out the other.

I had no idea where or when she'd decided her odd squint was fierce. I also really tried not to laugh when she did it.

"Do you know why he is the problem?" Covey had changed in the last few years; she was actually trying to ask Garbage a question.

Garbage stomped onto Grillion, peered closely at his face, then nodded. "Dead ones."

I waited to see if she was going to add anything, but she didn't.

Foxy flailed about and I stepped back. He would never

hurt any of us, but his eyes weren't open. And he kept grabbing for his leg. Specifically, the vine and leaf tattoo on his lower leg.

I put my hand on the twin tattoo I had on my upper arm and tried to mentally reach Foxy's dryad wife, Amara.

"Taryn? What's wrong? I'm trying to contact Foxmorton but he's not responding." Amara was a powerful dryad—one who had been the last tree goddess until she sacrificed her status to bring Alric back to life.

She needed to remain in Beccia with her tree, but she made tattoos for Foxy and me to remain in touch. Foxy contacted her at least once a day.

"There's a spell of some kind keeping him asleep. Everyone was hit with it. We're working on getting Grillion and Foxy to wake up."

"That's not good. Walk to him and take his hand. I'm going to try something."

I shrugged and took Foxy's hand. "Okay, what—" My words ended in a scream as a jolt shot down my arms, through the hand touching Foxy, and sent me flying backward.

"Taryn!" Covey ran over and helped me to my feet.

"I think I'm okay." I shook out my still-tingling arm and went back to Foxy.

"Amara?" He sounded like himself but still hadn't opened his eyes.

"Open your eyes, Foxy." I patted his arm as Covey returned to Grillion.

"Taryn? I heard Amara." He smiled. "And she's here too. Ah, she says we've all been spelled, and need to leave here immediately."

"Tell her thank you, but we need to figure out what happened before we do anything." If it was something about this place, leaving made sense. But if it was something about one of us, we'd be taking the problem with us. I watched Covey and Grillion for a few moments. Garbage was leading her faeries to march across him, but aside from more whimpering, he wasn't responding. Even when a bunch of faeries jumped on his side.

"Amara understands but says to hurry. She can't sort out what's happened." Foxy frowned and moved away to finish speaking with her in private. Unlike the rest, once he woke up, he was fully awake. Too bad I didn't think Amara would be able to zap everyone. Nor did I think I would enjoy it if I had to be the one to help.

"This one needs wakes—noes more deads in head." Leaf had a scowl almost on the level of Garbage's and they both started hitting him in the head.

"Girls, I don't think that's going to help." I picked them up, then dropped them when Garbage looked ready to bite me.

Mathilda and Cwin came into the room. Both were now awake, but looking disgruntled and extremely annoyed. Being enormously powerful magic users meant they didn't fall prey to spells often.

"What did this? Padraig and Alric didn't have answers and went outside to see if they could find anything there." Mathilda stomped around the room as if she might see what attacked everyone if she glared hard enough.

Cwin looked annoyed as well, but calmer than she had when asleep. Maybe the massive number of years spent on the top of a mountain contemplating reality gave her calm. Or she simply wasn't awake enough yet.

She was the first grimarian I met who wasn't a homicidal hilstrike mage out to control the world. But I had a feeling that once she felt more like herself, she might join Mathilda in the pissed-off magic-user status.

"This!" Garbage stomped on Grillion's head. "This things in head. Needs outs."

Mathilda nodded to Garbage and came to Grillion's bed. Cwin narrowed her eyes and slowly walked around the perimeters of the room.

"How do you know?" Mathilda's voice was gentle now.

"Is heres." Garbage pointed to her head, and then hit Grillion's head. It wasn't a hard hit, more like a gentle touch. She watched Mathilda closely with a massive smile.

Mathilda dumped Garbage, Leaf, and Crusty with me when I first landed in Beccia all those years ago. I didn't know where I was, or who I was, and she saved me. Then she took off, leaving the three faeries with me. They were fine living with me, but they always treated her with more respect.

I was mostly over it.

"Can I see?" Mathilda held her hand over Grillion's head but it was currently covered in faeries. They stopped hitting him but were sprawled over him.

At Mathilda's words, and Garbage's shouts, they moved off. Grillion continued to twitch and curled up tighter.

Mathilda gently put both hands on his head and murmured a spell so soft that I didn't hear the specific words.

"No! They're coming! Defend the castle!" It was Grillion, but his voice was pitched far lower than normal. He also flailed his hands around as if he held a sword.

"It's okay. Release this man. Go back to sleep. Your time is done."

"Never! We fight!" Again, a variation of Grillion, but so high it sounded like a woman.

"Easy. Rest. Be at peace." Cwin came over from her walk around the room.

I wasn't the best magic user, but the power these two were demonstrating made the hair on my arms stand up.

"We…can't…" This voice was different from the other two and faded away.

The faeries all ran forward and hugged Grillion's arms and chest.

"Garbage? Are you crying?" I'd only seen her this sad once when Crusty and Leaf were missing.

She wiped her eyes. "Noes. Yes. Sads."

This was new. Foxy and Covey looked at me as the strange tableau continued but I shrugged. I had no idea what was happening, magically or normally.

Grillion slowly uncurled and opened his eyes. "Thank you. I was screaming, but no one heard me."

"I hears." Garbage beamed and marched closer to him. "Is okays nows." The tone in her voice implied saving him had been all her doing.

The smiles on Cwin's and Mathilda's faces said they weren't going to say otherwise. They also no longer appeared sleepy.

"Do I want to know what happened?" Grillion slowly sat up, looking impaired more by the current faery infestation than sleepiness.

"Probably not," Cwin said. "But as we're not completely certain, you're safe from knowing for a while." Her smile was almost believable.

Grillion paused, then nodded. "Fine by me. Has anyone set up breakfast yet? I'm starving."

"It's lunchtime now." Mathilda laughed. "I think it's Padraig's turn, but we've all had a rough start today. What say we go make a bunch of food?" Mathilda seemed cheerful, but I caught a look at her face as she turned toward the doorway. She was concerned but didn't want to share. At least not yet.

The faeries jumped to the ground and ran into the kitchen to help Padraig, along with everyone else. I continued to the courtyard where Alric glared at a tree branch crossing high over the yard.

"Did that branch threaten you?" I went to where he stood and looked up. Yup, the branch looked normal from this angle too.

"Not directly. But it wasn't there yesterday."

Bunky and Irving were flying close enough to it, but not actually approaching it, I knew Alric must have ordered them to stay back.

The branch was long, but no wider than my thumb. "It's a branch. How can you tell? And how was it a threat unless it was thick enough to fall on one of us?" Alric was naturally a suspicious guy—it came with what he used to do for his people before they came out of a thousand years of hiding. But this seemed a bit much.

"I know trees. This type wasn't here before."

Bunky warbled and I felt what he was saying. He wanted to go see it. I didn't often understand his words, but his sentiments came across to me now.

"Why not let Bunky and Irving check it out?" Constructs weren't impervious to harm, but they were extremely tough.

"I wanted to see what I sensed first." Alric shot a glare at both constructs. "And they're too willing to charge into things."

I covered my mouth to hide my laugh. Alric had slowed down on charging into things from when I'd met him, but he was definitely one to charge forward and figure it out later. Padraig said he'd been like that as a child as well. And as an adult. The idea he was finally growing out of it decades later was a bit suspicious.

Most likely he decided that being cautious pertained to others, but not him.

"Bunky? Do you promise to only go as close to the dangerous branch as Alric says is okay?" Bunky listened to Alric as much as me. But there might be some loyalty since I now recalled our time together when I was a kid.

Bunky bobbed his entire little flying goat body and sent a warm feeling of agreement.

Good enough for me. "Alric, Bunky and Irving can get a better sense of what it is with less risk. Have you been staring at it the entire time you've been out here?" I couldn't say whether the branch was there when I'd been contemplating my tea a short while ago. It looked like a normal branch from an unremarkable tree to me.

"Not the entire time. I sent a query spell at it, a subtle one which was deflected. There is something wrong about that tree." His eyes were barely slits as he refocused on the branch.

Magic worked in our hidden spot, but only inside the shield. An invisible bubble made up of magic so old that even Cwin wasn't completely sure how it worked, protected the entire section of ruins we were hiding in.

The tree branch was inside the bubble. Therefore, any magic Alric used should have worked on it.

"First we're all knocked out, and now this branch invasion?" It now seemed nefarious even to me.

Bunky and Irving gronked. Bunky was asking to be allowed to approach it. I wasn't sure what Irving said, but it seemed to echo Bunky.

Alric glared at the branch for a few more moments, then nodded to the two hovering constructs. "Okay, but fly slowly, and when I say stop, or something comes out of the branch, you stop."

Bunky gave the equivalent of a yes, and then he and Irving flew up to it. Knowing how fast both constructs normally flew, I was impressed at how slowly they went.

Then a bit of wind moved the branch. Only there wasn't any wind. Almost faster than I saw, the branch twisted like a snake and tried to grab the constructs.

CHAPTER THREE

—————

I DIDN'T THINK, I FLUNG MY strongest spell, push, at the branch and put the weight of my fear for Bunky and Irving into it.

The branch screamed as it flew away under the power of my spell. Bunky and Irving came zipping down to me as I dropped to my knees.

Alric swore and cast his spells, then swore some more and helped me to my feet. "That was a dangerous thing to do." He grabbed me in a tight hug and then held me at arm's length. "It looks as if the thing poked through the shield."

I rubbed my face. My normal spells didn't usually drop me—especially push. "And my spell probably made the tear larger." I didn't regret what I did—the spelled branch was going to crush my construct friends. "How did I know what was going to happen?" I barely said the words out loud, but that was enough for sharp elven ears to hear.

"Know what?" Alric released my arms but hadn't moved away.

"I sensed something when the branch moved toward them. The spell on the branch was going to destroy Bunky and Irving." I shook my head. "I have no idea *how* I felt it though." It was as if I just knew. Not helpful for me or anyone trying to figure me out.

Such as the love of my life currently watching me like an experiment gone wrong.

"What? I felt something and cast the spell in reflex. I honestly don't know more than that." I looked up, but if there was a crack in the shield hiding us, I didn't see it.

Bunky and Irving stayed above us. It was hard to tell on their metal faces, but both looked furious as they glared up into the sky.

"We need to tell the others." Alric spun me around and marched us toward the kitchen, then paused and looked back to Irving and Bunky. "Under no circumstances do you fly higher than you currently are. In fact, come closer to the kitchen and stay low."

Neither construct appeared happy, but they followed his orders.

Since the entire bunch of faeries was in the kitchen, there was no way things were going to be quiet in there—and they weren't.

Alric whistled to get them to shut up. He quickly told everyone about the branch, the attempted attack on Bunky and Irving, and my spell reaction.

"We've been found." Padraig was awake now and his usual immaculate self. He also made an enormous amount of food, far larger than needed for all of us and the faeries.

"I can get the rest of our food supplies packed away. Grab what you want now though." Mathilda stepped back and added the last comment as Grillion looked ready to start ripping food from her hands. She darted forward to slide a huge bowl of meat and vegetables along with a thick slab of bread in front of him. He nodded in thanks, but I swore I heard him growl as he shoveled food in.

I caught Mathilda's look of concern. There was still something wrong with him, even if whatever had been speaking through him vanished.

Unfortunately, our option of staying here if the initial problem was one of our own was lost when the branch tried to take out Bunky and Irving.

Good or bad, our time to hide here was over.

Once everyone except Grillion was finished, the faeries ran around grabbing food and stuffing it into their tiny black bags. I looked at Mathilda, but she shrugged. Less for her to pack.

The rest of us went to our rooms and packed everything. From the sounds of slightly annoyed neighs, our horses weren't happy at being rousted from their little bit of paradise. The back of the enclosed area of the ruins was a field which contained everything a horse would like. I didn't blame them for being unhappy about leaving.

"How do we know whoever was behind that branch isn't out there waiting for us? Maybe we should try to defend this place." I was whining and I knew it. But we'd been on the run for far too long and this rest wasn't long enough to recover from it.

Having assorted people and groups hunting you down to kill you, or worse, didn't make for a relaxing trip through the countryside.

"We don't. Which is one of the reasons we won't be going out the way we came in." Alric was faster than I was and had everything of his secured in his pack while I was still waving around my first shirt.

"There's only one way in or out. You and Padraig made it clear during the first few days here." Okay, they made it clear to me. After what happened in the late town of Yosi, and the woods not far from these ruins, I was a bit hysterical about this not being a safe place when we first got here.

"We found another way two weeks ago. It leads into the mountains and isn't going to be easy to cross. We set up warding spells to see if anyone passed through. In the time we've been here no person has come near it. I didn't want to worry you."

I shoved the shirt and a few more into my pack. Wrinkles were fine. I wasn't happy about the lack of information, but he'd made the right choice. I wouldn't have reacted well.

"And the horses will be okay with it?" I finished packing and looked around the room to make certain nothing had been left behind. I'd kept my belongings neat for the first week, but after that, I'd sprawled out.

"The horses will be fine. It's an actual trail. Narrow, but they've had worse." He handed me a sock I missed.

"We can ride them up though, right?" My mind went to the trip up the Devils' Path right after we'd crossed the channel between the north and south continents. It was so precarious, we had to lead the horses up, not ride them. Alric hadn't been with us—we'd been coming south to find and rescue him—but he'd heard enough about the trip to know what I was talking about.

"Yes. The faeries can ride, you can ride, we can all ride."

"We's rides!" Garbage yelled as she, Crusty, and Leaf came riding in along with a half dozen other cat-riding faeries. The faery who was allergic to cats must not have been riding with them as the puppy wasn't out.

"Sweetie, wouldn't it be easier if you rode with us on the horses?" I had a horrible vision of a narrow trail, horses, and faery-driven cats. It wasn't going to end well.

"Noes. We's rides guards. Others guards yous." Garbage shoved her war stick into the air, spun her war cat around, and led her troop outside.

Alric slipped on his cloak and laughed. "You tried. And the cats are smart enough to stay away from the horses' hooves regardless of what their faery riders say."

My look of doubt bounced off his back as he followed the faeries. We were being hunted by sentient spelled tree branches, something might have been working through Grillion to put us all to sleep permanently, and now a sneaky trail with the faeries on cats.

I wasn't looking forward to it.

Everyone was with the horses—even Bunky and Irving. Both continued to glare in the general direction of the front courtyard but remained near us. The horses were loaded and ready to go. Including the non-cat-riding faeries. Garbage must have given specific orders as they'd divided up with some on each person.

"Where's Garbage and the cats?"

"They took off. She said they'd scout ahead for us." Mathilda got on her horse and nodded to her escort faeries sitting politely on the saddle.

My assigned faeries waved hello and they placed themselves, fully armed with war sticks, although not wearing their war feathers, around my horse and settled in to protect me.

Bunky and Irving stayed at the back of our group and flew low. Again, probably under Alric's orders. Having them scout upfront might be helpful, but I agreed with caution. Whoever sent the branch after us knew about them and it would be better not to give our movement away.

Padraig led with Mathilda, then Alric, me, Covey, Grillion, Foxy, and Cwin. Strategic placement of our strongest magic users. As a siramage, Cwin balanced out the three in the front. The trail was wide at first, but steep. A glance up indicated it was going to get narrow fast. Thick trees hid the trail well. Here and there I saw flashes of color racing through the dense trees at cat height. I assumed it was Garbage and her entourage. They weren't going far off to the sides but were clearly in search mode.

I still wasn't sure how I felt about that.

"They'll be okay," Covey said from behind me.

"What? I didn't say anything."

"You saw the girls, sighed, and shook your head. Which seems like concern to me."

I turned back to her. "It is concerning. Everything about this entire trip is concerning. And not only today—since we left Beccia." I kept my voice low but the words came fast.

"True, it is. But it's for a good cause." She gave me one of her profound slow nods and went back to watching the woods around us as we ascended the mountain.

Padraig and Mathilda were speaking softly as they rode, but I couldn't hear their words. One of them was using a blocking spell of some kind. Unless I focused tightly, I wasn't sure anyone was speaking.

I mentally added the silence spell to the ever-growing list of ones I needed to have the others teach me. I'd been hoping my reconnection with my past via Bunky's stored memories might trigger my recall of more of the spells I used to know.

Sadly, so far nothing new had popped into my head. And delving too much into Bunky's storage left me feeling sad and anxious. There also hadn't been any way for me to find more information on where my two older brothers had gone after they came south to get help when the Paili attacked our people.

I was glad to not only have remembered I had two brothers but also that there was a chance they were still alive somewhere.

However, the reality of finding them was overwhelming me.

Padraig froze and held up his closed fist and I noticed the woods around us were silent. I hadn't paid much attention to the birds as we rode, but I noticed the quiet now.

I didn't see any flashes of color in the surrounding trees, but the faeries might be ahead. I noticed none of the faeries guarding us on horseback seemed concerned.

Then they all stood and raised their war sticks.

CHAPTER FOUR

THE FAERIES DIDN'T YELL THOUGH. But either the entire episode was freaking me out, or I was picking up on what caused them to raise their war sticks. I felt like someone had a crossbow aimed at my back.

My sword remained with me, so I took it out of its sheath.

The faeries on my horse all moved closer to me. Dingle Bottom and Penqow were on my thighs and poised to jump off if they needed to attack something.

"What do you sense?" I whispered to them but Alric glanced back at me. He didn't say anything. But he got off his horse, gave Padraig a nod, and vanished into the woods. It happened so quickly, that unless I wanted to yell, I couldn't find out what he was doing.

Well, I knew what he was doing—I didn't know why he felt he had to do it. From what I saw, neither did Padraig as he watched the direction Alric had disappeared with a growing frown. And a tic in his cheek.

The faeries were busy scowling at the woods around us. At first, I didn't think they were going to respond beyond raising their war sticks. Then Penqow nodded my way and scampered up to my shoulder. Faery whispering was usually closer to slightly louder than normal speech for other people. But Penqow kept her voice low as she whispered in my ear.

"Is a *bad* thing." She pulled back to show me her serious face as she nodded.

"Do we know what it is?" The horses were restless which wasn't a good sign. Mathilda got off her horse and collected the reins of Alric's horse. The elves were great at dealing with horses, and Alric often left his free, but something was spooking everyone.

"Is…baaaaad." The tiny black and white faery leaned forward and over-enunciated the last word as if doing so would answer all of my questions.

"Ah. Thanks." I turned around to Covey and shrugged.

"I should go check." Covey's fingers appeared decidedly claw-like and her shoulders seemed to be getting broader. She was slowly going berserker.

Cwin was at the end of the line, but her hearing was good. And her ability to have a whisper carry past Grillion and Foxy to reach Covey and me was equally impressive.

"No. Covey, stay where you are. Alric shouldn't have taken off. There's something foul in these woods. But I believe it is only passing through. Taryn, if you can call back the missing faeries, this would be the time."

"I can try." Getting them to respond to things they liked was hard. But pulling them from an adventure was usually impossible. What I wanted to do was reach Garbage and have her and the other cat riders find Alric and help him.

It was good to know Cwin agreed with my assessment that Alric shouldn't have taken off, but it didn't reduce my worry. The silence of the woods was getting to me.

I tried mentally calling Garbage, Leaf, and Crusty, but there was no response. "Hey Penqow, can you tell Garbage I'm in danger and they need to come back here?" I hated doing it, but the weird feeling was getting worse. If I could, I'd grab everyone and take us all back to the ruins until whatever this was passed.

"Yous noes dangered?" She tilted her head and squinted at me as if there was something she was missing.

"I might be and you can't see it." I gave her a slow nod.

She closed her eyes and squinched up her face.

"Also tell them to be silent. The danger likes noise." I didn't know if that was true, as I didn't know what was out there. But it wouldn't hurt.

She cracked open one eye, then closed it, and went back to squinching up her face.

I didn't think her attempt was doing any better than mine when Garbage and the rest of the cat riders came silently out of the woods.

Garbage scrambled off her feline steed and ran up my horse. She poked my chest. "Whats?"

"There's something dangerous coming. We need you and all of the faeries to keep us safe." I made my voice sound scared but kept it low. Telling her to stay to keep her safe wouldn't work—she knew she and the faeries were able to beat anything.

Playing on her protective side might though.

"Rides?"

"Around us only," Mathilda said. "We need you to stay close."

Garbage nodded but then saw Alric's empty horse. "Missing? Goes saves?"

"No, sweetie, he's fine." I put all the calmness about Alric being missing that I didn't feel into my face and words.

Garbage's glare softened and I almost thought she understood. She might have, as she jumped off of me and ran to her war cat.

A stillness even stronger than before filled the area. I felt like I was disturbing it by breathing. I had no clue as to what was coming, but it wasn't good. Garbage rode around the group, stationing her cat riding faeries to circle us and barking soft orders in native faery.

"Protects." Penqow was still on my shoulder and beamed proudly at Garbage's moves.

"From what?" I wanted Alric back before I got the answer to that question, but I wouldn't mind a hint.

"The bads."

That was useless.

Padraig and Mathilda got off their horses but motioned for the rest to remain in our saddles. They stayed next to each other at the front of the line and both were crackling with magical energy.

"Everyone remain where you are, yes, that includes the faeries. Cwin? Can you anchor the back?" Mathilda's voice traveled down the line.

"Yes." Cwin remained on her horse but had both hands out. Even from here, I felt the magic rolling off of her.

"What do you want us to do? Besides staying on our horses?" I felt like I should be prepping some big magical spell, but I didn't want to interfere with those three.

"Just sit as still as possible," Padraig said softly.

"And don't change. No matter what happens," Cwin's voice was also low.

I'd run into spells that either forced me to turn into my dragon form or kept me from changing into it. We still hadn't determined who or what had that ability.

"I'll try." Turning into a massive dragon against my will, while covered in faeries who couldn't fly, on a horse, in a dense forest, would be an extremely bad thing.

Those were my last words before the darkness slammed into us.

It was thicker than normal smoke and as it bashed against the shield held by Padraig, Mathilda, and Cwin,

I swore I saw tiny bugs inside it. Either they were the darkness or they rode within it.

The cats hissed at the initial strike, but the faeries calmed them down. Garbage happened to turn my way briefly and I saw fear on her face before she shook it off.

I couldn't recall how many times I'd seen fear on the face of any faery—but it wasn't a lot.

Garbage knew what the smoke bugs were and didn't like it. As one, the faeries on cats moved their steeds closer to the horses.

I almost felt sick. Alric was out there alone.

"Taryn! Come to me! Save me!" The voice sounded like Alric but was weak as it came to me. Part of my mind pointed out that Alric would never risk me or the others even if he was dying. He'd shown me that a few times.

That didn't help right now.

I swung my leg over to get off my horse.

Penqow and the other faeries on me tried pulling on me. Then all the faeries, aside from the cat riders, were on me pushing me back into my saddle. Silently.

"Taryn, whatever you heard, it's not him. You can't go out there." Padraig was calm, but his jaw was clenched and his eyes held tears.

Damn—he heard someone else calling to him. Probably his late wife.

I glanced around and all of my friends appeared to be fighting something inside their heads. If they stayed, I could too.

Bunky and Irving were behind Cwin but hovering close to her as she whispered something to them. She was the only one who didn't look emotionally tortured.

"Now!" Cwin yelled and Bunky and Irving shot out of the shield and it closed back up before anything got in. "Fire!"

Both constructs let loose crackling arcs of energy and Cwin added some nasty-feeling spell that rode alongside the electricity coming from the constructs. The increased bolts slammed into the dark cloud.

A scream of a thousand voices echoed around us.

"This is not your time or place. Return to slumber or I will destroy you. Feel the truth in my words." Cwin rose in her stirrups and lifted her face and hands to the sky as she shouted. Another bolt of lightning from Bunky and Irving struck the dark mass.

"Ours." The voice was unified all around us and sounded frightening and mournful at the same time.

"Never yours," Cwin's voice was powerful and shook the black swarm. The tiny bugs I thought I'd seen were dropping to the ground and not moving. "Leave now. Return to your tomb." One more strike from Bunky and Irving, followed by another lightning strike from the sky, punctuated her words.

"Nooo!" The voice separated into a thousand as it faded. The cloud was completely gone, bugs and all, a few moments later.

"What was that? We need to find Alric." I was shaking as if I'd run ten miles.

"Give it a few minutes to vanish completely. Not all of that thing was visible to your eyes. Then we can find Alric, although I believe he is safe." Cwin patted down her fur which was sticking up. "As for what it was…I won't speak of it until we are in a secure location."

Padraig and Mathilda might have had a hint as to what it was, but they both looked extremely rattled and said nothing as they climbed back on their horses.

I was at the point of ignoring Cwin and taking off to find Alric when she spoke.

"Taryn, Padraig, and Covey should find Alric on foot—the horses wouldn't be happy in that forest right now. I believe he sought shelter up and to the right, but he shouldn't be far. Mathilda and I will maintain the shield. Everyone, keep your weapons ready."

That wasn't reassuring and the forest was still too silent for my liking. But I quickly got off my horse. Garbage and the cat brigade came up behind me while Padraig and Covey joined me.

"We's goes. Kittahs finds." She might have been scared for a moment, but Garbage folded her arms and glared as if daring me to say no.

When I looked at Cwin and she shrugged, I nodded. "Okay, but you have to stay with us. No taking off. *At all.*"

"Fines. They needs stays heres." Garbage nodded to Bunky and Irving who were buzzing around the group.

"I agree. They need to remain with us." Mathilda nodded.

Bunky gronked in protest, but I cut him off and waved for him to come closer. "Bunky, we need to save Alric and I know you want to help, but it seems that you two are targets as well. You might endanger our rescue mission." I was hoping that Cwin was right and Alric had gone to ground and wasn't trapped or injured. But it would be better if the constructs remained here.

Bunky bobbed in reluctant agreement and he and Irving flew back to Cwin.

"Let's go." I thought that Padraig would lead, but he waved for me to instead. I figured that if he or Covey sensed something, they'd tell me. With Garbage on her cat riding alongside me, and Crusty and Leaf on their mounts on the other side, I headed into the thick trees.

I like trees. There weren't many in Beccia, at least there hadn't been before Amara moved in. Along with the remains of a protective hedge she created around the town when Foxy had once been kidnapped, and her own tree, she'd been encouraging trees to spread out over the town.

But these trees didn't feel nice. I couldn't explain it, but they almost reminded me of the creepy forest in the *tir cudd* that we found the diamond sphinx in—the final piece of the relic staff I used to protect my people. And send them somewhere in time by accident.

The trees there were weird and not normal. I found myself looking for odd moss-covered square blocks as we went further in. Along with the trees, those things were dangerous.

Thinking of Amara gave me an idea and I pushed my sleeve back from the vine tattoo she'd put on me. Aside from communication, it seemed to show a connection to the dryad. Hopefully, it was something these trees recognized.

A slight ruffling of leaves, even though there wasn't a breeze that I felt, and the trees suddenly felt less hostile. Or I might be imagining it. Either way, I continued in the direction that Cwin pointed.

"Should we call for him?" I turned back to Padraig.

"Not yet. Besides, if he was out here when that beast was, he might have heard voices calling him like the rest of us did. I don't think we're far. Just need to find something he'd hide in…like those." He pointed further up the hill where a group of boulders sat.

When I first met Alric, he'd shown a tendency for creating hideouts in rocks. Clearly, it was something he'd also been prone to when living in the elven enclave.

Garbage, Leaf, and Crusty were slowly having their cats creep ahead of me but trying not to be noticeable.

"Girls, stay with us. We're almost there." The remaining cat-riding faeries stayed behind us as they were supposed to. Sadly, I had a feeling that Garbage told them to do that to confuse me. The idea of faeries listening to me without constant watching was laughable.

Garbage's sigh as she and the other two let their cats drop back to me was loud.

Covey brought up the rear, but when I turned back, she was a lot closer to full berserker than she was when we left the horses. I might try to control what trouble the faeries got into, but controlling Covey was never going to happen.

Not to mention that she scared me when she changed. Even though I was able to turn into a full dragon. She was truly frightening.

"Maybe I should lead as we go in? Just in case?" Padraig asked as we approached the boulders. A small entrance appeared to the right. Although his going first as the more powerful magic user was smart, I knew he'd stand back if I said no.

As much as I wanted to see Alric as soon as possible, I also didn't want to get spelled by him if he was in there and didn't recognize us. "By all means."

"We's goes?" Now all the cat-riding faeries were clumped behind Garbage, Crusty, and Leaf. I shook my head, but Padraig gave me a small nod.

"Fine, but you do what Padraig says. We'll be right behind you."

If Covey was upset at being relegated to the back she gave no sign. Then again, if something happened, she'd probably go full berserker and fling herself past Padraig and me.

The entrance was short and narrow, but if Padraig fit, then Alric would have also. It was completely dark inside until Padraig called up a trio of glows and sent them forward.

Alric was there all right, but he was curled up in a corner and not moving.

CHAPTER FIVE

I RAN PAST PADRAIG SO FAST he didn't have a chance to step out of the way. "Alric!" I dropped down next to him and gently rolled him over.

His face and arms had tiny dark marks all over, but they looked more like splotches of dirt than bites.

Or really tiny bites from really tiny bugs.

"Alric? Wake up." I wasn't going to cry, but it was taking all I had not to. The smoke monster which attacked us was full of what looked like the tiniest bugs I'd ever seen. Had they done this?

I felt a cat rub against my arm and Garbage, Leaf, and Crusty slid off their cats and ran to Alric. The rest of the faeries remained on their feline steeds but had their war sticks at the ready.

"We's fix." Garbage nodded seriously, turned her war stick upside down, and went to poke Alric.

"No!" I grabbed her. "What are you doing? It's Alric, don't hurt him."

"Stick noes hurts," Leaf explained as Garbage twisted around in my grasp to get free. "She backwards it. Is goods."

I looked at Garbage and her war stick. One end was two-pronged, and was what they hit their enemies with. The other end was rounded. And was the one she was about to poke Alric with.

"It will help him?"

Garbage twisted again then gave me an annoyed glare. "Is yes. Heals him."

"Do you know what did this to him?" Padraig stood behind me with Covey flexing her claws next to him.

"Yesssss. Maybes. This fix." Garbage took advantage of my watching Padraig to bite my hand to make me drop her and ran to Alric and start poking him. Crusty and Leaf had reversed their sticks and were tapping him as well.

Crusty was hitting a small rock near Alric's arm on many of her strikes, but she meant well.

Alric moaned and all three faeries ran back to their cats.

I held him up gently. It looked like the marks were fading, but even with the glows, it was hard to see well enough to be certain.

Padraig sent another ten glows up toward the ceiling.

The marks *were* fading. I turned to the faeries. "Thank you." Later I needed to ask them about this. There had been plenty of times where magic healing war sticks could have been handy. But they never brought them out. They'd been developing new-old tricks in the past few months. Things they claimed they used to be able to do, then couldn't, then could again. Sometimes. This might be another one of those, but could prove extremely helpful.

"I feel awful." Alric blinked his eyes, then closed them again. "There are three of each of you. And I feel like a dozen people stomped on me and beat me up with clubs."

Padraig helped me get Alric into a sitting position. Then he slowly moved his hand about an inch away from Alric's body as he did some sort of magical search. "Whatever hit you was bad, I can't tell more here. But it's leaving." He looked down at the three faeries. "Good work, ladies." He also looked like he wanted to find out how they did what they did, but, like me, decided this wasn't the place for it.

Alric cautiously opened his eyes again. Since they remained open, I assumed there were no longer split visions of all of us. "I still feel like a herd of horses ran over me. A black cloud chased me as I was returning to you. It attacked me not far from here but stopped when I came into this cave. Then I passed out."

"Did you hear anyone calling for you? One of us?" I knew who I had heard and the fact most of the rest clearly heard other people was also on the list of things to talk about when we were safe.

"Not a thing until you came in here, but I didn't wake up until then either. Is everyone okay?"

"Yes, but we need to get moving again," Padraig said. "The swarm was chased off, but it might come back."

I helped Alric to his feet although he was already looking stronger.

The faeries were showing signs of boredom and quickly led the way out. They went further up the hill, but I called them back. At first, Garbage tried to pretend she didn't hear me, then, with a heavy sigh, she turned her troop around and came back to go around us and take the lead back to our friends.

Alric had his arm around my shoulders but was lost in his thoughts as we went down the hill. He finally came out of them once we saw the others through the trees. "I don't understand how I've recovered so well. I'm not completely sure what went after me, but it wasn't good. It felt like I was in serious trouble."

Garbage spun her cat around and rode back to us. "*I* dids it. Fix yous."

Leaf didn't come back to us but she turned to look back. "Us toos!"

Crusty and her cat were drifting toward a tree. She was humming loudly and ignoring everyone else.

Alric's eyebrow lifted and he looked at me. I shrugged and nodded.

"Thank you, ladies. Once we stop for the night, I'd like you to tell me about it."

Good thinking on his part. Even though with luck the cloud-smoke thing was gone, the faeries could take a while to tell things. Especially if they were things where they were the important focus. We needed everyone to pay attention on the trail.

Garbage led her faeries toward the rest of our group.

"You found him. Good. We need to get back on the trail. Immediately." Mathilda pointed down the hill to the ruins we'd left. From the smoke rising in the air, someone was attacking it.

Mathilda and Cwin dropped their shield and everyone got on their horses. Garbage started to lead her cat riders back into the woods.

"Not this time," Mathilda called out before they got to the first trees. "It's too dangerous for us if you're not here to protect us. Please stay near to guard."

I kept my face as neutral as possible as Garbage appeared to think it over.

"We's stays. Takes positions!" She waved her war stick over her head and the cat riders spread themselves out.

Penqow nodded seriously as I climbed back on my horse. "We's saves. Faeries saves him." She pointed to Alric. He was a little slower than usual getting into the saddle but mostly seemed normal.

Garbage must have told the other faeries mentally.

"Yes, you did. Thank you."

Padraig led as we resumed heading up the winding trail.

I glanced back a few times before we were out of sight

of the ruins. It was sad seeing them fall after being a safe place for so long.

The mountain became steeper and rougher. We had to stop and put all the war cats into their bag; their paws were taking a beating and they were slowing down.

Adjustments of faeries followed as the former cat riders now climbed up to ride on the horses. I almost suggested the faeries ride in the tiny black bags as well, but there was no way Garbage would agree. She took a seat between the ears of my horse and kept an eye on everything with a stern glare.

Whether it was fear of the weird smoke thing, or others were feeling the sadness of the echoes of the ruins being destroyed behind us, everyone was silent.

Even the faeries. Except for Crusty. She and Leaf had joined Garbage and my original guards on my horse. Leaf was watching the trees as we rode by—Crusty was still humming the same melody she'd been doing when we came back from rescuing Alric.

"Sweetie? What is the song you're humming?" I'd originally thought it was something random, but hearing it again indicated it was a melody from a song.

"Is song of travels. Importants." Then she went back to humming.

Crusty had always been drifty. But in the past year she'd shown something of a more serious nature. While her hummed tune sounded light, there was a sadness in her eyes as she continued it.

"Is it an old song?" Cwin asked from the back of the group.

"Is. Yes." Crusty gave a small sad smile and went back to her song.

I glanced back toward Cwin. Her thoughtful look indicated she might know something about Crusty's melody, but it would wait until we got off the trail.

We stopped for a short break a few hours after the attack. We were deep in the mountains now and as much as I loved trees, I was getting tired of them. The forest we were riding through was massive and old. Amara would love it, but I felt like it was closing in on us.

Alric was in a quiet, but intense, conversation with Padraig, Mathilda, and Cwin. Well, Cwin was listening but I noticed that unlike the others, she wasn't saying anything.

I grabbed some food and stayed near the horses along with Foxy, Covey, and Grillion. Yes, I was a magic user and they were probably talking about magic. But it would most likely go over my head. My relearning of the abilities I had twenty-five hundred years ago wasn't happening yet.

Bunky and Irving swung by and sat on my horse's saddle.

"Hi, guys. Thank you for staying behind and guarding the others. You need to stick close to us for now."

Bunky gronked and made a sharp move for my hand.

I used to have to wear gloves to touch him because the flood of images would literally knock me on my butt. However, in the past month either I'd grown used to it, or he was controlling it better. This time it was more like a short shock—like during the summer when I'd shock myself because it was so dry.

But he startled me this time and the images were sharp. Me as a kid going through a mountain like this with my parents and brothers. It was before the attacks by the Paili. We were going to stay at a cabin nearby and I was excited.

And it was *here*?

I had no memories of ever being in the southern continent before we came down on this trip. Then again, there were a lot of things I'd forgotten. Dragons could cover far distances when flying. And the water crossing between the continents wasn't long enough to have caused danger for a group of them.

Did we spend time down here?

I closed my eyes while I was going through the flashes of memories Bunky shared with me but opened them again.

"I know this place."

CHAPTER SIX

———

COVEY CAUGHT IT FIRST. "YOU know this path or the mountain? I thought you'd never been in the south before?"

"This specific area. I didn't recognize it from below because we came from the top when I was here. Flew down here when I was a kid." I smiled as more memories surfaced. "We did it fairly often. And there's a cabin nearby, or there was." I shrugged. "As for not remembering about ever being down here, there's a lot I still don't recall." I wasn't sure if it was the length of time that had gone by or what I did to myself when I flung myself into the future. But I was glad some of the memories were coming back—with an assist from Bunky.

Who was now buzzing around like a drunk bumblebee. He wanted to go to the cabin.

"Easy there. I seriously doubt the cabin is still standing after this long."

"What's going on?" Alric came over to us, dodging when Bunky dove for his head. "Why is he so excited? He keeps saying we found it."

I only got feelings from Bunky, even now. But Alric was right. Bunky was sure the cabin was still here. "We came here when I was a kid and Bunky thinks the cabin we had is still around. After twenty-five hundred years." Bunky had been underground hibernating with the rest of his kind for those years—his sense of time passing was sometimes off.

Crusty stopped humming and nodded. "Is heres."

"You were there too?"

"Noes. Knows of its. Is thats way. Song tells." She pointed in the direction Bunky kept wanting to go—to the right and into the deep woods. Or deeper. The trees were already thick and close. They formed an almost solid wall in the direction she was pointing.

Padraig, Mathilda, and Cwin joined us so I repeated the story.

Grillion looked around the dark trees. "If it is still around it might be a nice place to stay for the night. I don't feel comfortable with these trees. And even I can tell we wouldn't make the top of the mountain before nightfall."

I looked at my friends' faces. They agreed with Grillion.

"It's over twenty-five hundred years old. We probably couldn't even see where it stood." I wasn't sure how I'd feel about standing in a place with so many memories and seeing nothing there. Logically, I knew it had to be gone. Emotionally, it felt like I was there only a few years ago.

"Your parents were powerful magic users. They might have left protective spells on it," Cwin said softly.

I shook her off before her words caught up to me. "You never said you knew my parents." Cwin was old enough to have known the Ancients. And possibly even my parents. But she'd never hinted at such knowledge before.

"I didn't think I did. But I once knew some Ancients who came south and stayed on this mountain, it was a popular place during the summer. One family had three children. Two older boys and one tiny girl. Which I now believe was you."

Bunky gave a happy gronk and zipped over to her.

"Yes, my friend. I remember you now." She pet him and he rumbled happily.

"I don't even know what to say. But once we're somewhere safe, wherever that is, you're telling me everything you remember." Just hearing stories about my family would be amazing—sad, but wonderful. I didn't realize how much I'd lost until it started coming back to me.

Alric put his arm around me. "Do you want to try to find it?" His emphasis on the word 'you' told me if I said no, he'd convince the others not to try.

I sighed. I didn't want to get my hopes up. Not to mention that I wasn't certain if I would be more upset if there was nothing there, or if there was.

"Yes. But I reserve the right to cry," I said it loud enough so all of my friends could hear. It was getting late in the day and even if the cabin wasn't there—getting off this trail would be safer for camping.

My friends nodded with varying levels of sympathy. The faeries cheered. Crusty climbed up me and hugged and kissed my face.

"Is goods. Travelings." Her smile was still tinged with a bit of sadness and I wondered if it was tied to the song she'd been humming or to the cabin.

I knew asking her probably wouldn't get me anything useful, and I was still fighting myself on going to where the cabin was. Had been.

"Okay, if everyone is done with their break, let's go." Padraig gracefully leaped on his horse, and the rest of us followed at our own skill level. He motioned for me to lead, or at least ride up near him. I felt a slight pull for the direction.

Bunky and Irving flew low over me and gronked reassuringly.

We were a few minutes out when an explosion shook the ground. A cloud of smoke rose from the ruins far below us.

I rubbed the side of my horse's neck to settle her down. It didn't look like whatever it was had impacted anything up here. But whatever it was had been strong.

"Good to see the ruins fought back." Cwin turned her horse to look down at the rising green smoke. "I hope all of those hooligans were destroyed."

"The ruins fought back?" Grillion was riding in front of her but turned back as well.

"With some help. I didn't have time to do much, but what's left of the ruins should be safe now. We can discuss details once we're off the trail." Cwin turned back to us and Padraig got us moving again.

A tiny trail went toward the right. It was so narrow that I figured Foxy would be picking tree branches off him and his horse.

I thought I felt a tug, but I didn't like the look of the new trail. Bunky's excitement and exceedingly happy gronking pushed the matter. "It looks like we go on the new one."

"You remember this?" Padraig asked as we went down the new trail.

"Not specifically. Remember, we traveled differently. Landed on the top of the mountain and hiked down. But it feels familiar. And Bunky insists we're near."

He gronked a few times, then he and Irving flew even lower.

Alric laughed. "But he doesn't remember the trees being so close. He's politely asking them to move out of the way."

Bunky might have asked nicely, but the trees didn't respond. More trees to remind me of the creepy ones in that other *tir cudd*. If any trees or rocks came toward us, I was turning around. Memories or not.

The sounds of snapping branches, and a variety of low-voiced swear words, told me Foxy wasn't the only one finding the trail a bit too close.

The faeries were loving it. The looks on their tiny faces, as they stared up into the trees, made me wish I could make them fly again.

Then again, it would be too easy to lose them in here if they were flying. We reached a fork and the trail to the right of this one was even thinner. Nothing had used it for a long time, not even wild animals. "This way." I sounded a lot more confident than I felt, but Padraig nodded and we went through the narrower trail.

Cwin muttered a few words behind us and the shield from before surrounded us. It was lower this time, but it worked to keep the tree limbs from us and the horses.

We rode for what felt like days, but was probably only a few hours. We were still climbing, but not at the same steepness as our original path.

Bunky had been sticking close to me, he and Irving needed to stay within the shield, but he suddenly zipped forward.

"Bunky, come back!" I didn't shout, the stillness around us was heavy and it felt like shouting would be a bad idea. But I put a lot of force into my words.

He turned back and charged me. I put up both hands to grab him and almost fell off my horse as the flood of memories smacked into me. The family running through the woods, in human form, then zipping over the trees in aerial games of tag. The images seemed so real I nudged my horse forward.

"Drop the shield," Padraig called out to Cwin but stayed where he was.

There was a clearing ahead, I was seeing both as it was then and now. But the images from the past were stronger—a cabin, picnic tables in the clearing. Then it was only a clearing. No cabins, no family. I'd warned my friends that I might cry, but I'd been hoping not to.

Nope, tears went down my cheeks as I saw the empty clearing.

Crusty pulled my hair to make me look to the right. "Theres."

A clump of trees intruded upon the clearing—long ago the clearing had been larger. Big oak trees, which was weird enough as everything up here so far had been pine.

Then I noticed the trees were shimmering. I got off my horse and walked toward the shimmer. Crusty climbed to my shoulder. At some point, Garbage and Leaf joined and took positions on my head and the other shoulder.

"Taryn? Where are you going?" Padraig asked, but a glance back showed me Alric was already off his horse.

"There's something here. Can't you see it?" I walked slowly, but it seemed my friends were dropping further behind me at a fast rate. I stopped.

"Keeps. Yes. Keeps," Garbage said from on top of my head and soon all the faeries jumped off their horses and ran after us.

"It could be a trap!" Foxy yelled as he got off his horse. "It looks like fire!"

I still saw a shimmer over the oaks, but nothing looked like fire. Or smoke. "Are you sure this is safe?" I asked the three faeries currently on me. My friends were moving in slow motion. Or I was moving at a crazy fast speed.

"This right. Noes pays attentions." Normally that tone from Garbage would be followed by her flying an inch away from my nose. Since she couldn't fly, she settled for swinging down on strands of my hair and waving her finger in my face.

With one more glance at my slow-moving friends,

and a tiny voice in my head pointing out they had some serious magic and yet were still stuck in whatever was slowing them down, I touched the closest oak.

CHAPTER SEVEN

A SHOCK WENT THROUGH MY ARM. It didn't hurt really, more like it itched. Then I stepped forward and saw the cabin.

I knew this had to be my memories playing with my mind, but the sense of joy as I stepped toward the mirage made it too hard to stop. This had been our vacation home. A place to go to return to nature. A place for family.

Like the places I'd seen in my vision in Yosi, this building was made to accommodate beings who were both human-sized and dragon-sized. It was built of huge logs and was rustic, but bright spots of color along the window sills broke up the solid wood. I remembered this now, although just a few minutes ago I couldn't tell anyone what it looked like.

It looked like it had been built a few years ago.

I wanted to go inside, to see if the inside was as familiar as the outside. The faeries and constructs joined me but held back and watched me carefully. Just seeing any restraint from the faeries was amazing. My friends, with Alric in the lead, were barely moving now.

"Girls? Do you know why the rest are stuck back there?"

"Is spells. Yous okay. We's okays. Thems nots. Noes sees." Crusty was serious as she nodded.

"Yous musts lets in," Garbage added as she kept watching the cabin. She wanted to go inside so badly it was rolling off her.

I looked back at my friends. If this cabin was here, and not a shared hallucination, then obviously I wanted Alric and the rest here too.

After I saw it.

I darted forward and the human-sized door opened at my touch. The inside was exactly as I remembered it— again, I couldn't have described it to anyone a moment ago. But seeing it made me drop into one of the human-sized chairs and start crying.

"Is goods! Safes here." Leaf came running over and hugged my ankle. She was still looking around though.

"So, this is real?" I knew without walking around the rest of this side what I would see. The same would be behind the larger dragon-sized door. I couldn't go home again, but this was the next best thing. "My parents protected it."

"Taryn? Can you invite us in?" Cwin's voice sounded like she was miles away, not only across the clearing.

"Reals." Garbage's smiles were usually scary, but this time it was genuine.

"Okay, let's get everyone else in here too."

This time I saw the shield covering the cabin, a pair of barns, and the grounds around them. And my friends all standing on the edge trying to look in. I paused at the shimmering walls of the shield. I wanted to let them in, but not drop the shield. I had no idea if my parents made it automatic or not. But after it remained in place for this long, I didn't want to mess with it.

Cwin stepped forward and smiled. "Just touch it and think about all of us and our horses. It will let us pass and keep the shield up."

I shrugged and did what she said. Cwin and Alric, along with my horse and theirs, were the first through.

Within a few moments everyone, along with their horses, was on this side and the shimmering shield was still in place.

Alric dropped the reins to our horses and ran to me. "Are you okay? You've been crying." He wiped a stray tear with his thumb.

"Happy tears. A bit sad too, but mostly happy." I hugged him and then turned to my friends. "This was my family's vacation home. Welcome." I motioned for them to follow and took them inside. Since I now recalled this place, I gave them all a tour of both sides.

Bunky and Irving zipped around on their own, especially paying attention to the high rafters on the dragon side. They looped around in a game of chase. Seeing them relaxed and playing was nice.

Grillion, however, couldn't get over the dragon-sized side. "I know you're big, I've seen it. But your whole family was that big?" He staggered as he almost fell over while looking at the high ceiling.

Mathilda laughed. "All of her people were that big. I heard tales of some Ancients being twice the size of our Taryn. She's still young for her people."

Kind of disturbing to know. I hadn't thought about it, but I'd been the equivalent of a late teenager when I built the relic staff twenty-five hundred years ago and messed everything up. "I don't need to get larger."

Cwin patted my arm. "Your parents and brothers were larger than you, but there were a lot of variances in the sizes of Ancients, like any species."

"So, I could stay the size I am?" I didn't know why I was so freaked out—I was already massive compared to everyone else when I changed. What was a few more feet?

"You might." Cwin's smile was too big. She figured I wasn't done growing but didn't want to disturb me further.

Probably a good idea. Being back here was amazing and sad at the same time. I was already an emotional mess.

"Changes! Fixes us!" Garbage yelled as she stomped around me.

Looking down, I realized that while I'd been worried about getting larger, I'd been circled by all the faeries. And they were all looking at me with far too much hope on their tiny faces.

"Girls, I don't know how to fix you. And I'm the same person whether I look like this or not." Back in the ruins, the girls had said I could change and fix them. I was hoping this was one of those times they forgot.

Mathilda and Cwin shared a look. One I didn't think boded well for me.

"There are differences when you change. You can't fly or breathe fire when you're like you are right now, for instance," Mathilda said.

"Okay. Um, how is that going to help break the spell on the faeries? And why didn't this come up before?"

"Tooks longs thinkings." Garbage nodded sagely and reminded me of Covey when she was working with a particularly dense student.

"We weren't keeping anything from you," Mathilda said. Just as someone who regularly keeps secrets might say.

I folded my arms. "Do you know what I have to do?"

"No, but maybe the faeries can help?" Mathilda leaned down toward them. "Ladies? What does Taryn need to do to fix you?"

"Gets big. Stomps like this." Garbage held up her arms in a crude copy of me on my back legs as a dragon. "Say words. Poof, bads gone. We's flies."

I rubbed the side of my face. It had been a horrifically long day. Lots of emotions. Sorting out faery-speak wasn't on my agenda until I got food and rest.

Alric must have noticed my look as he dropped down to Garbage. "We're all exhausted. You want her to fix you correctly, right? She needs rest."

Leaf looked at me, then Alric, then me again. "Is wrongs? Wings still noes works?"

"It could be." I caught on a bit slower than usual, but Alric had a good idea. "If I do it wrong because I'm hungry and tired, you could be worse off. Your wings could fall off." I seriously doubted that. Most likely whatever spell breaker I tried would fail. But from the looks of horror on all the faeries' faces, aside from Crusty, it was the right thing to say.

"We's waits. Get feds! Sleeps!" Garbage announced as she and the rest of her pack ran back toward the human-sized part of the cabin.

The rest of us, including Bunky and Irving who gave up their game, followed. Luckily for me, Mathilda and Padraig headed toward the kitchen after waving for the rest of us to sit. This might be my family's place, but I was never a great cook. Not even when I was younger. I recalled that at least.

Alric, Foxy, and Grillion went out to stable the horses. There wasn't a separate stable per se, but the nearest barn inside the shield had stalls.

The rest of us took over the large comfy living room. Bunky and Irving settled on a beam designed for chimeras. They both nodded, then went to their version of sleep.

"How are you holding up?" Covey dropped onto the couch next to me. The sympathy in her eyes was genuine and again spoke to how much Covey had changed in the past year. She'd not been uncaring, but she usually simply didn't notice things that were emotion-based.

In anyone, including herself.

"About as expected. Although I have a feeling I'm unique in my situation." I sighed. "It's weird though. I recognize this place now, but I'm not recalling a lot of distinct memories. Just a vague feeling of contentment. Maybe we should hide out here until everything blows over."

Covey laughed and gave me a sideways hug. "I know you wouldn't do that. Deep inside of your pub-going-digger is a true protector."

"You take that back. I want to be lazy." I tried to keep my face straight but it didn't work. As much as remaining here sounded wonderful, I knew I couldn't abandon the rest of the world. Not to mention, I had many friends who weren't with us right now.

"Right." Covey smiled and leaned back.

Garbage and her mob ran to our feet. "Ready?"

"Sweetie, I need food and rest." I had no idea how I would break the spell on the faeries and also needed to have a serious chat with the other magic users.

I wasn't sure how Garbage thought I could change into my dragon form, stomp around, and remove a rare, contagious spell designed for the faeries specifically.

We didn't get much information within the ruins, but Amara received some and passed it along to Foxy during their talks. No other known group of faeries, including the wilds who sometimes came into Beccia, had been affected by the spell.

At least that was something.

"We's halps food." Garbage raised her arms, then ran toward the kitchen with her brightly colored mob behind her.

Except Crusty.

She watched the rest go, then climbed up my legs and sat on me. The look she gave me, as if those large golden eyes saw far more than they should, was more than a little disturbing.

"What's going on, Crusty?"

"Yous change." She didn't seem happy, but nor was she sad. She was stating a fact.

And I didn't think she meant the way I needed to change to fix the faeries.

"I know I change, but you mean something else?"

"Noes." She held up her tiny hands, closed them into fists, and stretched them out to either side of her as far as she could. "This goods." Her left fist waved about. "This ungoods." Then her right fist shook around. "Yous need boths." She scampered up my chest and patted my heart. "Heres."

Before I could respond, or try to sort out what she was saying, she kissed my cheek then ran off me and followed her friends into the kitchen.

CHAPTER EIGHT

COVEY WAS THE ONLY ONE near me and watched Crusty race off with a fond smile. "Do you have a clue as to what she's talking about?"

"Not at all. I'm not sure if the old clueless Crusty was better or worse than the current enigmatic one." I was pretty certain that having a very bad side wasn't mitigated by having a very good one. Whatever she was talking about, I needed to know. Eventually.

Just not now.

Alric and Grillion joined us.

"Foxy stayed in the barn for now, he can reach Amara better there and wanted to update her on our move." Alric sat to the other side of me and Grillion took a chair near Cwin.

Cwin appeared to be sleeping.

"Where are the faeries?" Grillion tried to engage Bunky and Irving, but they were still turned off—their version of being asleep.

"They went to help in the kitchen." Covey winced as a loud crash came from the back. "And there they go."

There wasn't any yelling from them or Mathilda and Padraig, but the faeries raced through the living room and into the hall which led to the dragon-sized side of the cabin.

"We probably don't want to know." I was used to the girls yelling when they ran, but silence was good. I hoped.

Foxy came in from the outside looking somber and thoughtful. He flopped down on another chair but remained silent.

"Is everything okay?" Grillion stopped watching the resting constructs and turned to Foxy.

"Yes. I think. I'm thinking Amara might be keeping things from me." He frowned. "She be claiming all is fine in Beccia. But she didn't have information about Lorcan and Siabiane. She didn't sound completely herself."

Foxy and Amara had kept secrets about the dangers they were in from each other in the past. And both promised not to do it again. I couldn't blame him for being suspicious though.

Covey leaned forward. "When was the last time you spoke to her?"

"Right before we left the ruins. Sounded fine then." He folded his massive arms and his scowl grew deeper.

"Did she use any odd phrases or terms?" Now Alric leaned forward.

Foxy shook his head, then stopped. "Now that you mention it. She said some names wrong. Carlan instead of Harlan. And Logmaela instead of Dogmaela. Were she spelled?"

Alric shook his head. "Not sure, but we need to talk to the others. Your link might have been compromised."

"Or she is." Foxy lumbered to his feet. "We have to go there."

"We need to know what we're getting into," Cwin spoke but didn't open her eyes. "Using a fada path makes ripples in the magic of the world. It can also be tracked by strong enough magic users. Something we don't want to happen." The alertness in her eyes when she opened them indicated she'd been awake the entire time.

"But what if she's in danger? The last time—"

"Things have changed since then. Orenda and her people are keeping an eye on things, and so are the mages and knights." I gently cut him off. "Faeries are stationed with everyone and some of the chimeras go by to check on them also. The faeries would have sent the chimeras to us if there was something wrong."

Not all of Bunky's chimera friends were working with us, but the twenty or so who had helped us in Yosi, and spread the word to the faery groups to stay away from ours, had kept lines of communication open. Granted, there had only been three visits in the entire month. But I trusted them.

Even if Amara was compromised, the rest of our friends, including Ceithera, a powerful elven healer, would have sent word.

"I'd not be liking this." Foxy turned to Cwin. "When we leave here, can you open the path? There's something wrong."

Cwin shrugged. "I can try. But again, it's risky for many reasons to do it. Let's see how things go."

Foxy looked ready to argue, then instead let out a massive sigh. "Okay. But after we eat, I think Taryn should try to reach Amara as well. See what she thinks."

Foxy had a better nose than I did. A few moments later Mathilda and Padraig came out to the huge heavy dining room table and put down platters of food.

"The least I can do is get dishes." I got up and Alric followed me.

"There's still more food to come out." Mathilda fixed a look on Grillion.

"I will never say no to helping bring out food." Grillion grinned and followed us in.

It took a few tries but I finally found where the dishes, glasses, and silverware were. Of course, I also got a bit misty-eyed as more memories trotted back.

Alric followed me in, and held me as Grillion grabbed a pair of loaded dishes and ran out.

"Are you sure you're okay staying here? It won't be for long; we do need to find out what the empress and whoever was behind the destruction of Yosi has been up to. But we could camp in the forest." Alric hadn't liked that we stayed in the ruins as long as we did. He understood it, we didn't have as many injuries as we would have if the ghosts hadn't been spelled to help us in that fight after fleeing Yosi. But most of us were weary.

"I'll be fine. And the memories are lovely once I get used to them. It's weird not to have them for my entire time in this period and suddenly have them start popping up." I handed him half of the plates. "What do you think about Foxy and Amara?" I noticed Alric had given a tiny twinge when Foxy said Amara got two of our friends' names wrong.

If anyone would see suspicion in that—it would be Alric. Although I found it odd as well.

"I think I'll wait until you contact her after dinner to make any opinions. The last thing we need is a distracted Foxy. And Cwin was right. That fada path of hers is powerful, but every time we use it, we run the risk of it leading our enemies to us. Or worse. Understanding a bit more of how it works now, I realize how dangerous it is. And why it's almost unheard of."

Those were cheerful thoughts. I plastered on a smile and led the way to the dining area.

The faeries showed up and were watching the big table. Mathilda pointed down to a faery feast on a low table near the couch. They scrambled over each other grabbing food, but there was enough for about ten times as many faeries as we had.

The food was plentiful and good, so the table fell silent. Finally, everyone finished and started chatting.

Except Foxy. He kept watching me with an encouraging smile as I finished the last bit on my plate. I knew he wanted me to contact Amara.

"We need a reason." I pushed my plate away so I wouldn't be tempted to fill it again. I hadn't been using much magic, and that was usually a big food drain. But I'd been starving.

"For?" Covey asked.

"For me to contact Amara." I held up my hands as Foxy appeared ready to protest. "I'm fine with doing it. But either something is wrong up there, or everything's fine. Whichever it is, my calling an hour after Foxy did will seem odd. If things are bad, it tips our hand that we suspect something. If they're good then it's going to worry Amara. I need a cover story."

"She's right. Cons always have to have a good understory or they don't work." Grillion looked around the table at the reactions to his words. "What? I wasn't saying this was a con job, but some elements are the same."

Alric grinned. "They are indeed. How about Taryn wants to ask Amara about the other goddesses? We know Ageora is alive and stuck in her *tir cudd*, maybe you could ask her about another one?"

I frowned. "That's a great idea but I have no idea about what deities were floating around all that time ago. It needs to be realistic."

"I could help." Cwin nodded. "How about Lissera?"

Mathilda clapped her hands. "She was one of my favorites. Lovely singing voice. She was one of the bird goddesses. I do wonder if she's trapped in a *tir cudd* down here."

"That might work. I had a bunch of birds appear to help me fight off evil birds on that weird Dragon Day a few months ago. Maybe calling the good birds was her attribute? I can already fly, but I can't call birds."

"Tell Amara that you've been having bird dreams and that you feel like someone is talking to you." Even Covey was getting into it.

"Okay, but I want to keep it simple. Foxy? Is there anything that I could ask her, that others wouldn't know, but she should?" He might not be paranoid; Amara could be spelled or have been replaced by a changeling. Or something else that we hadn't run across yet.

He pulled on his left ear in thought. "Yes. But I'll need to whisper it to you when we go out to the barn." He got to his feet and I followed him out.

Technically, he didn't need to be with me. My communication tattoo would let me speak to Amara. But I knew he'd be edgy if he wasn't involved. And having him nearby might be good if something came up that I didn't know.

The barn wasn't as large as I remembered, but I'd been smaller the last time I was here. Our last trip was a year or so before the Paili began attacking our people. I now wonder if they'd begun earlier but my parents kept it from us.

I shook off the feelings. I was furious and heartbroken at the same time. Neither of which was going to help me at all right now. The horses seemed happy roaming around the barn and only a few went into the open stalls. Thanks to some efforts from the elves, none of them appeared to want to leave.

"So, what's this secret that no one else will know?"

"When you mention that bird goddess, say your dream had falcons in it. She hates them for reasons she won't share, but that should get a rise out of her." He frowned and a huge line carved itself between his eyes. "If it is her. I don't care about what they say—if I need to, I'll run all the way back to Beccia."

I hugged him and patted his back. "I know you would. But we might want to look at other options before that. Everything could be over by the time you got there. We can try to get some of Bunky's friends to find the others in Beccia if needed." I wasn't going to send Bunky or Irving, there were too many people who wanted them. Or so it seemed.

"Might be right about that. Okay, I won't worry. Call her." We were already standing close to each other but I moved closer to him. Amara's voice would appear out of the air near the tattoo. In my case, it was my left bicep.

I put my hand over the tattoo and thought of Amara. That was one thing, yes, we were contacting her. But would it even work if she was a changeling? Changelings could mimic people, but not their magic.

Unfortunately, I didn't have a clue as to how these tattoos of ours worked, let alone if an imposter could access them if we contacted her. Foxy had contacted *someone* earlier.

"Taryn? Is everything okay?" It sounded like Amara was in the middle of the lunch rush.

"Yeah, sort of. Sorry to bug you so soon, but I had a weird dream about birds. Kind of like when I met Ageora. Some birds helped me out during Dragon Day, and I was wondering if this was another goddess like Ageora?"

"It might be Lissera. She was one of the most powerful bird goddesses and if any of them survived, it would be her. Was there anything bad?"

"Just that I felt threatened by a pair of falcons. Good to have a name though in case we come across her."

"*Falcons.* Stay clear of them. And be careful of those *tir cudds.* They're dangerous. We need to figure out more about them before any of you go into any more." She paused, but already I realized that she was the real Amara.

"Is Foxy okay? I know I spoke to him this morning, but

he said he'd check in once you all found a place to camp for the night. I thought you might have been him."

I looked to Foxy and his eyes widened.

"Yeah, he's here somewhere. Let me tell him to call you. We just got settled. Oh, how are Saline and Coran?"

"Your connection isn't great. It sounded like you said Saline and Coran. Siabiane and Lorcan drop in every few days. Mostly they stay in the house they rented doing magical experiments. They talk more to Ceithera and her crew than myself."

This was definitely Amara. Then who did Foxy speak to an hour ago? And how did they intercept his contact?

Foxy looked about as freaked out as I felt, but he nodded and began to put his hand on the tattoo on his leg. I waved him off.

"Foxy just came in the room, but he's filthy from the stuff we had to move. I know it won't be private, but I promise to ignore you two if you want to go through my tattoo to speak." Foxy frowned, then slowly nodded.

This was the real Amara and whoever he tried to contact before wasn't. There was a chance that Amara was fine but someone or something had taken over Foxy's tattoo.

"That would be wonderful. We're in the lunch rush right now, but I would dearly love to hear his voice."

Foxy told her simple things about the trip and that we'd found a good place to stop for the night but her responses brought back his smile. Finally, they said their goodbyes.

"We need to have our powerful magic users sort out what happened to your tattoo." I spun him around and marched us out of the barn. I was grateful that Amara was fine, but worried that something broke into Foxy's tattoo.

The group was spread throughout the cabin. Covey

and Grillion were debating something on the sofa, and everyone else was gone.

"The others are doing the dishes and storing the leftovers. It got too crowded in there," Covey said as we walked in. "Glad you're back. Mathilda said you should get the first pick of the rooms, and I want to go to bed."

I peered closely at her. It was still fairly early and Covey never was the first for bed. "Are you okay?"

"I should be with all the extra sleeping I had. But I think that while we were unconscious, we weren't getting rest. Padraig is working to figure out what did it. But consequently, I need to go to bed now."

"Okay, but we need to talk to everyone first. Then I'll grab one of the rooms on the dragon side. There won't be enough rooms for everyone if we don't use those as well."

Foxy ran to the kitchen and chased everyone back into the living room. "Important things are happening." He was still visibly upset, but far less than before, after speaking to the real Amara.

CHAPTER NINE

———◆———

FOXY AND I QUICKLY FILLED everyone in on our conversations.

Padraig looked the most concerned, but the other three magic users were as well.

"That link should be unbreakable. Amara said that she spoke to you in the ruins?" Padraig asked.

Foxy nodded. "Aye, and this one sounded right, like the one I spoke to this morning before we left."

"When and how did something get to Foxy's tattoo? And how do we stop it? Is there any way that they, whoever they are, can hear us through it? Like now?" I added the last part as a whisper with a glare at Foxy's leg.

Mathilda, Padraig, Alric, and Cwin looked at each other. Then all four shrugged.

"No idea, as that's not a spell any of us know. Even me," Cwin said with regret. "But based on other old spells sort of like it, I'd say probably not. I also have no idea how it was compromised."

The four magic users stared at Foxy's leg.

Padraig moved forward. "Can you pull your pants leg up? I think I can put a magic-blocking patch over it. Just temporarily until we sort this out. If whoever spoke to you is trying to use it to find us or listen in, this will stop it."

Foxy's scowl was going to become permanent if he kept using it, but he finally nodded.

Padraig spoke a few words then stepped back as a thin shield covered Foxy's tattoo.

"Can we now sort out the rooms?" Grillion yawned and Covey followed a moment later.

"I think it might be a good idea." Mathilda stifled her yawn. "I feel oddly drained. It could be the spell in the ruins, or that smoke thing that hit us."

"I can stay up to guard if need be. It didn't hit me like all of you. After I pick my room." I had been so focused that I didn't notice that Bunky, Irving, and all the faeries were missing. "Where are the faeries and constructs?" Foxy and I weren't gone that long and Bunky and Irving had looked completely out of it when we left.

"They're touring the cottage. I think they're on the dragon side." Grillion got to his feet. "But do we need a guard? This place is safe, right? *Right?*" He looked stressed on the final word.

"Yes, unless another Taryn is roaming around, or her brothers are out in the woods somewhere, no one else can get in." Padraig flashed me a smile. "I know we'll find your brothers, but they probably aren't lurking around here."

"Agreed. And my standing guard is more because I'm not tired." If I was lucky, the faeries *would* be tired and I could sort some things out in my head without their help. I led everyone up the stairs in the human-sized side of the cabin. First, I checked to make sure there were no personal items left behind—we usually took everything private back home. While seeing my old human-sized room did give my heart a twinge, the rooms were empty of everything beyond a bed and chairs.

"There are four rooms here and four on the other side. Alric and I will be over there, so the first four of you can pick any of these."

Covey and Grillion moved fast to claim the first two rooms. Cwin and Foxy took the other two.

"Sleep well." I then led Mathilda, Padraig, and Alric to the dragon-sized side. Even though I didn't recall being a dragon until fairly recently, this side hit me even harder. Most Ancients had homes for both sizes, and my parents had replicated that here. For some reason, this side felt more like home.

I found my old room and claimed it for Alric and me. "All of the beds on this side will be big, but there should be step-stools underneath them."

Mathilda and Padraig took my brothers' rooms.

Alric rubbed my arms. "I can stand guard with you." Then a yawn attacked him.

"Yeah, you woke up before the others, but that spell was still working on you. Go to sleep. I'll be in later." I gave him a long kiss that almost made me rethink staying. Until he fought off another yawn. "Sleep."

He finally gave in and climbed into the massive bed. I shut the door and went to the room at the end of the hall. My parents' room. The door was shut, and there wasn't a lot of sound coming out, but I recognized a few of the louder giggling snorts.

The faeries had taken it over.

I didn't knock but slowly opened the door. Bunky and Irving were sitting on the top of the headboard while the faeries had set up an amusement park. They'd taken a number of the slides that Ageora set up for them in her *tir cudd*. They hadn't used them much in the ruins because there were plenty of other places to play in. But they had them out now. Along with a dozen half-empty ale bottles.

And they were significantly louder than they'd sounded in the hall.

"How are you doing that?" The faeries hadn't ever shown the ability to hide their noise. And if they had it and had never used it, there were going to be serious words.

"Is in walls." Leaf ran over and pounded on the nearest wall. There was hardly a sound.

"All of you need to stay in here until morning, you understand? Bunky and Irving, you two as well. I'm going to be looking for a way to fix the faeries tomorrow, but I need you all to remain here." That wasn't what I'd intended to say, but an image of the library my parents left here—duplicates of many of the books back home—popped into my head while I was talking to the faeries. There could be books on magic in it. I was still remembering the times we were here and my parents didn't want to drag the books back and forth while flying, so they set up a smaller collection here.

Garbage was on the top of a long slide and nodded at my words. The rest of the faeries duplicated the move although many of them were probably too drunk already to realize what they were nodding about.

I was turning to the door when another thought hit me. "Wait, can I have one of your black bags? I might want to bring some of the books from here along with us."

Garbage squinted at me, then finally nodded to Leaf. She dug out a handful of bags from the small pocket in the front of her overalls, searching inside each one before finally running over and handing one to me.

"Is empty. Yous keeps." The rest of the non-empty bags were shoved back into her pocket and she ran back to the others.

Bunky and Irving gronked in agreement as I shut the door.

I hadn't thought about magic books until now, but images ran through my head. The last time we were here, my folks were having me work on various spells. I doubted that any of them were directly related to reversing a contagion to stop faeries from flying, but I might get something useful.

And I wanted those books.

The library was human-sized and tucked behind the kitchen—probably why I didn't see it or think of it when I was showing the others around.

The downstairs was silent, but glows on the tables and in the rafters made it feel homey and cozy. For a moment I could imagine that I was sneaking out to get a snack with my family none the wiser. Like many of my recently recovered memories, the emotions that brought were happy and sad.

The library's lights came on as I passed through the kitchen. It wasn't huge, the flashed memory of the one we'd had back home pointed out that this was a mini-version.

But there were still over a hundred books there. Covey and the rest of the book junkies were going to be extremely excited about this.

I originally hadn't thought of taking anything with me when we left here. I was hoping that the magic around this place would keep it safe until we sorted the empress and her cronies out. But I needed these books. Hopefully, since I had been studying at least some of them in the past, the spells would come easier.

Even though the entire library was smaller than my living room in Beccia, it still took me a while to find books that I recognized. I finally found a shelf of ten books that I immediately remembered. Not completely happily. Even back then, apparently, I had more magical power than knowledge. From what I recalled, the younger me wasn't a huge fan of studying.

I grabbed the ten books and staggered out to the living room. A nice big chair with a sturdy table next to it and a big lamp called to me. I did pop into the kitchen and grab some bread from Mathilda's stash and fresh brewed tea before I settled in.

The first book seemed familiar but the spells I saw were way over my current understanding. Same for the next three that I picked up. I knew them, but I hadn't read much of them.

The fifth one was a winner though. The wording was simplified, almost childlike. But it had spells that I knew.

Many of them were similar to the ones my friends had been trying to teach me. Including a fancy version of my push spell. I re-read that one a few times and an almost sick feeling hit me.

This was the spell that I modified to send my people into the future. Which hadn't been my plan at all. My spell was targeted at the syclarions we were fighting. But I'd used part of this spell as the base for it.

It was good to know why push was my strongest spell, but bad to think about what past me had done with it. Even unintentionally.

There were a few other simple spells that I recalled and practiced. I had furniture bobbing about the room, not bobbing per se, but the pieces were moving a few inches off the ground. I even magically reached into the kitchen for another piece of bread.

I was grateful for recognizing this book, but flipping through didn't reveal any secret way to heal the faeries. Two more books and two more pieces of bread, as well as a pot of diluted tea, and I found something that might work.

Part of the problem was because the faeries *were* magic. I had to sort out how they were spelled in the first place, and then work on a way to cure them.

The spell I finally found that might work, lytleian spaking, was a way to spell magical beings. The reason the girls' spell was contagious was because it was the only way to make the magic work. Faery bodies could normally shake off a bad spell. But with a contagion, it would keep replicating itself. Even separating the already exposed girls from each other wouldn't work to stop it.

But the spell I found might.

I laughed when I saw a drawing on the next page— an Ancient in dragon form, on back legs, performing a spell in a circle.

At least the girls had been on the right track, even if they'd missed a few important parts.

The spell was more complicated than simply marching around and unfortunately, my tea hadn't been strong. My eyes kept sliding shut.

"Taryn? You should come to bed. You fell asleep reading." I felt the shake on my shoulder and heard the words. But for a moment they sounded as if both Alric and my mother said them.

I forced my eyes open and pried the writing stick off my face as I sat up. At some point, I'd pulled the small table in front of my chair and fell asleep over the books on it.

"I found the spell." The words made sense to me, but Alric looked at me as if I'd spoken gibberish.

I might have mumbled. I'd also had some weird dreams that were already fleeing too fast for me to catch.

"Come on." He helped me out of the chair, and then picked me up to carry me upstairs.

"Can walk." *That* I knew I mumbled.

"Um, hmm. Sure, you can. I'm making sure you don't fall down the stairs. You will have to climb into the bed on your own though."

I nodded and leaned into his chest as we went up.

I must have climbed into the bed on my own and

passed out, because the next thing I knew the sun was shining, the bedroom was being attacked by tiny rampaging hordes, and Alric was missing.

CHAPTER TEN

—◆—

"WAKES! FIXS! NOWS!"

My eyes slid shut when the chant began, and what felt like a million tiny feet bounced on the bed and ran across me.

Cracking open one eye was a bad idea as there were a lot of faeries far too close to my face. I shut my eye again.

"Noes! Yous fix nows!" A tiny hand grabbed my cheek and squeezed.

"Ow!" I opened my eyes and glared at Garbage. I knew it had most likely been her. "Let me sleep a bit more."

"Yous needs foods. Done. Rests. Done. Reads books. Done. Fixs nows!" Now she was giving me her fierce one-eye-almost-closed-and-one-bulging-out glare.

Normally it was cute. That changed when it was an inch from your face.

"Back off, all of you, and I'll get up." My stomach rumbled. "But breakfast before the spell. And there's no promise this will work. You have to understand that."

Garbage backed off and nodded slowly. "Yous fix."

"I'll try." I looked down at my rumpled clothing. "I also need a bath and fresh clothes. Wait for me downstairs." I sat up and swung my legs over the edge of the bed, luckily Alric had left the step-stool up.

I gathered my things, got in a quick bath, which would have been easier on the human side of the cabin as the tub over here was massive, and went downstairs. The smell of breakfast cooking made my stomach rumble more and everyone else was already around the table.

"We were wondering when you'd get up." Covey nodded to the tea. "Food is on its way."

"I was up reading late last night."

Alric poured me tea and I settled in next to him.

"Yes. I wanted to ask you where those books came from. But I was told it would be rude to wake you up for that." Covey smiled, but it clearly had taken a lot to hold her back. Books were her favorite things in the world.

"In the library." I took a long sip of tea and looked up to see all of my bookish friends staring at me as if I were a tasty snack. "I forgot about it. But we have a small library behind the kitchen." I'd barely finished speaking when Covey was out of her chair and gone.

Mathilda and Padraig came out with breakfast and both were shaking their heads.

"What's happened to her? She almost slammed into both of us." Padraig sat down plates of eggs and potatoes.

"Taryn recalled where the family library was," Alric said. "That's where those magic books came from."

"Excellent." Padraig looked like he wanted to join Covey, but he and my other bookish companions settled in for food first.

Cwin smiled. "Did those books help figure out fixing the faeries?"

I looked up from shoveling food in. "None of you looked at them?"

"They tried," Grillion said. "Couldn't get them open. Kid-you put a spell on them."

"I did what? Oh. I forgot. My brothers were always playing tricks with my studies. So, I spelled the books.

Sorry about that, I can remove it after breakfast. But I found a spell, the lytleian spaking, that should release the faeries from the contagion that's grounding them. I can show you after we eat." I looked around but the faeries and constructs were missing. They could have gone back to my parent's old room when they left me, but they'd been pretty excited earlier.

"They went outside. Forcibly." Mathilda gave a tense smile. "I adore those girls, but they were driving me crazy. Don't worry, I made sure they understood that if they went through the shield, you wouldn't be able to make them fly again."

"Is that true?" I didn't know what the shield around this place was made of, but that would be bad.

Mathilda laughed. "It shouldn't be. But we have to think as if others are following us. We understand that, but the faeries refuse to. I've only vaguely heard of the lytleian spaking. They were old when I was born." She looked at Cwin and Padraig, but they both shook their heads.

That was disturbing. The spell made more sense in my head now, but it was still complicated. I'd counted on those three, and maybe Alric, to help me with it.

A yell came from the kitchen, then Covey came out with a massive pile of books. "I dropped one in the kitchen—it tried to bite me."

"That was probably one of Griff's books. He was always putting in traps." I smiled at the memory of him and our older brother Elgar running around the cabin that flashed in my head.

"Well, it can stay on the floor for now." Covey glared at the crowded dining table. "I require more room."

Padraig got up, took half of the books off her precarious pile, and then walked over and put them on the sofa. "We'll all go through them after we eat. As lovely as this place is, we can't stay here long. The shield hides us, but if we don't keep moving people will find us—and eventually find a way in."

"I was thinking that a few faery bags could move the entire lot?" We might not need all of them, but I didn't think we had time to sort them out. I was starting to get an itchy feeling between my shoulder blades. One that got worse at Padraig's words. Our time here *was* limited.

"Good thinking." Mathilda nodded to Covey who was still standing with her remaining books. "Put them down, eat, then you can dig into some. But Taryn's right, we should take them all with us. Even the biting ones. Your brothers didn't trap them with anything more dangerous?"

I shrugged. "Not that I recall." I was amazed at what I did remember. But I doubted that my parents would have let them do anything too dangerous. Hopefully.

Covey reluctantly put the books on the sofa, then came and ate. I noticed all of my bookish friends were either watching the pile of books on the sofa or trying to see the library itself by staring through the kitchen walls.

Foxy and Grillion shook their heads and kept eating. I agreed with them and finished a second plate.

The faeries were starting to make noise in front of the cabin now, and I realized I needed to try the spell. I'd explained it in more detail to the other four magic users, hoping that something would sound familiar. Cwin nodded at some parts, but couldn't give much guidance.

"We'll all help where we can, but I think you're the only one who can do it," Alric said as we put the dishes into the kitchen.

"Which doesn't make me happy. And the faeries are getting louder." I came back into the front room and pulled out the book with the spell. The faeries were reaching screeching levels of laughter. Even the shield around this place might not be enough to block the sound of them for long if they kept that up.

"Might want to use the barn behind the one the horses are in. Seeing through that shield is almost impossible, but better not to take chances," Cwin said as we headed for the door.

The faeries swarmed me as I went out. Bunky and Irving held back but were still hovering close. They wanted their faery friends in the air again.

"Okay, girls, settle down and follow me." I should have moved faster before I spoke, as soon I was tripping over faeries running around my legs.

Following was a loose concept for them.

The rest of my friends, including Alric, followed at a safe distance and Bunky and Irving zipped ahead once they realized where we were going.

Padraig released a wave of glows once we went inside the barn. It was larger than the one the horses were currently in, but in worse shape. I felt a pang of loss as I recalled my father saying he was going to fix this one on our next trip. Then the war with the syclarions ended everything.

I took a long slow breath and changed into my dragon form. It came faster this time, and more or less as I wanted.

My friends scrambled backward. I probably should have warned them. To be honest, I didn't think it would work on the first try. The ruins were spacious, but not enough for someone my current size, so I didn't even try to change while we were there.

The faeries squealed and ran around me, flapping their wings even though they couldn't fly. Another tug at my heart. None of them had made a big deal about being stuck without being able to fly during our month in the ruins. But I knew how hard it was for them.

I hoped this worked.

I felt a hand on my front leg and Alric looked up at me.

"You can do this; I know you can." His grin gave me hope.

"Okay, faeries gather in front of me in a circle, but not too close to me. I will need to stomp around all of you for this. Everyone else, I suggest the edges of the barn." While I walked on two legs in my human form, I wasn't quite used to it in my dragon form. Sort of like flying, I knew I'd figure it out eventually.

Right now, I wanted to refrain from squishing my friends. The faeries could survive being squashed; the others weren't as sturdy.

I might have waited a bit longer than necessary for everyone to move back. I had the spell book open on the ground in front of me, but I'd memorized it on the walk over. Nerves were hitting me though.

The trick was to focus. The spell was going to change the faeries on a very basic level, then return them as they were before the contagion spell hit them. Thus, removing all traces of the contagion spell. Easy peasy.

I took another deep breath to settle my racing heart and churning stomach. Then I reared back on my hind legs. And became unbalanced, staggered a bit, and then landed on my behind.

At least I didn't fall completely.

"It's okay, I got this." I raised a front leg toward Alric to keep him back as he moved to come to me. I focused on my back legs and the spell and was finally bipedal.

The faeries cheered with a bit more surprise than I thought was warranted.

I spoke the spell, softly at first, then louder. It had to be repeated six times, then released. The faeries had been still when I began, and remaining in the middle of the circle I was stomping around, but they were fidgeting by the final pass.

Focusing on them returning to their flying status, with no spells or contagions to pass to others, I released the final spell.

A soft light flowed over the entire group of faeries and they began singing. Usually, faery singing was something that could be used to torture miscreants, but like their humming, this was something soft and lovely.

I smiled down at them as they slowly lifted off the ground.

Then everything went dark and I collapsed.

Moments later, I felt tiny hands lightly tapping my face before I opened my eyes. Pretty sure it was the faeries, but if I'd remained in dragon form when I passed out it could have been Alric and the others. "Did it work?" I felt like I'd raced from one end of Beccia to the other a dozen times.

Unlike Covey, I didn't run for fun.

"Open your eyes." Alric was next to me, but I didn't think those were his hands slapping me.

"Urgh. Everything hurts." I forced open both eyes and grinned. I was back in human form and it was the faeries who were tapping me. They did fly-bys overhead and took turns dipping low enough to hit me—softly, luckily. "You're fixed!"

Mathilda came into view. "They're flying, but we'll need to run tests to make sure there's no contagion left." She frowned. "We might need to recruit some test faeries from outside the group."

Which meant potentially dooming them to being exposed to the contagion if my spell hadn't cleared everything out. I pushed myself up and Alric helped me pick straw out of my hair.

"We's gets!" Crusty was flying upside down but looked quite happy about it.

"No, sweetie. All of you have to be checked out first by Mathilda and the others. Maybe Bunky and Irving could bring back some test subject faeries?" I was still exhausted, but the feeling that we needed to get moving was still hitting me.

"Good idea." Padraig nodded to the constructs. "Let us do our tests and if everything works out, we'll send you two to get three or four domesticated faeries—no wilds. But they need to understand the risk of coming here."

I got to my feet and hid my laugh. Even after almost twenty years of living with faeries, I had my doubts concerning their understanding the concept of risk. About anything.

Mathilda, Padraig, and Cwin were already conferring in a corner.

"Do you need the rest of us right now?" I wanted to go inside and crash somewhere soft. And probably drink a pot or two of tea. Covey was already edging toward the barn door and her books.

"What? Oh no, just us three." Mathilda raised her voice as the faeries flew for the door. "And the faeries. Sorry girls. We need to make certain you won't get sick again or infect others. You don't want other faeries being stuck on the ground, do you?"

Garbage had been in the lead to escape, but turned around at Mathilda's words. She held her glare for a few moments, then sighed. "Noes. We's stays."

I was shocked.

"Okay then, we'll be in the house." I left before the three of them could rope me into something else. That spell seriously sucker-punched me.

Foxy and Grillion muttered something about checking the horses and detoured to the other barn. Most likely to get away from the book talk. They might be planning on gambling, but Foxy always won if the faeries weren't there.

Covey raced inside the cabin and by the time Alric

and I joined her, she had a dozen books spread open on the dining room table and was gleefully bouncing between them. She flung one hand toward the pile still on the sofa. The ones I'd been going through, plus some friends. "Those over there seem to be magic spells only, or at least predominately spells. But there are Ancient history books here! Do you know how rare these are?" If she hadn't started drooling yet, it was only a matter of time. "I have a faery bag, so unless any of you object, I'll pack up these when we leave." She was already back to looking at the pages.

"Well, since it's Alric and I, you're fine. And I doubt if the others will fight you to carry them, but they probably want to know what you found." I shared a glance with Alric but he shrugged. He wasn't the history aficionado that many of our friends were.

We shoved aside enough books to sit on the sofa, but I didn't like the way Alric was looking at me.

"What?"

"You still look pale. And no one said anything yet, but after you collapsed you sort of half changed. You were both dragon and human until right before you woke up. Mathilda said you'd be fine, but she and the others were worried too."

"I just feel tired. As for the weird change? Who knows? I've only known who and what I am for a short while. I would like some tea though. And maybe those cookies they had out last night." It sounded like I was whining, even to me, but I smiled to balance it out.

"I'll get them, you stay seated." Alric was gone and came back with more cookies, fruit, and tea than a herd of faeries could eat.

"Hmmm?" Covey hadn't moved as Alric went back and forth but finally looked up. "Oh, you do look pale. Eat lots." She nodded and dove back into her books.

We were going to have a hard time getting her to

leave those books long enough to get them into their bag. She would also need to be watched to make sure she didn't sneak one or two out on the trail.

The door swung open and the faeries, Mathilda, Padraig, and Cwin came in. Bunky and Irving flew in behind them.

"They appear to be fine. Excellent work with a tricky spell." Mathilda moved for the table, then turned and took a seat near the sofa instead.

Covey might have growled softly at her approach, but I wasn't sure.

"We's goes!" Leaf flew through the room so quickly that she was little more than a green blur.

"Not yet." Mathilda held out her hand and Leaf buzzed over to land on it. "We need to make certain it's not going to affect other faeries."

"Bunky and Irving, please go borrow some faeries from Tag in Notlianda, he's probably the closest." Padraig held up a slip of paper. "Give him this. If he can't spare them, try others, but don't go too far. Only go north if there is no other choice." He handed over the paper and Bunky ate it with a nod. "Remember, no wilds."

Padraig held open the door and the constructs zipped out.

I watched through the window as they flew high, but they made it through the shield without a ripple. "Maybe we should start packing up the books? Be ready, just in case?" The tea, cookies, and fruit had helped, but I still felt off. And I didn't like the way Alric and the others were looking at me when they thought I didn't notice.

I also still had the skin-crawling feeling that we needed to leave. This was as close as I was ever going to get to being home. But I wanted to leave soon.

"Good idea." Cwin moved toward Covey's table.

This time all of us heard the low growl.

"Maybe we'll start with bringing out the rest of the books in the library." Cwin smiled and stepped back. "Could the faeries give us a few more bags?"

Garbage must like Cwin, because she flew right over, reached into her tiny pocket on the bib of her overalls, and handed Cwin a bunch of black bags.

Considering how stingy they were with giving them to me, I figured they were in limited supply.

Nope, it was just me. Or they'd restocked them somehow.

Alric and I went through the books I had and he brought out a few more spell-focused ones. The other three worked on sorting the rest of the library. Covey must have already brought out all she wanted as she wasn't going for more. She did manage to pack away the ones she had in a pile on the table, while still pawing through the open books.

Cwin, Mathilda, and Padraig brought out armfuls of books with the faeries mostly staying out of their way. Wisely, none of them went near Covey and her table.

We'd packed away everything from the library, even Covey only had a pair of books still out, when Foxy and Grillion came in.

As expected, Grillion looked annoyed. Most likely he'd been trying to gamble against Foxy again. Alric repeatedly tried to explain to him why that wasn't a good idea. Grillion would smile, nod, and go right back to it.

Then again, he also still thought he might win in cards against the faeries someday. Even though I told him they were most likely cheating.

"Are we getting ready to go then?" Foxy nodded to the books still on Covey's table. Somehow Covey's pair had turned into five. And she was scowling as she flipped through pages.

"Yes, in theory. Covey?" I walked over to her, slowly. "We need to get moving."

"No, no, no. There's something here that we never knew about your people."

"And? What is it?"

"I'm not sure. I need more time."

A thunk came at the door. Alric opened it and Bunky and Irving came flying in with four faeries zipping behind them.

I had trouble just telling apart all the ones with us, so these could be some of the ones who went with Tag back to Notlianda, or not.

All of our faeries swarmed the newcomers completely before Mathilda could say a thing.

"Hopefully there's no contagion left." I watched as the newcomers were greeted as long-lost family. Which was sort of what they were. Faeries normally interacted without concern for distance. The issue of not being able to see more of their kind had probably been as hard on them as the lack of flying.

Mathilda, Cwin, and Padraig moved closer to the flying ball of faeries. Mathilda held out her right hand and closed her eyes. The other two continued the circle around the faeries and did the same.

"They're fine." Mathilda opened her eyes. "The contagion would have spread by now and not only are they still flying, they have nothing in their system that shouldn't be there."

"We's goes!" Garbage had been focusing on the four new faeries, but heard Mathilda.

Padraig smiled. "Yes, but not until we all leave. And I think it might be best to do so when it's still dark, early tomorrow morning would be the safest. We can't be certain that whoever attacked the ruins didn't follow us. And we don't want anyone to see us coming out of an illusion."

"Is fine. I guess." Garbage went into full pout mode for about two seconds, then she and the rest of the mob flew off to the dragon side of the cabin. Bunky and Irving followed them. There was more room on that side for flying and from the screams and laughter coming from there, the girls were making up for lost flying time.

The rest of us broke up to finish our packing, eat, and grab snacks for the road. One advantage of being there for only a short while, only a few things had been taken out.

"Is there anything else you want to take? I have a few more faery bags." Alric's pack was ready to go and by the door of my old room. We'd sleep in our travel clothes to make it easier to leave early.

I looked around. There were no personal things here. My parents made us only bring what we would take back when we went home. Something that made sense at the time, but was sad as my home was now long gone.

"No, but thank you. I'm hoping that we can come back here once things are settled. The books are probably the most personal things here for me and I know I only read a handful of them before."

He hugged me. Then stepped back. "You still look a bit grayish."

"You say the sweetest things." I forced a larger smile than I felt. "I'll be fine. That spell I did was tricky and took a lot out of me."

We went back downstairs to finalize the routes, which I couldn't weigh in on really, the plan was to go over the top of the mountain, then loop down a hidden trail to the northern plain.

Padraig and Alric spent over an hour creating and sending out spell balls through the shield. In theory, they would be waiting for us with warnings if anything passed along the intended trail during the night. It was a serious modification of an Ancient spell and Mathilda and Cwin expressed doubts about its success.

That didn't stop them from trying, and I didn't blame them. We needed to get back out there, find out what the empress was up to, recruit more people to our side, and find a way to free Ageora and any other deities who were trapped in the *tir cudds*.

Not to mention, find my brothers. I didn't bring that up very often, but even with Amara's warning, I'd be checking every *tir cudd* we came across.

And searching those magic books for anything that might help.

This was still the calm before the execution of the empress's plans. She'd been pushed back in those, but even I didn't feel that she'd stay back for long.

The brutal destruction of the town of Yosi pointed that out.

By mutual agreement, we went to bed as the sun was setting in order to leave long before the sun even thought about getting up.

CHAPTER ELEVEN

———

"WAKIES!" CRUSTY'S VOICE IN MY ear after what only felt like a few moments of sleep wasn't a great way to wake up.

I reached up to grab her, expecting to find more faeries as well, but my hand only closed on her.

"Not yet. Need more sleep. Where are the others?" I knew it wasn't time to get up. Mathilda and Padraig had rigged alarms in the hall to get us all moving. I kept my voice to a whisper, but Alric was snoring. It was too dark to see anything, and I didn't feel like calling up a glow if we were still going to be able to sleep for a few more minutes.

Crusty took a deep breath, held it, and glowed. The blue light from her body indicated that she was the only faery in the room.

"Thanks, sweetie. But I think we have more time."

"Nots haves times. Comes." She squirmed out of my hand and pulled on my fingers.

"What are you doing?"

"Needs goes. Sees before leaves."

I glanced at Alric, but he was still sound asleep. And I didn't know what time it was, nor why she was here but not the rest.

"Fine. Let me get my boots on first." I got them on and patted down my hair a bit. I doubted that any of my friends were up yet. Alric was one of the lightest sleepers usually and if he was still out, we couldn't have gone to bed too long before. I also created a glow. Having a glowing faery was handy, but not completely trustworthy. Especially going down stairs.

I waited until we'd left my room and were halfway down the stairs to speak again, still in a whisper. "What do I need to see and why couldn't I have seen it before we went to bed? And where are your friends?" I'd expected to see the rest of her horde out in the main part of the cabin, but they weren't anywhere to be seen.

Neither were Bunky and Irving. Hopefully, they were trying to keep the girls under control.

Or they were part of whatever mayhem the girls were currently involved with.

The curtains in the front room were drawn but a faint flickering of colored light still shone along the edges.

"Nots times then. Times nows." Crusty pulled on my hand as I reached for the door. "Yous needs believes." Her tiny blue face, usually laughing, was extremely serious. And even sad. "This importants."

"Okay, sweetie. What do I need to believe?" I held on to the door handle but didn't turn it.

"Whats yous sees." She released my hand and nodded toward the door.

I cautiously opened the door.

The faeries were doing some sort of dance in the air. The lights came from them holding their breath and flashing their colors.

Bunky and Irving were on a nearby stump, watching.

"What am I supposed to believe?" I felt relief, honestly. Crusty had worried me. A weird faery dance I could handle. If I was lucky, I could go back to my room and get a bit more sleep before we had to leave.

"New olds. Yous too. New olds. Importants." Crusty

remaining extremely serious wasn't as nice as I thought it would be.

"New old tricks? But you already could glow." I hoped she wasn't saying that I could glow. Okay, it might be fun, but also weird.

"Noes. This." Crusty flew off to her friends. The faeries continued to glow as they formed a circle in the air. Between their glowing and the soft light coming from the shield behind them, it was a bit odd to watch. As if they were creating a portal to some distant land.

Then it turned bad.

Images appeared in the center of the faery circle that were vague and indistinct, yet still strangely disturbing. I wanted to run back into the cabin but forced myself to stay. Then the faeries began to hum. Not one of the songs they'd gathered from me, but it was still mostly soothing.

The images solidified and I bit back a scream.

Desolation filled everything I saw. It began where we'd initially landed on the Southern continent. Even the solid fortress Alric almost died in was rubble. The stretch of water between the two continents was littered with broken ships that bobbed in the water—including Jadiera's *Dangerous Lady*. It was as if something was preventing them from sinking but there were no signs of life anywhere.

The visions moved faster and I turned to get away from them, but I was tied to them somehow.

The entire southern continent was destroyed. Then it changed to the north and I almost screamed again as an indescribable horde raced through the land. Literally indescribable. They shifted forms as they ran, but destroyed everything in their path.

"The empress..." I felt the tears rolling down my face but I couldn't stop the images. And the feelings.

"Noes." The images returned to the south. Rows of

slaughtered fighters, all wearing the empress's colors and many holding the banners of the Dark covered a wide plain.

"What happened?"

"Yous dids." Crusty broke the circle and flew to me. "We's stops."

"I do this?" I was hiccupping with sobs. "I wouldn't do this." I couldn't do this. I wanted to save the world, not destroy it.

Crusty cut me off with a hand across my mouth. "We's halps. Yous knows. Heres." She flew to my heart and patted it. "And heres." Then back up and tapped my head. "Nows noes happens."

I wiped away my tears as the images faded and the faeries all came around me.

"So, it won't happen? That's all it took?" I had a flash of that evil out-of-control feeling when I had the canfydd crown and the power I'd wielded. But this was far beyond that. I looked around for a place to be sick.

Garbage flew up to my face. "Noes. Is goods yous believes. Could stills happens." Her being serious wasn't shocking, but the compassion on that tiny orange face was.

"Okay, what do I need to do?" I forced myself not to throw up. "Leave the others? Go into hiding? What?"

"Waits. You'll knows and we's halps. Bonds." Garbage motioned between her and me then kissed my cheek.

That was a sign for the rest of the faeries and soon I was covered in hugging and kissing faeries.

"Wait, there are a lot more here than before." And many appeared to be wilds judging by their leaf wardrobes.

"We's calls. Needs mores." Leaf ensconced herself on my shoulder and looked like she wasn't letting go.

"What about Queen Mungoosey?" The faeries had a cat-faery queen and although tiny, like all of them, she was not one to be messed with. She didn't agree with Garbage and her group and resented the domestication of the wild faeries.

"She understands. Halps." Garbage pulled back and waved to the wilds. "Nows we's noes sicks."

I might be the one to destroy the entire world. Even though the visions only showed the northern and southern continents, the feeling that hit my gut was that the destruction was everywhere. And while I might have accidentally sent my people out of time, and thrown back the evolution of the syclarions by a few thousand years, this wasn't an accident.

This was going to be hard to get over. I wanted to tell the others. I needed to in case they had to lock me up or destroy me. But I needed to process it first.

"Okay. What do I need to do?" I didn't feel quite as ill as before, but I needed to do something to stop this.

"Goes to sleeps." Leaf, Crusty, and Garbage stayed near me as the other faeries flew away.

"Thanks, but I don't think that's going to be possible after what I just saw." I didn't think I'd ever be sleeping again after that.

"Sleeps." Garbage gave me a huge smile and then poked me in the middle of my forehead.

The world went black and I collapsed.

◆

"Taryn!" Alric's voice cut through the fog of sleep although I couldn't figure out why he was yelling since we were in the same bed.

Then a rock jabbed into my side as I turned to roll over. It was still mostly dark, but a faint dawn was peeking through on the horizon. Alric, Covey, and Foxy were hovering over me and I was on the ground outside of the cabin.

"What happened?" I sat up with help and brushed grass, dirt, and twigs out of my hair.

"We were going to ask you. Why were you out here? Were you attacked?" Covey looked ready to trounce any hidden attackers at my word.

The reality of why I was out there slammed into my mind. "No. I came out here because of the faeries. They needed to show me something. Then decided I needed to sleep. Here, apparently." I rubbed the middle of my forehead where Garbage had touched me. That was a new trick. Or an old-new one. Either way, knowing the faeries had that ability was good and bad. If it could be used against enemies—good. If they continued using it against us, or in this case, me—bad.

Alric was checking me for injuries but pulled back at my words. "The faeries put you to sleep?" From the look of concern in his green eyes, he'd made the same connection that I had. And was equally worried about it.

"Near as I can tell. They said I needed to go back to sleep, Garbage poked my forehead, and then boom, I woke up here." I looked around. "Where are they?" Bunky and Irving were missing as well.

"In the barn with the horses, helping Padraig load them," Alric said with enough emphasis on 'helping' I knew they were doing their version of it. "When I woke and you were missing, we searched the cabin for you. Padraig and the others were loading the horses in case you'd left the shielded area."

"But I was right…outside the front door." I looked around where I was. I thought the vision from the faeries had taken place immediately outside the front door. But I was now off to the side in a clump of trees and shrubs. The shield glowed softly about a foot from where I sat.

"The faeries woke you up, led you out here, and then

knocked you out?" Covey sounded disappointed that there was no one for her to beat up.

"Yup. They said we're getting more support from Queen Mungoosey—more wild faeries." I blinked a few times when I swore I heard Queen Mungoosey's voice in my mind giving directions. "And we need to go north." I shook my head as Foxy's eyes went wide. He dearly wanted to be with Amara, but he was committed to this fight. And he still was dealing with the fallout from his wanted status by the Klipu mob.

"Not to the northern continent. But toward the northern part of this one." I frowned. The voice was no longer in my head, but a strong tug of direction was. I knew where we needed to go, even if I wasn't sure why. I also didn't know that I could explain it to others. "Do we have a map of the entire southern continent?"

"Padraig has one." Alric helped me get up when I tried to do so, but he didn't look happy about it. "Should you be getting up right now?"

"I fell asleep out here." I dusted off my clothes. "It wasn't fun, and I intend to talk to Garbage and the faeries about not doing that again, but really, that was all. If they'd done it when I was back in bed, I wouldn't have even noticed." Of course, now that the thought crept in, I wondered if they'd done it other times and I *hadn't* noticed.

Once I processed the visions I'd seen, I'd tell Alric and the others. But right now, I simply couldn't.

The girls and I were going to have a long talk in the near future about a lot of things.

We walked toward the barn as Padraig and Mathilda came riding out.

"You found her!" Mathilda jumped off her horse and ran to me. "Are you okay? We were afraid you'd been taken."

Padraig got off his horse and Cwin came out as well,

with Grillion leading the rest of the horses. They also ran to me.

"I'm fine." I held up my hands. "The faeries wanted to tell me about their new additions and Queen Mungoosey somehow gave me a direction to go to next. Unfortunately, Garbage decided to put me back to sleep. Out in the trees. Have you ever heard of them having that ability? She touched my forehead and dropped me."

Mathilda frowned at my words. I figured that it was more at my weak story of why the faeries brought me out there than what Garbage had done. Or at least a combination of both. "No. But they do keep rediscovering old tricks and that might be one." Her eyes narrowed and I was afraid she was going to ask for a better explanation. Then she shook her head. I was pretty sure that she knew I wasn't saying something, but could tell that I was holding back for a reason and wasn't going to call me on it. Yet.

"Where did Queen Mungoosey say to go?" Padraig also appeared to have suspicions but was also holding back.

Even though it was difficult to read Cwin's face—I was sure she held the same thoughts as the other two. I wasn't a great liar, even through omission.

I smiled and ignored them for now. "I need a map of the southern continent. It was more an impression than actual directions. Beyond north, anyway."

Grillion frowned. "Back up to Beccia?"

"No, just north of here. But not where we rescued Alric. Over more." I waved my hand to the left as if that would help. It was hard to explain what I felt in my head. Made even more so by the faint flashes of the visions of destruction. Those were going to haunt me for a long time.

I shoved them aside for now. I needed more information to process what I saw. Even with that evil crown, a single Ancient couldn't do that much damage. Some element was missing.

Padraig opened one of his faery bags and brought out a collection of scrolls. "There's not a lot of details on these, at least not about where we currently are. But this one has the entire continent." He handed over a large scroll and Alric and I unrolled it.

"This works. We need to go here." I unerringly tapped the far left northern corner of the southern continent. It looked like a village on a plain, not far from the water separating the northern and southern continents, was the destination. It was bordered by a steep mountain range. There were no indications of any large cities, but the map was very old.

"What's there?" Cwin tilted her head to look at the map and tapped the sharp mountains. "The Lledir mountains are one of the few mountain ranges the siramages have never occupied."

My smile faded. "I'm not sure. I'm sorry, this is all from the faeries and their queen. Maybe we shouldn't use them as guides." The tug I felt meant there was something important about that village. But without knowing what or why, I was starting to have doubts.

"Yous awakes!" Garbage led her inflated flock out of the barn with Bunky and Irving zipping alongside them. "Yays!" The faeries and constructs circled overhead. It was a good thing that our horses were used to the girls. They didn't bolt, but a few ears did go back when some faeries dropped lower.

"Garbage? Do you know why Queen Mungoosey said to go here?" I tapped the corner of the map while all the faeries repeated their queen's full name, "High Queen Princess Buttercup Turtledove RatBatZee Growltigerious Mungoosey, empress of all". If they were dropping back into saying that when her name was mentioned, I was going to ban the use of her name completely.

"Is where gets stuffs." She nodded sagely as if I now knew the secret of the universe.

"What stuff?" Alric asked.

"The. Stuffs. Importants. Dangerous. Mights dies." She shrugged. "Needs it."

"That's not helpful." Mathilda stepped forward. "Can you clarify a bit? That's a long way to go, and we're trying to prepare to stop the empress and the Dark from taking over everything."

Garbage shot me a somber look, but it was so quick that I wasn't sure that anyone else noticed it.

Probably for the best.

"This importants. Needs or bads things happens." This time her look at me lasted longer and a few of my friends switched from watching her to watching me. Whatever was there, it was most likely tied to keeping me from destroying the world—or allowing it to be destroyed.

"I think we should at least see what's there. If we don't want to all go, maybe I could fly up there with the faeries on my own."

Alric gave me a look that said I was crazy. "That's not a good idea. There are still too many people who want you."

My blood specifically, to create a race of crazed super monsters, but I was grateful for him not saying it.

"Needs goes." Garbage sighed and looked around with a scowl. "Most needs goes."

"We're going to listen to them now? That's not an easy route. Qianru sent me up that way with a message for her sister once. It wasn't easy. The locals aren't friendly to outsiders, or anyone not a former pirate anyway." Grillion was looking at the map so he didn't see Garbage narrow her eyes at his comment.

"They goes. Yous noes goes." She folded her arms and flew up to Grillion's face.

"Now, you can't just send others off," Mathilda said.

Grillion got an odd look and nodded to Garbage. "You know something about me?"

"Yous needs to works. Then brings togethers everyone." She looked sad as she turned to Foxy. "Hims too. Not longs though." The faeries from Beccia loved Foxy. Mostly because of the free ale he gave them, but he was also gentle, and never chastised them.

Covey had been watching silently but spoke up now. "So, all of us, except Grillion and Foxy, are going to this mysterious place to get the things we need to save the world?"

"Yes. Yous goes with us. Thems goes to bird lady." She waved to a group of ten wild faeries that separated from the pack. "These goes with yous twos. Stays togethers." The last part was aimed at Grillion and Foxy.

Bird lady was the term the faeries used for Qianru, my former patron.

"I don't be knowing about separating. If it's dangerous, we could be needed." Foxy wasn't happy.

But Grillion was okay. Oddly. "No, I think this is right. It's to do with what that goddess told me in my head. Not sure why you're being included, Foxy, but I think I do need to go to Qianru."

Garbage nodded and grinned.

Grillion watched Garbage carefully. "But I didn't need to go when Tag left us?" He'd thought he was supposed to go with Tag at the time, but then decided against it. He looked more at peace with going now.

She nodded, smiled, and scowled but didn't add anything.

I rubbed the heels of my hands on my forehead as my headache grew worse. It could have been like the rest of my aches—coming from my time spent sleeping on the ground. Or it was an unwelcome side effect of the current issues with the faeries.

"Let's grab some food to eat on the trail and get going. The sun will be up soon and this is already later than I'd wanted to leave," Padraig said.

"I have your things." Alric nodded to the packs sitting on the front stoop.

"Thank you. Let's get going." I gave the cabin a quick look then turned away. If I took too long, I might not leave.

We were ready to cross the shield a half hour later. Grillion and Foxy would ride with us over the mountain, then they would turn down another trail and across the plains to the south to Notlianda.

I was sad at their leaving. Foxy was one of my oldest friends, along with Covey and Harlan. Even Grillion had become a good friend. I understood what we were facing was massive and potentially world-changing— even more after the faeries' vision last night—but I still hated that we were separating our group again.

"They'll be fine," Alric said as I swung onto my horse.

"I know. But I'd feel better if we were together. Not only them, but everyone." I shrugged. "I'll be okay, but spreading us out means widening the worries as well."

He patted my hand and then went to his horse.

I felt bad about not telling anyone about what Garbage and the faeries had shown me. But I couldn't talk about it until I sorted it more in my head. Finding out that you might be the one who destroys everything was unnerving. Especially with my record. It could be an accident, like what I did to myself and my people twenty-five hundred years ago.

Or I could be hiding a really evil side that was going to come out. That was a cheerful thought.

"What's wrong?"

I hadn't noticed that I'd stopped my horse until Covey spoke up from behind me.

"Sorry, thought I'd forgotten something." I nudged my horse to the shield, then waited off to the side to go last.

Padraig led everyone else through the shield and I was the last. The collective magic users weren't sure if it made a difference since they'd been allowed in, but Padraig felt it might be good if I closed things out as it were. First one in, last one out.

The faeries zipped through the shield with Padraig, but Garbage, Leaf, and Crusty flew back to me as Alric passed through ahead of me.

"Yous be okays. No sads. Place happy yous came." Garbage smiled and waved to the cabin. "It stays safe."

I tried to memorize every windowsill, then smiled. "Thank you. We do need to talk by the way. Alone."

She kissed my cheek then she and the other two flew back out of the shield.

I sighed and rode through.

The spell balls Padraig and Alric sent to check around us didn't show any riders coming through in the past day. Nor anything larger than a fox appearing to pass through. It could be because of something being out in the forest scaring off wildlife. Or a slow evening. The spell balls were limited, so the details weren't great. I hoped they were right about no riders though.

The trail was wider now, but steeper, so we mostly remained in single file.

Foxy was ahead of me and reached down for his tattoo to call Amara.

"Is that a good idea? We still don't know what happened when you tried to call her yesterday." That could be one problem of us separating. Foxy wasn't happy having to go through me each time to speak to his wife, but he'd not last long if he couldn't speak to her at all.

"Ach. I forgot." He tugged on one long floppy ear.

"I want to work on sorting out what happened with that before we separate." Cwin turned around and nodded to Foxy. "I have a feeling it's a simplistic spell that's latched onto the magic Amara created. Once I fix it, I'll deal with Taryn's tattoo as well to make it secure."

"Thank ye on that. I don't mind a side trip, but not speaking to Amara would be bad." He turned back to me. "I did tell her I'd contact her when we left."

I looked to Cwin who was forming some spell in the air. She nodded. "Go ahead, but keep it short."

I touched my tattoo.

"Taryn? Is Foxy okay?" Amara's voice sounded far away, but aside from that it sounded like her.

"He's fine, he's just moving some rocks on our trail." I shrugged as Foxy gave me an odd look. I had to say something and right now telling her that Foxy's communication tattoo had been waylaid wasn't a great idea. "He asked me to let you know we're on the trail."

"Thank you. That is a relief. We're all fine here as well. Tell him that I will speak to him later."

"She's fine and she'll speak to you later." Amara's voice had sort of floated in the air near my arm, but Foxy would have been too far away to hear her. I hoped that Cwin could fix this before Amara tried to contact him.

I was a big fan of sleeping in, something I so rarely got to do that the concept was like a mythical creature—I wasn't sure it existed at all. But I had to admit that watching the sun come up while on a forest trail with people I loved, was amazing in its own right. It got even better when Padraig led us around a steep bend that flattened out to a lookout over the plains.

It was truly lovely. Until I looked to the south. "That dark smudge is Yosi, isn't it?" I kept my voice low but the others heard me. Yosi survived more than a thousand years, and through a major war. I couldn't help but feel that if we hadn't gone there it would still be standing.

"It's not your fault." Covey rode up next to me. "I know what you're thinking. You didn't destroy Yosi. The empress and the Dark did."

"Yeah, but what if they were only there because we were? Because *I* was?"

Covey moved her horse forward to block my morose staring. "No. And don't even think about taking off on us again. Ever." She was still upset from when I'd taken off a while ago. *Just* because I'd turned into a dragon for the first time, had no idea what I was, and was afraid I would stomp on all of my friends.

It wasn't my best decision, but given the circumstances at the time, I stood by it.

"I'm not going to take off. But don't you think it's suspicious that people were after us there, you became a piece of statuary, the faeries lost their ability to fly, and then the town fell? It had magical protection that had lasted over a thousand years. Then poof. Gone." I was settling into a good funk, one fed by those images the faeries showed me.

"I'd say the forces that destroyed Yosi had been planning it long before we got there." Mathilda had been off to the side, looking to the north, but came over at my words. "They knew how to break down the spells protecting the town. Yes, I do believe we, *all of us*, were a target. But that was only after the town was set up to be destroyed."

"And there is probably more than one group involved." Covey nodded.

"I'm still going to feel bad about it." I folded my arms.

"As long as it makes you happy and doesn't distract you from what we have to do." Mathilda turned to go, then added, "And Covey is right. Don't take off on your own." Then she joined Padraig, Cwin, and Alric as they debated some point of the map.

Map. "Hey, do we still have that weird map that could show the past?" It freaked me out when we were in Yosi, but it might give a clue as to what we were looking for when we got to the Lledir mountains and the plains beyond them.

Padraig looked up. "We do, but it's fairly location specific and will change as we travel. Did you want to see something on this mountain?"

"Not really, how close do we have to get to an area for it to work?"

"I'd say we won't see much of the plains where the village is until we're almost there," Alric said. "But good thinking. Just going there and hoping the faeries know what we're looking for isn't the best plan."

The faeries were busy looping out over the side of the mountain in a twisted game of tag with Bunky and Irving so didn't hear him.

"Just a thought." I looked to Yosi again and made a silent vow. The more I recalled who I really was, and what my people were, the more responsible for things I felt. My people had been protectors. The main reason the syclarions, specifically the Paili, declared war on us was because we wouldn't stand by and let them destroy others.

CHAPTER TWELVE

"THAT'S A FIERCE LOOK." COVEY nudged her horse alongside mine.

"I can't bring back the people of Yosi, but I can avenge them. We can't let the empress and her flunkies win." Even though I had become fairly proficient at it in the past few years, I wasn't a fighter. In fact, up until a minute ago, I wouldn't have thought of myself as such. But the sorrow about what happened to Yosi had turned to anger. This couldn't be allowed to happen again.

"Just don't go overboard. This isn't going to be taken care of quickly." But there was a tone of pride in Covey's voice. She *was* a fighter. Even when she denied her berserker side, she would always fight injustice when she saw it.

"Agreed. And I'm glad you're with me on this." I pulled myself away from staring at the smudge that was once Yosi. It could live with the images the faeries showed me until we stopped all of this.

Covey grinned back. "We've come a long way, you and me. I've no intention of leaving you now. Someone needs to keep you out of trouble."

"Let's get moving. Not sure if it's coming our way or not, but there's a thin trail of dust coming from the bottom of this mountain." Padraig and the others were already in line, it was just Covey, myself, the constructs, and the faeries—who were lagging.

"Coming. Girls? Come on, we need to get back on the trail." A chorus of whines was their response, but they joined us. With some nudging from Bunky and Irving.

Covey was the last to turn away from the view below and when she did, she wasn't smiling anymore. "Whatever is down there is moving too fast to be natural."

Padraig and Alric brought out long glasses and both swore in unison.

"You're right. It was hard to tell before." Alric looked around the mostly open area we were in. "We can't protect ourselves well here. I say we go into the woods and find a place to defend." From the tone of his voice, outrunning whatever was behind us wasn't an option.

Padraig spun his horse around and we followed him as fast as was safe to go.

While that brief open area would have been harder to defend, it was easier to ride in. Within an hour we were in the deep forest. Better to hide in, more difficult to move through.

Bunky, Irving, and the faeries stayed low under the trees, but every once in a while a pair of faeries would dart up above the tree line, and then rejoin a few moments later.

So far Garbage hadn't said anything to any of us. But she was scowling and speaking softly to her commanders.

"I hear something." Grillion was in the middle of us. "I can't be the only one." He probably had the most limited hearing of our group, but I hadn't heard anything.

"Damn it, so do I." Covey turned her horse around but Cwin and her horse blocked her.

"We can't outrun them. We need to find a place to defend ourselves. They can't be allowed to get past us."

Padraig caught her words at the same time I did. "You know what's coming." It wasn't a question.

"Flinms. They shouldn't be down here. But they will devour us, our horses, the faeries if they can catch them, and then continue as far as they can get. We can't let them get past us." Cwin rarely reminded me of the other grimarians I'd run into, but she did now. Her fur poofed making her twice as large, her eyes went red, and her fangs, not normally visible, grew longer.

"Those are myths," Mathilda's voice remained low, but there wasn't much belief behind her words.

"I've never heard of them, and I doubt Taryn and the others have." Alric kept his words soft as he looked through the trees. "But I can see a rock wall not far from here."

Covey went pale, not an easy thing for a trellian to do. "Do you mean cothiflinms? Children's stories, nothing more." But her fingers were already becoming claws and her shoulders were broadening.

"Whats does?" Garbage dropped down between Mathilda and me. The faeries briefly returned to flying higher, but all of them, along with Bunky and Irving, dropped to right above our heads. That and their silence were scaring me almost more than the others' reactions to Cwin's words. Not to mention Covey's words.

"Girls, we are facing a vile enemy. One that none of you can fight. *No matter what.* You must not fight." Mathilda kept her voice steady but there was way too much fear in her voice.

Bunky and Irving buzzed closer and gronked at Mathilda.

"You two can fight, but stay near us. The faeries need to flee."

Even I was shocked at that. "But—"

"No. I thought they could stay, but they can't. The flinms are magic eaters. They can't be allowed to take the faeries."

I held out my hand and waited until Garbage landed on it. "You have to take your faeries and fly to the top of the mountain, maybe beyond."

"We's fights?"

The subdued tone of her voice hit hard.

"You have to leave, so you can fight another day. This foe wants you, and if you're with us, it will kill us all. I need you to stay alive, no matter what."

"This nots foreseen," she said in a real whisper that I didn't think any of them could do.

"No, it's not. Can you do this? Go away? Actually, forget this mountain, find the rest of the faeries with Tag." That idea hit me in the moment, but it was a safer location for them and we could find them later.

Provided we survived.

Something of the seriousness of the situation reached her. She nodded solemnly. "We goes. Stays safes." She flew over, kissed my cheek, then she and the rest of her group vanished.

I was surprised it had been that easy, but if there was a time for her to listen to us, this was it.

A sudden flash of insight as to what we were facing hit me, and I was furious. "Bunky and Irving, listen to Alric and Padraig. They'll tell you what to do."

"Taryn, what are you doing?" Alric was still at the edge of the forest, looking toward the boulders they'd make their stand at. But he was already getting off his horse.

I was faster. I jumped off my horse as my sword appeared and I held it up. "Not this time, but thank you." It vanished. Then I turned to Alric and the others. "I have to buy you all time. Those things want magic, let them meet mine." I didn't have time to explain, but I now knew what those things were. As a little kid, they'd attacked our town and done some serious damage before they were stopped. To reinforce my words, I locked a shield around the entire group. I knew with the amount of magic they had it wouldn't take them long to break it.

By then I'd be gone.

I ran to another clearing I'd seen while they were trying to call me back without making a lot of noise. A low buzzing behind me told me that Bunky and Irving were staying with me. I almost sent them back but changed my mind as we hit the clearing.

Another part of a memory hit me. My father pointing out that while they were magical creations, constructs couldn't feed the creatures coming after us. The chimeras had fought to save our town. "You two can stay with me, but if I tell you to leave, you go back to the others. Got it?"

Both constructs bobbed in agreement. It only took two tries to change into my dragon form and get the wings on. Staying in our summer home might have helped in more ways than one.

The clearing was tighter than I would have liked, but I kicked off hard with my back legs before I began flapping. Bunky and Irving remained nearby, but far away enough not to be caught in the draft of my wings.

Or my wildly flapping tail. I took a calming breath and willed it to stay in place.

The trail of smoke was much closer now, but still not thick. Although I recalled the creatures, my people called them jailanks, I didn't know what they looked like. I was only about five or six when they attacked our town. My brothers, both much older, joined in the fight. I was left with a powerful old guardian and not even allowed to look out the windows.

Bunky flew closer to my head as we moved toward the trail of dust. He gronked forcefully and while I didn't understand specific words, the sentiment came across—he really hoped that I knew what I was doing.

"So do I, Bunky." A delayed thought hit me. To be fair, I was working on my wings, flying, and a tail that was still twitching more than I liked. I wasn't going to blame myself for not thinking of this sooner. "Can you reach your people? Even just the ones that helped in Yosi would be useful."

Bunky gronked in agreement, then turned to Irving. As far as I could tell, he was telling Irving to defend me while he left. Irving's responding gronk didn't sound happy but Bunky vanished a moment later.

I flew higher to get a better view, but also because fear was hitting me. I had no idea of the size of the group of creatures I was about to take on, nor how it compared to the swarm that hit my hometown eons ago.

But I did recall it took most of the town's adults to stop them.

Then I saw the smudge of Yosi in the distance. There was a chance that those magic-eating monsters weren't related to the empress and the Dark. But the way things had been going, I seriously doubted it.

An unintended burst of flame startled both Irving and me—I was pissed again. Also afraid for Alric and the rest of my friends, but fear wasn't going to work as well as anger right now.

Ideally we'd wait at least until Bunky brought back the reinforcements—but at the rate that 'dust' was coming up the mountain, we were out of time. "Let's do this, Irving." I flexed my front claws. I had no idea if the creatures we were after were large enough to grab, but I felt like ripping something evil apart.

Irving stayed close to me as we dove. The trail of dust rising into the sky was masking the creatures, but they seemed small. Or it was that I was currently massive. Something I still wasn't used to.

A weird tingling hit the back of my mind and told me to give up. The feeling grew stronger, but after the initial surprise it made me angrier. I mentally grabbed ahold of what was poking at me and sent back a command of my own—drop dead. I didn't remember the flinms being telepathic, but I had been a kid at the time. Plus, there could be a magic user with them trying to get me to back down.

Which wouldn't be done if I wasn't seen as a threat.

There was a brief feeling of shock from more minds than I could count, then nothing. I should have had a plan, but while rage motivated me, it didn't leave much room for anything else.

I went lower, flaming as I went. The dust cleared and dozens of pony-sized creatures with massive fangs and wicked horns burst into flame.

Then the survivors grew wings that looked a lot like tiny dragon wings. Damn it. They not only tried to snack on my magic, they used it to adapt themselves. They'd picked up my ability from that brief incursion into my mind and now they could fly.

I might have destroyed a bunch of them, but I'd now made the ones left far more dangerous. I flew over them again, but they were so much smaller than me that flaming them wasn't working well when they scattered. Luckily, none of them flamed back, but I didn't know how long that would last.

A cloud appeared to my right, too fast to be natural, but too far to see if there was anything inside it. I pulled back so I could keep an eye on it and the flinms coming toward me. At least they weren't able to fly fast.

Irving's gronk startled me as the monsters flying below charged up to attack us. Before I could respond, the cloud on my right burst into a massive group of chimeras. I'd been hoping for the twenty who'd helped us in Yosi, but there were probably over a hundred.

They were silent at first, but were now buzzing and crackling as lightning strikes shot out toward the flinms flying toward us.

Most of the flinms burst into flame and drifted to the ground as dust. Unfortunately, more of them rose toward us. They were focusing on me and trying to avoid the constructs.

Bunky led the chimeras around me. Good in terms of protection, but not so great for me to help with the fight. I'd already inadvertently given those beasts the ability to fly, I needed to stop them.

Some of the flinms still on the ground were also taking the opportunity to continue up the trail toward Alric and my friends.

"Bunky, you and Irving plus your people need to keep fighting the ones here. I can't let those things get to our friends." Bunky gronked in what sounded like disagreement, but ten of the chimeras flew closer to me while Irving moved closer to Bunky. "Thank you."

My escorts and I swung around and flew after the flinms racing up the trail. I hadn't seen any signs of my friends following me, and I was hoping they stayed where they could defend themselves.

The flinms turned to fly down the trail my friends were on.

Damn it. The very reason we'd gone on that path into the forest was what was causing a major problem now. I was way too large to fly under that canopy.

The chimeras were able to do so, however, and crackles of lightning were seen through the trees.

I felt like Covey when she wasn't allowed to fight—I wanted to be in the thick of it. The scattered memories of the damage those flinms caused were making me angrier.

Something from one of the magic books popped into my head. It had to do with size. I didn't pay much attention at the time because I was looking for a way to fix the faeries. A flash of me as a kid, scaring both of my brothers by making myself into an adapted dragon form. One small enough to ambush them from under the table, almost smacked me out of the air.

Oh yes, I now recalled this spell. It took three times to get right, but then I was a much smaller, but still as powerful, pissed-off dragon. I followed the chimeras through the tree line. I was about twice the size of them now, but they didn't appear surprised at my appearance.

I flew low over the running flinms and released my flame. The chimeras zipped alongside me and continued sending electric currents at the flinms. The monsters exploded into dust.

I was congratulating myself on stopping the evil things when a massive boom filled the air.

A black-cloaked mage appeared in a show of fire and smoke in the middle of the dusted flinms.

I pulled back and called for the chimeras to do the same. "Really? Hiding under a black cloak?"

"It's good to see an Ancient with her constructs. They will come under our control when we bring you in. These were nothing more than a gambit. You won this time. But we will win eventually." The voice sounded male, but there was nothing to be seen through the cloak. A long arm, also wearing black, protruded. I pulled back and motioned for the chimeras to as well, but the arm pointed to a tree and heavy, painful words filled the air as it burst into flame.

Then the mage and what was left of the flinms vanished and the chimeras and I tumbled out of the sky.

CHAPTER THIRTEEN

I TRANSFORMED BACK TO MY HUMAN form as I fell, but I wasn't sure if I did it, or if the person in that dark and brooding cloak did. I scrambled to my feet armed with my push spell in case they hadn't really left.

The chimeras appeared to be stunned but were shaking themselves and slowly lifting off the ground. Understanding what Bunky was trying to communicate was one thing. Ten pissed-off chimeras were impossible. Beyond the fact that they wanted to zap that person in the cloak.

"Taryn? Are you okay?" Alric came running up behind me as I was trying to calm down the chimeras. I was grateful that they wanted to destroy the person behind this, but one of them almost zapped Alric as he stepped out from the trees.

"I am, did any of them get to you?" I ran to him after shaking my finger at the aggressive chimera.

"No, but we heard the chimeras. Where are Bunky and Irving?"

"They were taking care of the flying ones."

"No one said anything about them flying."

I winced. "Yeah, they hit me when we first found them and might have pulled that ability from me. On a plus side, I remembered the spell to change my size so I could fly in here." I turned and waved to the surrounding trees.

"They stole part of your magic?" Alric spun me back to him. "Are you okay?"

I loved that he cared about me so much, but this was the "I need to lock you up somewhere safe" look. Not a big fan of that.

"They *copied* it more than stole anything. And it seemed like only some of them got it. By the way, they look like monster ponies that want to rip your throat out." I gave him my largest, most convincing smile. "I'm fine."

"You know that you look anything except fine when you do that." He folded his arms. "And taking off like that—"

I put one finger across his lips to cut him off. I also dropped my attempt at a smile. "I won't back down on that. I can't explain it, but *I* needed to stop them. And while there were about fifty or so, they can travel in packs that would fill the valley floor." I shuddered. I saw them briefly before my parents locked me up in our house. There were thousands. "This might have been a test. Someone is trying to bring them back. My people destroyed them when I was young and that mage had to be behind this." I was even more annoyed at not knowing who the mage was. They'd not been upset about their creatures being destroyed, because they were expecting it. They wanted to see what we'd do.

What I'd do.

"Mage? There was someone with them?"

Bunky and Irving were gronking as they made their way toward us but weren't in the trees yet. Once I'd been certain none of the flinms made it to our friends, I'd planned on going back to find them.

"Not with them during the attack, but after. All in black, with a cloak and hood, and might have been disguising their voice. They didn't seem upset or surprised that their creatures lost the fight."

Bunky, Irving, and the rest of the chimeras swooped under the treetops and came over to us.

"Thank you, Bunky. You, Irving, and your friends saved the day." He didn't need to know that this was a ruse. If we hadn't stopped the flinms where we did, the attacks could have been deadly, even if they were only a test.

Alric looked between Bunky, who gronked at him too fast for me to understand, and me. "He says that you're right, but it was still a big risk." He put his arm around my shoulders and turned us back toward the woods.

"But we now know there is at least one powerful mage behind them, and that they can mimic stolen magic even if they don't eat it."

"Point, but it was still a risk."

I pulled on his arm and looked up into his eyes. "Our lives have been risky since we met. And I still wouldn't change anything." Okay, that sounded good, but I would change a lot of things if I could. However, having Alric in my life wasn't one of them.

"Sigh. Agreed. You're worth the stress." He squeezed my shoulder.

The constructs followed behind us as we got to the massive rock outcropping where our friends were waiting. The horses must have been spelled and hidden, as there wasn't any sign of them.

"Halt!" A massive Padraig appeared before us, waving an equally massive sword. He and it were almost completely see-through against the rock face, however.

"You got the spell to work! Still needs development though, the rocks are showing through." Alric walked up to the figure and swung his hand through one of the tree-sized legs. "But I haven't seen a dilana spell since I was a kid."

The image laughed then vanished and the real Padraig, along with everyone else, came out from behind a short rock wall. One that was so well blended with the rock wall behind it, that I hadn't even known it was there.

I tapped it and it felt like a rock—then it crumbled and vanished.

"I haven't tried one of those in hundreds of years." Cwin grinned. "Easier to do non-animated objects than people. Even with help." She winked at Padraig.

"I take it the flinms are gone?" Covey flexed her fingers but seemed to be less berserk than when I ran off. "I was looking forward to a fight, but *they* said you needed to do this on your own." She focused on Mathilda and Cwin.

I looked to Alric—he'd been seriously annoyed at me for taking off, but I thought that his not coming after me until everything was finished meant he'd understood. The shield spell I'd flung as I fled wouldn't have held more than a few minutes. He gave a small shrug.

Mathilda and Cwin called all of them off from following me—although neither looked happy when I jumped off my horse.

"Yes, Cwin and I were the big meanies on this." Mathilda grinned. "Not to discount the flinms but there didn't seem that many of them. Since your people destroyed them a few thousand years ago, we felt it would be good for you to take care of these now."

I briefly explained Bunky's chimera friends' and my fight with the flinms. As well as the mysterious mage behind them.

The magic users were interested in the fact that some of the creatures copied my wings, while the rest didn't. They noted the information on the mage, but I didn't have enough information for them to sort out who it might be.

Padraig came closer to me. "I'd like to make sure that

they didn't compromise your magic. The stories said they were magic eaters—but that was a few thousand years ago."

I nodded and he carefully held his hand over me and slowly moved around me. After a few minutes, he shrugged.

"You seem fine. But when we stop tonight, I'd like Mathilda and Cwin to check as well."

I shrugged but glanced at Alric. He wasn't as powerful as the other three, but it was still surprising he wasn't included.

Padraig gave a soft laugh. "Nope. He's got too much bias. A good healer needs to distance himself, and that's not one of Alric's gifts. Especially with you."

I hadn't said anything to the chimeras, but Bunky seemed to be having a meeting with them. Two groups of five took off in different directions, then he came near me and gronked.

"The rest are staying with us? For the entire trip?" He gave one of his head bobs. "Where'd the others go?"

Alric had to answer that one as Bunky was speaking far too fast. "The two groups are going to find reinforcements and spread the word. The return of the flinms was something the chimeras were waiting for. They like them even less than the sceanra anams."

"That's reassuring and terrifying at the same time. But thank you Bunky and all." I forced a smile I didn't feel and joined the others in getting my horse ready. "Can I call the faeries back now?" I agreed that the faeries needed to be kept away from the flinms, but I missed them. And knowing they were rampaging across Notlianda made me nervous.

Mathilda tilted her head as if sensing something—or not sensing something. "Yes, it would be good to have them with us. I believe Padraig and Alric were debating stopping near the top of the mountain for the night?"

Both elves were on their horses and nodded.

"It'll be an early night but we've had a long day." Padraig's tight smile told me which side of the debate he was on.

Alric stayed quiet but didn't look happy.

It was still a few hours before dusk and from what I'd seen while flying during my fight against the flinms, we weren't more than an hour from the top of the mountain.

Padraig was worried about something on the other side of it.

I closed my eyes and called to Garbage. Nothing. After the fifth time, I was worried. "I can't reach them." They'd been gone an hour at the most, I would say even they couldn't have gotten into too much trouble that quickly.

But I knew them. They could bring down a building in less than a minute.

Mathilda tried as well, then she opened her eyes. "Nothing. I can't reach—" Her words were cut off by a screaming blue rock breaking through the tree branches above us and hitting my arm with enough force to knock me off my horse.

I grabbed the rock or tried to. It was hot. And not a rock. "Crusty?" She had her wings wrapped tightly around her toasted body but unwrapped them at my touch.

"Funs! Dos again?" She had soot all over her but otherwise seemed unharmed.

"What happened? Where are the others?"

She scowled. "Not fun. Big boom. Captured. Yous halps."

I looked up, but Mathilda was already off her horse. "Sweetie? Where? Who captured them?"

"Nasty bads. Place yous sends us. Friend said hi. OH!" Her golden eyes grew huge and she reached into her pocket on the front of her overalls. "This yous." She handed me a crumbled paper with writing on one side that she jabbed at with her index finger. "Needs nows."

I unwrapped the paper. "It's from Tag. Notlianda is under attack. Qianru, Locksead, and her compound are holding but won't last long." I crumpled the edges of the note as I read the next line. "And the enemy locked up my faeries along with the ones with Tag and Qianru." I looked up. "We need one of those weird paths now. Or Crusty and I will fly back on our own."

CHAPTER FOURTEEN

THE SILENCE AROUND ME WAS punctuated by the clinking of Crusty fishing for a bottle of ale in one of her tiny bags. She stopped when I took the bag out of her hands. "We have to save your friends. No ale until we do." When she shrugged and didn't try to grab her bag back, I knew she realized how serious things were. "How did you get here anyway?" The faeries could fly extremely long distances, but they'd popped out when they left to go to Notlianda. I'd never seen one of them come in hot and crispy before.

"Threw mes." She tugged on her flower hat which had somehow come through untouched.

"Who threw you?" Mathilda held out her hand and I moved Crusty over to her. She needed a bath but otherwise seemed okay.

"The friend of friend of bird lady." She tilted her head. "Yous likes him." She smiled at Mathilda.

"An elf?" None of our friends who were in Notlianda were magic users.

Crusty nodded. "Has growly friend who noes growl."

Alric caught it first. "Nasif and Dueble?"

Crusty bounced in Mathilda's hand. "Is yes! He throws mes fast to get heres. Going to sends a magic letter, but thems attacked." She frowned. "Wants friends backs."

Nasif and Dueble had remained with our resident

ghost, Zaelian, in the *tir cudd* where the nature goddess Ageora was trapped. From the looks on the faces of my friends, no one else had a clue as to why they were in Notlianda either.

Padraig looked at me. "I know that faery queen told you to go north—"

"But we have to save them. They took my faeries." I still felt an odd tug about going over the mountain and toward the place where Queen Mungoosey's voice said we needed to go. But it wasn't as strong now. Not to mention, *they had my faeries.* "Can any of you open a chawsia path? Now?"

Padraig nodded. "Yes. We need to get everyone together. Are the chimeras all coming?"

Bunky gronked at them and the flock moved in closer. He understood us better than we understood him, and he knew his faeries were in trouble.

He might have grown up with me, but he loved his faeries fiercely.

"He says yes." Alric turned to Grillion and Foxy. "Well, now you don't need to take the long way there. Unless you'd rather?"

Grillion shook his head with force. "No thank you. Not a huge fan of those weird tunnels, but crossing those plains isn't fun even when a war isn't brewing. Tunnel sounds nice."

"I agree. But after we get the girls back, can we sort out the tattoo issue?" Foxy was on his horse but stuck out his covered leg for emphasis.

"We haven't forgotten. Cwin and I think we have a way to see what happened as well as block both of your tattoos from leaking again." Mathilda frowned. "But it will take time and a safe place to hide while we do it. Let's free Notlianda and get our friends back. Then fix you two." She handed Crusty back to me and for a moment I thought the faery couldn't fly again.

Then Crusty flew up from my hand to my shoulder and kissed my cheek. "Is fines. Just dirty. Was funs!" The last bit had way too much enthusiasm behind it. I didn't know what spell Nasif used to send her to us this way, or why she couldn't pop here, but she liked being thrown far too much.

"Let's not do that again, okay?" My attempt at being stern was lost as she shrugged and hummed to herself.

I climbed back on my horse and we gathered behind Padraig. We kept the chimeras spread out within us, so we'd all arrive together. Earlier, I'd heard Padraig and Cwin have a brief discussion—most likely over which type of tunnel to use. Cwin's fada path was more powerful in terms of distance, but it was more noticeable to other powerful magic users.

Since Padraig was taking the lead on this, we were using the chawsia path. I had to admit, after the last time we'd used that thing—and someone attacked it and sent Alric and me into a trap—I wasn't happy about it now. But I needed to save the faeries, and if this was the way, so be it.

I knew I couldn't fly faster than the chawsia path, not to mention, I wasn't sure exactly where Notlianda was compared to our current location.

Padraig and his horse, along with a large portion of the chimeras, went in first. The rest of us followed and I noticed Bunky and Irving stayed near Crusty and me.

I finally released my held breath when the path swirled around us in what I felt was a normal manner. And I saw nice, normal trees outside the other end of it.

Cwin and Covey were bringing up the rear when Cwin yelled, "Move faster! We're being attacked back here!"

A glance around didn't reveal anything except for them pushing everyone forward and vague darkness growing behind them. A few of the chimeras turned back, but I shouted to Bunky, "Keep them with us!" I didn't know what was trying to follow us into the tunnel, but if Covey and Cwin were freaked out, so was I.

Padraig picked up the pace and the horses ran for the end of the tunnel. We made it through but a buzzing roar tried to follow us out. Padraig and Alric released the tunnel the moment Covey's and Cwin's horses cleared it.

Normally the chawsia paths just vanished. This one exploded. Most of us barely held onto our horses as their ears went back and they tried to run. The chimeras and Irving tumbled in the air as the wave hit them, but quickly came back.

"What was that?" I had grabbed Crusty before the explosion hit to keep her safe, but she seemed unfazed by the ruckus, wiggled her way out of my grasp, and flew back to my shoulder.

"Goods. Theys goes booms. *Nots* nice things." She even turned and stuck her tongue out at the general location where the tunnel had been.

"I don't think we have time to sort out what that was. Incoming!" Alric yelled as he raised a shield spell over all of us when a volley of arrows flew our way. "Run!" He held the shield a few more minutes as we raced into the woods outside Notlianda, but had to eventually drop it.

I was impressed that he had been able to create one that large and ride with it.

There was no sign of the archers, or anyone else for that matter. But the arrows came from the wall that surrounded the town.

Alric slowed down after about ten minutes riding in the forest. Bunky moved up to him and kept giving gronk suggestions, but Alric shook his head and kept going.

Alric finally held up his fist and we all stopped. He

waited until we'd gathered closer and then looked over everyone. "Is everyone okay? What almost got us in the path?" He turned to Padraig on the second question.

Padraig rarely showed his temper but it was revealing itself now. "They breached my path. Whatever those tiny things were that chased Alric into that cave in the mountains, they broke through all of my spells. I hope that explosion destroyed them." He dropped his voice, "or at least some of them." Padraig was confident in his magic, once he'd gotten over his brief crisis that things weren't how he'd always thought they were. But there was self-doubt in his last words.

From the glances around me, I wasn't the only one to catch it.

"We're outside Notlianda though, right? I think I know the spot we landed in. Those arrows came from the town guards." Grillion lived in Notlianda for a few years and knew it well.

"Or from whoever took over the town." Covey scowled behind us.

"She's right," Alric kept his voice pitched low even though night was falling and there were no sounds that we'd been followed. "I wasn't going to lower my shield to grab one of the arrows, but they looked shorter than most southern longbows like the Notlianda guards carried when we were here before."

"We're not that far from the smaller entrance closer to Qianru's place." Grillion twisted around looking through the dim forest. "Or we weren't when we came out here. But if the city has been overrun, I'm not sure if going in when it's dark or staying out here is better. We could be hit by allies."

I agreed but wanted my faeries back. Not to mention, I had no idea how much danger my friends in town were in. Nasif and Dueble were planning on staying with Zaelian and Ageora and working on finding ways to track the rest of the presumed dead, but not, deities stuck in various *tir cudds*. They wouldn't have left without a really good reason.

But if they left, maybe Zaelian left as well. I closed my eyes and mentally reached out to our long-dead ghost librarian.

"Are you okay? You tilted to the side." Covey propped me up.

"I was trying to reach Zaelian. But nothing." It was a long shot, but she'd popped into my head before.

"Good idea, though." Padraig waved toward the direction we'd ridden. "I am open to discussion, but I think we should try to get inside the walls tonight if Grillion can lead us in the sneakier way. Yes, Qianru's people might be tricky if they're in full defense mode, but we're going to be too noticeable during the day." He motioned toward Bunky and the other chimeras.

I agreed. They would take way too much magic to hide and I wasn't going to send them off somewhere else. That was how the faeries got caught.

The discussion was quiet and quick. Everyone seemed to be of the same mind—get into Notlianda. Which was weird since we had three elves with us and they usually loved the woods.

Convincing the chimeras, and Irving, to fly in a low formation between us was harder. Especially since from the bits that I caught, Bunky wanted to storm the town walls and get his faeries back. Now.

CHAPTER FIFTEEN

WE EVENTUALLY GOT EVERYONE SPACED out, and enough light magic spells were dropped on all of us by our four strongest magic users—they didn't ask me and I didn't offer—to keep us mostly hidden through layers of deflection spells.

Needless to say, everyone had their hoods up and weapons out. It was difficult for Foxy to ride a horse quietly, and the way we were sneaking in was narrow and going to be tough going. Foxy tied his horse to the back of Alric's saddle and walked ahead of us.

Since we were closer, I tried to call Garbage, Leaf, or any faery—nothing.

Bunky and Irving hovered near Crusty and me, sticking extremely close to my horse. "Make sure you stay with us, Bunky. We can't afford to be seen until we know where the faeries were taken." Crusty flew off my shoulder at the same instant I realized my mistake. Part of it was because I didn't think she knew where her friends were, but I still should have known better.

"I knows!" It was the oddest, quietest yell I'd ever heard as Crusty landed on Bunky's back. "I shows!" Again, she sounded like she was yelling but it was so faint most people wouldn't hear it beyond me.

Unfortunately, Bunky heard it.

He gronked and then he, Irving, and the rest of the chimera horde flew off before we could stop them.

I tried mentally calling them back, but Crusty chose to ignore me.

"I'm sorry. I didn't think about Crusty knowing where they were." All the chimeras were flying fast. They were out of sight almost immediately.

"We need to get ourselves inside, and then deal with this. We can't roam around the town looking for them." Alric turned to me. "Unless Crusty said something to help us find them?"

"Not a thing. Let's get to Qianru." I was already working on a plan to take off on my own once we settled in Qianru's place. Alric narrowed his eyes but didn't say anything as we followed Foxy through the gap.

There were far more guards marching around the town than the last time we were here. And while they sort of looked like they were wearing the uniforms of the Notlianda guards, they seemed a bit off. Of course, I hadn't spent a lot of time studying them before.

Grillion moved up the line to ride behind Foxy. Good idea. He'd be a familiar face to anyone who spotted us—and to Qianru's houseboy troops. The wealthy people down here often had troops of houseboys who took care of running the homes, gardens, fields, and defending their rich patrons. Qianru's had shown to be quite resourceful in the past.

Aside from the guards, or fake guards, there were no other people out, and the two pubs we passed were closed. Lending credence to the occupied status of the town.

I happened to look up and thought I saw some flying black shapes pass over us as they blocked out the starlight briefly. I tried mentally reaching out to Crusty or Bunky, but no response.

Hopefully, they weren't a flock of sceanra anam. Every time I thought they'd all been killed, more of the flying snakes appeared.

Grillion came to a stop as Foxy and he paused for a whispered chat. They seemed to disagree about the direction, but Foxy finally nodded and motioned for Grillion to lead.

I again reached out to the faeries mentally. Someone could block them, but not easily. Unfortunately, like the other times I'd tried since they went missing, there was no response.

A series of low walls, sloppy ones at that, that I didn't remember from before, appeared in the final stretch to Qianru's compound. I doubted any of us were surprised when ten shortish dark forms rose from behind the final set of walls, all clearly armed with bows and arrows aimed in our direction.

They could be the invading troops, but even in the dark, they looked like houseboys. Aside from a taller one off to the far right, almost invisible, and holding a long bow. The houseboys were there for distraction, although I had no doubt they would fire if needed. The hidden man was the true threat.

Grillion tucked away his crossbow, threw back his hood, and slowly continued to move his horse forward. "It's me. Grillion. Is that you, Locksead?" He kept his voice low and continued to look forward, but he had spotted the hidden archer as well.

Locksead would have been my guess as well. A former relic thief up in the northern continent, Locksead had decided to take his chances turning legit and working for Qianru. When she came south to return home, he joined her.

Alric followed Grillion and likewise threw back his hood. He also released a few of the orange-tinted glows to hover around him and Grillion. He didn't sheath his sword, however. "You know who we are Locksead, let us in."

The houseboys didn't speak or lower their bows, but the tall shape to the side did.

"Damn good to see you both. I hope you brought an army with you; things are bad here."

Locksead was a tall slender man with black hair. And a few more scars on his face than the last time I'd seen him. He was heading toward Grillion and Alric but paused when he passed me. "I'm sorry about your faeries. They'd already grabbed Tag's and Qianru's faeries by the time yours came here and they were taken almost immediately. Did Nasif's trick work?" He waved his hand the moment the words were out of his mouth. "Never mind, we need to get you all out of sight." He gave a low whistle and four houseboys popped up from behind the ten standing guard and came up to Grillion.

"Follow them. We've got the front entrance well barricaded and getting in is more trouble than it's worth right now for the scum who invaded Notlianda. The others will tell you what happened and I'll see you in the morning." He stepped out of the way and Grillion and Alric followed the new houseboys.

The armed ones lowered their bows finally but watched us closely.

I didn't blame them. Now that I recalled some of what it was like to be their age, having to fight and defend your home shouldn't fall on them like this.

We twisted around the original entrance to Qianru's place—it was so fortified it looked like a solid armored wall. The new way went along the back and I saw the guest quarters we'd stayed in before as we looped around.

"Leave your horses here, if you would. They will be taken care of." The tallest houseboy's voice cracked as he pointed toward the stables attached to the guest quarters and another group of houseboys jogged out and gathered the reins of our horses.

"Are Nasif and Dueble here?" Mathilda asked as she removed her pack from her horse and a houseboy took it and ran toward the guest quarters.

The lead houseboy looked grim but shrugged. "The Mistress will explain everything. Follow me."

Not a great answer in my opinion. Nasif had used a spell of some kind to get Crusty out of there and get us the information. But he might not have been able to save himself or Dueble.

The horses were led to the stables, and all of our packs were already in the guest house when the houseboy took us down a low passage. I couldn't tell what exactly the spells were, but there were a lot coating every surface of the walls, ceiling, and floor and none of them felt welcoming.

Had we made a mistake? I looked around at my friends, but no one else appeared concerned. Even Foxy—and he wasn't a fan of Qianru. I readied my spells. My spirit sword was still with me, but I sheathed it so I'd have two hands free for spells.

The passage went even deeper before tilting back up. If I had to guess, we were coming up underneath Qianru's main house.

The houseboy stopped and said a few low words that I couldn't catch, and a narrow stairwell appeared in front of us.

Grillion moved to be in the front again and he took the boy's arm as he moved forward. "You know me, Dila, you wouldn't be doing any tricks, right? My friends have had a rough time of it, and might not take kindly to surprises."

I thought this was a bit late to make sure things were okay, but my doubts were also increasing. Maybe Grillion was sensing whatever was wrong too.

The boy smiled. "I know you, Grillion. And I miss taking your money at cards. It's been rough the past few weeks, but Mistress Qianru protects her people." He waited until Grillion nodded before going up the stairs.

Grillion looked to Alric, then shrugged and followed Dila up. The rest of us trooped up in single file. I changed my mind on keeping out a weapon, but I pulled out Rhyfel instead of my sword. For the first time since the fight in Yosi, he had an extremely faint, but definitely there, green glow.

Covey saw it and tapped my arm. "That's good, right?"

"I think so?" I didn't notice any lightning sparks coming off him, nor did I feel him in my head. If the faeries were here, I'd see if they could speak to him.

He flared a bit when I thought of the faeries. Maybe he *was* coming back.

The stairwell opened up into a small, empty room. Well, empty aside from the ten well-armed houseboys at any rate. I knew that Qianru had only taken a portion of her houseboys when she came to Beccia to look for the glass gargoyle. And there had been more than that when we were here a while ago. But at this rate, she must have recruited houseboys from across the entire southern continent.

Dila spoke fast with another heavier boy who was about his height. None of the ones facing us lowered their weapons.

Grillion raised his hands and took a small step forward. "Okay, at least three of you know who I am. And you were here when we came through before and saw the rest of my friends." He waved behind him to us.

Of course, Cwin hadn't been with us then, and a grimarian was fairly noticeable. I froze as I glanced back to where Cwin had been. A short, stocky, dwarf woman was there in her place. She flashed me a grin and a wink.

It made sense that Cwin could pull a glamor, but for some reason, I wasn't expecting it. Although she was the most powerful magic user with us.

Dila took a step back toward Grillion and faced the other houseboy. "It's like I said, it's them. Locksead sent us through and he knows them better than even Grillion does. Lady Qianru will be furious if you delay them." The last line was said with a low almost snarl and the other boy jumped back.

The other boy nodded. "It's okay, we can't keep the mistress waiting. Escort them to her." He paused as if to demand those of us with weapons to sheath them, but a cough from Dila stopped him from doing anything.

Dila and a few of the others went out the door that led into the middle of Qianru's house. Even if I didn't recognize the front room, the glaring white walls adorned by far too many portraits of Qianru would have made our location clear.

We turned to the right and I thought we were going to the row of bedrooms, but Dila stopped in front of a wide doorway and Qianru came racing out and grabbed Alric in a hug.

Considering that Grillion was still her employee, Padraig was toward the back, and Foxy made her nervous, Alric was the logical choice. Even if she did hold on much longer than necessary.

She finally stepped back and acted as if she'd just noticed the rest of us. "Thank goodness you're all here. We're under attack! The end of the world is coming!"

Blank looks all around. Things were bad, but there was still hope. And she shouldn't know how bad things were anyway.

"Qianru?" Padraig had stayed back with the houseboys, but Qianru knew him from her time in Beccia and the elven enclave. "What's happened?"

She gave me a nervous look, and stepped over a bit so I couldn't see her face—or she couldn't see mine. "I know Taryn isn't involved, but her people are back. And they're going to destroy everyone and everything."

CHAPTER SIXTEEN

"WHAT?" I HAD SO MANY emotions packed into that tiny word, it should have come out as more than a squeak. If someone had seen my people, even one, that meant I could find my brothers. But the fact that my people were being held up as killers and world destroyers wasn't good.

Covey grabbed my arm before I could jump forward.

Qianru minced through the group to stand before me. She was wearing a floofy lounge set of some kind, and even without her odd hat, she still looked like one of the watcher birds from Beccia. One that had gotten into a pile of white feathers and silks. "My dear child," Qianru gushed as she grabbed me in a fierce hug. "It is true. Dragons have been seen in the land. Several villages have been destroyed." The last word was the loudest, most dragged-out whisper I'd ever heard.

I patted her back but it took precious minutes of breathing in feathers to get her to release me.

"How do you know that?" Padraig was projecting charming elven prince now as he stepped between Qianru and I. Granted, he wasn't royalty, and Qianru knew that. But it didn't stop her from simpering as she looked up into his eyes.

"That's why the guards first moved in. To save us." She tilted her head to the side. "Of course, then they locked people up who might be working with the enemies. All the regular guards had to go. Then they took the faeries. Your elf friend Nasif and his syclarion friend were taken as well. Closed all the pubs…you don't think they were lying? I heard travelers say their towns were destroyed before the new guards came." There was now a lot of doubt in her voice. And annoyance that someone might have lied to her.

"Did they say the dragons did it?" Mathilda wasn't as well known to Qianru as Alric and Padraig, but she was an elf. Qianru was obsessed with elves.

"The first poor souls didn't say much as they kept moving past our town. Only that creatures came from underground and destroyed everyone. The new guards said it was the dragons coming back from the dead." Her eyes narrowed and she scowled as her mind caught on. "Right before they started locking everyone up. This is horrible!" Qianru spun and hugged me again even though she had to dodge around Padraig and I tried to slip away. "My poor child! Someone is blaming your long-dead people!"

Alric came and helped free me from Qianru.

Qianru knew what I was, but not that the rest of my people were probably around somewhere in time. Or, as I believed now, some place. The *tir cudds* were still our best place to search, in my opinion. None of which was going to be shared with my former patron.

"How long have these new guards been in place?" Padraig drew Qianru toward an overstuffed white sofa and motioned for her to sit. Then he joined her and clasped her hands.

"Two weeks. Your two friends showed up a few days ago, looking for you actually." She glanced around as if suddenly recalling the rest of us. "All of you." She paused as her glance hit Cwin. "I don't recall a dwarf with you before. Aren't your people usually in the mountains?"

Cwin gave a sideways grin and a quick curtsy. "Aye, that we are. But I think these people are the ones to save everyone. My name is Niwclin, Lady Qianru. I have heard much of your skills and beauty from my friends." Her accent was a perfect copy of the few times highland dwarves had come down into Beccia. Considering how long Cwin had lived in some very remote mountains, she probably knew many of them.

"Oh, you are too much. Welcome to my humble home." Qianru waved a feathered fan toward her houseboys. "Bring in more chairs and refreshments, we have much to discuss."

I pulled Alric aside under the guise of making room for the army of houseboys. "We need to rescue Nasif, Dueble, and the faeries. And possibly the chimeras if they got caught." Bunky and Irving had been here before and even if Crusty couldn't help them get back here, they could have found it. I wasn't happy that they'd taken off and were still missing. "And killer monsters coming from *underground*?" I found that I was digging into Alric's arms. I'd had to go full dragon and destroy a pack of Tjolia mountain dreks in Hassi, a few villages over from here, months ago when they'd attacked my friends and almost killed Alric. From under the ground. I'd also cast a magic spell that I still hadn't sorted out. It followed the monsters through their tunnel and turned them all to stone.

If there were more of them rampaging through the land, I was going to be sick.

Alric gave me a gentle smile, then removed my hands. I'd left red marks on his arms. "That was my thought too. We'll deal with them when the time comes. I agree we first need to free our friends and this town."

I took a few deep breaths and shook out my hands. "I wish I knew what I did to those dreks."

"We'll sort it out." He turned us around just in time for Dila to set down two chairs near us.

Qianru was chatting about something to Padraig and Mathilda, who sat on the other side of her on the sofa. She looked at Alric as if to wave him over, but then went back to the two elves she had. She adored elves, even after two of them turned out to be major followers of the Dark and almost destroyed Beccia. And all of us. Including her.

The trays and carts of food, lemonade, and tea made my mouth water and my stomach growl. Going after the flinms had taken more out of me than I thought. I tried to control myself as I took a plate and loaded it up.

Qianru's laugh could scare most adult mountain trolls. "Oh good! You're still doing your magic. Eat up, child."

I was too hungry to be annoyed at her little tiny finger movements when she said magic. In Qianru's mind, only elves could be true magic users. I wasn't going to argue with her about it. Especially with the amount of food she brought out.

I wasn't the only hungry one and even Padraig and Mathilda collected a fair amount of food.

Grillion waited until everyone was eating and chatting, and Qianru was focused on her conversation with Padraig and Mathilda, before motioning for Dila and three other houseboys to follow him into the main room. Hopefully, he could get some useful information.

I'd assumed the barricades and secret entrance here were due to a hostile takeover of Notlianda, but it seemed they were against the hypothetical dragons. Or in this case, the possibly not hypothetical dreks. A handy way to keep a populace complacent and ready to be knocked off.

The empress might have pulled back her sources a bit, but she was still in form.

I wasn't going to be the one to tell Qianru that dreks could go through solid rock. Someone was controlling them on behalf of the empress—that was who we needed to find.

Qianru yawned and blinked rapidly. "There simply isn't anything you can do tonight. The guards lock up anyone roaming outside of their homes once things go dark. It's amazing you all made it here. My houseboys have set up the guest quarters now. I will see you all in the morning." She let two houseboys help her to her feet and tottered out.

Alric waited until she was gone before shaking his head at Padraig. Three more houseboys were waiting to escort us, so Padraig also remained silent. But his wink told me Qianru had some help at suddenly becoming so tired.

Good thing. My yawns weren't spelled and every muscle in my body was starting to ache.

All of us, except Grillion, followed the houseboys out through the odd underground passage and across to the guest building. Grillion was still off with Dila and the other two houseboys.

It looked like I recalled from a few months ago. And I heard our horses nickering softly from the adjoining stable past the main room.

We picked up our packs and selected bedrooms. Not fancy, but that large bed in the room Alric picked for us looked like heaven.

Then I noticed Foxy setting up on the large sofa in the main room.

"Foxy? There are enough rooms for everyone." He'd been agitated since we came into town and I felt it was more than still not being able to contact Amara.

"I know. And it looks like your friend Locksead has the defenses well set up. But it's not all the same as having someone on watch. There's a lot wrong here and

I'll be making sure nothing gets in." He raised both his club-like sword and an even larger actual club.

One I'd never seen before. He must have found it on the ride through the forest.

"What do you feel?" I sat down next to him. The others were getting their rooms set up, but Alric was heading our way.

"It's hard to say. But even if I'd be able to contact Amara, I wouldn't right now. Not from here. Something foul be haunting the very air." He nodded to Alric as he took a nearby chair. "An I be seeing the two of you react earlier. You think there are dreks again." He tightened his grip on his club. He wanted a chance to bash them to bits judging by the look in his eyes. Foxy wasn't a violent person, imposing size aside. But right now, no one who didn't know him would come near him.

When the door opened and a distracted Grillion came inside, Foxy leaped to his feet and growled, I couldn't blame Grillion for squealing and jumping back out the door.

Alric ran after him, brought him back, and shut and locked the door.

"You shouldn't do that, Foxy." Grillion cautiously walked further inside but moved away from the sofa.

"Sorry about that. I was telling these two, there be something wrong here." Foxy lowered his club but still had it across his lap.

I think we all felt there was something wrong here—a lot of something. But this seemed like more than that. Foxy wasn't a magic user or someone sensitive to things like that, but he was acting like one now.

I was about to ask Cwin to check him out when I noticed a weird orange-red glow showing through his pant leg.

Right where his compromised tattoo of Amara's was.

"Padraig? Should that seal be glowing?" I saw Padraig

leave one room and go down the hall, but he came back immediately.

He dropped down next to Foxy's legs and pulled up the pant leg. "Does it hurt? Because no, it shouldn't be doing that."

"It feels…muffled." Foxy frowned and helped to pull up the fabric. "Like someone is yelling at me when I'm inside the Shimmering Dewdrop and they're down the street aways. I almost hear them, but not what they be saying."

"Do you want me to try to contact Amara?" An odd chill flowed across my tattoo as I spoke. "Or maybe not."

Foxy shook his head. "No. Can't say how I know, but I'm thinking someone is trying to get to her through me. And you."

I wasn't sure what getting to her would do—she wasn't a goddess anymore. She was a strong dryad, but the south had a lot of those. But we couldn't ignore that he might be right.

Padraig nodded as he poked around the tattoo. "The shield is holding, but I do feel that something is trying to reach through." He turned to me. "Let me see your arm." I kept my sleeve up as I leaned closer to him. He nodded then said a few words. My arm tingled and then went numb from the tattoo down.

He was repeating the words on top of the shield over Foxy's tattoo when everyone else came back. We were all tired, but this needed to be dealt with.

"Someone was trying to break through Foxy and Taryn's tattoos." Alric stayed out of the way but remained close to me.

Mathilda and Cwin shared a concerned glance that they didn't share with the rest of us and came closer.

Covey drifted to the door, unlocked it, peeked out, and shut it. Then leaned against it. Whatever was in the air, our non-magic users were feeling it too. "It feels like when my family pod would be on the edge of a major sandstorm when I was young and lived in the desert. Something is seriously wrong, more than we thought." She held up her arm. It was changing colors like the slightly mottled pattern on it was being controlled. "I'm fighting going berserker right now, by the way."

Cwin left Mathilda and Padraig to continue examining our tattoos and went to the door. "I'd say Covey's family intuition isn't off. Something is coming to Notlianda, something that none of us felt on the way in here. And something we might not survive."

CHAPTER SEVENTEEN

CWIN STILL WORE HER DWARF glamor, so maybe that was why the look of fear on her face as she turned to us was noticeable. The normal grimarian fur covered most facial expressions similar to a chataling. Unlike Harlan, she was usually an expert at not letting any of them show.

My eyes must have given my shock away as she quickly hid her concern. "We can't get out in time, even if we were willing to try." She gave all of us kind looks. There was no way we would leave any of our friends behind, even if she'd never met Nasif and Dueble.

"Then we defend ourselves here. The tattoos are safe and can't be used to get to us or Amara." Padraig got up after securing our tattoos. From the way Foxy kept tapping at his leg, it probably felt as numb as my arm.

But better numb than something using them to get to Amara. Or us.

"We defend to the death." Cwin put her hands behind her back and stalked through the entire building, looking like a dwarf mimicking an extremely annoyed grimarian. She came back, nodding to herself. "I put heavy spells on the stables, those are the weakest portion of this place. I've also spelled the horses to keep them calm. The best place for them, and us, is inside here."

Grillion pulled back the curtain and looked toward the main house. "Will Locksead and the houseboys be okay? Qianru's place is more secure than this, but they're outside."

"I think we need to get them inside. There's nothing they'd be able to do against what I now believe is coming." Back to Cwin briefly looking frightened. Twice in ten minutes was more than I ever wanted to see.

"Qianru would have secured her house already. Or Dila and his people would have." Mathilda also was concerned.

"What is it that's coming?" Grillion finally asked while the rest of us worked up our courage to do so.

"I can sense the edges of it now, it's a lictenspelt. A spell storm that raises the dead and sets them loose in the world to bring death and destruction to all. Or in this case, to destroy this town. Either those fake guards have left, or they were set up to die with the rest of us. It hasn't been used for over two thousand years, as it was believed that all of the mages who could call it were killed." Cwin's voice was flat. "At least not until those attacks Qianru spoke of happened to other villages. The only reason people would have been allowed to escape was to spread fear. Fear and depression fuel the spell."

The room dropped into silence.

"What do we do? They can't destroy this town. Or any others. We have to stop them." I finally broke the silence when I couldn't stand it anymore.

"We can get Locksead and the houseboys with him inside here, but I don't know what else we can do." Mathilda looked more beaten than she had when her sister and Lorcan were kidnapped.

I glanced around. Alric and Padraig also looked hopeless. The rest appeared freaked out, but ready to fight.

I was pissed. "Something is affecting the magic users; you're sliding into depression."

Covey shook herself and turned to me. "How come you're not?"

"I'm not sure. I'm just really, really pissed off. Maybe that lictenspelt thing can't hit Ancients. Don't know, but this is not happening." My arm with the tattoo lost its numbness as anger flowed through me.

All four of the other magic users slid to the floor. They weren't unconscious, they just seemed to have lost the energy to remain standing.

"They're using a Jhea spell." An insidious, and extremely old spell that could lock people into a depressed stupor. It could hit non-magic users also, but it seemed designed for mages. I'd been struck by it before but wasn't sure why it wasn't affecting me now.

Maybe rampaging fury kept it at bay.

"Damn it, that's why they took all of the faeries," Covey snarled. "Word got around that they could break that spell with their humming."

I tried to think of the song my parents used to sing at night when I was frightened, the one the faeries had hummed to break the Jhea spell. There was only one of me and I didn't have the strongest voice, but I wasn't letting anyone go down without a fight.

It took ten attempts, with Covey, Grillion, and even Foxy joining in. But we finally got through and slowly all four of the magic users blinked and shook themselves.

"They used a Jhea spell without even being near any of us." Padraig got to his feet, then helped the others. His jaw clenched in anger.

Cwin shook herself and a furious grimarian appeared in place of the dwarf. "That shouldn't have worked on *me*." There wasn't a question or doubt, only pure fury. "Stay angry everyone, it'll help keep it at bay."

Covey smiled. "Taryn sorted that out as well."

"Could they have left traps for that spell in town and we went through them on the way here?" There had been spell traps set up inside the cave where the empress and her Dark minions held Siabiane, Lorcan, and Tag a few months ago. They got me when I went inside, but the faeries and their humming saved me.

Mathilda shook her head. "I doubt it. That cave was specially prepared to hold those prisoners and grab the rest of us when we came to rescue them. This one hit us all at once." She looked around. "And was targeted at the magic users. The rest of you should have fallen but you were a lower target. We need to bring in Locksead and those houseboys. Now."

I was still full of too much anger and nothing to stomp on. "I'll do it."

Alric stood. "Me too." Everyone raised their hands and stood to go. Foxy beat all of us to the door.

Padraig and Mathilda moved forward to block the rest of us. "Taryn, Foxy, and Alric only. Taryn, I know you don't like changing—"

"But if I need to in order to bring them in, I will. I get to stomp on any members of the Dark out there though." I knew the empress could have other people running this, but many of the Dark were powerful magic users—they'd be needed for this level of spell. I had a bad feeling that most, if not all, of the people in Notlianda were falling under the sway of that Jhea spell by now.

I hated the Dark possibly as much as the elves did.

Mathilda and Padraig shared a look, but they both nodded.

"Now, I think we're missing something here." Cwin's fur was still sticking up and her eyes were red. "I am a siramage after all, I should be out there."

"Which is why you need to stay here with us," Mathilda said. "We may end up being the last defense if they fall." She nodded to the three of us. "Trust me, I'd rather I was going. But there are too many innocents in town who will need help."

Padraig clasped arms with Alric. "Keep your head down, let them focus on Taryn. And all three of you need to hum that song under your breath the moment you leave this building. They obviously thought only the faeries could sing it. That's a benefit for us."

I was already humming it before we left. My spirit sword stuck around, a good indication things were bad, and Rhyfel seemed to be a bit more alert and green light grew around his edge. He still wasn't crackling or mentally responding, but the green along his blade was stronger now.

I forced my fear for the faeries, chimeras, and everyone else back to a small dark corner of my mind. I needed anger not fear. Even though I was still in my human form, I found myself stomping as we approached the barricade.

No one was in sight.

Qianru wouldn't have called her protectors back, and I knew Locksead; he was stubborn enough not to truly hide.

We found them all on the ground. Tag was with them now, he looked roughed up, but alive. None of them would wake up. We all hummed the song, but there was no response.

"Oy! Bigguns! Helps!" The annoyed voice came from a pile of rubble at the edge of a barricade. It almost sounded like one of the faeries, but I'd never been called 'biggun' by them before.

"Keep humming, I'll see what this is." I stepped forward before Alric could and waved him back toward Locksead and Tag.

"Needs more lows, too highs." Now the voice reminded me of an annoyed Garbage. But it wasn't her.

"Hold on, I'm digging you out. Who are you?" I didn't even know all the faeries with us, let alone any new ones.

"Direidus Salvia. Moves faster. Please."

I stopped in shock. Not so much at the name, faery names ranged in complexity. However, most weren't the mouthful that was. The surprise was that she said, please. I needed to see this faery.

The final rock was removed and a squished sage green and deep purple faery twitched. "Goods. Song no works. Wrong spells." She removed her hat; a combination of fabric and leaves and I held back my surprise. She was a faery, there wasn't a doubt. But she was old. Her hair was wild and gray and her tiny face was lined.

"Are you okay, Deeridious?" I couldn't get much closer to it than that.

She climbed out of the pile, shook herself, and laughed. "Just call me Derry, easier for both of us. Never seen an old faery, have ya?" The faery pidgin, which she'd had earlier, was gone now. The faery queen didn't speak pidgin, maybe this one was related to her. "Don't be minding those things, you need to sing lower." She tilted her head toward Foxy. "Especially you. Sing from your toes." She dusted herself off and no longer appeared squished. "Bad things happening. Big bad things. I's fix." Right back to sounding like one of my girls.

Alric and Foxy didn't question Derry, but kept singing at a lower level.

Tag and Locksead both twitched and then the rest of the houseboys began to as well. We needed them to be able to walk. It would take too long to carry them all back.

"Where did you come from?" There were a lot of questions in my head, but that was the first that came to mind. According to Crusty, the faeries had been around forever. Yet, they all appeared young. Derry was definitely old.

"The beginning." Wrinkles deepened as she grinned and a twinkle came from her eyes. Then the twinkles landed on my foot and vanished. "Sorry, they have a mind of their own sometimes. I am where I needed to be." She marched over to the nearest houseboy and began poking at him. "Get along with you now. The dragon and I have people to stomp." She repeated it to the others and soon Locksead, Tag, and the rest were on their feet.

"We can fight." Locksead was listing to the side but kept a grip on his sword.

"I don't think you can fight this," I said. "You all need to get into the guest house." I shook off Tag, Alric, and Foxy as they moved toward Derry and me. "No. This is something she and I need to do." Oddly, I trusted Derry completely. Also, I really wanted to stomp the people behind this. "You have to save everyone if we fall." I grabbed Alric for a passionate kiss, danced out of reach when he tried to grab me afterward, and shook my head. "No."

Then I ran to an open spot and changed. For once it was quick and smooth.

"Taryn, you can't—"

"You're more being a danger to her by staying here. Go, young ones." Derry flew up to Alric's face, patted it like a fond grandmother, and flew to me. "We's rides!"

I couldn't look back at Alric and the rest, I might lose my anger. Actually, Derry had knocked the anger out of me, but it was coming back. She flew alongside my head as I ran toward the center of town.

"All of the faeries have been taken; can you tell where they are?" No idea why or how she'd shown up, but I'd take the help. My original plan of stomping bad people into dust only went so far when there was no one in sight to stomp.

"Yes. Turn left." She was furious now and I thought I saw white arcs of energy dancing between her hands. "They crossed lines."

I turned left and ran up to a large building. The fake guards must have known what was coming and left town. And the townspeople were too afraid to come out. Ancients in our dragon form were powerful, massive, and dangerous. But we were not silent unless we flew. I was making enough noise to wake the dead back in Beccia.

And ran into an invisible wall that knocked me on my tail. Derry kept going but flew back to me.

"Oops. That's okay. Upsie." She motioned for me to get to my feet and then flew where the invisible wall crackled.

Derry held up Rhyfel—he and the sword always vanished when I changed so I wasn't sure where she got him from. But he crackled as well and sent an arc of electric charges to the spell wall stopping me.

Derry laughed and followed his arcs, sending her own energy to the same spots Rhyfel was hitting.

Garbage and the rest had been pulling in new-old tricks lately, but this wasn't one I'd seen before. It was as if she was copying Rhyfel but in her way. Or she'd suddenly channeled a chimera.

I felt the spell wall crash, even though I couldn't see it. I walked through this time without anything more than a slight tingling.

Derry threw Rhyfel into the air and he vanished. I hoped he'd come back when I changed again, but this wasn't the time to worry about that.

A huge dark building rose in front of us. Derry snarled and zipped forward.

I assumed that was where the faeries were but she'd

gone inside before I could catch her. As large as the building was, I couldn't get inside in my current condition. Not unless I wanted to knock the entire structure down.

I shrunk back to my human size and let out a sigh as both my sword and Rhyfel came with me. My magic felt strong, but sometimes blades worked better.

I heard Derry before I saw her. She was humming yet another version of the anti-Jhea song, but there was a hard level of fury in it.

The building was dark and a chill flowed through my bones as I walked through the doorway. I fought not to change into my dragon form, but fear was almost forcing me to. Instead, I picked up on the changes Derry was humming and joined in. My fear channeled its way into anger.

There was no light at all—another reason to wish I could change. My eyesight as a dragon was better than in human form. During that odd Dragon Day, I'd been able to pick a few traits to modify, but not change them all. This wasn't the place to test that though. Nor my trick of becoming a smaller dragon. I didn't trust my memory of the spell to try it now.

Derry's humming grew louder and came from the left. After hitting the wall twice before putting my hands out to find it, I made it around the corner.

This room was more like a cavern and had an odd unhealthy glow. I doubted that the building had been built around the cavern, as I could faintly see the building's walls above the rocks. The cavern seemed to be growing inside the building.

Derry appeared next to me. "Now keep humming, no matter what you see. You can't stop." She grabbed my face and held onto it until I nodded. "Bad things come. I get peoples out. Then you change and stomp. Magic too. Use magic."

Her going back and forth between talking in the pidgin the faeries used and sounding more like Queen Mungoosey was disturbing, but not something to be dealt with now.

"You good." Her smile lit up the weird gloom, she kissed my cheek and flew to the top of the room/cavern so fast she was little more than a blur.

I kept humming. The new version had a rough edge to it because of the slightly off-key tones that were worked into it. It was disturbing and it was meant to be. It worked to keep my anger at whoever was behind this up.

An explosion echoed through the cavern, but I couldn't see anything until Derry came flying back. Rather, she had been flung and didn't appear to be in control of her trajectory. I grabbed her as she almost flew past me.

"Ha! It almost worked. Nice catchings. Need to change the plan. Keep humming." She studied me for an intense moment. Then grinned and tapped my nose.

The entire world went black and I felt like I was tumbling into a void. Then normal-sized hands were hitting my face.

"Flapping wings good idea."

My eyes flew open and a human-sized Derry was in front of me and I was about to crash to the jagged ground.

I didn't think, just flapped. Then I saw my wings out of the corner of my eye. They were dark green, but not at all like my dragon wings.

They were faery wings. And judging by the massively increased size of the cavern, I was a faery. Derry wasn't my size, I was hers.

"What—"

"Nope. Keep humming and keep flapping. Follow me." There was an evil twinkle in her eye—one that stayed there this time—and I was very glad it wasn't directed at me.

I obeyed the fierce faery and followed her to the top of the cavern. Fortunately, my faery wings worked better than my dragon ones, possibly due to whatever Derry had done to change me. I looked down and saw my clothing was now a pair of overalls.

Not going to ask how she did that—I kept flapping and humming.

The ceiling opened to another cavern. One that we were flying down into. Yet another reality twist that I didn't have time to face right now. Once we were inside, it was no longer upside down. Too much weirdness going on right now.

There were dozens of cages filled with faeries, chimeras, humans, elves, and others. Everyone, even the faeries, was slumped inside them. Not asleep, dead eyes watched us but didn't react.

I flew to one of the cages, I was going to blast them apart.

Derry grabbed my arm and shook her head. "Not yet. We listen. Come this way." She flew us behind a rock outcropping as deep voices came into the cavern.

"I told you; I heard something. We need to—"

"We need to finish this damn test. This is the fourth town and she's still not satisfied. We even have faeries and chimeras this time. I don't know what more she wants."

I didn't need to hear the name to know it was the empress. Whatever she was testing, she was being more cautious than her prior attacks. Adding rumors that my people were behind the destruction was a bonus for her.

"I know, but something triggered the sensor. This weirdly twisted cavern has problems we don't have the magic to sort out."

From the shuffling, and the voices, both people were big. Not my dragon-sized big, but probably Foxy-sized. Most of the Dark were elves, but they'd shown a recent tendency to branch out to other species. The only criteria were a dark heart and the ability to cast magic. Although they had recruited non-magic users before.

"There's no one else here. Let's open their path and get out of here."

I was still humming the modified Jhea-breaking song and turned to Derry in confusion. I wasn't loud, but they should have heard me.

She grinned and gave a nod. Then motioned for me to keep humming. Whatever she was doing, she'd not only transformed me into a faery, she was masking my humming.

I shrugged and continued to listen to the two people in the cavern. There was a lot of swearing and moving of rocks. Then a foul, and unfortunately familiar, odor of rotting meat filled the air.

Dreks. Coming through an odd modified chawsia path just like they'd done a few months ago in the village of Hassi. I hated being right. My humming stopped until Derry shook me. She was furious, but not at me.

The other time we'd run into these monsters, they managed to not only silence themselves but the sounds of their victims.

At Derry's look, I returned to humming. I was pretty sure there would be no sound, and without the humming the Jhea spell would get us all and then the dreks would kill us.

I was glad to be wrong. My humming was shaky at first, terror of a gruesome death did that, but I heard all of our hums.

No idea why one of the dreks' natural fighting abilities wasn't working this time, but I'd take it. But it still left their claws, tusks, and massive strength. Those monsters would destroy everyone in this cavern and then the rest of the town.

I needed to change into my dragon self.

My eyes must have given me away, and Derry grabbed my arms, looked into my eyes, and spoke in my head.

"*No. We end it like this. You can't be seen as the other. This will work.*"

"*We're only four inches tall. They have dreks. It's not a fair fight.*" I wasn't sure how I felt about her speaking in my head, I'd just met her. But it allowed me to keep humming.

She patted my cheek. "*I know. But we don't have time for them to get more fighters.*" She tilted her head. "*Six dreks are currently coming through the tunnel they uncovered. That will have to be enough for us for now. I'm sure there are more behind them that I'm not sensing yet.*"

I shook my head. I meant we were going to lose, but her confidence flowed from her like a wave.

Then little pops of air appeared around us. Queen Mungoosey and almost a thousand faeries surrounded us behind the rocks. That many faeries being silent and armed with unnaturally long war sticks was almost more disturbing than the dreks I could now hear pounding through the earth beneath us. The two people who'd called the dreks scrambled out of the cavern.

Queen Mungoosey nodded to myself and Derry and gave a short bow.

Derry grinned and gave the same move in return.

The dreks were almost to the surface and my humming wasn't waking anyone in the cages up. "*We need to free them.*"

"*Easier to fight with them safe. Just follow our lead, but don't stop humming, and don't forget who you are.*"

That was the only prep or warning I got as the faeries around us burst out of hiding, gave loud war cries, and followed Derry and Queen Mungoosey toward the massive hole in the floor of the cavern. I kept humming and flew along. I didn't have a war stick, but my sword and Rhyfel, both now shrunk to my current size, appeared as I flew.

The first drek was already climbing out as the Queen and Derry led the first wave of faeries down. Dreks were massive, brutish, pale fur-covered monsters, with huge tusks, beady glaring eyes, and arms longer than my leg that ended in dagger-like claws.

It took a lot of magic on my end to destroy the dreks when I faced them before, but the faeries dropped them with their oddly long war sticks this time.

I was with the next wave and flew with them. My spirit sword must have been envious of Rhyfel as it began glowing yellow. I kept humming but focused all of my pain, fear, and worries into my blades as I dropped low to the massive beasts and began stabbing the next one coming out.

It too fell, but when I flew up and out of the way, I noticed other dark shapes raising weapons and running to the cages that held the prisoners.

CHAPTER EIGHTEEN

———◆———

"*THEY'RE AFTER THE CAGES.*" I kept humming as I sent my panicked thoughts to Derry. I half expected her to command me to stay.

Instead, she gave me a serious look and nodded. "*Protect them. This is your job. Keep humming. Stay strong.*" Then went back to lead another flight of faeries against the dreks.

Humming as loudly as I could, only slightly modifying the tune to be more like the original Jhea bashing song, I raised my weapons, readied my magic, and flew to the cages.

And fought down the fear that being so small was causing. Being small never stopped the faeries even if many had been captured. I wasn't only powerful because I was a dragon.

The dark shapes weren't as large as they seemed, both my size and weird shadows made them appear that way. But they were waving axes and hatchets around.

Brownies.

The only brownies I'd run across who weren't greedy and borderline evil were the two brownie constructs Siabiane created. I flew to the closest cage and waved my weapons at the nearest brownies. I wasn't sure how to yell at them unless I stopped humming and that wasn't a good idea.

But magic was. Still waving my sword and dagger I cast the strongest version of my push spell I could. I wasn't sure whether my current size would weaken the spell or not. In hindsight, that wasn't the best assumption as the entire wave of brownies went flying backward and smashed into the wall. A little overkill.

I increased my humming and noticed the caged faeries nearest to me were blinking. Queen Mungoosey's bunch was humming as well as they fought the dreks.

Then the brownies began humming. The same song as they slowly picked themselves up from where I'd slammed them.

I spun to them, but they were humming the anti-Jhea song. Taking a chance that I had misjudged them, and the faeries in this cage looked fully aware now, I broke open their cage.

None of the faeries inside were ones I recognized, but they immediately flew to the brownies. After a brief standoff, the freed faeries nodded to the brownies, then flew back to me and joined in on the humming.

I glanced back but the brownies were slowly approaching with their axes down. I gave them a nod and we freed the remaining faeries. Garbage, Leaf, and Crusty recognized me right away and all flew over to hug me hard, before joining in on the attack of the dreks.

Still more dreks were coming out of their chawsia path tunnel.

More cages further back held Bunky, Irving, and the rest of the chimeras, as well as Nasif, Dueble, and a handful of villagers.

The chimeras and Irving recovered the quickest, but I wasn't completely sure how a spell like the Jhea could take out constructs. Questions for when we got back to the others.

Nasif was the most difficult to get moving. Once I'd

convinced Dueble that I was me, he picked up Nasif and came out.

Queen Mungoosey and the faeries were still taking down the dreks, but their tunnel remained open.

"That chawsia path tunnel needs to be closed. I need to be back to human-sized to do it." I mentally called out to Derry as I didn't think screeching across the cavern would work. I'd been in my dragon size when I'd shut their tunnel down months ago—but this cavern wasn't large enough for that.

Not to mention we had no idea what the people behind this would do when their pet dreks failed to appear to devour the town. Even if the two people who'd been in here were gone, the empress would have had someone watching things.

"You can change on your own. Just think of it like when you change into your dragon shape."

Aside from the fact that the dragon was part of who I was, and as far as I knew there wasn't faery in my family line. But arguing with someone when they were busy destroying monsters wasn't a great idea.

So, I focused on being a human. And ended up flopping to the ground, hard. But it seemed like I was full-sized and, aside from some bruises, more or less okay.

Next time I did that, I needed to make sure that I was closer to the ground before changing. If there was a next time. Being able to change into a faery was sort of fun, but also extremely disturbing.

I ran to the chawsia path entrance as the faeries fought off more dreks and the chimeras joined in. Dueble, still carrying Nasif, led the villagers out. The brownies trotted along after them.

Not that I blamed them—dreks were nasty and the faeries seemed to be slowing down in their attacks.

The Jhea spell permeated the cavern. Unfortunately, in the second I changed shapes and fell, depression and hopelessness hit me as I slammed into the ground and stopped humming. I fought back with anger and more humming.

I ran to the chawsia path mouth and pulled in the weird spell conglomeration I'd used before to turn the other drek to stone and close the path.

It stayed right out of reach.

"Anger! Fear! Use them!"

Derry was right. When I'd done it before, one of the monsters was trying to kill Alric and the rest of my friends were in danger. It took two more tries, and the faeries were definitely slowing down, but I blasted the tunnel. A single drek had been at the entrance, and he turned to stone. The tunnel cracked behind him and collapsed. Hopefully I got all of them.

"Needs to flee!" Derry yelled in my head as Queen Mungoosey led the faeries around the cavern, then out the way everyone else had gone.

I looked around in case we missed anyone, then climbed over the stone drek in front of me and raced out.

"You can stop humming now. Spell broken. But get further away." Derry flew next to me as I ran. Everyone else was past the nearest building to this one and seemed to be waiting.

Garbage, Leaf, and Crusty all flew back to me. Then they spotted Derry and froze in place.

"Is yous?!" Garbage had a serious level of surprise and hero worship in her voice. The other two couldn't even speak.

"Yes, child. It's me." Derry flew to where they hovered in mid-air, hugged all three, then turned back to me. "I have to go now. Things to do. But I'll be back." With a wink, she vanished.

Queen Mungoosey approached us before my girls had a chance to recover.

"I thank you for many things, including bringing Direidus Salvia back into our world. This town is safe now. But you have much work." All the faeries gathered around and bowed in the air to her. Then she and the troops she brought in vanished.

I looked around as townspeople slowly came out of their homes. It was the middle of the night, but they came out shaking their heads as if they'd just woken up. Which they sort of had.

Crusty flew up to me. "I saves!"

"Crusty, you and the chimeras took off and got captured. You all could have died." Part of me wanted to turn back into a faery so I could better hug and strangle her. Not that any of us in town would have been safe if those dreks got out, but she'd risked herself and the constructs.

"Noes. *Saves.* Me brings Direidus backs. She's oldest." She nodded sagely.

I sighed. This wasn't the place to deal with this. "We can debate things back at the guest house." I noticed there were about fifty more faeries than we had back at the mountain. "Are they all supposed to be here?" No idea if they'd been with the queen or not. Garbage had a bad tendency to annex wild faeries into her hoard— usually not good in the eyes of Queen Mungoosey.

"Bird lady and friends. Theys comes with us." Garbage recovered from her surprise at seeing Derry, and nodded. "Yous dids goods. Backs now." With a bow in my direction, Garbage flew up in the air and led the faeries back toward Qianru's compound. Bunky gronked and also bowed, then he, Irving, and the rest of the chimeras followed the faeries.

The freed townspeople left. Nasif seemed to be shaking off the spells that hit him and was now leaning on Dueble, but wasn't being carried.

Nasif smiled. "I've no idea what happened, we were

captured right after I threw Crusty to find you. But I believe we owe you our lives."

I ran and hugged them both. "Let's get back to Qianru's place and sort things out. I'm glad to see you both."

"Agreed." Nasif, still being held up by Dueble, put his other arm around me and we made our way through the town and the confused, but no longer spelled, townspeople.

"We'll need defenses for the town." Dueble looked at Nasif. "But we need to get back first."

I knew he meant to get Nasif to safety first, but I nodded. One thing that was constant with most of the elves I'd met in the past few years—they were all exceedingly stubborn. Especially when it came to their own injuries or health.

Alric, Foxy, and a recovered Locksead, stood at the entrance of the compound as we approached, swords at the ready. Alric held a nasty-looking spell ball that vanished once he saw us.

Alric ran to us and shook his head. "I'm glad to see you all. The faeries wouldn't say anything about where you were as they flew by and were gushing about a deer or something." He hugged me and then took my place assisting Nasif.

"Long story, but I think we can go inside once we do something to protect the town for the night." Nasif looked better but still sounded exhausted.

"We can help." Padraig came over with Mathilda and Cwin following. Covey was stalking behind them, but I didn't know if she could help set magic barriers.

She ran past them and grabbed me in a hug. "Stop doing that!" She set me down and gave a suspicious swipe near her eyes. "Okay, what can I do to help?"

Mathilda smiled and put a hand on Covey's shoulder. "As it happens, we will need people to set up relays around the town perimeter. Grillion is getting the houseboys. We'll need these placed at specific spots." She handed Covey a grayish cube about the size of the palm of her hand.

Covey narrowed her eyes and tilted it around. "What does it do? Will it blow up our enemies?"

"Probably not," Cwin said as she came over. "Just place it where I tell you, and come back. Once they're all in place, we'll run a protective spell through them. Nothing will be able to cross the line without getting a painful jolt." She briefly touched Covey's forehead.

Covey's eyes went wide. "What was that? Ooh. I know where to go now." She grinned and took off into the center of town.

"I gave her the one furthest away; she's fast and I doubt anyone will try to slow her down." Cwin looked at me closely, then nodded. "We have much to speak of. *You* won't be planting the cubes." With that dismissal, Mathilda and Cwin went through all the non-magic users. Mathilda gave each one a square and Cwin touched their forehead to tell them where to go. Handy, since while the houseboys probably knew Notlianda well, our people didn't.

Dueble stepped forward. "I can place one."

Mathilda hugged him. "We have enough runners and you should escort Nasif back to the guest house." She glared at Nasif as he opened his mouth to protest. "No. I can feel the exhaustion rolling off both of you. You haven't officially met her yet, but this is Cwin. She's a siramage and will physically move you if needed."

Cwin flashed a very old-school grimarian smile. "Nice to meet you both."

Dueble laughed and turned Nasif around. "We're outmatched, my friend. Surrender is the best choice."

Nasif gave Mathilda and Cwin a nod, then let Dueble lead him back. The fact he didn't challenge either

Mathilda or Cwin, siramage or not, spoke a lot about his condition.

Covey was the first of the runners back, even though she'd had to go all the way across the city. She had a bag with her—a big one that was squirming.

"I found these lurking around the edge of town." She opened the bag a little. "Now, one of you can come out, but no funny stuff."

The red cap appeared first.

"You grabbed the brownies?" I figured they were the ones from the cavern, but they all appeared the same to me.

"Yes, oddly they didn't fight when I bagged them." Covey watched as the one she released dusted himself off and bowed to me.

"Thank you for assisting us. We would like to help if we can." He gave another deep bow. If it wasn't that Siabiane probably wouldn't have had time to create a group of more Welsys and Delsys, I would have believed this one was a construct.

"Help? Assisting?" Covey scowled and tightened her hold on the bag as she looked at me. "You know these brownies?" She wasn't brownie-friendly. Especially after an evil group of them took over her house in Beccia, tied her up, and left a serious doily infestation on all of her furniture.

CHAPTER NINETEEN

I SHRUGGED AND TOOK A STEP closer to the brownie. Covey looked a bit wild. "Sort of. We met in the cavern where everyone was held. They were trying to help us." I wasn't going to bring up the fact that I'd tried to stop them when I thought they were going after everyone in the cages.

"We have learned the true path of our people. It is spreading throughout the land." The brownie winced. "Slowly, sadly. But we follow the brownie guardians' teachings. The ones who manifested in this world."

This time it was my turn to narrow my eyes. I'd been attacked by a group of brownies when we'd first come south. Welsy and Delsy had a serious meeting with them. The term brownie guardians had come up then too.

"You follow Welsy and Delsy?"

He nodded reverently. "Those were the names the chosen ones gave themselves. We left the rest of our group, who failed to see the changes needed after the leaders spoke to us a few months ago. The rest of the followers are in that bag. But they hold no grudges." He smiled at Covey who still appeared confused. "We know how greedy most of our people are. We will help in this time of heroes and battles. We will be remembered for what we gave."

I hid my smile. He was extremely melodramatic. But, when they weren't being greedy jerks, brownies could be handy in a fight. And I had a feeling that we needed everyone we could get on our side.

Mathilda stepped forward. "I am the sister of the one whom Welsy and Delsy follow." She held herself regally. Granted, Siabiane *created* the two brownie constructs, but that didn't need to be discussed now. "Will you allow me to examine you and your honorable brownies before you join our hallowed battle?" Her words were drawn out as if to add gravitas to them.

I again hid my smile.

"Oh, yes, honored one." The brownie's bow brought his head almost to the ground.

Covey sighed and set down her bag. She wasn't going to argue, even if she didn't trust any brownies beyond Welsy and Delsy further than she could kick them.

The brownie held himself up proudly. "I am now called Flower Weaver of the Night Sky, but you may call me Flower, oh regal one. I will bring forth my companions."

I shared a look with Covey. If they all had names this long and were going to be so stilted, we were going to be out here the rest of an already too-short night.

"Thank you, Flower." Mathilda kept her face serious. "I believe we can conduct all introductions once we have taken shelter. However, I would like to see your companions before we go inside."

Flower scurried to the bag and undid Covey's knot—I hadn't even noticed she re-tied it once she let him out.

It seemed there were more in the cavern, but I also thought they were much taller. Eight brownies tumbled out clutching their caps as they bowed to Mathilda. And to myself, Covey, Cwin, and a few piles of rubble that looked vaguely like people.

Mathilda gave a benevolent smile and walked through

them all, lightly holding her hands out as she searched them with magic.

I didn't know how she could look for intention, but that would be an extremely handy spell. I figured she was simply searching for any spells laid on them.

Then I noticed that while she hadn't moved, Cwin was also casting a low spell. I knew that siramages had different powers than everyone else, so she *could* be searching for intentions.

Cwin gave a small nod at the same time Mathilda did.

"You will join us, Flower and companions." Mathilda turned and led the way back to the guest house.

The last of the houseboy runners returned from setting the perimeter. Cwin thanked them and sent them back to Qianru. Along with a slightly protesting Locksead.

Foxy and Covey followed the brownies, and Alric and I trailed after them all.

The guest house was well lit and faery laughter hit us before we opened the door.

But the room went silent as Flower and the rest of the brownies trooped in.

Most appeared curious, but Grillion went for his blade.

"Easy all." Covey held up her hand. "These are friendly. So say Mathilda and Cwin."

Padraig dropped a spell that I hadn't noticed him carrying and Garbage looked up.

Faeries and brownies weren't friends at all. I prepared to defend the brownies when Garbage waved and her faeries all swarmed the brownies.

I was probably the most surprised when the attack turned into a hug fest.

"These goods! Saves us."

I opened my mouth to remind her that I'd been leading the charge to save them, then shrugged. This was for the better. And I wanted to go to sleep. Arguing would prolong getting there.

Mathilda introduced all of us by name, then Flower introduced his eight fellow brownies. I was fairly sure that the names were new and based on their changes from the rest of their people. The names were all plant-related and sounded more like faery names than brownies. But as long as they didn't expect me to recall them, I was fine.

Garbage was smiling at Flower, then folded her arms and tilted her head. "Needs things for difference. Noes like other brownies."

"She has a point," Cwin said. "No offense, good brownie brothers, but to us, you all do look the same."

All nine of them burst out laughing.

"We look the same to us as well. But maybe we could add something to our caps." Flower removed his cap and handed it to Mathilda.

Brownies were quite partial to two things—their doilies and their red caps. But he didn't flinch when Mathilda touched the top of the cap and it turned a deep green.

The brownies all leaned forward to look at the cap, then all of them stood in line to have Mathilda change theirs after she handed Flower back his.

"We shall wear these with honor! And if our enemies try to disguise themselves as us, ask them for the names of our leaders—Welsy and Delsy." Flower gave a solemn nod and placed his cap on his head.

I wasn't sure how Welsy and Delsy would take being their leaders, but it worked for us.

After the brownies' caps were changed, the faeries took over a corner table and pulled out their ale bottles. I wasn't going to argue with them, it had been a rough time for all of us. They called for the brownies to join them. Flower and his group stayed politely near them but waved off the offer of ale.

"That's actually disturbing." Covey dropped to the sofa as she watched the odd faery-brownie interaction.

"But handy." Padraig stretched and yawned. "I know a lot happened out there, and we do need to sort it out. But if we don't get sleep, we won't be able to deal with anything."

I kept my shock to myself. Padraig was more of the keep-running-all-the-time guy. For himself anyway.

"I'll take the first watch." Foxy remained near the door with his club.

Mathilda patted his cheek. "We're safe for tonight. The spell wall is set around the town and will last at least eight hours, possibly longer. The townspeople will find that they don't want to leave the town until then. The lictenspelt is further out than originally believed and might have been sent out to raise terror in magic users." She looked at the faeries and brownies. "Bunky, Irving, and the rest of the chimeras are resting in the stables. The faeries and brownies don't need much sleep. But the rest of us need it immediately."

While Mathilda had been dealing with the brownies, Padraig and Cwin used healing spells on Nasif. He fought them until Dueble threatened to sit on him.

Padraig smiled and put a hand on the nearest wall. "And for increased protection, this building and stable are now extra spelled. Sleep, all—she means it."

I sprinted for the room Alric and I dropped our stuff in. Or would have if a wave of exhaustion hadn't slapped me up the side of my head before I got three steps in. When I almost walked into a wall instead of the hall, Alric picked me up.

"I'm not sure what all happened out there, but our Taryn had some adventures." Mathilda patted the side of my cheek and nodded to Alric as he carried me into the room.

"I'm fine. Really," I tried to say more, but it sounded like mumbling even in my head. I fell over the moment Alric sat me on the bed.

Exhausted as I was, I still had scary, insane, and weird dreams. Not scary enough to wake me up and I knew they were dreams. But I couldn't figure out what they were trying to show me.

Probably something in the books at the cottage that I had skimmed. I needed a few weeks to work through them all.

Then Queen Mungoosey appeared in my dream world. She was so real in my mind that I reached out to touch her. She remained right out of reach.

"Good work. But you need to be at Bailinsea, by the time of calling, or all will be lost."

"What? What's the calling? Can you tell me when I'm awake? Seriously, I won't remember."

She grinned. "You will." Then she and my dreams vanished.

I woke up slowly searching for something in my mind, but there was nothing beyond an odd sense of disturbance. That weird feeling when you know you had some dream adventures but they remain out of reach.

Alric was sound asleep next to me. An uncommon enough occurrence that I curled into his side closer and pretended that we were back in Beccia in my little house. There was nothing to worry about beyond what we were going to do for fun that day.

Then the reality of the world right now pushed its way in, no matter how hard I fought to keep it at bay. Even though I had been content with my former simple life of digging for elven ruins in the day, and hanging out with my friends at the Shimmering Dewdrop during the evenings, I would dream of exploring the larger world. Especially if I found something exotic in the ruins.

I now figured it might have been my memories of my past poking in. But at the time I would drift into thoughts of exploring beyond Beccia for a bit, then get back to my life.

I never thought I'd have so much danger and excitement around me that I would pay anything to go back to my old life.

I looked at Alric and brushed one long blond strand of hair from his face. I wouldn't trade him or any of my new friends for that life though. I sighed.

"I felt that." Alric was more awake than I thought and he opened his eyes.

"Just imagining life when we're done with this." I hugged him close. "And trying to recall a dream I had." The bedroom had one small window and thin curtains so seeing that it was light outside was easy. "And now we have to get up." I snuggled closer.

Alric pushed himself up on his elbow and peered down at me. "Taryn? What happened to you when you took off?"

"I know it was risky. And I know you were upset, but you couldn't have gone where we went. I'll tell everyone today, but I became a faery." There were so many emotions behind that statement I wasn't sure how to deal with them yet. I was an Ancient—being two forms was sort of our thing. But the faery transition was really weird and bugging me. I first thought it had all been Derry's doing, but the more I searched, the more I had a bad feeling that she had activated something in me.

"You became a faery? At your size?" He wasn't shocked, I doubted much could shock either of us at this point. But curious.

"Nope. Same size as Garbage and the rest. That odd faery I found, I call her Derry, she's old. Really old. Wrinkled face, gray hair—old. She did something and changed me." I kissed him and then rolled out of bed. "Let's get ready and face the rest of them. I don't want to repeat everything."

I beat him to the bath, but we were out, dressed, and heading for the front room in ten minutes.

The smell of fresh buns, hot tea, and honey pulled me from Alric's arm and into the small kitchen. Padraig was cooking, this time along with Grillion. Although Grillion was helping bring food to the table, he was also tasting bits as he worked.

I gratefully took a cup of tea with a generous spoonful of honey and went to the table. The faeries and brownies were sound asleep where we'd left them. It said a lot that the faeries snored louder than the brownies did.

Of course, the brownies hadn't been drinking.

Mathilda and Cwin came in from the direction of the stables with Bunky and Irving buzzing along right after them.

I waved Bunky over. "I'm glad to see that you and your people are okay, but following Crusty's lead yesterday wasn't a good idea."

He gronked and I understood him. He hadn't been following her really—he had to rescue his faeries. He wasn't defensive in his gronk, but he made it clear that he'd do it again. That was a possibly disturbing change we didn't need.

"I know. We came here to save them too. But by going off without all of us, you could have been destroyed." I paused; I needed a different tactic. "The faeries might not have been saved." I didn't want to scare him, but things were going to get worse and he couldn't take those risks.

Bunky paused, bobbed, and gave a soft gronk of

acceptance. Then dove for Alric's head before darting up into the rafters.

Mathilda joined us. "The rest of the chimeras left a few hours ago. Bunky said the group will come when needed, but being in cities for too long makes them uncomfortable. They still remember the fall of the Ancients."

"Someday, I'll sit down and go through all of those memories." I kept my shudder to myself—it might be another fifty or so years before I was ready for that.

Everyone else stumbled in, more or less awake. None of us had more than a few hours of sleep. Unfortunately, we were all getting used to it again. After that month off in the ruins, it didn't take long to get back into panic all the time.

There was rustling behind us as the last platters of food were brought to the table.

Flower and his brownie companions were awake and looking hopefully toward the table.

"I've set up plates for you over here. I wasn't sure where you'd like to eat." Padraig motioned toward a low table off to the side, loaded down with the same food we had.

"Thank you very much. Yesterday was quite an adventure." Flower even took his cap off, and his fellow brownies followed suit, as they went to sit around the low table.

The faeries hadn't budged.

"I saved food for them too. Whenever they get up." Padraig took his seat just as there was a knock at the door.

Foxy was closest, so got up—he had left his club behind the door in case and grabbed it before opening the door.

"Morning, everyone. I told Locksead we should come to see what happened last night." Tag came in. "And tell you what happened to me." He and Locksead waved off offers of breakfast. "Thanks, we already ate." They sat on the sofa.

Foxy got them tea before sitting down and diving into his mountain of food.

I figured sorting things out would take place over breakfast, but everyone was not only exhausted but starving. Nasif and Dueble almost ate as much as Foxy. Impressive since, while neither of them was small, together they weren't close to Foxy's size.

The faeries were stirring by the time we finished eating, but they only ate a little food. After their third unsuccessful attempt at getting tea—something that put them into hyper mode—they muttered about stuffs and things and took off. Popping through the door before any of us could get up to open it.

Locksead shook his head as they vanished into the wood. "That's disturbing."

"Most things they do are." I looked at Bunky and Irving. They hadn't charged the door yet, but I could tell they were trying to be patient. Maybe some of what I told Bunky sunk in. I'd feel better if they were with the faeries to a point. I went to the door. "Bunky, you and Irving can go with the faeries, but you have to promise me that you will come get us if something goes wrong. Do not go after the faeries until you talk to us."

He gronked in reluctant agreement and I opened the door. They were out of sight immediately.

Once the dishes were put away, we gathered in the front room. Flower came up to me as I sat. "We would like to remain here if we can. We can explain why we were in the cavern."

I looked around but everyone either shrugged or nodded. "Sure. Flower and company, meet Tag and Locksead—friends of ours."

Mathilda called us to attention. "I think the first point

is Taryn's adventures and freeing the faeries and Nasif and Dueble."

I would have rather gone after the others; I knew Alric at least was worried at my running off with Derry. But might as well get it over.

I said Derry's full name once, and probably garbled it, but Mathilda and Cwin both reacted to it. They said nothing though and motioned for me to continue. I explained why I took off, where the cavern was, and about changing into a faery—there were a lot of questions at that point. The bulk of which I couldn't answer. Then I talked about Queen Mungoosey bringing a fleet in to help, fighting the dreks, destroying their chawsia path tunnel, almost beating up the brownies, then freeing everyone and fleeing. I also mentioned that sound wasn't compromised this time.

Nasif rubbed his head. "I don't recall your appearance or that of the faeries, or brownies. At least not until you broke our cage. Whoever was behind this used a tricky pair of Jhea spells. An extremely targeted one against magic users, and a weaker general one on the main populace. That could be why they modified the dreks. Or some other ability they gave them that required them to remove the dreks' natural silence when hunting ability."

Dueble gave a tight smile, for once appearing like the more vicious, modern syclarions. "Apparently, syclarions are immune to it. Or at least the general version. I'm not sure what it would do to a syclarion mage. I was subdued, but not as bad as anyone else."

Padraig leaned forward. "That's interesting. However, there was speculation that the Jhea spell was created by the Paili. They wouldn't want to hit their people."

Paili were brutal and powerful syclarion mages who'd almost destroyed my people. Yet another reason to hate them.

Nasif briefly spoke of how he and Dueble were captured, and his spell on Crusty to get us the message.

He didn't mention why he and Dueble had left Ageora's *tir cudd* though.

Mathilda waited as he finished speaking, then folded her arms. "Nasif, I've known you for centuries. There's something you don't want to tell us. What happened in the *tir cudd*?"

"Thank you." He smiled. "Ageora put a geas on us that we couldn't speak of what happened until one of you asked. I'm not completely sure why, but she didn't want the information to get out." His smile faded. "It's a short tale and hopefully one that will eventually have a happy ending. After you all left, we managed to destroy the attackers who had invaded the *tir cudd*. Zaelian might be a ghost, but she has some useful tricks. Once they were gone, we settled in to work through the *tir cudd* information, and where the other surviving deities might be." He paused and looked down.

"It wasn't your fault." Dueble patted his arm. "We were attacked, but not on our level. It was an attack aimed at Ageora and Zaelian. Nothing Nasif or I did stopped them. Ageora told us to come here, she had information you'd all be here. She and Zaelian took off to another *tir cudd* but we can't travel like they do. Once they're safe they'll contact us."

Covey patted Nasif's shoulder. "I'm sure they're fine. They're both powerful and neither is actually alive. That's got to help."

Nasif gave a small smile. "True. I'm concerned about what was after them and why Ageora was so sure you'd be here. She's not usually wrong about such things."

"I was here," Tag said. "Maybe she somehow focused on that? And I came here based on what she said to me when we were in the *tir cudd*."

Mathilda shook her head. "It could be, but I think there was something else at work in her directing you here. How pressed for time were they when she and Zaelian left?"

"Very. The final attack was unexpectedly swift. She was trying to get Dueble and me out. She even created a chawsia path to help us. She might have realized something bad was going on out here, but didn't have time to explain—so she said you were here."

Dueble smiled. "Which they now are, so she was sort of right."

Tag's tale was last. He'd been captured at the same time as Nasif and Dueble, but fought free before they were able to lock him up. "They were taking me somewhere other than the building Taryn mentioned though. There was something their leader wanted from me."

I leaned forward; so far no one had seen the people behind this beyond vague shapes. "Who were they?"

"I wish I could tell you. I know they were magic users of some kind. But they were using a spell so that I couldn't see them. They were taking me outside of town though—that's when I broke away." Tag was young, but it was clear in his eyes how close he'd come to not getting free.

"There are spells to do that, but they're rare," Padraig said as he watched Tag closely. "You aren't a magic user, but you should have still been impacted by the general Jhea spell. Did you feel different?"

"No. They were concerned about that as well, though. I think that was why they didn't take me to the cavern building."

"Could his prior Jhea exposure change him?" I had no idea how the evil spell worked; I just wanted it to go away.

Mathilda came over to Tag. "It shouldn't have. But maybe? We don't know that much about the old spells, even us older people." She looked to Cwin who was squinting at Tag, then finally frowned.

"I can't sense anything."

"Maybe it was because of us," Flower said. He and the rest of the brownies had sat still, politely listening, but he stood up now. "Here's our tale, maybe it will help." He bowed to the room as if doing a formal presentation.

Covey gave an approving nod. He sounded like an academic and that was extremely valuable in her mind.

"My troop and I followed the destruction of the other towns. We arrived after the towns were destroyed and did what we could to help the few survivors." His voice cracked. "There weren't many."

CHAPTER TWENTY

—◆—

THE ROOM WENT SILENT AT the start of Flower's tale.

"The first town was Dunian. A small place to the north. It fell with only a handful of survivors." Flower patted his pockets searching for something until Alric unrolled one of our maps and handed Flower a charcoal stick. The brownie studied the map, then made a neat 'x' off the main road.

I wasn't great at map reading, but I'd gotten better over the past year. It appeared that the town was about two weeks' ride north of us.

"How did you and your companions find this place?" Mathilda was still using her slightly regal tone.

"We have been wandering and doing good deeds since we met with the leaders. Nothing grand enough for a story, but helping where we could. We arrived at Dunian hours after the attack." Flower took a deep breath to steady himself, then continued. "The next two towns were larger and fell quickly." He marked them on the map. "They had tales of dragons, but there was no sign. Lots of booted foot trails though. And no dead guards that we saw. But many dead townspeople. By the time we reached Kanik, the former town a day north of here, we figured their pattern and told the survivors not to come to Notlianda, or any of the towns to the south following the line of attacks."

Padraig tilted his head. "But you did."

"Aye. We still had no idea as to what was destroying these places, or why. Then we saw people here being taken, and then the faeries and chimeras. We knew we had to leap into action to save everyone." He gave an embarrassed smile. "We thought perhaps Welsy and Delsy were with them, as they traveled with the faeries. But we still would have fought to save everyone."

"That was very gallant of you. I will make sure my sister knows." Mathilda gave a slight bow.

Padraig, Mathilda, and Cwin added questions, but most of them were ones I was clueless about. They involved spells I'd never heard of.

"Can brownies do magic?" I kept my voice low as I leaned into Alric.

Flower had excellent hearing, however. "Sadly, no. Or at least most of us cannot. Some of us can carry spell stones though. Ones we found in the north at great peril." He reached into his shirt and pulled out a chain attached to a glowing green stone. The other eight brownies did the same, but their stones were all different colors. "They protect us from many magics."

"I've never heard of those." I leaned closer to the stones. Waves of light magic flowed from them, calling to me. They might protect the brownies, but I felt like one of the faeries and their love of shiny objects.

"You wouldn't have." Padraig reached toward Flower's stone but didn't touch it. "These are an old magic of long ago and only known in the southern continent. It was thought they were all lost two thousand years ago, during the last battle." His smile dropped as he watched Flower's face. "There were more of you linked together."

Flower and his friends nodded sadly. "We saved some of their stones when they fell, but the nine of us are all who remain of the twenty who began this journey. More of our people did head further north to find Welsy and Delsy prior to these attacks. But we aren't sure if they survived or not." He rummaged around in a sack I hadn't seen before and pulled out ten more stones on chains. All were different colors but lacked the brightness of the ones on Flower and his friends. "We would be honored to have their stones carried by those who traveled with Welsy and Delsy."

I sat on my hand to stop it from grabbing them. This wasn't like me at all. Ancients weren't hoarders, but I found myself needing those stones. Maybe a side effect from turning into a faery.

I sat on my other hand and ignored the odd look from Alric. This was a really disturbing feeling.

"I will hold them and give them to my sister when we next meet." Mathilda smiled at the brownies but I noticed she kept sneaking looks at me.

Flower handed the chains over, tucked his own stone back into his shirt, and finished his tale.

Which, until Mathilda dropped the stones inside one of the faery bags that she carried, I didn't hear at all. Those stones were almost singing to me.

The moment she closed the bag I was fine again. And I stopped sitting on my hands. I did continue to ignore Alric's inquiring looks, however.

"And that's when we followed the Ancient one into the cave. But they vanished by the time we arrived inside."

I looked around. If the brownies were staying with us, they needed to know what I was. Finding out shocking realities in the middle of a battle could prove deadly.

Padraig, Mathilda, Alric, and Cwin all shared quick looks that made me worried. Then Alric nodded to me.

I gave the briefest introduction that I could as to what I was.

"You were both the Ancient and the faery? That is great power indeed." Flower clapped his hands.

"Now that we know what happened, what's next?" Covey had been silently listening along with the others, but she looked ready to fight something.

Or to deliver a soul-crushing lecture.

"We need to know why these towns are being targeted." Padraig pointed to the map. The line of 'x's where the attacks had occurred was distinct. "We can assume part of the campaign is to control the remaining towns by destroying others as a lesson. And to build a fear of Ancients should they come into battle. Along with creating an army of dead for the lictenspelt." He looked at me and I controlled my glee. If the empress feared the return of Ancients, she had information we needed.

And I had more hope of finding my brothers.

"But there is probably a strategic reason for these towns. They're too specifically placed to be chance." Alric scowled at the map as the rest clustered around.

Tag and Locksead had listened to the rest of our tales, but both leaned forward to look at the map. Tag turned white, muttered something under his breath, and stepped back. Locksead didn't look as bad but he shook his head and joined Tag.

"What is it?" Grillion studied the map as well, but either it was because he was upside down from the map, or wasn't seeing what the other two did, he didn't appear concerned.

Tag took a deep breath. "I grew up here in Notlianda. There were always old wives' tales about the cauldron of death. A great mage battle took place there long ago. It was said that we were on the rim of the cauldron and that one day great mages would come back and control its power. In order to rule the world." He gave a hollow laugh. "It was stuff to say, nothing more."

"And where is the cauldron?" Padraig was using his talking-to-scared-horses voice and I felt the calming magic he was sending wash over all of us.

Tag didn't move forward at first, then went to the map. He didn't use a charcoal stick, just his finger. But the circle he drew went through the destroyed towns. And Notlianda. It was large enough that it would take out the entire plain if something big, explosive, and evil came out of it.

"Damn." Grillion stared down and shook his head. "I'd never even heard of that. Then again, I've only been down here a few years. Locksead? You?"

"Nothing except rumors from drunks in the pub." Locksead had his arms tightly folded and remained away from the map.

Alric watched Locksead. They'd worked together for years when Alric was hunting the glass gargoyle as a disguised relic thief in Locksead's gang. He knew him better than anyone here.

Locksead finally sighed. "Fine. Yes, I had heard of it. Mostly when I was helping Qianru move back down here. She had some relics she didn't want to touch but also didn't want to get rid of. They were supposedly related to this destroyer of worlds. The cauldron."

"So Qianru knows of it? Where are these relics?" Cwin leaned forward and watched Tag and Locksead carefully.

"Honestly, Qianru gathers things without fully knowing what they are." Locksead continued to glare at the map. "As for where they are, I think they were stolen by that fake elf changeling a few months ago. I'd have to ask her. Many things were taken."

"How do we stop this cauldron thing from creating

itself?" Now that we'd rescued the faeries and everyone, I felt the pull to go to the Lledir mountains, and the village below them, Bailinsea. But we couldn't let this thing do whatever it was going to do. If it did what Tag said, the empress would gain enormous amounts of power from it. Not to mention that too many people had already died because of this.

"We already started that." Mathilda tapped where Notlianda was on the map. "We ended the attempted attack here, there was no slaughter to generate the magic needed. They can try again, but it needs to be soon. Within a day they'll have missed their chance."

I looked around at my friends when none of them responded. "That's good news, right? We have those spell things surrounding the town. If they can't take this town, they can't open the cauldron." I didn't like the surrounding looks. "*Right*?"

"Correct, but the spell protection will only last a few more hours. That still leaves the empress's people time to destroy this town and continue the pattern." Cwin scowled at the map. "Or they could try from the other side. This area is north of Dunian. How many towns are in this circle?" Taking the charcoal stick she marked off an area that appeared to be in the mountains. "They have to continue the circle pattern once it's begun. They could use Notlianda as the final piece if they switch to the other direction."

Locksead squinted at the map. "Tag? Is that about where Maziline is? I've never been up there, but a pair of Qianru's houseboys came from that town."

"I think so. I went up there once for Qianru years ago before I joined your crew in Beccia. It's a nice little mountain town." His eyes went wide as some connection hit him. "They dig for lathisite. Huge mines for it."

I had never heard of whatever lathisite was, but the people around me had. And it even caused Cwin to twitch. I gauged my freak-out level by those around me. This wasn't good.

"Lathisite is a powerful metal but it's explosive, extremely so, until it's processed. Most likely the empress was saving it for the final push of opening the cauldron." Padraig continued to scowl at the map as if it could give him more options.

"Then they probably won't go there? So, we need to defend Notlianda for a few more hours?" I didn't want to be in a massive battle for this town, but was even less interested in being in one for an explosive town. No matter how lovely it was.

"Twelve hours at this point." Covey shared in the glaring at the map, but her focus was aimed at where we were. "We have to figure out which way they'll go. We can't protect both towns. Unless someone hid the real guards for this one, and they're still alive, we don't even have enough fighters to cover one town."

"Excellent points," Padraig said. "But we don't have time to look into the empress's thought process. She's taken a lot of hits lately and misjudged the people working for her. There's no way to tell what she might do."

"Lorcan might be able to help." Mathilda nodded. "He's very good at understanding behavior. A skill he developed after the betrayal of the Dark. And a few more magic users could help us defend whichever town we determine to be the target."

Alric shook his head. "We don't know what's going on in Beccia. They still need to protect those Pernasi library scrolls."

"We bring the scrolls here." Covey shrugged as everyone turned to her. "What are we saving them for? If this thing opens, the war is over. Our *world* is over. I'm all about saving the past, but there comes a time when it has to be used to save the future. We need help and information. The empress will have another plan if this one fails."

I almost fell over. Covey was the ultimate academic, only possibly surpassed by Zaelian, our ghost librarian. But as shocking as her words were, there was a lot of truth to them.

Mathilda shared a look with Padraig and he finally nodded. "I can attempt to reach Siabiane, she'll be easier than Lorcan when he gets into his studies. And I agree we need them. I hope they're both up to it. Cwin, I'll need you to help me contact them and to bring them back with the scrolls, if they can. A chawsia path is too slow for this distance."

Lorcan and Siabiane had returned to Beccia to help protect the town but also to recover from their prolonged time trapped in the Jhea spell. But both were powerful magic users and Lorcan had a researching skill that even outstripped Covey.

At Cwin's nod, Mathilda and she went toward the stables. "It'll be easier out of the way. And if they agree, I can bring them back immediately. I'd say we need to find out if Qianru has anything on this cauldron and warn her there might be another attack. We have about three hours before the spell walls fall."

CHAPTER TWENTY-ONE

THE FRONT ROOM WENT SILENT with their departure.

Until Flower coughed. "I don't want to interrupt, but my people and I can patrol this town while we wait. Most people fail to notice us when we don't wish to be seen. There could be things of importance to learn." His slow nod indicated he relished being a spy.

Padraig smiled. "That's a good idea. Stay out of sight and report back on any guards who remain. Or anything that appears out of place."

Flower nodded and his group trooped to the door. Foxy quickly opened it, looked outside, and shut it once the last brownie left.

"I'd like to talk to Amara if I could. There are oaks around this town, and those are her favorites." Foxy didn't reach for his tattoo, but his hand on that side twitched a bit.

"That's also a good idea, aside from the whole we're still not sure who was cutting into it," Alric said. "We could use her help but not if we're giving away something to the enemy."

"Maybe try mine?" I rubbed my upper arm where the vine tattoo was. "I know we aren't sure about that one either. But if Amara can help Notlianda, we need to ask her."

Nasif and Dueble remained silent after telling of how they came to Notlianda. But Nasif nodded slowly. "I think I can help remove the trackers on the tattoos for good if you are referring to a communications sigil. Right now, I feel they're being blocked from interference, but given time they could break through." He nodded to Padraig and Mathilda. The thousand years he and Dueble spent hiding from everyone, but conducting odd magic studies, had changed his magic outside of the elven norm. "I'll need Foxy and Taryn to stand in a circle with me. I'll use the power of your marks to reach Amara. There's truth to the power of trees and if we can get them to help defend this place, we should try."

Foxy, myself, and Nasif moved away from the others and closer to each other.

"Both of you should put your hand on the tattoo, but don't reach out to Amara yet." Nasif took some deep breaths—whatever he was going to do, it was more difficult than he implied. Or he was expecting problems.

Neither option made me happy.

I pushed up my sleeve and wrapped my hand around the vine tattoo and Foxy did the same with the one on his calf.

Nasif put his hands on our shoulders and began speaking a soft spell. Some magic needed words, but other spells didn't. "Now, both of you, reach out to Amara." He'd waited until whatever spell he was casting was in place and it settled over us like a cloak.

I mentally called for Amara and felt Foxy doing the same. It was as if all three of us were sharing the contact. Which hopefully protected us from whatever or whoever had broken into Foxy's connection before.

"Foxy? And Taryn? And…hello?"

"I'm Nasif, one of the elves from the enclave of Alric and Padraig. We fear there is a leak of some kind in the communication sigils you gave to Foxy and Taryn. I'm currently creating a permanent way to keep them out."

Amara was silent for long enough that I feared we'd lost the connection. "How long has this gone on? I spoke to Foxy a few hours ago."

Foxy's eyes went wide. "That wasn't me. What did they say?" The hand not on his calf clenched into a fist.

"Nothing much. He asked about the scrolls Alric hid. But there was something odd about his wording, so I said everything was fine. I should have realized something was wrong, but I didn't think my marks could be compromised."

"That someone was able to do so, is surprising. I'm using your spell as we speak to make sure they can't get in again." Nasif's voice was strained as he nodded to Foxy.

"Amara, we're in a town that's been under attack and might be again, Notlianda. There be a forest of mostly oak trees surrounding it. Could you reach them and ask if they could help defend this place?"

Amara hummed a light tune, an odd response, but pretty. "Yes. I can. And I was able to send a resonance spell through to you three. Even with Nasif's spells, I've added another layer. If anyone else tries to speak to me through the tattoos, I'll be able to tell they aren't you. Give me a few minutes to reach the oaks. I can feel them now and they are old trees. And they haven't liked what's been happening in their town. I'll have to drop this communication to speak with them, but you three will feel their acceptance or denial. Stay safe, all of you." Then the communication ended.

Nasif let out a long breath and the connection between us vanished. "I'm glad that worked, the tattoos are locked now, from our side and hers. I think I'd like to sit for a while though." Dueble was at his side immediately and led him to the sofa.

I shared a look of concern with Alric. Nasif had only been under the Jhea spell for a day at the most. Yet he looked washed out and wan. I had no idea how much effort the spell he did took, but I didn't think it should have done this to him.

Like most elves, Nasif was stubborn to a fault. I'd have to ask Dueble about what happened before they fled the *tir cudd* when Nasif was out of earshot.

From the look of concern on Alric's face, he was thinking the same.

A loud whooshing sound, followed by shaking strong enough to rattle the windows and doors brought us back to the current situation.

It came from the stables but stopped as quickly as it began. Padraig and Covey raced there with the rest of us following. Foxy only went a few feet from the front door but kept his club ready.

The horses were under a calming spell, so they were fine. The pile of bodies, chests, and bundles that greeted us was disturbing.

Until the people involved sorted themselves out.

Lorcan, Siabiane, Mathilda, and Cwin all shook straw out of their hair and clothing.

"Sorry about that," Cwin said. "I think something might have interfered with our return trip."

"But we made it." Lorcan's smile was back to its normal self and Siabiane's was as well. Two much smaller shapes crawled out of the pile and bowed to all of us. Welsy and Delsy.

I was happy to see all of them, but would need to warn the two constructs about their worshippers before Flower and crew came back to the guest house.

After all the hugs were finished, and the packs and chests—one was Alric's, were sorted, we returned to the living room.

Lorcan looked around with a smile that quickly

dropped. "It's very good to see you all, but I wish it wasn't in this situation. Don't worry about Beccia; Ceithera and Flarinen are calling for reinforcements. Although aside from some more dwarves and llweins passing through the area, there's been no trouble. We left our assigned faeries with Amara. We'll remain here until this is done."

Alric released the spells he'd placed on the chest with the scrolls from the Pernasi library. "What's the second chest?"

"Some more research I found. Not sure how much of it will help the current situation, but I do have a few books about the cauldron, but that's all I had time to take." Lorcan looked around. "Where are the faeries, by the way?"

"They had stuff to do." I shrugged. No matter how long I lived with them, understanding why they did what they did the majority of the time was going to remain a mystery to me. "I know they'll fill you in on *everything*." That it would most likely be partially insensible and would go on for way too long was a given. "But I should warn Welsy, Delsy, and possibly Siabiane. A group of brownies helped us out recently. They are followers of Welsy and Delsy as they say that you two saved them." Both constructs had been sitting politely off to the side but jumped to their feet in concern at my words. "I think they were part of that group you spoke to after they tried to kidnap me. They claim to be doing deeds to help others during this time of sorrow. They're a bit formal."

"That could be good, or they could be lying to gain access to you all." Delsy rubbed his chin. I'd given both of them name tags a while ago because I was tired of trying to sort them out. Luckily, Siabiane made them permanently part of their appearance. Living brownies looked a lot alike, these two were identical.

"We will have to speak to them. Did they leave with the faeries?" Welsy looked toward the door. "And how do they get along?"

"They went on a recon of the town a short while ago." Grillion, like Locksead and Tag, had been sitting back and watching things. But he smiled at Welsy and Delsy.

"They get along very well," I said. "The faeries, along with a pack of chimeras and Irving, were captured by our enemies. These brownies helped rescue them."

Both constructs looked at each other, then nodded in unison. "We will locate them and discuss the situation. They might have important information." They bowed to Siabiane, then marched to the door. Foxy had resumed his guarding of it after speaking to Amara and opened it.

"Their caps are now green, by the way," Mathilda called before they walked out.

Both turned with wide eyes.

"It was thought to help tell them from the bad ones."

"Very wise. Few brownies would dare change their caps. We'll return soon," Delsy said as they ran out the door.

"This could go well, or not so much." Siabiane laughed. "I know my constructs. Mathilda and Cwin gave us a summary of what was going on. But I believe we need more specifics."

Aside from my retelling of my adventures in the building, meeting Derry, and becoming a faery, I didn't have much to say. Lorcan and Siabiane looked intrigued at the mention of my transformation into a faery, especially Lorcan. But they didn't press the issue. Not yet anyway.

Padraig and Alric brought out tea for everyone. Good idea. After the lack of sleep, and way too much running around yesterday, I was ready for a nice mid-morning nap. I knew we were running out of time before that spell around the town fell, but I hoped once things settled, we could rest for a few days. Or even a few hours.

I covered my mouth as all eyes looked at me when my laugh at that idea jumped out. I waved them off and sipped more tea.

I worked on staying awake and not saying anything and eventually noticed everyone was moving the chests toward the table. Lorcan already had a few books from his faery pouch out on the table and plans were being made.

"Are you okay?" Covey came up next to me when I belatedly got to my feet to join them. "You looked odd a few moments ago."

I went to take a sip of tea then noticed there wasn't anything there. "Just a bit tired." My stomach rumbled. "And hungry. Again." We might have only eaten a short while ago, but my body was saying otherwise.

Covey nodded wisely and took us toward the kitchen. "I'd bet it's whatever you did in that weird cavern-building. Not to mention turning into a faery." She pushed me down on a stool next to the kitchen counter and shoved food my way. "What was that like? Did you think like them?"

I grabbed a roll and shuddered. "No. That would have been horrifying. I felt like myself, only a lot smaller. And with wings. I wanted to ask Derry more about it, but that might have been why she took off."

"The girls were more impressed with that older faery showing up than their queen, or you turning into one of them," Covey said.

"Which means we need to find out more about her. Somehow, I don't think she'll come if I call for her." It never worked with Queen Mungoosey, and I had a strong idea that Derry was her peer. Maybe some sort of adviser, but definitely not a subject.

The others were planning and debating the various books and scrolls. Grillion walked around them and joined Covey and me.

"Locksead, Tag, and I are going to find out what Qianru or any of the houseboys know. I'll warn them we might be facing another fight."

"Thank you." I nodded to the others locked in a debate. "I'll tell them if they ever come up for air." It was truly scary how quickly our magic users could process information. Even Dueble was involved. He wasn't a magic user, but after a thousand years of researching with Nasif, he had some great intuition about things. And he was a serious academic.

Grillion, Locksead, and Tag left and Foxy resumed his guarding of the door. That it was locked and there was a room of powerfully dangerous magic users a few feet from him didn't stop him from taking his duties seriously.

"Do you want to be with them?" I turned back to Covey and pointed to our friends at the table.

"I was about to ask you the same thing." Covey pulled over a stool for herself and picked through some of the food. "You are a magic user, after all."

"And you're an academic." I shrugged. "I don't recall enough of what I can or can't do yet to help them. And I still feel wiped out."

Covey stared into my eyes until I waved her off. "Sorry. But you seem to be getting more exhausted looking sitting here."

I shoved some more food in, along with two cups of strong tea. "It's odd. It's like a magic over-use, but on an epic scale."

"When they're done you need to have Mathilda look at you." She gave me her classic annoyed professor look and folded her arms. "You can do it, or I can tell her how you just drifted away a few minutes ago. And that I think there's something wrong with you."

"Not fair. But I'll do it. When they've sorted out if we're leaving or fighting here. It feels so long ago that we were hiding in those ruins." I gave a sad smile. "I miss it."

Covey got off her stool and came to my side. Then she hugged me, which was almost more disturbing than the way I felt.

"Thank you." I hugged her back before she zipped back to her seat.

"Could you two join us for a moment?" Padraig waved a scroll in the air. "This might pertain to Taryn."

Covey and I went over and Padraig gave the scroll to Covey. Alric appeared furious but didn't say anything.

That Covey reread the archaic script three times without saying anything didn't make me happy. It looked like an odd language, but she had full reading comprehension in at least ten languages that I knew of. Then I recognized the look on her face as she went for a fourth read. She wasn't reading to understand, she was reading for a way out.

CHAPTER TWENTY-TWO

"OKAY, WHAT'S IN THE SCROLL?" Fear and concern did a nice job of waking me up, so that was handy.

Lorcan glanced up as Covey did yet another read-through. "This is actually from the collection of items from the Dark we had. It speaks of one long lost, with unimaginable powers, who will find the sacred relics and use them to destroy everyone in the world. Part of it tells of this anam olc and their ability to change into anything—yet they are not a changeling. Which wasn't clear at first and might explain the Dark's interest in changelings. The Dark wants to control, but also fears, this being. It says they will be destroyed in the final battle as well."

I stumbled back to my stool and barely made it. I hadn't told anyone, not even Alric, about what the faeries had shown me a few nights ago. Yet this made all of those images from the faeries slam into my mind.

Alric was at my side immediately. "Taryn? You look like you saw a ghost. This is scary, but it can't refer to you." Never mind that Padraig said it might have something to do with me moments before.

I couldn't look into his eyes. "I hid information from you. All of you." I wiped away the tears that kept coming. "The morning we left my family's cabin the faeries brought me outside before sunrise. It wasn't only to tell me where we needed to go. They had a vision to share. Of me. Killing everyone. Good people, friends, loved ones, enemies, the empress, the Paili, and all of the Dark. I destroyed *everything*." I hiccupped as sobs made it hard to keep speaking. "You have to destroy me before I turn into whatever that was." My heart broke as all of my hopes for a nice calm life with Alric vanished before my eyes. Locking me up wouldn't work. Spells wouldn't work. They needed to kill me.

Alric grabbed me and held me so tight I stopped my hiccup-sobbing.

Popping sounds came from the door and we were flooded with faeries.

Garbage glared at everyone then pointed at me. "What. Yous. Do? Brokes it!" She zipped over to me and hummed the anti-Jhea song. Soon all the faeries, still over a hundred, were around Alric and me, humming.

"Garbage? Is what Taryn said about the vision you shared with her true?" Mathilda's voice was soft and soothing.

Which would have freaked me out more if Alric wasn't still holding me tight and rubbing my back.

"Yous tolds?" Garbage got into my face, dodging through Alric's hair as she shook her finger at me. "Yous noes tells yet. Bads for yous. Needs halps." She didn't wait for my answer, just flew to the door with her enlarged flock following her. They popped through the door before anyone could say anything.

"Okay, that was weird, even for them." I'd been chastised by the faeries before but this time Garbage was seriously worried. Which was good, so was I.

Mathilda and Siabiane came to Alric and me and hummed the anti-Jhea song. Soon all of my friends, even Foxy, were humming it.

I continued to hold on to Alric. "Thank you, I do feel a bit better. But that song won't change what I will do."

"*Might* do." Derry was suddenly in the middle of the room. "Visions can cause things to get worse. I disagreed with them showing it to you so soon. That's one reason why I came to help yesterday." She scowled as she flew around me. "This is not right."

Before either Alric or I could respond, she tapped me in the middle of my forehead and turned me into a faery. I might or might not have helped the change last night—this time it was all her.

Alric stumbled forward as I wasn't there anymore—at least not in a way to balance him holding me.

"Yup. She be a faery." Foxy nodded slowly.

"We'll be back. Maybe with answers." Derry grabbed my hand and flew us both through the door. I had no way of knowing if the faeries felt like this when they did it, but it wasn't fun. It was as if I felt every piece of wood sliding through me. Not painful, but extremely odd.

We popped out on the other side of the door, but Derry wouldn't release my hand. "There are many waves of realities that circle our world—all worlds. What they showed you was only one version. I won't lie, there are many connectors between the you here and the you in that vision. But it doesn't have to become real. Mungoosey agreed to you being made aware in the hope that the direction of things would change." She frowned as we flew around the edge of town. "Unfortunately, your arrival here lends itself to the version we don't want."

"How do I stop this? I almost fell to that side when I put that canfydd crown on to save my friends. If they hadn't saved me in return…I might have made that reality come true then." Granted the crown was currently being held by that Dark elf armed with a hopefully still not functioning Robukian knife. I didn't trust fate enough to think it wouldn't find a way to get the damn crown back to me. Or find some other way to make me all powerful and evil.

"That was a worry. We hadn't seen that happening. The faeries have seers but no one saw that." She kept flying and holding my hand.

"So, I might have destroyed everyone and everything at that point." I'd felt that at the time but had worked hard in the past few months to convince myself that I hadn't almost become a monster.

"Even I can't say for certain. And I'm the eldest of faeries. Not a true seer, but I have insight. Free will and love can move mountains. That's why we are fighting to save this world." She squeezed my hand. "On many fronts."

Notlianda was slowly waking up and regular people were going about their regular duties. If they knew how close they'd come to being destroyed, they weren't showing it.

They *were* staying away from the town walls.

"The spell?" I pointed to the closed gate and the people passing it as if it had never been open.

"Yes. It will fall soon, so hopefully your wise friends can sort out where the next attack will hit." She flew over a tall building and sat.

"If you have seers, and you know all of these different realities, can't your people see which town will be attacked next?" It was handy speaking to a faery who was able and willing to discuss things, but that seemed fairly obvious. They knew that I might go bad, the least they should know is where the next attack would fall. I was glad the enemies had a limited time to complete the next one, but it also made me twitchy.

Limited time could make them desperate.

"We can see multiple paths, but not always the right one. Tiny elements can change things. Both options are real, according to our seers. And I feel it in these old bones." She nodded sagely and looked out over the town.

I gave up for a moment and watched the townspeople go about their business of daily life. It was calming as long as I didn't think about how close they'd come to being drek food. "Here's something not related to this, how come you look old? Crusty and the others often say that the faeries have been around forever. Yet, all of them look young."

"And I don't. And Mungoosey is a cat." Her grin lit up her lined face. "We're magic beings, like the rest. Even the boy faeries—to a point." Her scowl echoed the one all of them had when mentioning the unfinished boy faeries. "Both the queen and I have the ability to change how we look to fit in with the rest. But we like being different. This is who we are."

"But where did you come from? You said you're the first faery—how did *you* become *you*?" Yes, I was being nosy, but it was an odd thing to be the first of anything.

"I was—look out!" Derry yelled and threw up a magic shield over us as a sceanra anam dove toward us.

I didn't know if my magic would work as a faery and within her shield, but I sent the strongest push spell I could at the evil flying snake.

It tumbled back a few feet in the air, then exploded. Luckily, thanks to Derry's shield, the pieces didn't hit us. Hopefully, the people below us that they did hit wouldn't know what smacked them.

"Damn it. Every time I think those things are all dead, they come back." I kept the push spell in my mind as I searched the sky for more of them.

"That's their nature. I will say it was nice for those few thousand years when they were hibernating in the ground with the chimeras. But the bigger worry is, how did it get in here? The spell your friends put up covers everything. The town is in a bubble with nothing able to go above or below the shield until it falls. Someone had them here in town before the spell on the walls was placed." Her eyes narrowed as she pointed to a building on the edge of town. It looked like a blacksmith's shop. Or it was at one point. It left that existence long ago.

Derry must have decided I wasn't a flight risk as she didn't grab my hand when we jumped off the roof and flew over. I did enjoy being able to fly with more ease and increased eyesight. Both were better as a faery than they were as a dragon.

While I had hoped to never see one of the flying snakes again, if evil was calling out their monsters, it made sense that these things were being brought into the towns they were destroying.

Both the faeries and the chimeras could destroy the sceanra anam fairly easily—it was difficult for even powerful magic users though. Most likely why grabbing the faeries and chimeras had to happen before the attack of last night.

I figured Derry was going to survey the smithy and then come back to destroy them with more troops.

Nope.

She did one loop around the structure, flying closer than I felt comfortable, then grinned like a mad woman and dove into it through a small hole in the roof.

I waited a moment, then shrugged and followed her. Yes, there were only two of us, but if I had to, I could turn into my dragon self.

The sceanra anam were everywhere. It was as if they'd been nesting in this place for years, not the probable weeks that they would have been here.

And they were sleeping.

I noticed it first when Derry flew under the noses of a clump of them, so close they had to have felt her. But not even a fin moved.

It was almost more disturbing than if we'd been fighting them.

Derry cackled and flew up to the top of the ceiling, then back down, slamming into the largest nest of sceanra anam.

The rest of my faeries were prone to acts like that, but I'd hoped since she sounded so rational, Derry wouldn't follow that pattern.

Judging by the way she was slugging the blinking sceanra anam, she was as bad or worse than Garbage and her crew.

The sceanra anam were waking up, and we were seriously outnumbered.

CHAPTER TWENTY-THREE

MY ORIGINAL IDEA OF TURNING into my dragon self was discarded based on the size of the smithy—if I changed, there would be no way everyone outside on the streets wouldn't see me when I destroyed the building.

Bad for many reasons, one being that these people had been told that dragons destroyed the other towns.

Instead, I called Garbage and her faeries to me. I extended the call to Leaf and Crusty as well, in case they'd split up. I added images of full ale bottles and piles of sugar.

Then added the sceanra anam.

I heard them before I saw them. So much for the element of surprise as a hundred or more faeries popped through the walls of the derelict building with whoops and yells.

There was no way to know how Derry would react. Most likely she could have called the faeries herself. She'd switched to using a war stick and continued fighting the sceanra anam on her own. But she grinned as the other faeries joined in the fight.

"Good idea! More fun for everyone!" She whirled with her war stick and five sceanra anam exploded.

I'd once seen what the sceanra anam could do to a non-faery person, and it was fast, ugly, and deadly for the victim. That it happened to someone about to try to kill me, on my very doorstep, didn't make it any less disturbing.

The mass of faeries swarmed around me, stabbing and attacking the sceanra anam with glee.

I tried to remain out of their way. I could try magic, but I didn't want to throw things off for the faeries. And I didn't have one of their war sticks.

If becoming a faery was going to become a thing, I needed one of those sticks. And instructions on how to use it.

The sceanra anam were all awake now but appeared to be focusing on trying to escape instead of fighting. Bunky and Irving crashed through the weak roof of the smithy and immediately zapped the evil flying snakes. Bunky must have felt that they and the faeries could destroy the sceanra anam as he hadn't called the other chimeras.

One of the reasons my people created the chimeras was to fight the sceanra anam. Irving might not be a chimera, but he'd proven to be a quick learner.

One sceanra anam flew right where I was staying out of the way. When it saw I was alone, it bared its teeth and charged me. I didn't even cast my spell, just popped him on the long, toothy snout with both of my tiny fists.

I hit it hard enough to send it slamming into the melee where it was dust moments later.

Either my punches as a faery were far more powerful than when I was human, or some of my push spell tagged along. Either way, it worked and I wasn't going to question it.

The faeries and constructs made short work of the sceanra anam while I kept an eye out for any that might try to escape. I felt more confident about fighting them now, but I still wanted one of the faery war sticks.

"Yous goods faery!" Crusty flew over and grabbed me

in a hug. Then she pulled back and tilted her head as she narrowed her eyes. "Needs stick."

My three hadn't had war sticks until a wild gave one to me to give to them. Now all the faeries had them. Possibly a sign of the times.

"Aye, that she does. And her own faery bags." Derry flew over. She appeared winded but couldn't stop grinning. "I haven't had that much fun in a few hundred years." She rubbed her hands together and a wooden war stick and a pair of black bags appeared in them.

"These are for you. We won't assign you a faery name, not yet anyway. The war stick can stay in one of the bags you'll keep in your pocket." Derry handed them to me and the rest of the faeries bowed in mid-air.

I had a feeling that something more momentous than giving me a stick and some bags happened. I bowed back to Derry and the girls, then, noticing the others had their sticks put away, I put mine into one of the bags and put both bags in the tiny pocket on the front of my overalls.

I had to admit, the overalls were comfortable.

"Yous goods!" Garbage yelled and she, Leaf, Crusty, and most of the group, excluding the wilds, surrounded me in hugs. Being eye-to-eye with my faeries was going to take some getting used to.

"Now, back to patrol! Taryn and I still have things to finish before the spell on the wall drops." Derry waved them aside and the faeries, along with Bunky and Irving, left.

I'd briefly forgotten about the spell protecting the town, the attacks, and the possibility of me destroying the entire world and everyone on it.

All of which almost knocked me out of the air when it came back to me.

"Word of warning as a faery—you have to keep flapping or you won't stay in the air." Derry grabbed my hand before I could drop into the pile of sceanra anam dust below us.

"Thanks." I flapped my wings, but it was half-hearted.

"I'll have the faeries come back and sing to you." Derry folded her arms and glared.

"I don't think this is a Jhea spell. Things are really messed up." Understatement of the centuries.

I was beginning to recognize the difference in Derry's smiles. This was a trouble making one.

"Oh, no. You're not under a Jhea spell. But you are feeling sorry for yourself. I think Crusty Bucket and a dozen or so faeries could lift you right out of that with a song about minkies."

"No!" I flew backward and raised both hands. The faeries usually found some interesting notes to sing, and none of them were friendly to anyone's ears. "Not that. However, I think finding out that one could be the destruction of everything is a good reason to feel bad." Even I heard the whine in my voice, but I chose to ignore it. "And how do you remember the minkies? I've seen them, but every time one of them shows up, the girls forget they've seen one."

"Eh, as we've established, I'm not like the rest. But all of that will wait. I dragged you away from your friends so you could sort yourself out. They love you and will do whatever they need to do to protect you." She flew closer to me. "They can't stop what needs to happen."

"They are supposed to stand by and watch me destroy the world? And them?" I felt sick but wasn't sure how throwing up while flying would work. And didn't want to find out right now.

"No. But the only one who can stop it from happening is you." She peered into my eyes and shook her head. "Nope, that doesn't mean that you go hide in a cave or whatever is going through your mind right now. I heard about that when you first remembered who you were. I'll grant that at the time you were scared and confused. But you don't have that luxury anymore. Not to mention, too many unsavory people know who and what you are now. Your friends aren't going to die defending you, so stop that right now. They are your strength. That and your secret weapon inside here." She poked my belly.

"Isn't my heart higher up?"

"Not your heart, that's not secret to anyone who knows you. The clarit. I'm surprised one of them survived, but not terribly shocked that it came to you." She moved closer to my belly and tilted her head. "That's probably the last of them, excellent hiding by the way. I can barely sense it in your current form, and didn't sense it at all when you were human. I don't know if we need the chalice for it to work for you when the time comes. But we will need the canfydd crown." Her grimace at saying the crown was nothing compared to how I felt about it.

"If I wear that crown, I *will* try to take over the world. I almost did once." I would ask her how she knew about the clarit, but she seemed to know a lot of things. The golden ball was hiding in my first gullet—as a dragon. It shouldn't even appear to exist when I'm not a dragon, but as she kept saying, Derry wasn't like the others. I'd hoped to get more information on the clarit before I had to use it since I'd swallowed it back in Yosi. But I needed to rest in those ruins. Then we were busy again.

Maybe Derry knew something.

She shrugged. "You weren't ready to control the crown then. The enemy pushed things by stealing your friends. We will get it back and your little friend will help us find the one who took it."

I looked around, but we were both about four inches high, so I wasn't sure who my little friend was.

She grinned. "Your dagger. He's slowly coming back

to his former self, which means the one who attacked him is as well."

"Can't you find where that elf is? You do have a lot of information for someone who's been hiding for so long." I was back in the whining range again. But I was short on sleep and there were a lot of topics I didn't want to deal with.

"I know some things, others remain hidden. Especially anything to do with the Dark." A worried look crossed her face until she shook it off. "Never fear, we'll find them. Now, are you feeling better? We have less than an hour before that spell falls and your friends might feel better if you were back with them."

"Oddly, I am feeling better. Still not liking being the bringer of the end of everything concept, but I'm not as pessimistic. But wasn't there a reason we came out here?" She'd been determined when she changed me and dragged me out.

"Oh, the sceanra anam helped with that. Otherwise, I was going to find something big and nasty to pick a fight with. Many times, realizing that there are options comes about the hard way."

"We're in the middle of," I waved my hands as I searched for the words, "*something*. You pulled me out of an important meeting so I could fight things?"

Derry's laugh would seem too large for someone Foxy's size. "How much of what they were speaking about before your part came in did you even notice? I see it in your eyes. You weren't paying attention. Don't carry heavy objects in life by yourself. They will destroy you." She dropped into a calm serene façade as she said the last. There were a lot of sides to this oldest of faeries.

"Okay, fine. They know and I have to face them. And possibly a horde of cranky take-over-the-world types." As we flew back to Qianru's, I felt that the attack would be against Notlianda, not the other town. No real way to know, but it grew stronger the closer we got to Qianru's guest house.

There were way more people inside than when we left, at least from what I saw through the window. I flew to the side and out of sight from those inside.

"I'm not sure who is in there, but I shouldn't show up looking like this if there are people besides my friends there." I waved to my faery self.

"Then change. I keep telling you that you are changing you, not me. Yes, even this time. I suggested it, but you did it. It's more subtle than when you change into your dragon form, just think of yourself as wanting to be human. Might want to drop closer to the ground. You're taller as one of them, but not that tall."

I glanced down and realized that I had drifted to over roof height now.

I dropped down a few feet, and then thought of myself as human. Even though I'd gone lower, it was still a jolt to fall out of the sky after flying for a while.

Derry circled me, and I swore that I heard laughter as she zipped off back in the direction we'd come. I presumed to join the other faeries, but she seemed used to doing what and going where she wanted.

I walked around the guest house to the front, holding a push spell ready. It wasn't deadly silent inside as would be the case if evil people had kidnapped my friends and set a trap. But it also didn't sound like a fight was happening. Just a low-level conversation.

I looked around for the faeries; the spell around the town would be down soon, and they should be back. But none of them were in sight.

I pushed open the door slowly. Partially in case I was wrong and there had been a horrible scenario that I missed and was now occurring—also because I wasn't sure how much room there was for me to open the door.

All of my friends were there, along with Welsy, Delsy, and the pack of brownies—all of which were hiding under the table. Tag, Locksead, Qianru, five of her houseboys, and a few elves filled in what gaps of space might have remained.

Why they hadn't moved everyone over to Qianru's home, I had no idea. Then I saw how protectively Cwin, Mathilda, and Padraig were guarding the items on the table. The rest of my magic and non-magic-using friends were placed around the room watching the other people. Foxy was behind the door and pulled me past some houseboys, then shut the door and blocked it again.

"I take it this just happened?" I wanted to add that Qianru probably forced her way in, but I was surrounded by her people. And Alric. He was too far away to touch, but the smile in his eyes was all I needed.

"Aye. Our friends were starting to put things away when she barged through. I shouldn't a opened the door." He dropped his voice at that one. Then lifted his lip in a snarl when two of the elves turned to look at us.

They quickly looked away.

I didn't recognize the two, nor the third who was standing closer to the table. But Qianru adored elves, so it wasn't surprising she had some in her compound.

The discussion seemed to be focused on the items from the chest and bags that were covering the table.

I was about to do something uncharacteristic and yell that we had a half hour to decide if this town needed to be defended again when a million pops came from all around us. Okay, maybe only a hundred, but it seemed like more. It was enough to make everyone except my friends jump.

Obviously, the faeries who came back here with Tag needed to work on going through walls more often to get people used to it.

"What. Yous. Do?!" Garbage hung in the middle of the room, better to be seen by everyone, folded her arms, and glared as she spun in a slow circle.

CHAPTER TWENTY-FOUR

I GRINNED AT GARBAGE'S ANTICS. USUALLY only I got that treatment. I almost choked when Garbage got to me in her spin and winked before continuing. That was disturbing.

Then she and her faery gang looked to me as if waiting.

"Ah, yes. That spell protecting the walls is coming down soon." I didn't like all of those eyes on me. It was only a desperate fear of Qianru deciding to take me as a pet that kept me from changing into a faery and zipping out.

"Taryn's right," Covey said. "You can sort out who gets access to these documents after everything's been resolved." She gave her extremely annoyed professor glare to the room.

Qianru started to protest, shot a look at Cwin, and closed her mouth. Cwin hadn't changed into the glamor of a dwarf. Even Qianru was thinking twice about messing with a grimarian.

She focused on Padraig instead. "Agreed. Is Notlianda about to be invaded again?" Qianru's regal nod and tone of a long-suffering matriarch would work better on people who didn't know her.

Padraig nodded. "Yes. And if you had let us speak, instead of demanding we hand over these priceless items, we could have been preparing for it." His tone not only matched Qianru's in force, it stomped on her. Padraig usually played more of a negotiator, but not this time.

"How soon will they attack?"

"Theys coming soon." Garbage did a faster spin this time. "Yous needs ready!"

"And that ends this." Mathilda began tucking away scrolls and items that had been taken out of the chest and bags.

Qianru was trying to get a better look at the items before they vanished, but Siabiane and Lorcan stepped in front of her. Good idea. Qianru was afraid of Cwin, but she respected the elves. She wouldn't go against them.

"We's gets ready." Garbage waved her hands in the air and the faeries flew through the door. I heard gronking and a quick peek out the window showed that not only were Bunky and Irving back—so was an entire flock of chimeras.

The faeries flew up out of sight, then came back wearing their war feathers and waving their sticks.

"I'm not sure what to do." Qianru addressed Padraig—obviously, his abruptness before was forgiven.

"Right now, we'll need as many of your people who can fight to gather out front. The rest of you should seek shelter in the safest portion of your home. Don't come out until this glows." He made a fancy move with his left hand and a light green flower appeared. It wasn't exotic, but I felt the magic coming off it.

She took the flower as if it were made of gold and gave a slight bow. "Thank you, Lord Padraig. I will have Locksead and Tag sort out my people. Please, all of you, be safe." She even managed a tiny tear as she turned toward the door.

Foxy kept a straight face as he whipped open the door for her.

Qianru's three elves left with her, but the houseboys remained with Locksead and Tag.

Locksead waited until Qianru and her entourage were almost to the secret entrance of her home before speaking. "I figure we can leave her with a handful of houseboys, there are some too young to be fighting. And those three elves with her are magic users. They aren't very brave though. They would do better to remain inside. She's got that place so locked up that once they're shut in, they'll be safe even if the entire town falls." He sighed. "I'll gather the rest of the houseboys and other staff and give them weapons." He nodded and he and the clump of houseboys left.

Tag frowned. "None of the other houseboys or militia came out of their households when we were attacked before. Granted, it was more subtle, but we did warn the nearest compounds. I'm thinking this time won't be subtle?"

"Not at all," Alric said. "The Dark has a limited time to destroy Notlianda to keep their pattern up in time to open the cauldron. The first time was using guile and the tendency of many people to stay out of things. This one will be brutal and swift."

Tag nodded. "We won't let this town fall." He started to head out when Grillion and Foxy stopped him.

"We might be able to convince the other homeowners that this is serious and they can't hide." Grillion winced. "Aside from the fact that Qianru is hiding. But that's probably better for everyone."

"Agreed. That woman would cause more difficulties if she were out here." Cwin had remained silent but there was no disguising her disgusted look now. "Good thing we don't need her."

Tag, Foxy, and Grillion went to speak to the other households. From what I heard as they left, they weren't planning on telling them who was invading—but that all the other households would be preparing for an attack, and the town guards had fled.

Both were at least partially true.

My sword popped up as I was changing into my worn black leathers for serious fighting. I was grateful to see it and put on the sword belt. Rhyfel crackled a bit in welcome when I added his sheath. I hoped Derry had been right. He seemed like he was coming back. I had a feeling I needed every advantage that I could get.

We were all dressed and armed within a few minutes. That was one advantage of having been on the run for so long. We adapted quickly.

Welsy, Delsy, and their followers, were also ready. They all had simple tools, but when used correctly, a hammer could be deadly. I overheard Welsy and Delsy telling Flower and the rest that they needed to stay behind them, but to give no ground.

I swore I heard the brownies growl in response, but tried not to stare.

A group of war feather-clad faeries dropped down as soon as we left the guest house. Bunky, Irving, and ten more chimeras joined us. More chimeras and faeries were flying high over the town.

"We's ready." Leaf was the leader of this group and looked far more bloodthirsty than her normal easy-going self. Garbage and Crusty were off leading other troops.

"Is there a plan?" I'd been focused on getting ready but hadn't heard anything specific before that.

"Bads outsides walls. Stops thems." Leaf nodded sagely and raised her war stick. A move echoed by the faeries around her. "Tree lady's trees help."

"Yup, what she said." Covey was already transforming into her berserker form. "They try to come in, we destroy them. Easy." She grinned at Leaf.

I wasn't certain what Amara's oak trees could do to armed fighters, but anything would help. Even if the trees were only able to slow them down.

Alric watched them both. He was dressed in all black leather like me. If it wasn't for such a deadly reason, I'd say we looked good together. "Not easy, but that's about how much of a plan we had. Right before Qianru barged in, we realized the Dark was definitely going to hit here. Nasif was able to send a projection into the forest. They're massed out there. No sign of the risen dead though. The lictenspelt hasn't kicked in yet, and hopefully won't if we can stop this town from falling."

"I was also able to send a projection to Maziline." Nasif looked better than he had and sounded strong. "There's no sign of any forces inside or outside of it. If the Dark succeeds, they will fall within a few weeks, but not today."

Even Dueble was armed and looking deadly. He might appear different compared to the modern-day syclarions, but right now there was no doubt he was one.

Lorcan pulled out a map, which would have probably been better while we were still inside, but it floated in the air and showed different levels as it hung there. "This area is fairly well protected." He tapped the back of the town. "There are also some nasty cliffs on the other side of the perimeter wall. Our focus will be on the front gates, as that's where the bulk of the enemies are massing. But these two sides will need coverage as well. Amara's trees will slow the attackers down, but they can't stop them." There were a few more details, but the main plan was to keep the Dark out of Notlianda at all costs.

Our group was divided up, with the majority going to the front gate and adjacent walls. The gates would be easier to breach than the solid walls everywhere else. Everyone was in groups except for me and Alric.

"And where are we going?" I looked around as I asked. Alric didn't appear concerned about it, but I was.

"We're going to look underground." Alric nodded to Lorcan. "Just because you and the faeries stopped the dreks before doesn't mean that more won't be coming. I'd like Covey and Foxy with us as well."

Lorcan nodded and Covey moved closer to Alric and me with a grin. She knew the odds of Alric and I seeing ugly fighting were strong—and she definitely wanted to kill some dreks. Foxy would be sent our way once he finished intimidating the other households.

"Not going to say I'm happy about this, but do we have a clue as to where any dreks would be coming from? They had a planned target before. We can't cover every inch of ground in this town." I looked around and folded my arms when I didn't like their looks of sympathy. "I'm not playing bait."

"We need something to focus them or they could come up anywhere." Siabiane looked apologetic, and so did the rest. If they could replace me, they would. But I was a tempting object for all the resident bad people. At least the ones affiliated with the Dark or the empress.

"You want me to go dragon and do something dragonish to bring them my way?" Part of me was pissed this had been discussed before I came back. The other part was oddly grateful. Had I known earlier, I'd have more time to worry about it. "I assume you have a building in mind?"

Derry came zipping over the house with a small armada of faeries—many of whom were wilds judging by their wearing of assorted leaves instead of feathers.

"I found one!" She moved Lorcan's finger on the map aside and landed a few inches over. "This here."

"Everyone, this is Derry. Derry, meet everyone." Her full name was lovely but hard to get right. And at this point, I needed to focus on fewer things.

"Nice to formally meet you." Lorcan bowed. "Is there a reason the building we selected won't work?"

"Ground not right." Derry was slipping into the faery pidgin but it might have been a side effect of being around so many other faeries.

Or she did it from time to time to confuse people.

"Dreks need specific ground?" That was news to me, but I was hoping to never face the monsters again.

"Yups," Leaf said. "No too squishy. No too crunchy. Needs rights. We's goes with yous."

Lorcan shrugged. "If it'll work, then use it. But get there now, the spell on the walls will fall in minutes and the Dark will want the distraction of the dreks to throw off the town's defenders."

I agreed with that. A single drek was terrifying, a bunch of them made me want to go be sick somewhere. "Then let's go." We didn't have Foxy back yet, but I wasn't sure if having him would make me more worried. I was glad to have my friends alongside me as we ran through the town, but the more of them I had to worry about, the more distracted I would be. Leaf, Derry, and the flock of faeries, chimeras, and Irving flew low overhead.

Even though when we'd come through here before I'd been four inches high and flying, I began to recognize where we were going—the smithy Derry and I had destroyed the sceanra anam in.

"Ah, Derry? That place can't hold me in my other shape." Then I whistled as we came around the corner. The building had changed. It was in the same spot, but it was a lot bigger. It was almost sitting on an abandoned storefront next to it.

"We fixed it. They will be expecting something here since it's where they left the sceanra anam. And the ground is perfect." She grinned as she sped up to fly inside.

"The adventure begins." Covey flexed her claws and ran after her, along with all of the faeries.

CHAPTER TWENTY-FIVE

A LRIC AND I WERE ABOUT to follow when the thudding of heavy footsteps headed our way. We both pulled out our swords and readied spells, but it was only Foxy.

"Good! I was afraid I'd missed the fighting." Foxy didn't run much; with his size he didn't need to. But he wasn't winded. "I'm ready to bash some dreks. After our last run-in with them, Amara told me if you aim for their face, they'll go right down." He swung his massive club with a grin.

That was good to know. The monsters were far too tall for me to hope to hit them accurately in the face in my current form. And I'd have to bend down to hit them when I changed.

"Okay, let's go." I glanced around. "But I'm not changing until I'm inside." There weren't many people on the streets; we had seen groups of household militia and older houseboys down side streets, but they'd been heading for the gates and walls.

Which was for the best. I still wasn't certain about us stopping the dreks. As much as I didn't want myself or my friends here, I knew the locals would have died.

The inside still looked sort of like a long-ago abandoned smithy, but it was a lot larger and sturdier.

Much of the wood appeared new. If we survived this, I was asking Derry how she did it.

She dove, and I noticed that she now had war feathers, but they were short, neat, and gray. She looked quite smart in them. "I don't want to tell you three what to do. But Taryn should move to the center, lots of ground there." She grinned as I slowly walked where she'd pointed. "Don't worry, when we expanded the size, I also relocated the sceanra anam dust into the forest." Her grin grew larger. "Even followers of the Dark aren't fond of that. Their screams were wonderful. I think I heard the trees laughing at them."

Alric laughed. "I don't blame them." He held me and gave me a fierce kiss then let me go and moved away. "Be safe. You're not invincible."

Understatement. In my original fight to destroy the dreks, I'd been clawed by one and almost died. It said a lot about Alric's growth that he didn't try to stop me this time.

Or he realized we didn't have other options.

"You too, all of you." I looked up to the faeries, Bunky, along with his chimeras, and Irving. "That goes for all of you. If you're injured, fall back." The faeries grinned manically, the chimeras, aside from Bunky, ignored me, Bunky and Irving gronked and gave their whole body bobs.

Once Foxy, Covey, and Alric were a safe distance away, I changed into a dragon. Or so I thought. Leaf laughed so hard she tumbled a few feet down in the air.

"What?" I pulled my hand up. I was the size of my dragon self, but a giant green-blue faery.

Derry dropped down to me and made a full circle. "While that is impressive, dreks don't react to one of us, even one this large, the way they do to the smell of a dragon. We need to make them only want to come here and leave the rest of the town alone."

"I thought that's what I was doing!" I shook myself and changed back to human. Then, ignoring the giggling and snorting faeries above me, I closed my eyes and focused on being a dragon. That was more familiar to me than becoming a faery, so this time it worked. Since, even with the expansion, the smithy was still small compared to me now, I left off my wings.

Derry nodded and rose higher, along with the rest of the flyers. Alric, Covey, and Foxy stayed off to the side with weapons ready.

Alric was packing so many spells that I felt the magic flow in waves off of him.

I wasn't certain what I should do, the opinion seemed to be that simply touching the ground in my dragon form would draw them to me. I stomped around a bit in case they were still far away. The spell protecting the town should have fallen about ten minutes ago. Not only were the walls unprotected now, but so was the sky and the ground. "I'm glad we killed the sceanra anam that were here. But what if they have more?"

Bunky gronked in response. A bunch of chimeras, with a few hundred who could be here in moments, were patrolling the town for that reason. Chimeras loved hunting sceanra anam.

"Good to know. Okay, anyone know some good drek jokes?" I wasn't stomping heavily but continued marching in a small circle. I didn't want to fight dreks, but I also didn't like the idea that if no dreks were coming, we could have been helping our friends protect the town.

The faeries continued giggling until the ground started shaking. They immediately flew lower, with Derry and Leaf in the front. No laughing now, all of them looked ready to kill.

I'd seen faeries take down a few of the dreks in that

cavern yesterday, but I still didn't like them facing dreks now.

I stopped stomping and rethought not having my wings. There wasn't a lot of room for me to go either in the air or the ground without impacting people around me, but the air might give me a better advantage. I popped my wings on and hovered in the air.

Derry zipped over. "You know you don't have to be quite this large, right? You made a dragon-sized faery, pretty sure you could make a slightly smaller dragon. Like you did before." She grinned at knowing something that happened before I met her, then she flew back up to join the rest.

Her logic seemed sound, if I didn't think about it too much. The spell from my old book came easier this time. I focused on still being a dragon, but a little smaller and sleeker. I wanted maneuverability.

And forgot that I was flying a few feet off the ground and stopped flapping. Luckily, the drop wasn't far.

I was smaller, not a lot, but it looked like my legs were actually longer. And had some impressive claws I'd never seen before but did remind me a little of Covey when she went berserker.

Before I could examine my changes further, the ground erupted under my feet, and hard dirt and rocks flew into the air.

A drek shoved its head through the chawsia path tunnel, all gray shaggy fur, nasty tusks, and murderous eyes. One clawed hand reached for me, but I flew higher. The thing shoved its way out of the tunnel too slowly, and a wave of faeries charged down yelling as they stabbed it with their war sticks. The chimeras held back, but were ready to come down when needed.

The drek exploded before any of the rest of us could get a chance to attack it.

"Back up, girls. We need to pace ourselves." Derry

called to the faeries and as one they flew to the highest rafters.

I wished they would listen to me like that.

Two more dreks widened the tunnel. I blasted them both with a belch of flame. Neither appeared happy, and their fur was singed off where the flame hit, but it didn't stop them the way I thought it would. Alric, Covey, and Foxy ran forward with sword, club, claws, and magic. The two dreks died at their attack and were pushed out of the way by the ones behind them.

One advantage, they seemed to be having trouble coming through the ground—at least coming through in more than this one area. I doubted the dreks cast the chawsia path spell, and the mage who did was most likely busy trying to break into this town.

I thought that too soon, as a second tunnel erupted behind me. Two more dreks climbed out, but instead of coming for me, they tried to get to my friends who were fighting another pair from the first tunnel.

I didn't try flame this time, but claws. I backed up my swinging clawed hand with enough magic to get through the monster's heavy, matted, white hair. Bunky, Irving, and a wave of chimeras dove at the same time. All of them crackled with electric shocks that jolted the dreks when they tried to pull back enough to fight me off as I kept hitting them.

I finally flew up to give the chimeras more room—besides, it was their turn.

I'd have to point out to Covey that I understood why she liked having claws when she went berserker.

Just as I thought we had them under control, the entire ground under the smithy exploded. Alric, Covey, and Foxy scrambled back to the walls of the building just in time to avoid falling in. Everyone else flew higher.

Eight dreks, all appearing larger than the ones before, roared and came out of the ground. For monsters supposedly rare and only living in the arctic regions, they were in good numbers down here.

Or bad numbers for us.

I dove to meet them and found myself surrounded by a wave of faeries and chimeras, and more of each were appearing.

Covey, Alric, and Foxy were yelling and fighting back, but it seemed like Alric's spells weren't hitting the monsters.

Then I noticed this group of dreks had collars, and there were large red gems on them. "Seriously? Alric, they're spell shielded!" We'd seen those red gems on evil squirrels and birds, but nothing this big.

Three dreks hit Alric, Covey, and Foxy so hard they went flying through the walls.

That got me. I tapped into when I'd faced the monsters months ago, when Alric almost died.

To be picky, I almost died then too, but I squished that thought as I dove for them.

I hit the largest drek hard, increasing my size and weight as I did so. The change was close, timing-wise, I felt a brief spasm of dizziness, but then the largest dragon I could imagine was biting, clawing, flaming, and even sending spells at the drek. I hoped my friends were all staying out of the way, my eyes had gone red and all I saw were the dreks. I grabbed ahold of the collar on the current drek with my teeth, tore it off, and shattered the red stone. Then used my claws, which I'd kept from my prior change, to slice the beast's throat.

No more dreks were coming through the ground, but all seven of the larger, spell-protected ones were still stomping toward me. And Alric, Covey, and Foxy hadn't come back inside.

Not that there was a lot of building left at this point. There were more holes than walls now.

The faeries dove but they were bounced back into the

ceiling. Those spell gems were as powerful as they were massive.

I waved the faeries back. "Those gems are protecting them. We need those off first." Of course, I had no idea how to do that. Dreks were a bit larger than possessed squirrels.

I thought about going even larger in hopes that I could get through their spell shields again by sheer force. Seven of them against one of me weren't great odds though.

"Smaller!" Derry remained up near the top of the ceiling with Leaf and the rest.

"Smaller? Make *them* smaller?" I didn't know if there was a spell for that, but I was pretty sure those red gems would block it even if I knew it.

"No, make yourself smaller. Still a dragon, with your full strength, but our size." Her grin was vicious. Like the rest of the faeries, she wanted to destroy these dreks. "Get those gems off and we and the chimeras can do the rest."

I looked where my friends had been flung out of the building, one of the spelled dreks was starting to move that way. If Alric and the others were unconscious, they'd be easy prey.

I didn't think, simply focused all of my dragon self into the size of a faery. It felt weird, but judging by the cheers from the faeries above, it worked. I zipped around the dreks in front of me and flew after the one going outside.

Alric was out cold, Covey was twitching slowly, and Foxy had been slammed into the building across the lane and taken half of it down with him. I saw part of him, but nothing was moving.

The drek was running for Alric.

I yelled and flew after it, aiming my strength and tiny claws at the leather strap holding the gem; the collar tore in my hands as a wave of faeries attacked the drek. I smashed the red gem against a rock and flew back inside the building. The remaining six dreks started to run out but didn't notice me. Their eyesight wasn't great and I was small. I needed them to stay inside.

Before I could decide what to do, Bunky, Irving, and a hundred or so chimeras flew down and waited. Bunky gronked loudly.

He told me that I needed to grab a drek's gem, not just the collar—and send a simple push spell into it. The gems were linked together. The chimeras and the rest of the faeries could take them out once the push spell killed it.

Easier said than done, but I'd try. The sound of marching feet outside sped up my decision. The odds of marching booted feet being on our side were slim and even with some of the faeries out there, Alric, Covey, and Foxy were unprotected, and not in any condition to fight.

I zipped down to the largest drek, dodging his massive paws once he realized I was there. It took four tries, but I got a hold of the red gem and focused on keeping my spell ready. If I sent it too soon the gem would block it. It had to be timed perfectly as the gem was being pulled away from the monster's fur. I released the spell into the gem as I sliced through the harness holding it. The drek roared and ended up smacking itself hard trying to get me. The other dreks had been poised to leave, but all turned back to our odd fight scene.

I finally got the gem off and smashed it with my full dragon strength into a nice boulder. It shattered, the stones on the other dreks shattered, and Bunky led the chimeras down, with enough lightning strikes it looked like the worst summer storm ever imagined.

The faeries who weren't still outside also dove in. I only killed one more drek as my flying friends took care of the rest.

They were all dead, and Derry sent flights of faeries into the tunnels to make sure there were no more.

Yelling came from out front as the smithy, expanded or not, groaned and collapsed.

CHAPTER TWENTY-SIX

IMMEDIATELY INCREASED MY SIZE, AND the pieces of wood slid off of me.

The sound of marching steps grew louder.

I paused. I could fight better in this massive dragon form; I was still even larger than my normal size. But I didn't need more people to know who and what I was.

Derry flew over to me and smiled. She knew what I was going to do, it would have been nice if she told me.

I took a deep breath and turned human. With a tail and wings. Dragon tail, faery wings. "What in the world?" I spun to get a better look until Derry flew into my face.

"Danger is outside, and while this is impressive, I don't know that's what you want the Dark to see."

"I was hoping our people stopped them at the walls?" I focused and the tail vanished. The wings grew smaller, but bright green and blue wings weren't going to be missed no matter the size. And I didn't have the time to figure out how to make them go away completely right now.

"They and the trees slowed the enemy. But some managed to get inside. Hurry!" She frowned and then zipped outside before I could explain I had no idea why I was stuck this way.

Two more attempts and the wings shrunk to only a

few inches and were barely visible. That was going to be as close as I could get.

None of my friends on the ground outside had moved, but Covey was still twitching. I hoped that was her fighting to regain consciousness and not something worse. Alric's sword was missing, but a spirit sword would vanish if its wielder lost consciousness. I found Foxy's massive club a few feet away from him.

For all of their noise, the owners of the marching boots weren't on this road yet. They could have been using a sound projection spell. Tricky, but it would make most people stay indoors.

It didn't mean they weren't coming here; they were just further away than they sounded.

I ran to Alric and gently pushed rocks and debris off him. He had a gash on his forehead and there was a thin trickle of blood on his side. I couldn't heal him here.

I waved to Leaf to fly down to me. "Can you do that healing trick with the sticks that you did for him before? We can't be here when those people get here."

Leaf shook her head and looked sad. "Nots for this. Different hurts."

"Okay." After this, we needed to discuss what they could and couldn't do with those sticks.

I looked around for places to move my friends. Another small building, next to the one Foxy had slammed into, was mostly intact.

With Leaf and the faeries' help in lifting him, although Derry was nowhere to be found, we got Alric over to the building. It looked like a food storage hut, but that worked, and I had the faeries put Alric down on some sort of greens.

"Thanks, we need to get the other two in here too."

Covey wasn't difficult, she'd stopped twitching, but her breathing was strong.

Even myself and all the faeries not fighting elsewhere

could only get Foxy an inch or two off the ground. He was going to have some bruises, but at least this way he might be alive to complain about them.

I started for the door once we got them all on beds of assorted vegetables, but Leaf flew up to block me.

"Yous stays. Dangerous."

My laugh escaped before I realized that she was serious. Everything we'd done today had been dangerous. It could be said that the past few years had all been dangerous. "I have to defend this place." I waved around the room. "They're going to look for survivors of the fight in the smithy. Those dead dreks are a bit obvious." Some had exploded due to the faeries war sticks but there were still bodies and parts lying around.

"Danger for yous. Bads wants." Leaf did a perfect Garbage impersonation and tightly folded her arms and glared. She couldn't get the one-eyed part of the glare right though.

I paused. The sounds of marching boots were getting closer and I didn't think it was only because of a spell. The truth was, the past me, from before I met Alric and got into all of this would have gladly remained in here.

That me was long gone.

"I'm sorry, but I can defend this place better from the outside. And a lot of our friends are still out there. We need to save them too."

"Bads follows yous. Take mores."

If the situation wasn't dire, I would have changed into a faery and hugged Leaf, she looked more upset than I'd ever seen. "That's a really good idea. Are Bunky, Irving, and his pack of chimeras still out there?"

"Yes." Leaf's scowl indicated she thought I was tricking her.

"Okay, we need a plan. Half of your faeries stay in here. No one in or out until I get back. If the others wake up, tell them they need to stay here…to keep me safe." A bit of a lie, but if I wasn't worried about them, then I'd be able to focus on my issues.

"The other half and the chimeras come with me. As soon as the enemy comes into sight, we run." Leaf looked down at her feet. "Okay, I run, you fly. We lead them as far from here as we can."

"No fightings? Just flyings?" She jutted her lip out and looked around at our three unconscious friends.

"Yes. No fighting." There was no way I could guarantee it but this would only work if we weren't seen coming out of the building. We needed to move.

"Okays." Leaf flew to the faeries and quickly split them up. The ones remaining in the room settled on Alric, Covey, and Foxy, looking fierce with their war sticks at the ready.

"Let's go." I cracked open the door. The sounds were closer, but the street out front was still empty. Aside from a destroyed smithy and the dead dreks.

There wasn't a plan, but I figured starting at the opposite end from the marchers was a good idea. I wanted them to see us, but not be close enough to catch us. I thought about turning into my faery self, but I wasn't certain they'd follow us then.

I mentally laughed at the thought that they might be good folks coming our way.

I jogged to the end of the street. There was a slight bend, so we would be further away but could still see them—and they would see me.

Another small house had taken some damage at some point, but aside from a few articles of clothing, it looked to be abandoned and empty. I waved at the clothes. "Leaf, can you, Bunky, Irving, and some of the others grab some of these and fly low enough to look like the clothes are running?"

Up close the clothing would appear ghostly, but if we

zig-zagged enough then it should look like there were more people with me.

"Tries." Leaf nodded to Bunky and Irving and between the faeries and constructs, they got a dress, a long vest, and three cloaks up and at about my height.

"There they are!" The yell startled me even though that's what we'd been waiting for.

"Run!" I took out my sword and waved it in the air. I felt a bit foolish running behind floating clothing, but with luck, they'd look like more troops.

A glance back told me that not only had the ones following us been using a spell to make them sound closer, but they'd also enhanced how many there were. There were only six battered elves running behind us.

And two feral dwollers on chains.

That was bad, very bad. We needed to lose them, but if those dwollers got loose in the town…I wasn't even certain that I could fight feral dwollers in my dragon form. They were little more than aggressive, mindless, eating machines.

"Gets bads?" Penqow, the little black and white faery, dropped next to my face and pointed behind us.

"No! No one goes back." I was grateful that it sounded like the six elves and two eating machines on chains were following us and not back attacking my friends we'd left behind, but there was no way anyone was going back to fight them.

"Noes funs. Okays." Penqow sighed and slammed into a low-hanging sign.

I slowed, but she spun out of it fine and flew up along me again. "Funs!"

She obviously spent too much time around Crusty. That thought wasn't good. I'd been too busy to think of the rest of the faeries and my friends fighting along the wall of the town—now those fears were coming in full force.

"Taryn!" A voice seemingly coming from the air around me made me slow down. Penqow pulled my shirt to keep running.

"Taryn! It's me, Amara! I can't reach Foxy, but you're in danger!"

Okay, now that she said who it was, I could tell the whispering voice was being shouted from the tattoo on my arm. "No time, Amara! Being chased!" I wasn't a runner at any point in my life and that hadn't changed over the past few years. I was losing speed. And my pursuers were gaining.

"I know. You're running in Notlianda. Town is under attack, local trees say you need to run to them."

I almost stopped at that, but the dwollers howled and I picked up speed. I had no idea how Amara knew that, but she understood trees. She might not be a tree goddess anymore, but the trees all still adored her.

"Where? In the middle of town?" The only trees I knew of were the ones at the front gate. The opposite way I was running.

"Left! Go left at the next street."

"Leaf! You all have to stay with me, we're turning." I couldn't yell too loudly; I didn't need to tip off our followers. Not to mention I didn't have enough air in my lungs. Fear was a good motivator, but eventually, body parts gave out.

I swore as I almost hit a pile of dropped baskets in the middle of the road. I jumped over them but that could have been a fatal mistake if I'd hit them. The dwollers were fighting at the ends of their chains and I heard their whining, and swearing from the Dark elves, closing in.

The turn Amara was talking about was dead ahead. "Here!" I yelled at the same time Amara added to take the next left at an old oak. There weren't many trees in town so that was easy. The faeries and chimeras were all more or less sticking with me, and when they overshot, they turned back to me. The ones holding the clothes were rising and dipping so much there was no way that anyone would have thought they were people.

Amara guided us through four more turns, all marked by trees, until I was extremely lost. Qianru's compound was close to the front gates, and even when we were here before I hadn't spent any time this far in the back.

"One more turn. Then jump over the wall." Amara yelled and I bolted for the wall. I heard the dwollers and their Dark companions easily now, they were almost close enough to catch me.

"Over the wall!" The faeries and constructs zipped over the low wall. It looked like it had been much higher at one time but bricks had been stolen over the years.

"Fly!" Amara's yell on that word was so loud that Foxy might have heard it in his sleep.

She wasn't kidding. I jumped over the wall, the Dark and the dwollers so close behind me I felt the dwollers' breath.

My tiny faery wings expanded awkwardly and I rose after a large dip. The six elves and two dwollers weren't so lucky and they dropped into the forest below us. Way below. I was concentrating on flapping, but it did seem like they fell for a very long time.

CHAPTER TWENTY-SEVEN

—◆—

"YOU MADE IT! STAY SAFE, this was difficult. Tell Foxy I'll reach him later." Then Amara's voice was gone.

Bunky looped around to me, flapping awkwardly. It was odd being human with faery wings. I couldn't get my balance right. The wings felt mismatched. One might be a dragon wing, but I couldn't stop trying not to fall long enough to look. They felt like they were different sizes though.

"Gronk!" He waved the cloak he'd borrowed as he asked if they needed to keep the clothes.

I was going to say to drop them but then realized the people of Notlianda had lost a lot, a few pieces of clothing might be needed. "Leave them where we found them. But could someone help me get turned around?" I swung out my legs but was still having trouble with my wings and only spun in an odd circle. It would be better if I could change completely into a faery or a dragon, but not when I was hanging in the air over a forest that was so far down it looked like a rug.

A small one.

Irving flew over and nudged me around with some help from Leaf and Penqow.

I dropped to the ground when we got over the wall

and was shaking so badly, I didn't know when I could get to my feet again.

At least I could look at my wings now. Yup, one was a faery wing, the other a small version of my dragon wing. If Irving and the faeries hadn't guided me, I'd still be spinning in circles.

Until exhaustion caught up to me and I dropped to the forest below the town.

That thought increased my shaking and I scuttled against the wall and curled over my knees. There better not be any more enemies coming or I was dead.

Bunky and the others with them had taken the clothing back but were now flying at me at top speed.

Not good. My sword was still here, so I took it and Rhyfel out of their sheaths. And braced myself. I'd look more impressive on my feet, but I wasn't certain that I could stand. Not to mention that even if I did, there was a good chance I'd tumble over the waist-high wall I was leaning against.

Bunky was right in front of me when he spun in the air and gronked at whatever was chasing them. Nice show of defiance, but not sure how helpful it would be.

Most of the faeries and chimeras were still playing in the air over the forest, but came zipping over at his gronk.

I held my weapons as best I could. I might be going down, but not without a fight. I was too exhausted to even think about a spell right now.

Footsteps running fast came down the street next to this one.

Padraig and Mathilda were the first two to appear, but everyone else, aside from the three we'd left in the vegetable pantry, was right behind them.

"Thank the stars! Bunky was frantic, but not clear about what happened." Padraig's spirit sword vanished and he dropped down in front of me. "Are you okay?"

I was laughing so hard I was crying. "Yep. Nope. Maybe? I'm so glad to see you all."

Mathilda sat next to me. "You're worn through. I felt it as soon as we saw you. Can you stand?" She took my weapons out of my hands. My sword vanished. It sounded like Rhyfel purred at Mathilda's touch.

I tried to get my legs under me and would have dropped back on my butt if Padraig and Mathilda hadn't each grabbed an arm.

"That would be a no. At least not without help." I let them pull me up with Cwin, Lorcan, Siabiane, Nasif, and Dueble all looking ready to grab me in a moment. "The battle is over?" There were no serious injuries that I saw, but they were all roughed up.

"Yes, it was hard fought, but the Dark and the empress lost this round. The cauldron will not be completed." Padraig looked around. "Where are the others?"

"We's locks up!" Leaf grinned as she and the faeries moved in closer. "Noes goings nowheres."

Mathilda turned to me. "Why did you lock them up?"

"And where?" Siabiane was distracted by Welsy, Delsy, Flower, and the brownie entourage joining them. The constructs even looked roughed up, but all the brownies were happy.

"Long story. They were injured and unconscious, six Dark and two feral dwollers were running in the streets and we had to keep them safe." I held up a shaking hand and pointed in the general direction of the building. Maybe.

I hadn't been paying much attention to where I was running on the way here. "It's across from where the smithy was."

"We's takes! Friends waiting." Leaf zipped off before I could stop her.

"The rest of the faeries raced off once the battle was over." Cwin looked up and closed her eyes. "But, dead dreks have a distinctive odor and feeling. They're that way." She pointed sort of the way I had, but I trusted her abilities far more than mine.

"What happened to the Dark and the ferals? I don't see any blood." Lorcan had held back but was all smiles as Padraig and Mathilda walked me forward.

I pointed to the wall. "We all went over that. None of them could fly, sadly."

Everyone except Mathilda and Padraig peered over the wall.

"Impressive. How did you get them to jump over?" Lorcan asked.

"I let them get right on my heels. Then jumped." It sounded far more heroic than it was, but I'd clarify things later.

"Let's get our friends and then move everyone back to Qianru's guest house." Siabiane nodded and turned to follow Cwin.

"I'm glad you're okay, but I am sorry that you had to face that alone." Mathilda kept me steady as she and Padraig helped me.

"I had the faeries, chimeras, Bunky, and Irving. But yeah, I'd rather not do that again."

Padraig stopped. "Would you be offended if I carried you? You're wearing yourself out even more trying to walk."

I raised my arms. "Carry away. I feel like I used up enough energy for three lives running away from them. After fighting those dreks."

We made much better time once Padraig scooped me up.

The road looked as I'd left it, the door to the vegetable cellar remained tightly shut and the drek bodies were still in the road. The smithy looked like what few parts hadn't fallen initially were now collapsed and it was a giant pancake. Except for where some of the other drek bodies were buried under it.

"How many dreks did you fight?" Dueble approached the nearest one and walked around it. From a safe distance.

"Not sure. Ten, maybe? It wasn't only me though." I explained about the faeries, chimeras, and Alric, Covey, and Foxy.

"They got knocked out and we put them in here." I waved at the vegetable cellar door and Padraig walked up and tried to push it open.

"Noes heres! Goes aways!" The voice was barely audible through the door. I looked around, Leaf and the rest had taken off to come here, where were they? Wait a minute. "Leaf? Is that you?"

"Noes heres!" Yup, her.

"It's us. Taryn, the rest. You just left us!"

"What's passwords?" Still hard to hear but this voice sounded like Garbage.

"Are all of you in there?" I looked to the people with me but they shrugged. "Let us in. Now."

"Taryn! They won't let any of us up!" That was Alric.

"Girls? This isn't the time for play. Open this door!" Mathilda didn't yell, but there was a lot of force behind those words.

A series of clicks, involving far more locks than had been on that door when we left, all popped and the door cracked open. A line of golden faery eyes filled the open space as they looked us up and down.

"Is thems!" Crusty yelled and tried squishing through the tiny space.

Mathilda grabbed the door and pushed it completely open before we saw if Crusty could do it.

"Thank goodness! They tied us up!" Foxy looked like he'd been covered in every rope, vine, and clothesline in at least three towns, not only in Notlianda.

I didn't ask where the faeries got their supplies. Or the locks that went the full length of the door.

Covey had a gag, Alric didn't, but shook his head. Both of them were almost as tied up as Foxy.

Padraig sat me down on top of a pile of turnips, then ran to help untie the three.

Mathilda had to chastise the faeries repeatedly as they kept trying to re-tie as quickly as the rest untied.

"Fines." Garbage waved her faeries back, and sent the bulk of them out into town on some mission—which was good as there were way too many inside such a small room. She had the remaining mob join me on the pile of turnips. "What's wrongs? Yous noes works." She gave me her one-sided stink eye but it was aimed more at my body than me specifically.

"I'm exhausted." I didn't feel up to explaining the entire thing to her. Especially since I knew the full series of events would be part of the discussion when we got back to the guest house.

Garbage flew up to my face, stopped an inch from my nose, and looked hard into my eyes. She finally nodded. "Okay. Talks later." Then she landed on my shoulder and watched as Covey, Alric, and Foxy were freed.

Alric beat the others to me, but at a growl from Garbage, refrained from pulling me to my feet. "What happened? Why was Padraig carrying you?" As he spoke, he patted down my arms, and the light hug that followed seemed more to see if anything was broken than affection.

"It's a long story, and one I know we'll have to go over back at the guest house. But I'm okay. I might still need help getting back though."

His beautiful green eyes narrowed, in case I was keeping something from him. Then he smiled. "I'll gladly carry you back."

Once everyone was free, we left the vegetable hut—after Padraig left some gold coins for the damage we caused.

I didn't even get a chance to stand up, as Alric had me in his arms before I could open my mouth.

Cwin and the faeries led the way, with Bunky and Irving close behind. The other chimeras had vanished again.

It was nice to know they'd come when called though.

The townsfolk were coming back to their homes, or in the cases of those who'd stayed behind, locked and boarded doors, starting to open them. We received a few odd looks, but then someone discovered the dead dreks in the street and they became the focus.

"Good thing they didn't see all of them," I muttered as we walked.

"Indeed." Alric's tone indicated that while he did recall some of what happened, he knew I'd gotten into some sort of mess.

Which I had. I buried my face in his shoulder until we got to Qianru's place. I looked up to see Locksead, Grillion, and a bunch of heavily armed houseboys standing guard.

Padraig nodded to Locksead. "The attackers were turned back at the wall after much fighting. But as a few that we didn't know about got inside the town walls in another section," he shot me a glance, "you probably want to stay on watch."

Locksead nodded. "That was my thinking. The real town guards, or the ones that survived, came by a few minutes ago. They'd been captured two weeks ago and only escaped when their captors abandoned them." He shook his head. "Glad to see them, but they all look rough."

"Good to know," Padraig said. "We'll be in the

guest house but need to rest for a bit. The fighting was harsh. Please tell Qianru we will be ready to visit her tomorrow."

Locksead opened his mouth, then shut it and shook his head. "She won't be happy, but I'll make sure she gets the point." From the wince on his face, he wasn't looking forward to that.

Grillion joined us as we trooped to the guest house. The brownies scurried in before us and ran, with their gardening implements raised, throughout the entire place, including the stables.

From the noises coming from the stables, the horses weren't sure what to think of the tiny warriors.

That was okay, I was still trying to get used to them being on our side.

Welsy and Delsy beamed as Flower and the rest returned and saluted.

"The building is cleared and secured." Flower gave a tight salute to Delsy and Welsy.

"Excellent work, men! Go rest and recover." Welsy bowed as Flower and the rest took off for the kitchen.

Everyone took seats, then Mathilda turned to me. "I believe that Taryn needs to fill us in on what happened with the dreks and why she ran herself to exhaustion. Before we deal with our side of things." Mathilda smiled but there was too much concern in her eyes for my taste.

With help from Alric, Covey, and Foxy, we filled in what happened at the smithy. Derry still hadn't returned, but I mentioned her help along with the faeries and chimeras.

Bunky and Irving gronked softly in agreement, but both were close to going into their sleep mode. Even the faeries seemed tired.

Attention focused back on me when I explained about the six elves with their attack feral dwollers and having to hide Alric, Covey, and Foxy. While we were talking,

Mathilda, Siabiane, Lorcan, Nasif, and Cwin began checking everyone for injuries.

"Did you see any other attackers? That's worrying that they got past us," Lorcan said.

"Amara told me they broke into town secretly, but didn't seem concerned about any more coming. Nor did she say from where." I shrugged. "I didn't have time for chatting. She and her connection to the town trees saved me though."

Foxy beamed. "That's my Amara."

There were more questions about the run and my subsequent awkward flight, but there wasn't much to tell.

Those at the wall of the town had faced a fair number of troops, but not as many as expected—and few seemed to have been magic users.

I looked around at the concerned faces. "That's not good." Even I sorted that out without their glum looks.

Padraig shook his head. "No. That means the focus was split. Cwin was able to determine that Maziline wasn't attacked, so the attempt at opening the cauldron is finished. For now, anyway. They can try again, but not for another year. But we don't know where the rest of the empress' forces went."

CHAPTER TWENTY-EIGHT

THE ROOM WENT SILENT, ASIDE from a few sub-dued giggling snorts coming from the corner the faeries took over. They only had three ale bottles out, and while there were fewer faeries than there had been, that wasn't up to their normal level of celebration.

I didn't try to get off the sofa, but I leaned toward their corner of the room. "Garbage? Are you and your people okay?"

She looked concerned, but not extremely worried. "Is yes. Buts bads things happens fars aways. Queen Mungoosey had to fights." The solemn tones of that last line were unheard of.

"What? Where?" I was grateful that Garbage hadn't said the queen's full name, and that the other faeries were too distracted to do so either. Queen Mungoosey had brought in faeries to help destroy the first round of dreks, but she usually maintained a policy of non-interference.

"Thataways." Crusty joined Garbage and pointed toward the right corner of the room.

I'd be lucky if I could tell the direction she was pointing to if we were in Beccia, there was no way I could tell here. I looked to Alric and the rest of my friends as Crusty remained standing with her hand up like a tiny, deranged, town crier.

"North." Alric wasn't sure, but he had been on the flung-in-the-air end of a fight with a drek. His head had to be rattled.

Padraig paused before answering, then nodded. "Northwest. That's not good." He ruffled through the maps near the table and found the one we'd had up at my family's cabin. "Was it here? Are they okay? Who were they fighting?"

Crusty shrugged, dropped her arm, and returned to the other faeries.

Garbage flew to the table and marched over to the map. Then she held up her thumb, squinted at both it and the map for a few moments, and then finally nodded. "Thinks so. Theys okays, noes happys, buts okays. Dunno."

"That's a few days' ride south of the Lledir mountains. Where Taryn was having us go before our trip here—per Queen Mungoosey's suggestion." Padraig started packing up the maps and scrolls, but Lorcan put his hand on Padraig's arm.

"I know you're thinking we should head out now, and yes, it seems that we might have been needed there." Siabiane shook her head. "But Notlianda would have fallen and the cauldron would have been unstoppable by now if we hadn't been here. And leaving without resting is a recipe for mistakes. Look around. Taryn can't stand. Even the constructs are exhausted. Plus, we need to verify that this town is secure before we can leave it."

Padraig didn't glower much, but he did now. "Fine. I just…"

"Wish we could have been in both places?" Mathilda smiled at him. "You were at the wall, any fewer of us, and we would have lost. The forces weren't as bad as expected, but they still could have decimated the local defenders."

"And as much as I hate to say this, if Taryn hadn't been there to fight the dreks, more than a few of the locals would have died." Covey had mostly been listening, and eating. She had an extremely fast metabolism.

"She's right. If we had lost that fight, a lot of townsfolk would have died." Alric put his arm around my shoulder.

Nasif looked up from the map. "I agree. This was where all of us were supposed to be."

Even Foxy nodded. "We were where we needed to be. Amara says that you can't play all the pieces at once." He nodded sagely.

A sharp knock came on the front door.

"If that is Qianru, I will toss her out myself." Mathilda was usually far more tolerant, but that was over. At least until we recovered.

Foxy was closest and cracked open the door—no doubt he intended to block Qianru from coming in himself. We'd all gotten beaten up, we needed rest, not to be hassled.

"Can we come in?" Tag's voice was subdued.

Foxy stepped back without question and Tag and Locksead came in.

I hadn't seen Tag at the front of Qianru's place when we came in, but he'd taken some hard hits and his right arm was in a sling.

Mathilda and Siabiane pulled up more chairs and all but pushed both men into them. Foxy did a glance outside, then shut and locked the door.

Locksead spoke first. "Qianru was not pleased at being 'shoved off' as she called it. But I convinced her that her valiant guests had done much to save the town and needed rest. She will wait until tomorrow."

Lorcan laughed. "Most likely she's now figuring out how being hostess to the heroes of the town will increase her standing. Too bad we'll be gone by then"

Tag looked surprised. "That soon? Alric had to carry Taryn back, you can't be ready to leave."

"There have been more attacks. We need to get there and see what can be done." Lorcan sounded more confident than I felt. We had no idea why I was sent to go to the Lledir mountains in the first place, or if the attack Queen Mungoosey and her faeries fought was connected to it.

Mathilda crouched in front of Tag. "Can I take the splint off? What happened?"

"I'll be fine. But you can't leave us." Tag was almost panicking as he pulled away from Mathilda.

"It's okay. I need to see what happened." Mathilda nodded to Siabiane standing behind Tag. Siabiane gently put her hands on his shoulders.

Or it appeared gentle. Tag twitched but couldn't free himself. He appeared to have a broken arm. The two elf sisters saw something I didn't.

Lorcan, Padraig, and Cwin also moved closer, but stayed behind Tag's chair.

Locksead watched them, then turned to Alric. "What's going on?"

"Were you fighting on the wall, Tag?" Cwin's voice was melodious and soft. I had to look twice to make sure it was her. She still looked like herself, sort of. But she was the sweetest grimarian I'd ever seen right now. Like someone's little old fluffy grandmother. Totally harmless.

Tag remained silent but kept watching Mathilda as she slowly reached for the sling on his arm.

Locksead stayed seated but appeared concerned as he watched Tag. His frown grew when Tag didn't answer. "He was. He left with five other houseboys to the south wall. He said he fell and broke his arm. It was in the sling when they came back."

"I'm fine." Tag's voice was so soft that I barely heard

it. He also sounded as if he was about to cry. "Help me!" That had more force to it, but the words were cut off sharply.

Grillion leaned toward his friend, but Mathilda blocked him. "What's happening to him?"

"It's not good." Alric held back but was wary.

Padraig and Lorcan spoke the same spell so quickly the words were gone a moment after they started and an iridescent spell bubble appeared over Tag. Mathilda and Siabiane stayed inside the dome as Mathilda took the sling off Tag's arm and Siabiane held him in place.

Cwin, no longer appearing sweet, stood right outside the dome muttering spell words under her breath.

I didn't know what the spell was, but the words sounded threatening.

Tag shook, but Siabiane didn't budge as Mathilda unwrapped the splint. The smell hit first: like a thousand bodies were buried days ago and were being dug up.

Luckily, I didn't know how that would smell specifically but it was pretty bad. Mathilda finished unwrapping and even the faeries gasped and moved back. Tag's arm was mummified.

Padraig pulled Locksead away. "Do you know who the other houseboys were with Tag? We need to see them. Now."

Locksead couldn't take his eyes away from Tag's arm. Tag twitched violently, but Siabiane freed one hand and placed it on his head. He passed out.

"What happened to him? The others seemed fine." Locksead was a strong man, but he looked ready to collapse.

Padraig forced Locksead to face him. "They're not fine. Tag was probably hit first. We need them to come here. And you need to make sure no one else comes near this place."

Locksead's eyes went wide. "It's contagious?"

Mathilda and Siabiane were working on a spell so quickly that their hands blurred. Cwin reinforced the spell bubble until it crackled with power.

"Not yet. But we need the others who were with Tag." Lorcan was also running spells but nodded to Foxy to open the door.

Padraig escorted Locksead out. "Quickly."

I finally pulled my gaze from the horror that was Tag's arm to look at the suspiciously silent faeries.

They'd all collapsed where they'd stood.

"The faeries!" I still didn't trust my legs well enough to get to my feet, but Alric saw them as I yelled and he ran to them.

"They're asleep. But it doesn't seem to be a good sleep—they're all twitching." He picked up Leaf, Garbage, and Crusty and brought them back to me.

"Mathilda! What's happened to them?" All three were tossing about and swinging out tiny fists as if fighting an enemy.

Mathilda glanced over but didn't stop working on Tag. "The spell that infected him was aimed at the faeries. I believe we blocked him quickly enough that they should recover. Gather all of them. Alric, drop a spell bubble on them." She glanced at me with a frown. "Over Taryn as well."

"What? I'm fine. I'm not a faery."

Alric slammed the spell bubble over me and the three faeries on my lap first, ignoring my protests. Then he did the same with the remaining faeries.

"No. But what did you turn into a short time ago?" Siabiane was still holding Tag's shoulders but now it was more to keep him from sliding out of the chair. "Your new-found changing ability is helpful, but it can also leave you vulnerable. The people who sent this spell attack might not have known about your change—or you could have been the primary target." The look of concern she flashed my way was more disturbing than her words.

I couldn't argue with that—not to mention she knew far more about whatever was going on with me than I did. And unfortunately, it seemed plausible. I might not be a faery right now, but whatever allowed me to change was still a part of me.

"What do we need to do?" Covey flexed her claws as she partially released her berserker side. Grillion didn't say anything but stood next to Foxy at the door with his short sword ready. Nasif and Dueble stayed nearby, with Nasif crackling with spells.

"Just stand by for now." Lorcan moved five chairs into a circle. "When Locksead brings the houseboys back, they might not be completely agreeable to the spell bubble. They shouldn't be able to get out, but once in, I need all of you to ensure they don't leave this room."

"There's no threat to us, is there?" Grillion looked around. "Or Locksead?" Although he didn't mention Tag, his eyes kept returning to his friend.

"I don't know," Cwin said. "This is an old spell. Almost older than me. It hasn't been seen or heard of for hundreds of years. We should be fine, but we will need the other exposed houseboys to resolve it. I've calculated the earliest Tag could have been affected based on when the attack on the wall came. We have a slim window to stop this."

A louder knock than before rattled the door and Foxy opened it with Grillion and Covey right behind him and ready to attack.

Locksead raised his hands. "Just me and my friends." He stepped aside and motioned for five older houseboys to come inside. Alric moved so that Tag wasn't visible from the doorway.

"What's the job you needed us for?" The tallest one

asked as the other four trooped in behind him. Locksead shut the door and Foxy, Covey, and Grillion moved to block it.

"How are you feeling?" Lorcan looked like a kindly grandfather type when he wanted to and he did so now.

"Fine? A bit sore from the fighting."

Another boy nodded. "And a headache. But we all got tossed about."

"Could you all sit? We need to look you over." Lorcan was sending a light spell of friendship over all of them, as Padraig motioned to the group of chairs.

"Take a chair so we can get this done and let's get back to work. You know how Qianru is." Locksead's voice didn't match the concern on his face. But the houseboys weren't looking at him as they took their seats.

Alric cast the bubble spell again, then stepped back.

"What did you do to Tag?" The tallest boy tried to jump to his feet when he saw his friend, but the chairs had been spelled as well.

"They're trying to save him. And all of you. Can you tell us what happened on the wall?" Nasif asked gently.

"We fought. Tag fell and we won. Why are you holding us?" The houseboys all shouted at once until Locksead and Grillion yelled at them to shut up.

Mathilda and Siabiane kept an eye on things from within their bubble, but they continued to work on Tag.

I watched the faeries. The three on my lap and the others in the corner didn't move. They weren't swinging out as if fighting anymore, but I wasn't certain if that was a good thing or not.

"Is that supposed to happen?" I happened to glance over to Tag and saw a thin trail of yellow smoke hovering around him. Neither Mathilda nor Siabiane reacted to it. "The smoke?"

I had no clue what they were doing and even if I regained all of my magical ability, I still wouldn't know.

But they both looked around their bubble and then back at me.

"What smoke?" Siabiane asked.

"Weird yellow smoke curling around Tag's head. It's thin, but you should be able to see it." I was already freaked out at the state of Tag and the faeries, that I was seeing something no one else was made things worse.

Cwin was outside the spell bubble but moved in close enough to almost touch it with her nose. "The spell is trying to escape!" She stepped back and fed more energy into the bubble.

The smoke moved toward Siabiane first then fled and turned toward Mathilda—same reaction. It seemed like a living thing as it tested the spell bubble for a way out.

I still didn't trust my legs, but a spell came to mind. One that should go through that bubble if I timed it right. The bubble had faint swirls and eddies like a soap bubble. I needed to wait for one of the spots where it was thin…. I sent a tricky little spell that had been in one of my old books. It was a hide-and-seek spell that my brothers and I would play with.

They were always much better at it than me, but the spell itself was fairly simple.

The spell slipped through the weak spot in the bubble, tagged the yellow smoke, and made it drop to the ground.

"What is that? What *was* that?" Mathilda looked at her sister as Siabiane used magic to lift the now solid and immobile spell up. "Did you do that?"

Siabiane shook her head. "But this is dead now. How's Tag?"

"He's breathing easier and his arm is slowly returning to normal. Cwin? Padraig? Lorcan? Any of you do that?"

Tag's arm looked better, but he was still unconscious. The houseboys were silent but all had extremely wide eyes as they watched the goings on.

"I did," I answered before the others could. "I'm not sure what that thing attacking Tag was, but it didn't like the spell my brothers and I used to play hide and seek with. The spell found the opponent and stunned them. Or in this case, killed the spell going after Tag." I shrugged. "You said whatever attacked Tag was old... well, so am I."

Garbage and Leaf stirred, but it seemed deliberate, not random dream fighting. Crusty didn't move at first, but then her eyes popped open and she sat up in my lap.

"Nots fun. Noes dos again." She frowned and rubbed the side of her head. "Sugar?" Her grin appeared as she held out her tiny hands.

Garbage and Leaf woke up a bit more slowly, and then the rest of the faeries. All of them wanted sugar.

Alric grinned and went to the kitchen after dropping the spell holding all of us. "Can you fly? Or should I bring it to you?" The faeries rose and flew over in answer. Many were wobbly, but that didn't stop any of them from shoving handfuls of sugar into their mouths and happily sitting all over the kitchen counters as they chewed.

"What...happened? Oh, my head." Tag was pale, but his arm was clear and his eyes appeared aware.

"If he's fine now, can we get up?" The tallest houseboy tugged on the invisible forces holding him in his chair.

Mathilda looked over. "Not yet. Lorcan and Nasif need to check you all out. Tag was infected by a virus which is gone now, but since you were with him, you all could have been infected as well." She looked to Siabiane, who nodded, and they dropped the spell bubble around themselves and Tag.

"Can I have something to drink? Maybe something sweet? Tea with a lot of honey?" The color was returning to Tag's face but he still looked drawn.

I had no idea what the spell was that hit him, but it

was a doozy. I hoped no one asked how I thought to use the hide-and-seek spell. I hated admitting when I guessed.

Alric poured two teas, added a bunch of honey to both, and brought them to Tag and me. "How did you know what spell to use?"

Of course, he'd ask. I delayed my response by a long sip of warm, honeyed tea. I couldn't recall when anything tasted that good. Finally, when it was clear that Alric wasn't leaving without an answer, I shrugged. "Not sure. Just came to mind."

Lorcan and Padraig carefully looked over the houseboys and even Locksead for good measure. All of them were clean. How the enemy managed to infect Tag was something the brainy magic users were going to look into.

The faeries were still shoving sugar into their mouths but seemed to be slowing down. Tag and I both held out our empty mugs for more honey tea.

"Were they attacked by something that drained sweetness?" Covey hadn't moved from her perch at the door but watched as Tag, myself, and the faeries went into sugar mania.

Cwin shook her head. "This spell drains the body, and sugar is the fastest energy replenishment. But all of them will need real food too—even the faeries."

CHAPTER TWENTY-NINE

IT DIDN'T TAKE LONG FOR the rest of the houseboys to be sent off with Locksead to do Qianru's bidding. Tag remained with us and he, myself, and the faeries ate enough food, with some more honey added, to feed five Foxys.

Everyone else ate normally.

Alric added another pile of food to my plate and peered at me cautiously.

"I'm fine, thank you, and full." I patted my belly. "Extremely full." I tried to fight the yawn but lost. "And tired. It's been a long and weird day." The curtains were closed, so I had no idea what time it was. But it felt like days since I'd woken up.

"I want to look you over before you head off for bed. Can you stand?" Lorcan stood near my seat at the table but didn't help me to my feet. I'd been hoping no one noticed I still had to be helped to my seat at the table when we went to eat. Or maybe they might think I was weak with hunger.

From the look on Lorcan's face, echoed by the rest of my friends, that was a big no. The faeries were no help as they'd pulled out more ale bottles after the sugar and food and were passed out in little drooling piles around the kitchen.

"Maybe?" I wasn't going to lie. I felt a lot better than

I had after my race through Notlianda and unexpected flying session—but I wasn't completely certain that I wouldn't fall on my behind once I moved the chair.

Alric reached for me, but Lorcan shook him off and I pushed the chair away from the table.

Taking a deep breath, I stood. "I'm up, but still feel oddly drained. Which, considering everything I ate, is probably not good," I said before Lorcan could.

"No, it's not. And don't forget you've fought dreks twice in two days. They carry their own issues, beyond trying to tear people apart." His voice was gentle, his face was concerned, and I knew I wasn't going to like whatever he found.

No one said anything as Lorcan held his hands over me. They stayed two inches or so above me, but I felt a tingle as they passed. Not a painful one, but a weird one.

"Okay, please go sit on the sofa. I need to speak to the others." The looks on Padraig, Mathilda, Nasif, and Siabiane's faces at his words also weren't good. Dueble stood to the side but his sympathetic smile hurt. He might not be a magic user, but he understood something was wrong.

Cwin was better at maintaining a neutral look, but even she twitched.

I made my way over to the sofa, grateful to be able to do it without help. I didn't know if Alric would be included in the spell user's conversation, but he followed me and sat to my left. Covey immediately sat to my right with a far too cheerful smile.

Those always made me nervous.

Foxy, Grillion, and Tag went off into the stable. I didn't think they weren't concerned for me, but they had their own things to discuss and also probably didn't want to get in the way of the magic users.

"You'll be fine. It was a lot of fighting in a short time. Plus, you fought off the flinms back in the mountains."

Covey patted my hand. That made me even more nervous. As a non-magic user, she wouldn't sense whatever the others did.

Alric didn't say anything but put his arm around my shoulders. His silence also didn't make me happy. He was too afraid to say anything.

A small debate broke out among the magic users. Specifically, Nasif and Lorcan, with the others mostly remaining silent.

They finally appeared to come to a compromise. And the entire group nodded and came over to the sofa.

"I'm tired, right?" Even I didn't believe that, but the concern all around was worrying me.

Lorcan gave a small smile. "You are drained far beyond tired. I heard everything that you did at your family's cabin. That alone would be exhausting. Then to add your new transmogrification into a faery and fighting off far too many dreks, you're depleted." He held up his hand before my smile of hope at a quick resolution got too big. "*But*, there's more than that. When you fought off the flinms, you were tagged by them as well. You did fight them off, and I would count that as a win. But they hit you with a tracking spell to drain your magic. The more you use it, the more it fades."

I looked around at my friends' faces in terror. I'd spent years believing I was a magic sink, someone without magic and who couldn't usually be impacted by most spells. I had a few other times of no magic since then. But with what we were facing, this was possibly the worst time for me to lose magic. Not to mention I'd started pulling in my old magic and relearning my old spells thanks to those books in my family's cabin.

"Can it be stopped? Can what's gone come back?" I couldn't look at Alric or anyone else. If I saw pity or sympathy, I was going to lose it.

Nasif didn't smile. "We believe so and possibly. I won't

lie. This is a tricky spell and it was created after your people vanished. There's no record of it ever being used against an Ancient. Let alone one who is now shifting into other forms. You were already a complicated and unique being, with the recent transmogrification you're even more so."

"What do we need to do?" Alric kept the pity out of his voice, but I still didn't trust looking at him.

"Taryn needs to refrain from using magic until we find the proper counterspell." Cwin was worried. "I think that could have been part of what was leading you to the location in the north. Queen Mungoosey often knows things that she can't share directly with others. One of the siramages, Fardoragh, the eldest of us, lives in the mountains near where I believe Queen Mungoosey was fighting, not far from the Lledir mountains. I think we'll need Fardoragh's help to break the spell, before we deal with whatever is in the Lledir mountains."

I felt myself crumble. These were incredibly powerful magic users. Cwin was even a siramage. But we needed someone stronger than them to fix me? I gave the floor a nice long study and then took a deep breath. "What happens if I don't change anything? If I keep using my magic? I'm feeling better and a good sleep or two should make me ready to fight again." Maybe if I believed it, I could make it so.

"The drain will continue." Nasif was serious. "You'll feel recovered after some rest, just as you're already feeling so. However, it won't last. Any fight you're in, or any magic you use to protect the people you love— could kill you."

That was blunt and hit me hard. I finally looked around. I wouldn't be happy if I died because of whatever those flinms did to me. This attack could have been the entire purpose of that mysterious mage sending them after me.

But what if that had happened today? The Dark would have claimed Alric, Covey, and Foxy.

Or let the feral dwollers kill them.

"Is there a spell you can put on me so I don't use magic? It's become part of me now, and I can't be certain I won't use it in a fight." Another thought hit me. "Does this mean that I can't change forms either?"

Siabiane shook her head. "As long as you don't use magic in your changed form—any of them—you'll be fine. The changes between human and dragon, or in your case, human, dragon, and faery, aren't magic. They're who you are. But you mustn't use magic in *any* form. The effects will be the same."

"I believe the Oleric spell would keep her from using magic," Padraig said. "But it will need an anchor to work best." He glanced around the room, but away from Alric.

"Which will be me." Alric shook his head before Padraig could do more than open his mouth. "I know the risks. We studied that archaic spell together. *I'm* the anchor."

I knew that tone. Alric was incredibly stubborn to begin with, but that tone was another level entirely.

"What's wrong with the person who's the anchor?" I didn't like the way Padraig still wouldn't look at either of us. Alric was like a brother to him and right now Padraig was envisioning a nasty demise for him.

"Nothing," Alric said.

"It could kill him," Padraig said a split second later.

"None of us might survive what's going on right now," Alric responded. "My death as the anchor would only come if Taryn dies. And I don't intend to let that happen."

"He'll be linked to me? How?" I didn't want to die, and I certainly didn't want to take the love of my life with me.

Padraig sighed. "The Oleric spell, the one to temporarily lock up your magic until we can find the siramage Fardoragh, is stronger with an anchor. That person is the base for your magic. But they can also allow you to break the spell if there's no other way out. You'd both be able to use magic until the tracker spell set by the flinms kills you both."

"Going out fighting, eh?" Covey nodded. "Something my people agree with."

Great. So, if I used magic, I would either be killing myself, or Alric *and* me. Not much of a choice.

"We have to do this." Alric took my hands. "The spell the flinms put on you will continue to grow. I'm surprised that you lasted as long as you did with the magic you've been using the past two days."

"But…"

Alric cut me off with a kiss. I returned it, then remembered we had an audience and a spell to cast.

"Fine. Let's cast this spell, get some sleep, and go find Cwin's friend. Then save the world." I sighed. Wishing for a little excitement when I was an out-of-work digger in Beccia was one thing—the past few years had made sure I would never wish for that again.

The spell was alarmingly simple, and Nasif and Lorcan cast it so fast I sat there waiting for it to hit after they stood back.

"Wait, was that it? I feel the same."

Mathilda laughed. "That's the point. Their spell tied your magic to Alric, so you can't accidentally cast a spell. But it's also working on keeping the drain at bay. For a week at least. That should be more than enough time for us to get up north and find this other siramage."

"I take it we're not riding there?" Covey wasn't a huge fan of long rides, but she also was wary of the chawsia paths.

"You'll be riding on the path," Padraig said. "We'll need the horses for later travel that we can't use the paths for, but the chawsia path can cut off a week."

"Which means all of you need to rest." Mathilda nodded to Alric and me as if we were five-year-olds. "Lots of sleep. The faeries have the right idea. When they wake up, I'll make sure they understand to leave you alone."

I nodded my thanks but she waved her hands at us.

"*Now.* You're feeling better but you need sleep." She folded her arms and glared at Alric and me.

Nice, get a chance to not be invaded by the wee loons for an evening, and we were under orders to sleep. I turned to Alric with a winsome smile, but he shook it off.

"Nope. We both need rest. I'd say everyone needs it. And we probably need to tell Tag, Foxy, and Grillion our plans." He rose and held out his hand for me. I wasn't certain that I needed it, but I took it.

Whatever the three had been doing, most likely gambling, they'd only come back into the living room long enough to grab plates of food, hear our plans to leave, and then vanish back to the stables.

I looked over the faeries, but all of them were still sound asleep. And snoring. It was a good thing no one had to sleep with them. Bunky and Irving were still turned off, their version of sleeping. And the brownies, along with Welsy and Delsy, had built an odd tent fort in the back of the room. From the deep snores coming from it, they were out as well. Like Bunky and Irving, Welsy and Delsy didn't sleep, but they did need downtime.

Alric escorted me to our room.

"I know we were all fighting for our lives, but should everyone be this wiped out? Even the faeries, brownies, and constructs?" I looked back as we left. Even Covey appeared fatigued and she was rarely tired.

Alric shut the door. "There was a lot of weird magic flying through town during the fighting. I have a feeling the enemy was hoping to wear down the defenders with exhaustion spells. Lorcan told me they sensed it on the wall, and he, Nasif, and Siabiane sent spells to mitigate it, but it still hit everyone at a reduced level."

I opened my mouth to mention there was more than that, but he kissed me before I could speak. Finally, we broke apart.

"It's okay. The spell was controlled; the guards and the majority of the townsfolk won't be too sleepy to protect this place after we leave. And, the spell of warding was put on the walls one last time. It's not as strong, as they're a limited use spell. But should protect them long enough to get their forces in place if needed."

Alric pushed me toward the bed, but sadly, not with romantic intent. "If we don't sleep, Lorcan will create something to make us sleep. He used to do it with students who were young and too stupid to realize they were exhausted. It usually tasted vile."

I sighed and gave him a lingering good-night kiss, one sadly broken by my yawn. Then we went to sleep.

◆

I woke to find myself in a dark room. On a dirt floor. Alone. I felt beaten and bruised and could barely get to my knees. Crawling slowly, I noticed a thin line of light along the floor and followed it. It was a narrow door, but wouldn't budge when I pushed or pulled.

What happened? Had we been captured in our sleep and no one noticed? I wasn't in the guest house anymore, the packed dirt floor pointed that out. Voices came from the other side of the door, but they were difficult to hear clearly.

"There's no way we can get her to change, she'll die first. The empress will have to sacrifice one of the other Ancients. She doesn't need all of them for her war." Low and gravely, it was probably a syclarion.

CHAPTER THIRTY

I FOUGHT DOWN MY PANIC AND tried to think through the words logically. Other Ancients? Who was out there besides the syclarion? How had they found my people? Were my brothers prisoners too? I tried to press my ear against the thin strip of light. A second voice spoke, but they were too far away to hear anything beyond a low level of mumbled words.

Then everything around me shook and invisible hands grabbed me. I fought not to scream, I might not know what was going on, but I knew that I didn't want those people to come in here.

"Taryn! Wake up!" Alric's voice registered before I opened my eyes. For a brief moment, the place I'd been and he and the bedroom occupied the same place.

"Wha…" My mouth wouldn't work right.

"You were screaming and hitting me." He didn't release my arms. "You were having a nightmare."

I shook my head as the dark images vanished. "That was worse than a nightmare. I felt the despair in my soul." I told him what I'd seen and heard as he held me. I didn't think he believed me that it wasn't a nightmare. It was a vision. It was real. At some point, that was going to be my reality. Or a reality. I clutched my stomach as a horrible feeling left from the vision hit me.

Everyone I knew was dead at that point.

"And now you're crying." Alric pulled my face up and looked into my eyes. "There's a darkness there. It's fading, but I think we need to see the other magic users. How do you feel?"

I was glad that he believed that hadn't been a nightmare, but a chill hit me and I couldn't stop shaking. "Cold." I got out before my teeth chattered.

"Not good." He scooped me and my blankets up and managed to get us out of the door.

Low voices were talking in the front room, but they were my friends.

Lorcan and Siabiane were quietly talking in the kitchen over cups of tea but stopped as Alric brought me to the sofa and deposited me, blankets and all, on the cushions. He tucked me in tightly before turning to the others.

"I thought she had a nightmare, but she's freezing now."

Both elves came over and all three of them peered at me.

I laughed. Three elves all worried about me. The old digger me would have loved this moment.

"Taryn? What's so funny?" Siabiane was gentle, but there was too much concern on her lovely face.

"Me with elves. We didn't think you were still around. I was digging up your salt shakers." It was difficult to laugh hysterically and shake at the same time, but I did it.

"She's delirious." Lorcan stepped forward, put his hand on my forehead, and frowned. "It's not a spell. Or not anything I recognize." He stepped back and Siabiane's hand replaced his.

"There is something there. But it's from Taryn. She cast this spell a very long time ago. One she made up." She pulled back her hand as if burned. "Taryn, let it go. That was you long ago. Let it go."

I looked up at the three elves looking down at me. We didn't see elves too often. They were still moving out of the southern lands and we were fairly far north. But my parents said they were friendly so far. "I'm Taryn. Well, I have a longer name but it's hard for outsiders to pronounce. Nice to meet you all." I looked down at my human body in a pile of blankets. "Did something happen to me?"

"Taryn, do you know us?" The pretty blond elf man's green eyes were worried.

"You're elves. From the south? My parents will be glad to meet you. My brothers too, but they can be difficult." I looked around more but the room I was in didn't seem at all familiar. "Where am I?"

The older male elf sat next to me and took my hands. "You're safe, Taryn, but you're in the wrong time. I'm Lorcan, this is Siabiane, and he's Alric. You need to let the past go."

I nodded hello to all three. "Let the past go? I'm only fifteen, I don't have a past."

I had never spoken to elves before, but concern was obvious on all three of their faces.

"This spell pulled her mind back to before she cast it?" The younger one, Alric, asked.

"I guess so? Has this happened before?" Siabiane had cool hands and they felt nice on my forehead.

"I would like to go home now." I shoved off the blankets, but my legs wouldn't move. Then the world shook around me.

The older man grabbed my shoulders as I shook. "Taryn, go back to when you were. Send your current self home."

"I can't...dead...all dead." I felt tears flowing down my face and the shaking grew worse.

New hands took my face and made me look up. It

was the younger elf. "Taryn, come back to me. To us. Release the spell, you have to."

I fought the overwhelming sadness. How could my family and my friends, all be dead? I saw them this morning. I just…something slammed into me, I fell over, and the world went dark.

"Taryn?" Alric's voice sounded like I was a scared kitten he was trying to rescue. Actually, I sort of felt that way. Everything hurt.

"What? I thought we were supposed to sleep?" I rolled over without opening my eyes and smacked into the back of the sofa. "Why am I out here?" I turned back to find Alric, Lorcan, and Siabiane watching me as if I'd grown two heads.

I patted my shoulders to make sure that I hadn't.

"Is backs!" Garbage yelled as she, Leaf, and Crusty flew over my friends' heads and dropped on me. "Noes dos. Bads spell." She shook her tiny finger at me but looked as concerned as the three elves. So did Leaf. Crusty gave a sad smile.

"Where did I go? Why are my blankets here? Why do you all look worried?" I wasn't sure whether to freak out or not, but I was leaning toward it.

"How do you feel?" Alric asked as he sat down next to me.

"Confused? That's about the best answer."

Crusty ran across my lap, flew up to my face, and kissed my cheek. "Yous noes dos agains. Gones!" She snapped her fingers.

"Gone…what just happened?" Crusty being worried was a sure way to freak me out.

The three faeries all jabbered but I couldn't sort out what they were saying.

"Thank you, ladies," Lorcan interrupted them. "Briefly, you had a terrifying nightmare—that was something other than a nightmare, woke up, then were yourself when you were fifteen. Do you remember casting a time spell when you were younger?"

"When I was fifteen? I was barely paying attention to magic lessons then. How do you know I was fifteen?" The good news was that I didn't feel exhausted anymore. The bad news was that I had no idea what my friends were talking about.

"You said you were. And you had no idea who we were." Alric's smile almost reached his eyes. I must have scared them badly.

"How can past me hop into now me?" My eyes went wide. "And I thought that Oleric spell wouldn't let me cast magic?" Alric appeared fine, but had I doomed both of us?

"It's something we'll need to look into. You didn't cast it when you were fifteen, it sent fifteen-year-old you mentally here," Siabiane said. "As for casting a spell, it wasn't the current you who did it, so you're fine on that front."

Garbage pinched my cheek to make me look at her. "Yous. Noes. Travel. In. Times." Her one-eyed scowl was the fiercest I'd ever seen.

"If I have any control over what occurred, in either situation, I'll try to not let it happen again." I wasn't sure which scenario was worse. I guessed that once they told me more about my non-nightmare terrors they were going to win. I was grateful that my groggy confusion was blocking it for the moment. But I did have a question. "If I came here mentally as a fifteen-year-old, wouldn't that have become part of my past and I would have recognized you three when we first met?"

Lorcan shrugged. "Time travel is odd; I doubt that even Nasif or Cwin would have a solid answer. Most likely your fifteen-year-old self passed it off as a dream and the interaction would quickly fade. It's almost dawn, so unless you think you can go back to sleep, we might as well get ready for our trip."

I had a feeling that he knew more about time travel than he was letting on, but I wasn't sure I wanted to know. Alric and I had gone back a thousand years to the time of the elven Breaking. But we'd physically gone back in time. It hadn't been fun, but far better than random past me jumping into my head. "Is there any way to block this spell? And you said that I cast it?"

Siabiane stepped up this time. "Yes, I traced it. It might have been not long before you flung yourself and your people out of your timeline during your peoples' fight with the syclarions. We won't push, but do you remember anything like that?"

I thought back, but I barely recalled putting together the relic staff and the magic in it to fight off the syclarions. "No. But if there was a time travel spell involved, unintentionally, that could explain how I came forward twenty-five hundred years. And sent the rest of my people somewhere and some when." I needed to look through those spell books for anything that could have done that. Yes, we had to save the world, but I needed my people, and my brothers to be a part of that saving.

Voices came down the hall and Foxy and Grillion came out. Foxy appeared awake but annoyed. Grillion appeared to have been dragged out of bed against his will and stumbled to one of the chairs.

"Why are you all awake this early?" Grillion managed to get out as Lorcan brought everyone tea.

"Lorcan and I were preparing for our upcoming trip." Siabiane turned to Alric and me. "When Nasif and Dueble were contacted by Zaelian. She and Ageora are in a new *tir cudd* and need their help. We helped them open a chawsia path. They will contact us when they can."

I wasn't happy about them leaving, I wanted my

friends together. But I knew they had important work to do with Ageora.

"And Taryn didn't sleep well. Why are you two awake?" Alric added.

"Amara called through the tattoo." Foxy held up his hand. "Yes, I confirmed it was her. There're some odd people moving through Beccia. I don't like it." His frown would make weaker people run in terror. It was a good thing we were friends.

"And he spoke very loudly. And aggressively. It woke me up." Grillion looked ready to fall asleep in his tea.

"What kind of people?" Alric ignored Grillion.

"Dwarves. And llweins from the deep mountains. Them ain't normal."

"Llweins aren't real." I laughed; my parents used to tell me stories of them. The four-foot-tall, whip-thin creatures were supposedly the builders of the mountains and also controlled the weather. And if you were a naughty Ancient child who kept sneaking out of bed, they were used to scare you back under your covers. They supposedly had long talon-like claws, could see in the dark, and were stronger than an army of dragons. The looks on Lorcan, Siabiane, and even Alric's faces weren't good. "Are they?"

"Is reals. Don't likes other peoples though." Crusty scowled. "Why leaves mountains?"

"And why go to Beccia?" Alric shook his head. "That town isn't near any of the major mountain ranges. Did she say how many there were or what they were doing?"

Foxy settled down, but I could still tell he wanted to race up to Beccia immediately. "She said Dogmaela followed a group of thirty through town to a camping location filled with a few dozen dwarves just past the ruins. They stopped for supplies but gave no answers as to what they were doing or where they be going. I don't like it."

I leaned forward. "Foxy, Amara is still a powerful dryad. Plus Ceithera, Flarinen, and a lot of very formidable elves are up there. They'll be fine."

His lower lip jutted out. "I still can be worried."

Siabiane smiled. "That you can, my friend. But Taryn is right. There's a lot of magic protecting Beccia. Do you think Lorcan and I would have come south if there was a danger?"

"Is noes!" Leaf jumped up and flew to Foxy. "Yous fines. Theys fines. We's fines. We's knows if bads happens." She pointed in what I assumed was the direction of Beccia.

Foxy gave a small but real smile. "You are being right as always, my friends. Thank you."

Mathilda, Cwin, Padraig, and Covey all came out, sleepy but awake.

Covey took some tea and dropped down next to me. "I know we were leaving early, but isn't this a bit much?" She yawned and gave a huge stretch. "I slept horribly with some odd dreams. Anyone else?"

"Taryn had some. I didn't really…" Alric tilted his head. "Actually, I had some weird dreams. Not like Taryn's, but I didn't even realize it until now."

One by one everyone else admitted they'd had odd dreams. No one would say nightmares, but it was clear that they'd been disturbing. Padraig didn't say much but nodded. The haunted look in his eyes said a lot though.

As they spoke, the events of earlier came back into my head. "So, it wasn't only me? Not that I recall it but there's a cold part in my mind." I shuddered and Alric tightened his grasp on my shoulders. Covey leaned closer on the other side.

"Apparently not." Cwin scowled. "But we can't discount that what you experienced didn't influence the rest of us." She raised her hand as everyone started to speak. "I know, you didn't all have the same experience.

Neither did I, but Taryn could have been so terrified that it sent fear to all of us."

"I'm sorry?" I really didn't want to be the cause of my friends' nightmares.

"It wasn't your fault." Covey shot a glance at Cwin. "There's nothing you could have done to change that." Although she wasn't a magic user, the tone in her voice defied any contradiction.

Cwin remained silent.

"Why you still here?" Derry asked as she popped in through the door and hovered in the air in the center of the room with her hands on her hips. "Should be on the way now."

All the faeries, including the three on me, squealed and flew up to the older faery. Direidus Salvia was as respected, if not more so, than their queen. And until a few days ago, I'd never heard of her.

"There have been things happening. And if you knew we needed to be somewhere at a specified time, you could have told us." I was annoyed at Derry simply coming and going. Especially since having her with me when the Dark and the dwollers showed up would have been extremely helpful.

"I know." Her face fell. "Sadly, I couldn't be here. My queen needed me. But you all do need to get moving. This town is safe now. Others aren't."

I wondered if the others noticed how she dropped her pidgin faery-speak from time to time.

"That was our plan," Cwin said. "We have to visit my friend Fardoragh and break the spell on Taryn, then we'll be on our way to the Lledir mountains."

Derry frowned and flew over to me. "This isn't good." She did a full circle in the air of my head. "Very not good. Why is she magic blocked?"

I explained what happened, but as soon as I got to the encounter with the flinms, she held up her hand.

"Those things need to be destroyed permanently; their powers are dangerous. Say no more. But we need to get you fixed."

That was obvious, but I had a bad feeling she was following something like a prophecy. I hated prophecies. Even more if they had anything to do with me.

Siabiane, Padraig, Lorcan, and Mathilda got to their feet.

Lorcan looked around the room. "We'll start setting up the chawsia path. Probably in the stables. Cwin and Alric will remain out of casting it in case we have problems. I recommend that everyone eat and pack quickly."

Grillion appeared torn after they left. "I'm not sure where I should go. Tag said last night that he was staying here. And I originally thought that was where I needed to be too. But now?" He shrugged. "I don't like the idea of you going into danger. I know I'm not a magic user, or fierce warrior, but still."

Foxy smiled. "You've saved us many times, my friend. You will be welcome with us now, or if you wish to gather forces here to join us in battle later." Foxy often knew the right thing to say. I figured it was from being a bartender for so long.

Grillion's face lit up. "Thank you. Either way, I need to pack. If I stay in town, Qianru will move me into her house with the rest. I have a lot to think about." He nodded and left the room.

"Are you okay?" Alric and Covey managed to get out at the same time.

"I will be." I looked over to the faeries as I stood. They'd dragged Derry off to their corner and were filling her in on what she missed. At least I assumed that's what they were doing. They weren't speaking native faery but were talking too high and fast for normal ears to understand. I wondered if I could comprehend them if I turned into a faery.

"What's that look? That's not a good look." Covey scowled.

"Nothing bad, just thinking. But until I eat, I won't do anything."

We quickly ate, left food for the others, then went to pack.

I paused midway through shoving a vest into my pack. "Do you think we'll survive?" I waved off Alric's look of concern. "No, I'm not feeling bad. Well, not any more than usual. But someday I'd really like to not be moving from place to place. To not have people trying to kill us. To sit and chat with friends over nothing important." My loud sigh even startled me.

Alric hugged me. "I believe we will. This will be nothing more than a tale we talk about around the fire in the pub." He peered into my eyes. "I promise."

I gave him a solid kiss. "I'm holding you to that. Okay, we'd better get out of here before Qianru shows up. Not sure how long Locksead can keep her back."

I shouldn't have spoken as a series of sharp knocks came from the front room. Alric and I finished our packs but left them in the bedroom.

Lorcan, Siabiane, and Mathilda were already there and he opened the door with a broad smile. They might have been working on setting up the chawsia path, but all appeared as relaxed as if they'd been sitting around over tea.

Qianru, followed by a frustrated Locksead, and three random houseboys, came into the room. "I wanted to congratulate you on saving the town. It's not much but it is dear to me. We will hold a ball in your honor this evening. Let the entire town know who brought in the saviors of Notlianda."

I hid my laugh. It wasn't us she wanted to celebrate; it

was herself for somehow being responsible for us being here to do so. At least she never changed.

"That is far too gracious of you, Lady Qianru." Siabiane practically fluttered over to her and took her hand. "We will be honored beyond measure to attend."

I hadn't been sure what the plan was, but lying and misdirection worked better than trying to explain this mess to Qianru.

"I do wonder if I could beg for a full tour of your lovely home? It would mean so much to me." Siabiane was full-on simpering and I had to look at her twice to make sure a changeling hadn't replaced her.

Lorcan and Mathilda stayed silent but both smiled appropriately.

"But of course! Do the rest of your companions wish to join? I'd hate to leave anyone out." She fired her smile to the rest of us and I tried to copy Lorcan's smile.

"Alas, we have many repairs to make after the fierce fighting. Magic to be restored and spells to be recast." Lorcan stepped forward and bowed. "But we will look forward to this evening. All of us."

Qianru tilted her head and gave a gracious smile. "It shall be an event for the ages. Come along, fair Siabiane." She held out her arm, which Siabiane took, and the group, except Locksead, left.

He shut the door behind them. "What are you really doing? There's no way that you would agree to this. I need to be warned what to expect."

Lorcan shook his head, but Alric stepped forward. "I trust him. And he's right. If we want to reduce the animosity of Qianru, he should be warned."

"Fine, but don't take too long." Lorcan and Mathilda went back to the stables.

Alric quickly told Locksead they had to leave immediately and that Qianru couldn't know until they were gone.

"Another life-or-death battle?" Locksead laughed. "Alric is a far cry from Carlton the relic thief with a nasty attitude in Beccia. But I'll do what I can. For one thing, I can stop the invites from going out, or at least slow them down. Nothing worse than Qianru left with no one to parade around and a full house expecting a show." He shook Alric's hand. "Try not to get killed. Carlton was a jerk, but I like this Alric fellow." He nodded to me and then left.

The faeries, including Derry, were now sitting with the brownies as Welsy and Delsy were telling them tales of Beccia. The faeries looked as enraptured as Flower and his brownies even though many of them had lived up there for a long time. The two brownie constructs were good storytellers. Soon Bunky and Irving woke up and joined the group.

I followed Alric into our room to grab our packs. "Are we taking Flower and his brownies on this trip? They were helpful here, and might be elsewhere."

"True. But every time we add more outsiders, we run the risk that someone isn't who they say they are."

I tilted my head and put my hands on my hips for emphasis.

"Fine, yes, if they want to come with us and the others agree, I won't say anything." He grabbed his pack and left.

I grinned. Alric was too stubborn. If he truly felt the brownies were a danger, he'd stop them regardless of what I said. He was trying to distract me from the morning's weirdness. I'd successfully shoved the issue of past me popping up without warning aside. The images of my night terrors were coming to me but were vague enough to shove aside as well. I didn't need more distractions as we headed into another battle, but I knew neither event was good.

The others were gathered in the front room, and Grillion was hugging people.

"You're staying here?" Grillion was an odd duck, but he had a big heart. I'd miss him.

"For now. Most likely you folks will come down this way after whatever you're doing on the coast. To be honest, I wouldn't be much help. I didn't learn anything when I passed through that area before."

"And he told me what he did notice." Covey grinned and hugged Grillion hard enough to make him pound her back to release him.

Grillion finished his goodbyes, after being swarmed with faery kisses, then left.

Garbage waited until he left, then whistled and three of the newer faeries flew to her. "Watches hims. If dangers, gets us." The three faeries nodded and popped out through the door.

I'd been surprised by Covey's hugging Grillion, but I was stunned by Garbage's reaction. But it was touching.

We'd all gathered, and the issue about Flower and crew joining us wasn't an issue. Welsy and Delsy had taken their training seriously and insisted they come along on this mission.

Mathilda brought out Siabiane's pack and was about to go free her sister from Qianru when the front door opened.

Siabiane appeared flustered but smiled when she saw her things were ready. "I had to knock her out. With a very tricky spell that should take her elves a few hours to sort out. She simply wouldn't let me go." She gave herself a shake and then was fine. "Shall we?"

The horses were nickering and pawing when we got into the stable. They didn't seem concerned about how we were getting there, they just wanted to be on their way. I rubbed the nose of my horse and thanked her for being so patient, then secured my pack and waited.

We'd walked them through chawsia paths before, but we also had ridden them.

"We're walking them through this time. The test tunnel seemed narrower than it should be," Padraig said as he and Mathilda cast the spell and then remained on either side of the opening. "Let's go."

I wasn't sure, but it did seem a bit smaller than usual. As long as it didn't dump any of us in some random deadly area, I was fine.

Siabiane led her horse through first with Delsy, Welsy, Flower, and the other eight brownies jogging behind. Mathilda nodded to Padraig and followed. The faeries chose that moment to fly after her, although Derry hung back. Bunky and Irving stayed near the faeries.

When Alric and I went, Derry flew up and landed on my horse's saddle.

"You're staying with us this time?"

"Seems prudent. Lots of trouble happening. But, if you don't mind, I'm going to nap." She didn't wait for my response, just curled in the saddle, and snored contentedly.

I shrugged. I'd never seen one of the faeries nap like that, but Derry was oldest.

The path shook a bit after ten minutes but stabilized.

"We're going slowly on this one. There's interference through these mountains, and we don't want to lose control as we cross one of them." Padraig was the last one and the tunnel gently closed behind him.

Considering how often these tunnels went wrong, I was fine with that.

A bright light ahead of us brought warmth as well as light and Siabiane left the tunnel with her brownie escorts.

Then Padraig yelled from behind us to get out.

CHAPTER THIRTY-ONE

I LOOKED BACK EVEN AS ALRIC started running. The tunnel had been closing gently behind Padraig's horse a moment ago, but that wasn't the case now.

It was crashing violently and picking up speed.

Covey was the only one between myself and Padraig, but she was soon on my heels.

My horse didn't need encouragement as either seeing the rest of her friends running, or the collapse behind us made her frantic.

Derry flew from the saddle to my horse's ear and whispered to her. The horse continued to run, but the wild-eyed panic was gone.

We all made it out before the path collapsed, but Padraig's horse had to jump the last two feet. The faeries swirled around us, almost like a protective wall, until the broken chawsia path vanished.

Derry and Garbage remained glaring at the space the path vanished from for a few moments, as if daring the chawsia path to reappear. Finally, they turned back to the rest of us.

"Not good. A grimlinspell got inside. They could have killed everyone." Derry was worried.

"Are you sure?" Cwin left her horse with Lorcan and walked back to us. "Those are older than Taryn and touchy to pull off." She looked at the rest of us. "They tend to explode on the spellcaster. Someone attached it to one of us."

"I've heard of them, as I'm sure the other magic users have. But they were said to drag their victims to the underworld." Lorcan appeared doubtful.

I'd never heard of it, or I'd forgotten it. But the looks on the other magic users, even Alric, said that they had. "Why are all of these old spells coming back now?" I finally asked. "One or two I could maybe understand. But there have been a lot aimed at us. Wouldn't you need to have some really old spell casters to know how to make them?"

I didn't like the looks aimed my way by Lorcan, Padraig, Mathilda, Siabiane, and Cwin. Alric was the only magic user who didn't look at me with concern and pity.

"Because of me? A confused, out-of-time, Ancient? That still doesn't explain how these people are finding these spells."

"That's going to take time to sort out, but I do believe it's connected to you." Padraig looked around where we'd landed. "Right now, we probably want to find shelter. This isn't where we were supposed to end up."

I noticed the deep snow and blustery winds for the first time. Which said a lot about how out of sorts I was. "This isn't the mountain your friend is on?" I asked Cwin. They'd said we couldn't take the tunnel directly to his mountain retreat because it was too dangerous. This looked fairly dangerous.

Cwin looked around and shook her head. "This looks like Clifton Mountain. The mountain that Fardoragh is on, is the Truijia mountain. We'll have to go down, then back up." She narrowed her eyes and studied a cliff near her. "Unless...Let me see what I can sort out while we get out of this storm. I recommend descending immediately."

The faeries were zipping around chattering to each other, but Garbage and Derry swooped over at Cwin's words.

"Yes. We can handle this weather. You and the horses can't." Derry pointed to a pile of rocks. "That way."

It was interesting that the faeries in their tiny overalls didn't seem affected by the cold. There were times in Beccia, that they'd acted unhappy in it, but like many things with them, that had changed. The constructs were metal, so unless it was cold enough to freeze their joints, they'd be fine. The brownies claimed to be fine, but there were drifts higher than them ahead of us.

I added both of my cloaks, as did the rest.

Actually, Foxy didn't seem to be bothered by the cold either.

As we bundled up, Siabiane cast a light warming spell over the horses and brownies—after we put Flower and crew on top of our horses, with only minor objections on the brownies' side and we followed Derry's path down.

Because of the trickiness in the trail, we were still leading the horses. But the snow was getting deeper and even with cloaks, none of us were dressed for this weather.

"Keep going. Will be right back." Derry whistled and ten faeries flew to her and they zipped off. Garbage was now leading the way down.

"Direidus finds ways," Leaf said as she flew alongside my head. "Is oldest. Very smarts."

"Yes, she is. So, you don't feel this cold at all?" I tried to think of any time in my fifteen-plus years of knowing the faeries that I'd seen them cold. Couldn't think of one.

She shrugged. "It feels fun. Slippy-slide. But not cold."

I sighed. Someday I'd find out who created the faeries and have a long talk with them.

Derry and five of the faeries came back through the increased snow flurries. "Shelter is ahead. Follow us."

I looked to Padraig and Lorcan, I knew they wanted to get off this mountain quickly. But I wasn't sure if the horses and the rest of us could make it. The snow was falling harder. It was still early morning, but the heavy dark clouds wallowing overhead made it feel like night was upon us.

"Lead on," Lorcan said as we followed the faeries.

The storm got worse before we could get to the shelter, and seeing the path became a problem. Then Leaf and Crusty held their breaths and lit up. All the faeries trailing behind them did the same, acting as markers for the trail. Garbage was in front and she and Derry both lit up. I wasn't too surprised that Derry's glow was brighter than the rest and a lovely swirl of green, purple, and blue.

The horses appeared calmer once the faeries flashed their colors, probably assisted by many of the faeries remaining near the horses' heads.

There was a sharp left turn and we went down a short but steep incline. The remaining five faeries who'd left with Derry flashed into their colors and a cozy cave was illuminated. Cozy in feel, it was large enough for all of us and our horses. As we walked inside, I noticed what looked like a wide fire pit and a darkened area in the ceiling far above it. The space appeared to be well-used.

"People normally go through this place? Why?" I took my pack off of my horse and removed her gear as the others sent glows to the ceiling and the edges of the cave.

And more warming spells to chase off the chill.

"There are travelers who visit the mountain villages with supplies and trinkets for sale. These stations were built for their comings and goings if the storms hit. But the weather has been getting worse over the past fifteen years, so many of the villages had to be abandoned." Cwin had a sad smile as she surveyed the cave. "Many things are changing for the worse, and I'm not as confident as I was about being able to bring them all back," she said the last part softly, but I heard it.

Everyone finished removing the gear from their horses and rubbed them down. We had some provisions for them, but things could get rough if we had to remain here too long.

"I'll get a fire started." Alric went directly to a dark wall in the back and came back with an armful of wood that I hadn't even seen. I might be an Ancient, with better eyesight than a pure human, but elven eyesight was better.

The faeries had stopped holding their breaths as more mage glows lit the cave. Derry found a nice rock not too far from the fire ring, settled in, then reached into her overall pocket and brought out a lot of sugar.

I expected the faeries to swarm her, but while they did move closer, they held back until she motioned them forward. "Come and have some treats. But, unless Taryn, Mathilda, or I say it's okay, you cannot leave this cavern." The faeries all nodded as one, zipped in and each respectfully grabbed a handful, then flew back a few feet.

I could have asked them to do the same, but with Derry it appeared they might stay put.

"Nice bag you have." Even though I hadn't seen the black bag, there was no way the amount of sugar Derry was bringing out had come from the pocket of her overalls.

"Thank you. I carry many emergency supplies." Her smile failed and she paused to glance at where other faeries were eating and chatting. "I am worried about the queen. I can't reach her."

"How far was she from here when you left her?" I

usually didn't ask my faeries those kinds of questions—I knew I wouldn't get anything useful. But Direidus Salvia was different.

"In the village of Rialone, it's in the valley between this mountain and the one Cwin's fellow siramage, Fardoragh, is on. I'd hoped we would have landed there when the chawsia path closed. That grimlinspell isn't a good sign."

We sat in silence for a bit as the others discussed guard spells for the evening. It might be early afternoon, but it looked like the dead of night outside and clearly, we weren't leaving until morning.

"Do you think that grimlinspell was tagged to me?" I kept my voice low. I was getting tired of everything coming after me specifically. But I didn't want any of my friends to be targeted either.

Derry looked at me carefully, her wise old face seemed to deeply ponder it. Then she shrugged and shook her head. "Don't know." She flashed a grin and held up a tiny hand before I could speak. "I know many things, child, but not everything. Even the wisest don't know it all. But I don't feel that it was aimed at you. They would have found an easier target, and until recently, you were a magic user and *not* an easy target." She looked at Foxy and Covey.

"You think someone planted that spell on one of them? When? How could whoever did it know we'd be using a chawsia path? We could have remained in Notlianda for weeks."

"That is one of the things that worries me. That storm outside? It appeared moments before we were dropped here. These mountains are dangerous and unpredictable, but that's too much for chance. As for when they might have been tagged? You said they were knocked out and on the street during the fight against the dreks. That would be when I'd do it."

I got to my feet. "We have to take it off, what if it does something else?"

"It'll dissolve in a short time if it hasn't already. Grimlinspell tags don't have long lives and if they complete their job, their victims die."

"I overheard part of that." Mathilda came over as I returned to my rock. "You don't think it was Taryn. And you could be right. But we need to see who it was."

Derry gave a short bow. "And you'd like my help."

"Yes, please. You're not as familiar with the others as I am." Mathilda turned to me. "Sometimes being familiar with someone can make searching for a spell difficult. The grimlinspell is one of those."

I nodded. I was closer to Covey and Foxy than anyone—not to mention I couldn't cast any magic.

Derry watched Covey and Foxy carefully, her deeply lined face pensive as she weighed out things in her head. "Let me go over alone first."

She barely waited for Mathilda's nod before she flew over to them. I couldn't hear what she said, but Covey picked her up. Then Foxy held her.

Derry kissed them both, then flew back to us. "I was wrong. Neither was tagged. But I don't believe I was wrong about the circumstance."

"Alric," Mathilda spoke before I could.

"Yes. The situation of the three being unconscious on the street was perfect even though they wouldn't have been there for long before Taryn moved them. I might need both of your help with him. Spells can act differently on magic users."

Mathilda nodded and she appeared to be aware of that. I hadn't been, but it made sense. Even unconscious, a mage would have more defenses than a non-magic user.

"What can I do since I can't use magic right now?"

"Change into a faery. I don't want to lie to Alric, but he might still have more activity left in the grimlinspell tag than a non-magic user would at this point. He wanted to get a better look at you when you were a faery and it will distract him enough for us to examine him."

I narrowed my eyes. "You don't think he's in danger, do you?"

"No." Mathilda.

"Maybe." Derry.

"Um, hmm." I folded my arms.

"Danger or not, the sooner we know if he's the one who was tagged, the quicker that we can resolve it," Derry said.

"Fine." I took a deep breath, closed my eyes, and thought of changing into a faery.

Garbage, and the girls who weren't already dozing, cheered me on but didn't join me as I flew over to Alric. He'd been talking to Padraig, but Padraig left to go check on the stew they had set up in a pot on the fire.

"You do make a lovely faery." Alric grinned and held out his hand for me to land on. "How does it feel?"

I settled on his hand as Derry and Mathilda sat nearby. "Thank you, I do like my wings. It feels normal until I get near anyone or anything larger than it should be."

We chatted for a bit while Mathilda and Derry did their spell.

Alric was mid-word when his eyes went wide, he looked ready to shout but then collapsed.

CHAPTER THIRTY-TWO

I FLEW FREE OF ALRIC'S HAND and spun on Mathilda and Derry as the rest of our group came running over.

"What happened?"

Mathilda shook her head. "Alric was the one they tagged, and the grimlinspell was still live. Its goal was to cause as much havoc as possible and follow us. That storm out there will make going anywhere impossible for us, but also for whoever set that spell. But they will find us if that thing remains active."

"Why did he collapse?" I flew to his face, he was breathing fine, simply unresponsive.

"I had to do it to block the tag." Mathilda looked at Padraig, Lorcan, Siabiane, and Cwin. "We need to remove it before we can wake him up."

Derry patted Alric's cheek and murmured a few words in his ear, then flew to me. "I agree that you make a lovely faery, but you don't need to remain that way now."

I flew back a few feet and changed, then ran back to Alric. "What can I do?" I knew I couldn't use magic, and by the concerned looks on the faces around me, the spell they were going to cast would have been over my level even if I could. But I needed to do something.

"Set up his bedroll, then Padraig can carry him over.

Keep him comfortable." Cwin nodded, then gave a small smile. "He will be okay, I promise."

I set up his bedroll, pulling out extra blankets for him. Padraig scooped him up and gently placed him on the pile before turning to me. "You know he's like a brother to me. He will be fine." His smile was sincere and made me relax.

I took Alric's hand as the magic users huddled together. Covey, Foxy, the faeries, Bunky, and Irving came over to help me keep watch. Well, the faeries who weren't in a sugar stupor yet.

Welsy, Delsy, and Flower's crew stood guard. Not sure against what, but it was comforting. Siabiane gave them a warm smile before turning back to Lorcan and the rest.

"This magic business," Covey said as she and Foxy sat near me. "I've always been so interested in the elves' use of magic. However, I honestly think I've seen enough of it in the past couple of years to last a few lifetimes."

"Me as well. Although, to be honest, never really had much interest until I met my Amara." Foxy watched Alric, but his thoughts were elsewhere. "You're certain she's being okay up there?"

I grabbed his massive hand in both of mine. "She's better off than we are right now. Not to mention the faeries in Beccia have orders to come to Garbage if things go wrong. None of them have." Of course, my paranoid mind filled in, 'yet'. But he didn't need that.

"Truth of that. I don't like any of this."

Covey put her arm around his shoulders—or as far as she could reach. "None of us do. Never thought I'd say I miss my university students, but I do. We'll get through this. Save the world again, and go back home for good."

Foxy sighed and nodded. "I do miss my pub."

Alric twitched but his eyes didn't open. It was as if he was fighting in his sleep.

I let go of Foxy's hand and grabbed Alric's fist as he swung it around. He was too strong for me, and Foxy also took hold.

Derry had been speaking to Garbage, but both came over and began humming. It wasn't the Jhea spell-breaking song, nor one I'd heard before, but it was light and bright and it lifted my spirits.

Alric calmed immediately as he stopped flailing and went back to a calm sleep.

Padraig and the rest of the magic users circled Alric and sat down. They all touched him and murmured an odd spell that vanished from my memory the moment after they said it.

Alric twitched again, but neither I nor Foxy touched him—I was afraid to mess up whatever spell was being cast.

They apparently didn't like his twitching as the words of the spell were louder now, still vanishing, but this time Derry came forward. At a nod from Mathilda, she sat on Alric's chest. Garbage called in more faeries and they all continued their soothing song.

Alric tried to sit up and his eyes flashed open when he was held down. But instead of his beautiful leaf-green eyes, dark heavy gray ones lurked there. The no-pupil bit was even more disturbing than the color.

"I will find you. This one is mine now." The voice sounded as if it came out of the depths of the abyss and echoed oddly.

Something about it triggered a memory, but I had no idea where it was from. I almost called my magic, but instead changed shape into a Xoti. A mythical magic eater. I wasn't using magic; like the faeries, right now, I was magic.

I leaned over Alric's face and growled. "Go now." The Xoti's mouth was full of nasty long teeth so even getting that out was hard. I put my clawed hands on Alric's chest and pulled on the evil magic inside him. There was more than just a tag on Alric.

"You do not exist." The gray eyes were slowly fading to green, but Alric's body was still trying to get up.

"Try her." Derry grinned and flew to my hands. Strength flowed from her into what I was doing.

"No. You can't..." Alric's eyes shut.

"Might want to change form, that's disturbing," Covey said as I rocked back on my heels.

I dropped the Xoti image and watched as the magic users finished their spell.

Alric sighed and opened his nice green eyes. "What happened? I feel like an avalanche hit me."

Padraig smiled. "Long story and we'll tell you around dinner." He got up and went to check the stew.

"He's completely clear." Cwin's smile didn't reach her eyes, but she released the spell she'd been building.

I smiled but noticed that Cwin and the rest of the magic users were watching me far more than Alric. Their collective faces were the studied neutral of when they were analyzing something in a book or scroll. Then they released whatever spells they'd been working on to fight the grimlinspell tag and went about setting up their bedrolls.

Those thinking looks still being flashed my way didn't make me feel calmer though.

Great. I shoved that aside with the rest of my issues and hugged Alric as he sat up. I didn't know how I pulled up, as far as I knew, a made-up creature. But it worked and didn't pull on any of my magic.

"What was it that spoke to us?" I asked anyone.

"A beast that we shouldn't mention here." Derry looked around at the other magic users and they all nodded. "It is gone for now, and once we are in a safer place we do need to discuss it. I am afraid I have to leave you. That thing being around and my inability to reach the queen concerns me. I must find her."

The faeries protested, but Garbage whistled for them to quiet. "War. We's at war. We's fights. We's obey." She bowed to Derry. "Call if needs."

I was surprised that Garbage didn't offer to send faeries with Derry, but from the look on Derry's face, she wouldn't have accepted.

"Thank you. Stay safe and get off this mountain at daybreak. I will find you." She flew toward the entrance. "If I can." Then she was gone.

"Without risking anything, can someone please tell me what happened? And why every muscle in my body aches?" Alric moved stiffly, but I was happy he was himself again.

"Bluntly?" Padraig walked over. "When you were knocked out on the streets of Notlianda you were hit with a grimlinspell tag, one that had an extra passenger. We got rid of both, but Direidus was correct, this isn't the place to name names."

"We's halps!" Garbage yelled as she and the rest of her flock swarmed forward—all clad in their war feathers and waving their war sticks. Derry's sugar hadn't been enough to keep them down for long. "Sings and soothes."

"You all did wonderfully," Mathilda said. "But I don't think you need to be in your war garb yet."

"Is ready!" Garbage zipped up to the ceiling with her faeries flying behind and all chanting.

"Yes, you are. But right now, being quiet and calm might be more important." Lorcan kept his voice low so the faeries had to shut up to hear him.

If I'd tried that, they would have kept yelling.

"Ohs." Garbage drifted down slowly with the rest. "Is fines." She shrugged and stuffed her feathers and war stick into her black bag inside her overall pocket. "Ales?"

"Don't you have some?" I knew they had a lot, and as far as I knew, we hadn't packed any.

"Maybes…checkings." She whistled and led her flock toward the entrance of the cave. Then took out the slides they'd taken from Ageora's *tir cudd*, and from the sounds, several ale bottles from her black bag and proceeded to ignore us. Welsy and Delsy sent Flower and his brownies to go with the faeries, but the two constructs joined Siabiane.

"That's a good sign." Lorcan created chairs, basic, but better than the ground, for us around the fire. "The faeries are far more in touch with danger around us than they used to be. Being willing to drink and play means we're safe for now."

As if in a threat response, a massive gale of snow slammed up against the shield covering the entrance to the cave.

"I wouldn't tempt things." Siabiane smiled as she handed him a bowl of stew.

Cwin frowned at the ice and snow whirling outside. "I agree. We need to rest and get off this mountain." She gave me a sharp glance. "Then sort things out."

I knew they were going to ask me how I changed into the Xoti, but the truth was I wasn't sure. I panicked at the thing inside Alric and reached for a creature out of my childhood to help fix the problem on instinct. I didn't even really recall that it was another childhood tale until I was already chasing that gray thing out.

Maybe I should come up with a better story by the time we could talk about what had attacked Alric.

CHAPTER THIRTY-THREE

NO ONE SPOKE MUCH AND the faeries soon exhausted themselves and passed out. The brownies returned to Welsy and Delsy's leadership.

No guard was officially set, but Foxy remained close to the entrance of the cave.

Alric seemed distracted as we cuddled in our bedrolls, but with what had happened to him, I couldn't blame him.

"Stop blaming yourself." He gently kissed my forehead.

"I wasn't. I mean, for what?" Truth was I was kicking myself for not being able to get him out of harm's way fast enough from the spell that had grabbed him.

"Because I was attacked while we were fighting the dreks. You're blaming yourself."

I pulled back. "Are you in my head?" I hadn't thought of the possible repercussions of my changing into the Xoti, were we now sharing thoughts?

His laugh was good to hear. "No, but it's all over your face. Especially since we laid down. It's not your fault. We could have been killed out there, but thanks to you, we weren't." He gave me a nice, but far too short, kiss. "Now go to sleep."

I was too tired to argue, so went to sleep.

Waking to the sound of faeries carrying on loud

conversations made me forget where I was for a few blissful moments.

With a sigh at reality, I opened my eyes. Alric was gone and most of my friends were already having tea and breakfast by the fire.

It might be me, but the mountain trail outside the shield looked only marginally brighter than when we went to sleep. I sat up and pointed to the chattering faeries. "Has anything changed? Why are they so worked up?" It was especially annoying since I knew most of them had drunk themselves into a stupor last night, and I'd had nothing to drink but my head felt like I'd had more than a few rounds at the Shimmering Dewdrop.

"Derry contacted Garbage and said we needed to be careful going down into the valley. She also forbade Garbage and the rest from joining her right now. Again." Lorcan raised an eyebrow as Garbage paused and glared at him. "Which was perfectly timed as they were getting ready to flee."

"Is Queen Mungoosey and Direidus Salvia!" Garbage flew over to him and shook her finger.

"And they both want you to stay with us," Mathilda said. "You need to do what they need you to do. We're at war."

That last sentence got Garbage and she slumped. Up until yesterday, I wasn't completely certain the faeries even knew what war was. But they did now and felt about the same as the rest of us did about it.

"Fines. We's waits." With an annoyed look directed at all of us, Garbage flew back to the rest of the faeries.

I joined the others at the fire. Foxy had taken food and tea and resumed his post near the entrance. I wasn't sure if it was that he didn't trust the magic users, or if he wanted to be alone with his thoughts.

"We're leaving in that?" I wanted to get off this

mountain as much as anyone, but the short trip from where the chawsia path was attacked and here had been rough. I didn't think the way down to this valley was going to be better.

"Yes, but I think we won't have the same issues as yesterday." Padraig was studying a map and now turned it around. "This way won't be as long as the main trail we were on, it is still large enough for the horses and will get us down to the village in less time. And it should be more protected from the cold."

I watched the rest of my friend's faces, but none of them were happy. "And? There's definitely an 'and' or 'but' in there." I inhaled my food, I might not be using magic right now, but I was eating like I was.

"And, the entrance is guarded by stone monsters. And the exit is dangerous. So, if we make it onto the trail, we might not get back out." Covey shrugged as she responded before Padraig did. "He would have taken too long. Personally, I'd rather face stone monsters than a few more hours of cold. My people are from the deserts." She did have probably every item of clothing she had with her on—aside from her heavy cloak.

"She makes a good point," Siabiane said. "And the longer we're on this mountain the more of a target we are. Whoever hit our chawsia path with that grimlinspell knows where we are, they made us crash here for a reason. I believe that the additional rider on the tag that hit Alric was from some other group, but even though we removed it, they also know where we are. Our strength is not to be where our enemies think we are."

I was too tired to debate things—not to mention I wasn't sure which side was right. "When do we leave?"

Mathilda grinned. "That's my girl! Let's finish here and load up."

I never thought I'd miss a cave, but after a half hour or so leading the horses down the mountain, I rethought my agreement to leave. Aside from the faeries and the constructs, everyone was bundled up, and no one was happy.

Aside from the faeries.

They were diving through the snow flurries, each still holding their breath to flash colors as they lined the trail. Bunky and Irving didn't seem to mind the snow or cold but flew close to us. Siabiane made sure Flower and the other living brownies were secured on horses, and Welsy and Delsy trooped along the mountainside of the trail.

Hopefully, Padraig's map was right and this alternative path would be less exposed to the cold. I kept Covey walking her horse ahead of me, but she was slowing down quickly and her movements were stiff.

I was about to suggest she should ride for a short while when Padraig raised his fist to stop and the faeries ended blinking their colors.

Covey's shaking was worse and I walked up to her. "Get on your horse." We'd been leading the horses for their safety, but I swore that her mount turned and bobbed his head in agreement. Since Leaf was whispering in his ear, he probably understood and agreed.

Covey shook her head when Alric came up and put his hands on her horse's head. He looked up a moment later. "I can't do it for all of them, but I made sure your horse won't suffer ill effects from your riding." He folded his arms as she opened her mouth to protest. "Who do you think will have to carry you when you collapse?" His tone was perfect University professor.

"Fine. I might need some help getting up." Covey hated being helpless, but this weather was brutal. Trellians *were* desert people and I was amazed she'd lasted this long. Alric easily got her onto her horse.

Garbage frowned at Covey curling over her horse and a large group of faeries swarmed her. They spread out their wings and covered as much of her as they could in a cloak of faeries.

It could have been due to the faery blanket she now wore, but Covey seemed to sit up straighter and wasn't shivering anymore.

Lorcan joined Cwin and Padraig and they began a low-volume spell aimed at the side of the trail. Their words seemed to be whipped away by the winds.

Siabiane went to Covey and handed her a small glowing rock; I felt the warmth coming from it even where I was. Then Siabiane and Mathilda gave smaller rocks to the rest of us with the whispered admonishment that they wouldn't last long and to keep them close.

Padraig and Lorcan finished their part of whatever they were doing as they pulled back to the rest of us with their and Cwin's horses.

Cwin stepped forward between two pillars of snow on the side of the trail that I swore hadn't been there before.

A strange voice drifted over the wind, but it wasn't Cwin's. I had no idea what the words said, but they felt old.

Older than me.

The sky grew darker and the biting wind increased, it felt more like the dead of night than early morning. I pulled my cloak's hood down tight as snow flurries raced around us.

Cwin spoke in the same weird language as the mystical voice and appeared to be having an argument with the two pillars and whoever the chanting voice was. Both pillars were now glowing under their coating of ice.

Alric took the reins of Covey's horse and moved us further back. I couldn't see much of his face, but what I saw wasn't good.

The faeries continued hugging Covey and not even a head came up to see what was happening as everyone except Padraig kept moving back. And Foxy. He sent his horse back but he remained next to Padraig with his club out, standing as a barrier between Cwin and the rest of us.

The world around us, aside from the words spoken by Cwin and whoever she was speaking to, became so silent it felt like we were in a bottle.

The ground gave a low rumble and the ice covering on both pillars exploded. Ice shards shot toward Cwin.

She snarled something in that weird language and the shards melted in the air. Then the snow under her boots melted and rapidly spread to the sides of the trail.

"I can keep going," Cwin now spoke Common. "Or you can let us pass. We'd rather not fight you and you are outmatched. We won't harm anything; we just need to get off your mountain."

The two pillars grew stone arms and orange eyes peered through the rock. Both pillars reached for her but the snow under them began to melt and they wobbled.

"If you fall, you die. I know what you are and don't want to be the cause of your demise. But I will if I have no choice. This is your final chance." The melting slowed down but didn't stop.

The air around us froze; not cold-froze, but halted-froze. The sky lightened and the wind stopped.

Then everything came back with an odd popping sound.

Cwin bowed to both of the pillars and thick snow reappeared at their feet. "Thank you. The siramages will sing of you. Guard the way, more will be coming, and they aren't on the side of good." There were a few more words after that but they were in the strange language.

Padraig motioned us all forward. "We need to move quickly through this pass. Don't veer off the trail and ignore anything you see." He shuddered and turned to Cwin. "Unless the myths aren't true?"

Cwin took the reins of her horse back from him

and shrugged. "They're true, but they can't hurt you. However, what you see might make you hurt yourself. Keep your eyes on the person ahead of you. They aren't ghosts; they're beings who became trapped here a long time ago. Yes, there's a difference, and now is not the time to discuss it." With a nod, she led us between the now still pillars on the side of the main trail.

Of course, if someone tells me to not look at things, I needed to look. Watching the faeries as they adjusted themselves on Covey distracted me for a few moments, and then I really wanted to look. A glance couldn't hurt, right?

I jumped and screamed as two vague forms charged me. Or seemed like they were going to, and then they vanished.

"Are you sure those aren't ghosts?" Yeah, I shouldn't have looked, but I did. And those looked like ghosts to me.

"Not ghosts, don't look, and no loud noises." Padraig was ahead of Covey and pointed up.

Sharp slabs of ice hung over us. They shouldn't be able to do that and appeared ready to collapse at any moment.

I nodded and went back to watching the faeries on Covey.

"What are they?" Foxy had changed to take the spot at the end, behind Alric.

Lorcan didn't look up. "They are bariards. Creatures trapped here long ago because they tried to take over the world."

"Why weren't they destroyed?" Covey's voice only chattered a little, so hopefully that was good.

"They can't be. They aren't truly alive, but illegal and unnatural spells created long ago during a mage war." Mathilda added as she raised her hands ahead of us and it seemed as if the air above her cleared.

At least from what I could tell without actually looking at what surrounded us.

"But they can't hurt us, right?" I was back to wanting to look at them again.

"No, but they can make their victims run off cliffs, run into walls of stone, and if you go off this trail, you'll never get out," Mathilda said the last bit sharply.

I looked down at my feet. My right foot was about to step off the trail. I swore and pulled back. My horse had been smarter and was already trying to tug me over. Great.

A thin haze began to grow over everything. I was aware of still walking next to my horse, and the sounds of the horses of my friends broke the stillness. But I also felt as if I was falling asleep.

While still moving.

I didn't know how the magic of this place worked and, for once, I didn't think I wanted to.

CHAPTER THIRTY-FOUR

SLOWLY, THE WORLD BEGAN TO reappear. My eyes cleared and I became aware of aches in my back and legs. The snow around us vanished and we were now coming down a rock-strewn trail. I thought we were in the clear, having gotten through the ravine of the bariards intact and as sane as we began. But the three rows of kneeling, masked archers in front of us as we exited the trail convinced me otherwise. The weather warmed up the moment we cleared the last two markers from the path and I was shocked at how far down we'd come. We were still in the mountains, but they were more like rolling hills at this point. The massive snow-covered peaks loomed above us until they vanished into a bank of clouds.

"Don't move." The voice came from somewhere in the three rows of arrows pointed our way, but with masks over the lower half of their faces, there was no way to tell the speaker.

Or so I thought.

Garbage zipped off Covey and flew directly to the middle of the archers. "Yous noes blocks! Important things to dos!" As she spoke, the other faeries also flew forward and hovered in front of the archers' arrows. Bunky and Irving joined them, both buzzing angrily as they flew back and forth.

"Should we go as well?" Delsy asked Siabiane as he

and Welsy pulled out their small hammers. Flower and his brownies sat up in the saddles of the horses they rode on, also ready to attack if needed.

"No, wait a bit." Siabiane raised her right hand slightly and appeared to be casting a sneaky spell.

"Call off your foul demons or we'll fire!" The voice didn't sound as confident as it had moments before.

Most likely the faeries were grimacing at them.

"Fowls? We's nots chickens! Goes away!" I hadn't seen Garbage or the others pull out their war sticks, but they were all waving in the air now.

"Not fowl, foul…as in evil." The speaker sighed. "Fine, you have us. Just call off the winged ones. Please." He rose and removed his mask and dark hood. He was a tall elf with deep red hair tied back in a braid. He reminded me of a male version of Orenda.

Siabiane dropped whatever spell she had been pulling up.

Derry and ten new faeries came flying over their heads from the village. "We've protected your village and you attack our friends?" Granted, she didn't have Garbage's fierce look, but from the way the first row of archers flinched away from her, she was fierce enough.

"These are the villagers you were defending?" I was going to say the queen was defending, but it wasn't always good to let people know that.

Derry folded her arms as Garbage mimicked her stance. "Yes. Many faeries were injured in the battle."

"I'm sorry!" As the original speaker for the archers moved away and put down his bow, he motioned for the rest of them to do the same. "We've been through a lot and are grateful for the faery assistance. But no one comes through that path. I thought these new faeries were spells." He gave a slight nod to Siabiane and she tilted her head. He'd caught her spell prep—which meant he probably was a magic user as well.

Or was extremely used to being around them.

Derry flew closer to the elf and glared at him. "Are you recovered now? These are my friends—all of them. They have important work to do."

He bowed to her and us. "Yes, I'm Gailen, hunt leader of the Rialone village. Welcome. We will ready the guest houses for you."

"We don't have time." Padraig introduced everyone briefly. "We still have far to go."

"Northern elves, and two from the south," Gailen sounded intrigued but simply bowed. "We are pleased to meet you all. But you won't want to keep going right now. It's almost night."

I looked around. It didn't seem like night, and we'd only been on that path for an hour or so.

Gailen gave me a small smile. "Now I know you did pass through the path. What time of day did you start?"

"An hour after sunrise," Padraig said.

"The sun sets oddly in this valley, but it will be setting within a half hour. Time is distorted on the path you came through, but as I said, no one comes through it. Be grateful that you're alive." He smiled and motioned for us to follow as his archers dispersed. "You were in there for over eight hours."

Padraig nodded to Derry. "These are good people? I wasn't planning on stopping here."

"Yes, they are. They're also extremely isolated and the attack hit them hard. Don't judge them too harshly."

He turned to the rest of us. "Let's get a night's rest. If we were on that trail for that long, we will start to feel it soon. And the horses need to be taken care of." He and Cwin took the lead.

Covey already looked better but still had most of her extra clothing on, just looser.

"How did it take that long to travel and no one noticed? We have serious magic users here. And the faeries? How did they not notice?" I walked with my horse alongside Alric, but I was becoming more upset about the time thing as we approached the village of Rialone. A large part of my tentative sense of security was based on the strength of the people around me. Even the faeries and the constructs. That they didn't notice the time issue was upsetting.

"There are some magics that are beyond living beings of today," Lorcan answered before Alric did. "Even people like us. However, I was as surprised as you about the lost time. Now, the sky does look like it's getting darker, but I would have said we were on that trail for two hours at the most."

"Nopities!" Crusty sang out as she flew around us. "I knews!"

I held out my hand for her to land on. "You knew how long we were on the trail? Did Garbage as well?" It had seemed as if she and the others hadn't, but faeries were weird.

"Noes. Only mes." Crusty ran from my open hand to my shoulder. "Minkies tells mes things. Buts alls secrets." She nodded as solemnly as I'd ever seen and I got the feeling that whatever was going on with my perpetually confused blue faery, there was a secret or two that she wasn't letting go of. Not now at least.

"The minkies didn't speak to Garbage?"

A long deep sigh. "Noes. Not yets. Buts is okay!" She smiled, kissed my cheek, and zipped off to join her friends.

"That was interesting." Alric watched Crusty join the rest. "Once we're on our way, maybe check with Derry and see what she knows."

I wasn't able to ask why we couldn't ask Derry now as Gailen turned to introduce us to villagers as we passed through.

Rialone wasn't a large village, but the buildings looked

old and solid and there was a feeling of permanence to them. Then I saw two huge buildings at the far edge of the village. As we moved closer, I had to fight to not run to them. Both had two sides that couldn't be seen at first—one our size and one the size used by Ancients in dragon form.

Those two were Ancient homes.

I pulled on Alric's sleeve and pointed. There was no way I was leaving Rialone without finding out about those two houses—and who used to live there. The houses appeared well preserved, but not currently lived in.

"They had Ancients here? Why only two?" He kept his voice down as we drifted a bit behind the rest. Gailen was giving brief histories of everything we passed— aside from those two houses.

"My people preferred living mostly with our kind. Either there were two living separate from our people for some reason, or this was once an Ancient village and those are the only two left." In my excitement, I spoke a bit too loudly, and Gailen turned around.

"You know of the Ancients?" He smiled. "We had two who lived here at the founding of Rialone thousands of years ago. They promised to return, so we keep their homes safe. Few even know they existed."

I smiled and let out a quick breath. He hadn't heard the 'my people' part. I was glad these people were friends with the faeries and seemed to be fine, but no one else needed to know what I was.

"Yes, I'm a digger up north. There are ruins of them there. I recognize the split homes from a few tattered texts." I was pretty sure I didn't look like I was about to race to them. "Do you have any stories of who they were? Did they live here full time?"

"I believe our historian can answer all of those questions and more. Plus, he can give a tour to any who wants one. After we get you settled." Gailen nodded to three elves standing near a clump of buildings. There appeared to be a near equal number of elves and humans, but no one else.

Aside from a mass of faeries heading our way.

"I'll send them back when we're done!" Derry yelled as she and our faeries flew out to join the new mob. I didn't see the small gray cat faery in the group, but the queen might have moved on to another place.

"We'd love to meet your historian and tour the homes," Alric said when I failed to respond.

"Excellent. There's a stable for your horses and the guest homes are right there. Again, sorry about panicking when you appeared." Gailen flashed a smile and then left us to sort things out.

The horses were extremely happy to be warm, dry, rubbed down, and with food at the ready. They, at least, were grateful for the stop. I flung my packs into one of the basic bedrooms and turned to race back out.

"Might as well wait; you know everyone is going to want to go." Alric stopped me as he put down his pack as opposed to flinging it.

"I want to go before my body realizes how tired it should be." I sighed and went to the common room to sit. I'd wait up to a point, then I was finding that historian.

"I doubt there's much information after all this time." Alric forced a smile when I glared at him. "Maybe I'm wrong. You did find things in your family's vacation cabin."

Covey, Foxy, and Siabiane then joined us. Covey was down a layer or two in her clothing pile and didn't look any worse for wear.

"Who attacked this village? I saw a few signs of fighting, but not much." Covey sat next to me.

"That's a good question, and I noticed that as well." Alric turned to Siabiane as she and Foxy sat. "How heavy is the magic protection around this place?" He was a powerful magic user but Siabiane was far beyond that.

"Good spotting. There are layers upon layers here that are far beyond most magic users; even I can't tell much more beyond the fact they are there. I would love to have a chance to explore this place, but I realize that isn't an option right now. With the defenses they have, no one should have gotten through. We need to get a basic understanding of what happened and who was behind it before we leave."

Lorcan, Mathilda, and Padraig were in a serious conversation as they came in from the second guesthouse.

"Does anyone else feel an overwhelming urge to leave this place?" Padraig frowned. "Actually, it's gone now, but all three of us felt it in the other house."

I shook my head. "No? In fact, I feel oddly at home here." I hadn't thought about it or even noticed until Padraig pointed it out, but it felt comforting here.

All the magic users peered at me closely, but didn't say anything.

"I hate it when you guys do that. It's not a magic thing; I'm not going to risk Alric and me by casting a spell. It feels…homey."

"When did that feeling begin?" Lorcan leaned closer.

"I don't know. When we got here?" I shrugged my head. "When I saw the Ancient homes? But I didn't notice it until you said something about feeling the opposite. I think I need to see those two places and find out who lived here."

Covey shook her head. "I think this is more than simply seeing the homes of your lost people. I'm not a magic user, but I'm feeling it too. Not a threat, just an urge to move on."

"I think we need to stay open to this magic, and we should speak to this historian."

I was on my feet and almost to the door before Lorcan finished speaking. I wasn't sure what everyone else felt, but I wanted answers about my people.

The historian was a wizened elf who appeared older than Lorcan. He gave a deep bow, took both Siabiane and Mathilda's hands, and smiled. "I am honored to see two of our sisters return. I am Jae, the historian of Rialone. I will be pleased to tell you what I can of our missing Ancients."

I knew there were two types of elves, the Alioth in the south, which was what Siabiane and Mathilda were, and the Mcallini of the north, which included Lorcan, Padraig, and Alric. But even after the past few years of being with all of them, I still couldn't tell the two types apart.

Obviously, the elves themselves could.

"Thank you, Jae. Taryn studied the Ancients and will probably have many questions." Siabiane gave a gentle smile.

That was a good way to explain why I was going to be extra nosy to an outsider.

Jae smiled at me as we walked toward the Ancient houses. "I will gladly help such a scholar. These two homes were built by a pair of Ancient brothers from the northern continent. There was a war brewing long ago up there and they were gathering reinforcements for a fierce battle. They helped prepare the village where they could and I believe you are feeling the effects of their shielding. It's not as strong as it was long ago, and you'll feel a mild discomfort. But before they left, they wanted to make sure we were safe. They feared it wouldn't be long before the war came to the south."

I froze when he said, 'brothers'. It might not be them,

but... "What were their names?" My throat was so tight I was amazed that the words came out.

"We recorded their full Ancient names, but they are long and hard to pronounce." Jae smiled. "They allowed us to call them Griff and Elgar. The stories tell of the times they helped this village when it was new. They would come and go, but after a few years they left to prepare for the final battle in the north." His smile fell. "They never returned. Since you are here, I presume the world outside our land did not fall?"

I'd been hoping for my brothers' names but didn't believe that I'd hear them. The world around me spun as I grinned foolishly. Then I collapsed.

CHAPTER THIRTY-FIVE

TINY HANDS PATTING MY CHEEK told me the faeries were back. But my eyes were sluggish in responding and I couldn't lift my eyelids.

"Wake up, Taryn," Alric's voice sounded far away. Did I change into a faery? But the hands didn't feel like they were the same size as me. I tried and failed again to open my eyes.

"Everyone needs to move back. Yes, this is fascinating, but only Jae and Taryn's friends should be here. We'll tell everyone about this at tonight's council." That was Gailen. Talking about me.

I tried to reach up to my eyes, but my movements there were sluggish too. I finally forced my eyes to open.

It wasn't the faeries who were tapping my face, but Alric. I'd changed into my dragon self in an unknown village in front of strangers.

Not a good thing.

"What happened?" Yup. Mouth was as sluggish as the rest, and even those two words were garbled. It was a good thing we were in hopefully friendly territory because if I was attacked right now, I'd lose. Against a snail.

"We don't know. Jae said the names of the Ancients who used to live here and you collapsed." Mathilda was almost standing on Alric and the concern on her face wasn't a good sign.

I didn't want anyone else to know who and what I was, and here I'd exposed myself to an entire village.

"No way we could make them think this was a trick?"

Jae hovered into my range of sight but stayed behind my friends. "I'm sorry, but that wouldn't work. Too many people saw you, and our village, better than most, knows what you are. Did you know Griff and Elgar? Are you that old? Have the Ancients returned?"

I looked around at my friends. There wasn't going to be a good way out of this, so I might as well go for the truth. "They were my brothers. And no, my people are gone. I'm the only one left. It's a long story." I'd been trying to hold my head up, but let it drop.

Jae practically drooled until Mathilda stepped in front of him.

"One that we can't share with anyone right now. Taryn's true nature can't go outside of your village. War has returned, as seen by the attack on your village. We'll share what we can, and promise to come back here after the war is over."

I must have looked worse than I felt as Jae watched me, then nodded in agreement. "Can she change back? Knowing what she is and seeing what she is are two different things."

Mathilda and Alric turned to me. Along with most of my friends.

"I'd like to, but I can't move and my head hurts too much to focus on changing back. I have no idea what changed me to start with."

War cries came from the far end of town and soon my faeries and Derry were racing toward us.

"Oh noes!" Crusty zipped forward and flew over me with a worried face. "This noes goods."

"I agree," Derry said as she followed Crusty's trail. The

rest of the faeries held back under Garbage's command. "How did this happen?" She hovered over my face with her hands on her hips.

"You can't think that I did this on purpose? I can't move."

Derry narrowed her eyes and frowned. "Crusty, touch Taryn on the nose."

I had no idea behind the strange order, but Crusty did it.

"Boop!" She laughed as she repeatedly bopped the end of my dragon nose with her hands.

Derry's scowl faded and she rubbed her hands together rapidly. "Okay, everyone who is not a faery take ten big steps back."

Jae and all of my friends, including Alric, obeyed the tiny gray-haired faery. I would have as well if I could move.

"Better." Derry waved for the faeries to come forward. "Ladies, on my count, dive, and touch. No bruises." The last bit seemed to be directed at Garbage, but it was hard to tell.

Before I could voice any concern, the faeries dove on me at once and it felt like ants were patting me down. I shrunk, and my strength came back. I kept shrinking until I was the same size as Crusty, but she scowled and tapped my face. With a jolt, I suddenly was human-sized.

"Am I human?" I held up my hand, and it looked human to me. I'd gone from human to dragon to faery and back to human. I was grateful that the Xoti hadn't been in the rotation. There hadn't been time to discuss that disturbing change with any of the other magic users—but I hoped it had been a one-time thing.

Alric and Mathilda helped me up as Jae watched with his jaw hanging low.

"You look like you," Mathilda said and turned to Jae

and the villagers trying to watch without being caught from a distance. "Nothing to see here. But we need to investigate the Ancient houses."

They both pulled me along as we all but ran toward the two split-side buildings.

Derry and Garbage kept the villagers back by pretending to engage in an elaborate game with the rest of the faeries between them and my brothers' houses.

Or they could be actually playing a game. Derry and Garbage aside, the faeries weren't known for being terribly focused.

The designs of both homes were close enough to my family's vacation cabin that even if I didn't know they were built by my brothers, I might have suspected. I looked around inside the first one. Jae tried to tell me things about it, but I wasn't paying attention. I felt *them*.

Or him. This side had been Elgar's.

I laughed and both Mathilda and Alric—who had remained on either side of me—appeared ready to carry me out.

Or spell me.

I waved my hands at them. "No, sorry, I'm fine. My parents always complained about my brothers fighting when we were younger. Guess they took care of it here. There's no trace of Griff in this house. It belonged to Elgar."

Jae's eyes were huge as he grabbed the stylus and a bunch of paper he'd brought and started writing. "You can tell that? Our stories said that while the two Ancient brothers loved and supported each other when they were here, they couldn't live together."

"Griff was a serious slob. Elgar was extremely neat. I'm happy they sorted it out. I'd like to go through both houses alone if no one minds. Then I want to hear everything about my brothers."

Jae settled down but nodded excitedly. "I can do better.

Copies of their history, that we knew, were made. I hold one as the historian. But the Ancients wanted copies for those who would come after them. I say who receives one. I would be honored for you to have one when you leave."

"Thank you, that will mean a lot." I wanted him to get it now, but I wanted to go through the houses alone first. These might have been the last places anywhere, not only in the southern lands, that my brothers had been seen.

Mathilda and Siabiane escorted everyone, even Alric, out. The faeries were still entertaining the villagers from what I heard, so within moments it was just me.

And faint feelings of Elgar.

Elgar was the eldest and more somber than Griff. But he indulged his little sister when we got older. I was a lot younger than even Griff, so I knew I was a pest to them as a kid. I walked through the dragon-sized side, slowly soaking in the faint feelings of my brother. Even though I'd accidentally sent away all of my people twenty-five hundred years ago, it had only been twenty or so years for me since I'd last seen my brothers. The more I remembered them, the more I missed them.

There were books and scrolls, but aside from running my fingers along them, I didn't move them. Many were copies of the ones in our home and also in the vacation cabin. But these were more worn and I felt Elgar's presence on each one. They would remain safe here.

The remainder of the house, both sides, had faint feelings of him, but the books and the library were the strongest.

I walked out the front door and waved to my waiting friends so that they could go into Elgar's as I walked to Griff's place.

The laugh that hit me when I came inside startled me. It also brought images of my second brother that I'd forgotten. Griff was loud and boisterous, and once I was old enough to tease, he loved having a younger sister. His place was far more chaotic, although I knew that centuries of curators had cleaned things up somewhat.

The books and scrolls here were neatly spread about, but still far more organized than he would have left them. I was about to leave after walking through the entire place when I saw a small journal. Even though it was on the dragon-sized side of the house, it was a human-sized journal. There was even a long dried-out quill next to the open pages.

I picked it up and started sobbing as soon as I read the words on the final entry.

"Elgar and I have done what we can to protect the south and gather our people for the war in the north. We were notified that our parents were killed weeks ago and Taryn stands alone. We leave to save her and fight this war, although I fear this final battle will not end well. Our people are still too far outnumbered and allies have been slow in coming. If you read this, let Taryn know that we love her."

My sobs grew worse. Our parents had been lured into a fatal trap over the ocean by agents of the Paili, including Edana. The news traveled slowly to Elgar and Griff, probably due to the fighting. Left without my parents or my brothers and lost in grief, I created the staff.

I did end the war. But all of my people, including the brothers I feared at the time were already dead, were lost in time.

"Is okays." Crusty had been so silent flying in that I hadn't noticed her. Or Derry, Garbage, Leaf, and the rest of the faeries all hovering outside the open door.

I dropped to the couch and sobbed harder—after waving for the rest of the faeries to come inside.

Soon I was covered in faeries all cooing at me. Except

Derry. She fluttered in front of me with a look of such profound sadness that it stabbed my heart.

I took a few deep breaths, then nodded to her. "What?"

"I was the one tasked with telling your brothers of your parents' deaths. I hadn't been certain you were the one until now, it was long ago, even for us. Myself and my chimera escorts were captured on the way down here by syclarion enforcers and it took too long to get free. I am truly sorry."

I gave a small smile. "It probably wouldn't have changed the outcome. You might or might not have known, but I'm the one who lost the rest of my people. I was so adrift and in pain that I'm not even certain having Griff and Elgar with me would have changed my actions." Saying the words made me certain. I didn't know that anything could have stopped me after my parents were lost.

I wiped away my tears and gently closed the journal. I'd ask Jae about one from Elgar, but he might have taken it with him when they left. I was keeping this one.

Tucking the journal into my vest, I looked around the house. Like Elgar's, Griff's belongings would be safer here. But if we survived the coming war, I'd come back.

"Okay girls, let's go see what Jae can tell us." I left Griff's house.

Alric and Padraig were discussing something as they came out of Elgar's house and saw me coming out of Griff's house. I motioned for them to come over.

"I'm taking this journal, it was Griff's." I briefly showed it to them then tucked it away again.

Alric said nothing as he walked to me and held me tight. I fought it at first, but I ended up sobbing against his chest.

"Sorry." I finally pulled back as the rest of our friends came out of Elgar's place.

Alric gently wiped away my tears. "This would be an emotional hit for anyone. Cry any time you need to."

"Thank you. It wasn't all sad, it was amazing feeling them again. I didn't even remember that I had brothers until a few months ago, and now it's flooding back." A laugh hit. "They were brats growing up. But so was I."

Bunky and Irving had been staying on patrol around the edge of the village, along with Welsy, Delsy, Flower, and the other eight brownies, but the two of them flew over, and Bunky dove right for me.

I laughed and hugged him. In my memories of my brothers, I remembered more about Bunky as well. "Thank you for always taking my side in our fights." Unlike before, I could now control the images that came from Bunky when I touched him. I let a wave of them flow over me.

"Okay, these were definitely my brothers' homes, and I want to take everything with me," I paused when I heard the collective intakes of breath around me. I doubted the entire faery kingdom had enough little black bags to move all of it. "But I know that won't work. Is there any way we can strengthen the protections my brothers left around the village and their homes before we leave?" It was a big ask—I couldn't help. Hopefully, Cwin's fellow siramage could fix my magic, but we still had to climb another mountain and find him.

"I think we can. And I will make sure we come back after this battle is won." Padraig bowed to Jae and again looked like what I'd imagined the elven kings of old to be like.

"Thank you." Jae smiled but kept looking at me as if he was trying to memorize every aspect. "I wish you could stay." He looked to everyone else. "All of you. But I know you are on a mission, as were your brothers. I'll get you their histories, and then I believe there is a massive village dinner being prepared for all of you. We would like to hear of the world beyond our mountains."

"That we can do, especially if you're willing to feed this hungry bunch." Padraig even sounded royal now as he took Jae's arm. "The others can get ready, but I can help you set up."

I shared a glance with Alric. Padraig hadn't said he suspected anything about Jae or the villagers, but there was a reason he wanted to stay close to him. The same brief looks passed to Lorcan, Mathilda, and Siabiane. Cwin openly scowled until she caught herself.

Foxy was oblivious but nodded. "Aye, I could use a bath before being in tight quarters."

Padraig nodded and left with Jae. Derry and Garbage circled the faeries overhead, then took off, and the rest of us went back to the guest houses.

Bunky and Irving remained near me, but neither said anything until we were almost at the door.

Bunky's gronks were soft, but he told me to be happy and careful. Memories could be a trap.

Interesting, considering that his people were created by my people to store memories. I nodded and he and Irving left for their patrols.

CHAPTER THIRTY-SIX

I'D EXPECTED TO FIND OUT more about my brothers after the evening's dinner when everyone gathered in a huge cavern. But mostly it was a history of the village. And my brothers' participation in that. I was fine about it once Jae handed me the history book my brothers put together and two massive tomes that were copies of the villagers' collected memories of my brothers.

After my reaction in Griff's house, I decided that it might be better if I read about them in private, rather than hearing about them in a group.

The village had been created and hidden long ago, in part, at the urging of my brothers. The war with the syclarions in the north was a long time brewing, but I now remembered my parents and brothers having serious late-night discussions.

After my bedtime.

Of course, I would sneak out anyway. But the discussions were dull and way over my head. And years before my brothers left and my parents were killed.

I'd ended a war that had been building since I was a kid but wasn't aware of. For the first time since I'd learned the truth of what I'd done twenty-five hundred years ago, I felt a brief flash of almost acceptance.

I knew the pain and loss I felt when I used the staff.

I also knew that I'd ended a war that could have swallowed the entire world.

Lost in my thoughts, I didn't hear my name called until Alric touched my shoulder. The faeries had been up front showing off but were now sitting politely off to the side and Jae was looking at me pointedly.

"He's introducing you." Alric gave me a nudge. "Just say who you are, where you're from, that sort of stuff. I'm pretty certain most of the villagers know what you are." He grinned, kissed me, and gave me another nudge.

I dropped the books into his lap and then went to the front of the cavern.

The village appeared small from our approach and brief time walking around. But there were close to two thousand folks in this massive cavern.

I introduced myself, ignored the people who called for me to transform, and answered basic questions.

Jae smiled, but then began twitching and foaming at the mouth.

Before the villagers could react, a wall of faeries rose to block the stage. Padraig, Alric, Mathilda, and Siabiane all ran past the faeries and surrounded Jae.

Lorcan and Cwin stood outside the wall of faeries.

Siabiane motioned for me to move away from Jae. I would, but there was no way I was leaving the others to face this. Something was extremely wrong with him.

Jae dropped to the floor but then rose and pushed my friends back with a spell. "No. She has come, she is mine. I am the spirit of the Ancients."

"The what of the who now?" I stuck my head through the curtain of faeries to the rest of the cave. The majority of the villagers were still there, but Gailen was helping the faeries reinforce their staying back. "Hey, do your people have a history of possession? Specifically, by something claiming to be the spirit of the Ancients?"

"It's a myth." Gailen's face paled. "In times of danger, the spirit of the Ancients would save us. They've never appeared though, even when we were attacked."

Lorcan and Cwin moved closer to him, with Covey and Foxy appearing ready to bust heads behind him. The villagers weren't armed, but there were far more of them than us.

"Is there a current danger? I can assure you, my friends will find out what is wrong with your historian, but it's not a spirit of the Ancients," Lorcan kept his voice steady, then looked to me, still peeking out of the faery mass. "Right, Taryn?" I felt a slight tinge of an agreement spell ride along on Lorcan's words aimed at the villagers.

"Yes. I am the last Ancient. Sister to the two you honor here. There is no spirit of my people in this place." I tried to sound solemn, but they already appeared to believe me.

Gailen nodded to a group of his archers. "We'll make sure everyone leaves, then come back to help you." He turned and his people began pushing the confused villagers out.

I pulled my head back behind the wall of faeries. The tableau hadn't changed, four of my friends were still circling Jae. His face fluctuated from angry to confused. "I am the spirit of the Ancients." He sounded far less sure about that now.

I'd had enough, especially after my emotional bit with Griff's journal. I stomped forward, clueless as to what I could do without magic, but knowing I needed to take care of this. Then my spirit sword popped into my hand. No sword belt this time, but it had been so sporadic recently that I wasn't certain that it hadn't finally realized that I wasn't an elf and had moved on.

I held the point of my sword at Jae. "You agree that I am an Ancient?"

"Yes, you are, but they…*we* are the last of the Ancients." The words had begun as Jae but then they switched over to the weird multi-voice of before.

"Look, you might not realize this, but I've had a rough week. Actually, a rough few years. I do not need another issue!" I took a step forward, almost touching his neck with my sword.

"I'd talk if I were you." Alric had spells in both hands, like the other three, but tilted his head toward me. "Whoever is there in Jae's body, you do not want to mess with a Xoti."

Jae's eyes went round and he tried to step away from me.

I hadn't wanted to change into the Xoti again, but the thing inside Jae hadn't been impressed at my being an Ancient. I focused on the fear I'd felt when Alric was attacked. The Xoti were almost as tall as me, so the size difference wasn't noticeable. But the vision was different. I tilted my head, then clacked my sharp teeth at Jae.

I saw two images. Xoti were myths, but seeing the true essence of someone was part of what they did. If they'd been real.

Jae was there in faded colors of what my normal eyes could see. Then there was a dark gray shadow shape, also an elf, hovering inside Jae somehow.

Rhyfel had been quiet as of late, and he was still recovering, but he crackled loudly as the dark gray shape emitted a similar blue spark.

I grabbed Rhyfel and blocked the blue arc with his green one. Whatever the shadow elf facing us was, he wasn't actually there, and his blade had less power. I knew who it was now; the elf who'd attacked Irving in the battle of Yosi and stolen the canfydd crown from Irving.

He and his Robukian blade were much stronger the

last time we fought. But because he wasn't actually here didn't mean he couldn't cause damage. I felt a jolt of pain go through the hand I held Rhyfel with. Rhyfel paused, then shot back a much stronger green arc that made the shadow elf scream.

"You have to give me the stones. Or I will destroy this place!"

From the looks on my friends' faces, they heard him as well, but unlike me, they might not have a clue as to what stones he was talking about.

I was sure he was looking for Crusty's jewels—the ones he needed to control the canfydd crown. I'd managed to use the cursed thing without them, but I was an exception. Crusty spent a lot of time in her own world, but she'd been certain that anyone else would need her gems to control the crown.

"The stones were lost. Leave now." I flexed my elongated Xoti fingers over the hilts of my weapons. Xoti were pretty nasty looking. "I will eat your soul." Wasn't sure if Xoti did that or not, but it sounded good.

At that moment, Cwin and Lorcan came through the faery wall and hit Jae with a barrage of spells. I stepped back, but the other magic users held on to Jae tightly.

The shadow elf appeared solid; his arm raised to send a spell. With a wild leap, Cwin flung herself at him, now that he was no longer a shadow. I expected magic and maybe there was some, but she was also punching him. A lot.

"Go back to your master and tell him this is from me!" She gave rapid blows to his face and then the elf vanished.

"That was refreshing." Cwin grinned and scrabbled to her feet before anyone could help her up.

Jae slumped to the floor and looked up with bleary eyes. "That wasn't me. I would never...no."

Gailen came through the faery wall and dropped

down in front of Jae. "How long ago did you begin feeling odd?"

Jae took a shaking breath. "During the fight. I didn't think anything of it, sometimes an odd bit of gravy can cause strange feelings. And we were defending the village. But my thoughts have been growing darker the past two days." He looked up to all of us. "I am so sorry. It was me talking to you all before. But that other elf was there too."

"Were you able to sense anything from him?" Padraig asked in his most soothing voice.

Padraig must have realized something was wrong when he escorted Jae earlier.

Jae paused, looking like an exhausted old man for a moment, then he shook his head. "I might have? But nothing I remember. The past few days are fading."

Before any of us could do anything, Garbage, Leaf, Crusty, and five more faeries swooped down and landed on Jae.

He did the smart thing and froze. But the girls crooned a low song. Derry and the rest of the faery mob flew closer, also singing. But they didn't land on Jae.

Jae's eyes widened and he got to his feet, with the faeries still on him. "Yes! Thank you, lovely faeries. I know his name, Psycian, he's a leader of the Dark. He's looking for a key." He frowned. "But not a key. He thinks Taryn has it."

I nodded. The gems weren't a key, but they would act like one to make the crown work.

"And some rocks. He's working for someone, but wants it all for himself." Jae's eyes rolled back and he stumbled, but Padraig caught him. Jae came back with a sharp smile. "I know his magic now. I can block him from everyone in this village. And all of you. But I will need to anchor the spell to one of you when you leave. Or perhaps two."

Cwin grinned. "I'll be one. I felt part of his master when I beat him up. Tygathis. First lieutenant to the empress, and a known enemy to the siramages. Also, a member of the Dark. But there was no feeling of loyalty to the empress in what I sensed."

"So Tygathis and this elf are working toward betraying her?" Covey shared Cwin's grin. "We can use that. I thought she'd unified her fighting crews?"

"Apparently not." Siabiane smiled. "And yes, I'd say we could use this. Is there anything else that you recall?"

Jae paused then shook his head. "No. But if anything comes back, I'll find a way to contact you."

"Thems." Garbage pointed to the new faeries who came in with Derry earlier. "Theys stays heres."

"Thank you. And thank your queen. Again. Not many of my people saw her or knew who she was during the fight, but I knew." Jae sighed. "I was hoping that your arrival was a good sign. But I fear our hiding and protections won't keep this place safe anymore."

Padraig and Lorcan each took one of Jae's arms as he was standing, but still unsteady.

"We have some ideas for that, along with the faeries who will be protecting you. They'll find us if things go wrong. Let's go somewhere private and discuss this further." Lorcan's smile wasn't as convincing as I'd seen before.

Padraig nodded for Gailen to join them. I wasn't sure who the true leader of this place was, they didn't seem to have one, but those two were close to it.

Cwin watched them go, then spun to the rest of us with a frown as we left the cavern. "It's too late to leave tonight, but I think we should be ready to ride at dawn. The path through this valley is relatively flat, but when we hit the mountain, we'll have to walk the horses again. Oh, no." She pointed to the far side of the village, toward the next mountain. Night had fallen, but a thin line of smoke was visible drifting toward the heavens from the mountain.

"What's that? It's glowing?" Foxy squinted at the weird smoke.

"That's a mage fire. Fardoragh is calling for help. This changes things. I'd leave now, but it's not safe and most likely a trap." Cwin sounded concerned, but also resolute.

Alric watched the thin, glowing line of smoke. "I've never seen a fire create that. Is it safe for us to go up?"

"You wouldn't have. Only a siramage can create them. They also reach a deeper level, beyond sight. Any of my fellow siramages would have felt it, even if they're not close enough to see it. As for safety? Fardoragh has the strongest powers in daylight." She shrugged. "We all have slightly different strengths. The fire is a call, but also a warning. We wait until daylight, then I'm going to do something I don't want to. Use a fada path to get us directly to the top of his mountain." She looked around and then nodded to herself. "Let's sleep while we can. Lorcan and Padraig will join us when they're through."

Even the faeries were subdued as we went to the guest houses. Rather, they were until they'd escorted us inside.

"Yous stays. Others patrolling. We's have things." Garbage flew an inch away from my face and waved her tiny finger at me. "Noes goes!"

Obviously, she'd decided that out of our bunch, I was the flight risk. Fatigue from our extended hike down that weird passageway was hitting me hard now, I didn't want to do anything but fall into bed.

"Noes leaves." Garbage leaned even closer. "*Stays.*"

"I'm not going anywhere, I promise. But all of you keep safe out there." I didn't have a real sense of foreboding, and the faeries were extremely tough, but too many things had happened in a short time. I felt jumpy and on edge. As well as exhausted.

Garbage softened, darted forward, and kissed my cheek. "Yous too." Then she whistled loudly and led the rest of the faeries out.

I'd seen Irving and Bunky flying low over the village on patrol and Siabiane said Welsy, Delsy, and Flower's brownie troop were doing the same around the edges of the village.

"Is there anything we need to do to be ready for tomorrow?" Siabiane asked.

Foxy nodded as he secured the door, pulled up a seat, and then sat next to it with his giant club.

"Not really, and don't worry, once Padraig and Lorcan are back, we'll have enough spells on both houses to keep out an army. When we leave, the spells will circle the village." Cwin turned to me. "I have a feeling that your brothers wanted to protect this place for many reasons. We don't have time to find out what they are now, but we can make sure the village remains safe. The fact that their spells lasted over two thousand years is extremely impressive."

I hadn't thought about that, but it was. "They were good. Thank you for helping to protect their legacy." I wanted to go to bed, but everyone else was waiting for Padraig and Lorcan, and Mathilda and Siabiane were putting together tea and toast. Luckily it wasn't long before they came in.

Foxy made sure it was them and let them in. He wasn't violent, but with everything going on he was hanging on to his club more and more. He still had his large sword, but I figured he felt more at ease with the club. It was similar to the one he kept behind the bar at the Shimmering Dewdrop.

"Good idea, Foxy. But I think once the full spells on this house are finished, we'll be fine," Lorcan said. "Tomorrow will be long; we all need sleep."

"About that." Cwin quickly brought Lorcan and Padraig up to speed about the attack on her fellow siramage.

"We didn't see any strange smoke coming back from clearing Jae." Padraig looked ready to go back out.

"You wouldn't. He was reaching out to the siramages. It stopped after all of us were aware." Cwin paced. "I fear he might not be the only one of us under attack."

"Can you check on them?" I'd never heard of siramages before meeting Cwin, but she'd said there weren't many of them.

"I could have before Fardoragh sent his call. When one of us sends that, we automatically lock down any communication. If he, or others, have been compromised, any mental or magical contact between us could lead to more of us being attacked. I only felt his warning, but others could have been hit also." Usually, I forgot that Cwin was a grimarian, but she was angry enough to make me take a step back now. I trusted her, but my past luck with grimarians wasn't good.

Padraig got up. "Tomorrow will be long, even if we use the dorchadais path. I think we need to get rest." He didn't sound happy when he mentioned Cwin's path. The chawsia paths were dangerous, but the an' cosán fada an dorchadais paths were a lot worse.

Cwin set up a few more layers of spells around the guest house and went to her room.

The rest of us left as well, even Foxy finally admitted he needed sleep. He kept his club with him though.

Alric waited until we were standing in our room, then came up and rubbed my arms. "How are you doing? I don't remember a lot about you turning Xoti before, but it was impressive this time. I'm not even sure if they're real." He paused. "Can you become anything now?" There was a little fear in his eyes, something I could count on my hand how many times I'd seen before.

I wanted to tell him no, but lying wasn't an option at this point. The fact that no one else had questioned me about it was only a matter of time. "I don't know. I thought the Xoti was a one-time, panic-mode thing. But it was too easy to pull up when we were facing that Dark elf inside Jae." Keeping my freaking out about this new change away from everyone was going to be fun.

Although, maybe if it scared me too much, I wouldn't be able to change into other things. I sighed. Not with my luck.

"What was the sigh for?"

"Wishful thinking. What if I can't control things and I start flipping into different shapes? What if this becomes like Dragon Day again? I didn't have control."

Alric kissed me to stop the words. That was fine by me and I shoved my panic aside. There were too many things to be frightened about—random shapeshifting was going to have to wait its turn.

We broke apart and he caressed the side of my face. "Better? We'll sort this out, don't worry."

I smiled. "Better." Then another thought hit me. "A person can't *become* a changeling, right? You have to be born that way?" Changelings were more than a little disturbing. Their base self was a blank form and they took on the image of their target person. One had copied Alric so well up in Beccia that I hadn't noticed— even after speaking with it in Covey's kitchen.

"You're not a changeling." He gave a gentle smile. "Yes, they are born that way and I'm pretty certain that your parents would have noticed at the time."

"Okay. I feel better. Or I would if I knew why this was happening to me. I'm still working on remembering my people and my former life, but I don't recall anyone changing into anything beyond dragon or human. The faery bit was weird, but I convinced myself it was something Derry did. Or helped with." I sighed when I saw his face. "Wishful thinking?"

Alric laughed. "I'm afraid so. You're unique among your people. There's no way to know what happened to you when you flung yourself into the future."

"Fine. Let's get to bed, I have a bad feeling that Cwin's going to have us out of here as soon as the sun comes up."

CHAPTER THIRTY-SEVEN

—◆—

SOMETIMES I HATED BEING RIGHT.

Cwin sent the faeries, tiny traitors, to wake everyone up when the night was just thinking of fleeing the sky. We weren't leaving now, but she wanted to ensure we were awake, fed, and ready to fight when we went through her an' cosán fada an dorchadais path.

I grumbled my way out of bed. As I got ready and checked everything in the room, Alric woke up bright, alert, and ignored my constant grumbling. The faeries assigned to us this morning: Leaf, Dingle Bottom, Penqow, and Morning Glory spent the entire time zooming around the room and telling us to hurry.

If I had the energy to catch one of them, I would have squished them.

Not that it would have done any good.

We made our way to the main room and finished off basic travel breakfast food. More importantly, pots of tea so strong I could smell it from our room.

The only other one of our band who was a slow morning riser was Grillion. Without him here, it was me and a bunch of morning people.

Aside from the horses, everyone was in the front room. Including all the faeries who would travel with us, plus the ones who would remain here. Not Queen Mungoosey or Derry, though. Flower and his brownies were happily chatting as they got ready. The four constructs were sitting in a corner talking in their way—Welsy and Delsy used words and Bunky and Irving responded in gronks. None of them needed to eat, although Irving did like a tasty bit of gold from time to time.

Cwin was pacing, muttering in a few different languages, and swearing to herself. Everyone stayed away from her and I figured that was a good idea. Part of me wanted to ask her if there was a chance that her friend Fardoragh might still be able to fix this magic issue I had, but her nerves were clearly shot.

Fixing me had been the original reason for visiting him, but now it was a rescue. Considering how powerful Cwin was, it was too scary to think about who or what could take down someone stronger than her.

Alric sat next to me and dropped his voice when he noticed me watching Cwin.

"She's nervous about using the an' cosán fada an dorchadais path, but her friend might be in serious trouble."

"Can you, Padraig, Mathilda, Siabiane, and Lorcan help cast it?" I knew I couldn't, but the five of them had some serious magic.

"I know I can't, not without a few years of training. Padraig and the others are discussing it, but with this short notice and the high stakes, it probably wouldn't be a great idea. Lorcan would be the best to try it, and he doesn't feel ready."

"So, we just charge to the top of the mountain, rescue this siramage, and hope he can fix me?" Yup, needed more tea; the whine in my voice sounded pathetic even to me.

"As far as I can tell, that's the plan."

Cwin faced the group. "This is as ready as I'm getting. Gailen suggested a hidden clearing in a grove right outside of the village that would be best to leave from. I'd like to trust these villagers, but Jae being compromised gives me pause. We don't have time to check all of them."

Foxy pulled back the curtain. "It still being dark. How long does this path take?" He'd missed the first time she used one since he'd been kidnapped and turned to stone at the time.

"Good point." Cwin glared at the dark window as if by sheer force she could make the sun rise faster. "Everyone finish your food, then head for the stables, load up your horses, and join me in the clearing. The fada path won't take long at all—as long as there are no complications." She hoisted her pack and left for the stables.

Mathilda watched her go, then put her things away. "Siabiane and I will keep an eye on her. She's extremely upset."

Welsy, Delsy, Flower, and his brownies trooped out after them. Bunky and Irving flew to where the faeries were having tearful farewells. Then they all laughed hysterically.

We went to gather our horses. The horses were saddled and Gailen was waiting with them.

"I wanted to thank you again. We'll keep the village safe and the spells you've cast will help. But come back when you're able." He handed my reins to me. "It was an honor meeting someone from our past. Stay safe, Taryn." With a bow to all of us, he went back into the dark village.

The faeries that were remaining to protect the village split off and Garbage flew alongside me.

"Is Derry staying with us?" I loved my faeries, but it had been nice having one who I could actually talk to.

"Noes. She doings things. She comes when cans." She'd been laughing with her friends moments before but was now somber.

I watched her for a moment. "What's wrong?" Garbage, even more than the other faeries, was fearless. But something was bugging her.

"This nots goods. Bad things tryings to wins. Nots times for thats. Big fights *laters*." Her golden eyes widened and she covered her mouth. "Nopes, never mind."

Before I could say anything, or grab her, she flew up and back to the flock of faeries bringing up our rear. She'd let something slip, which was more than a little unusual.

I often wondered if the faeries knew more than they acted like they did, but there was no way to find out now. Maybe when Derry came back.

The clearing was past a few clumps of trees, but it looked fairly long. I was pretty sure that casting the spell for the chawsia path wasn't something I'd ever done when I was younger. I knew there was no way I'd even heard of the fada path. Or siramages.

Cwin, Mathilda, and Siabiane were discussing something intensely while their horses waited off to the side.

The faeries remained behind us on the way here, but they swooped forward now.

"We goes!"

"Zooms!"

"Fights!"

Garbage had been concerned about what was happening a few minutes ago, but none of them were now. I shook my head. Figuring out faery motivation was hard back when I thought my three were the only ones. And their biggest issue was declaring war against a family of squirrels.

Now that I knew they were far more complicated, it was impossible.

Cwin smiled as they flew up—she'd come to terms

with her issues as well. "Yes! Garbage, we will need all the flyers to lead the charge the moment the fada path is secured. Whoever attacked Fardoragh will be expecting someone to come to rescue him. Fly fast and high. Don't engage until I yell to. Just distract at first. Got it?"

"IS YES!" Garbage and the rest of the faeries shouted so many times that I turned around, waiting for the villagers to come running out with arrows drawn.

Mathilda simply held up her hand and the faeries settled down.

Aside from Crusty, who continued zipping about doing rolls in the air silently for a few moments after the rest stopped. She bowed to a nonexistent audience and flew down to my horse. "We goes nows."

I nodded as she settled herself on my horse's saddle. All the brownies, construct or not, climbed up the horses as well.

Cwin, Mathilda, and Siabiane walked to the end of the clearing. Padraig, Lorcan, and Alric took their horses to the back of the line. Covey, Foxy, and I all looked at each other and shrugged. We'd stay in the middle unless someone said otherwise.

Bunky and Irving remained with the bulk of the faeries.

My sword reappeared, with the sheath this time, so I buckled it on. I still wished I could control it like Padraig and Alric controlled theirs, but I was grateful it showed up.

Rhyfel cracked in what seemed to be a hello to the sword, but Crusty giggled.

"Hims ready, but wants the one that hurts hims first." She added something too fast for me to understand and I swore I heard Rhyfel say he understood.

"Mathilda and Siabiane will help me anchor the opening. Alric, Lorcan, and Padraig will secure the closing. Don't try to control anything, just treat it like a chawsia path. Taryn, no matter what you see or feel, do *not* access your magic." I nodded but she must not have believed me as she continued. "I believe that the being attacking Fardoragh is the one who sent the flinms after you. He will try to get you to use your magic. You can't. It's not only a risk to you and Alric; it could destroy us all."

That didn't make me feel better, but I tried to agree. Nope, nothing but a squeak came out when I opened my mouth.

"Excellent." Cwin nodded at my lack of voice, then set her fada path spell.

The chawsia paths took a more ornate setup, so I was shocked when Cwin uttered a few words and the dorchadais path appeared. The an' cosán fada an dorchadais, or fada, for relative shortness, was much more colorful than a chawsia path. And like the other time I'd been through one—it was raining inside it.

"Go quickly, the rain won't hit you." Cwin, Mathilda, and Siabiane led their horses through with the flyers zipping overhead and Foxy, Covey, and I bringing our horses after.

I frowned when I tried to say something calming to my horse and still no sound came out. Cwin spelled my voice to help keep me from using magic. Doing that would stop some spells, but I didn't use words for all of my magic.

The path was short and uneventful, but running out of it at the end wasn't.

An army faced us at the end of the path.

CHAPTER THIRTY-EIGHT

———◆———

THE FAERIES, ALONG WITH BUNKY and Irving, did what Cwin asked and zipped high over the mob facing us while yelling and screeching.

It got the attention of a few groups facing us, and the enemy archers fired arrows after the speeding faeries. Crusty remained on my horse but cheered for her friends and laughed as the arrows failed to come close to their marks.

Padraig and Alric were on their horses as they charged through the attackers, both swinging their spirit swords as they hit the enemy ranks. Lorcan rode behind them with a long pike that he clearly knew how to use. Cwin did some odd contortions and flung the closing fada path into the army as a blob of melting colors. I wasn't sure what it did, but the people hit by it collapsed.

Mathilda blasted the blob with a series of spells and the entire thing, people and path, vanished.

That was weird, but Mathilda didn't pause and joined Siabiane in following the lead of Padraig, Lorcan, and Alric.

Foxy and Covey nodded to each other—Covey was in full berserker mode now—and they charged forward as well. Foxy swung his club with abandon, but the attackers disappeared as soon as he got a single strike into them.

I held back a moment, unsure where to attack that might not get me killed, nor convince me to use my magic. There was something odd about the army facing us, and I'd grown wary of odd. The group of fighters seemed to be shrinking rapidly and I saw more of them blink out of existence the moment after my friends hit them. Regardless of what they were hit with.

"Waits good." Crusty watched the fighting like she was directing it.

The rest of the faeries, along with Bunky and Irving, swooped low and attacked just as Welsy and Delsy led the brownie brigade into the mess.

Rhyfel kept crackling but his green arcs were too far away from the army to hit anything.

I got off my horse, patted her to stay put, and ran forward. Crusty flew to my hair and hung on.

"This goods too!" She had her war stick out and was waving it around but gave no indication she was going to join her friends.

I raised Rhyfel as I saw that the group I was running toward had metal armor. Rhyfel loved metal.

His green arc of energy struck the fighter closest to us. I'd seen what happened when he did that before in fights, but I wasn't expecting what happened this time. The arc jumped from the person he struck, then bounced to every fighter wearing metal armor. As one, they froze, then vanished.

"Okay, that was definitely weird," I said the words, but no sound came out. I understood why Cwin cast the spell, but it was still annoying.

All around us, the army we faced continued to fight, but then vanished when hit.

Foxy continued to swing his massive club around, then frowned when every person he hit disappeared before he could get a good fight going.

"What is this? A trick?" Covey yelled as she sliced through two fighters who flickered and then disappeared. "I've never read of a spell that could do this."

"It's a spell, yes. But they can still kill you! Don't drop your guard!" Cwin yelled and I spun to see a full-sized giant stomping toward me. Rhyfel hit him with a solid green crackling arc at the same time the brownies used ropes to bring him down.

He didn't vanish as he crashed to the ground, so I ran forward and stabbed him with my sword. I felt it go through him, but then before I could remove it, his body vanished and I was holding my sword over nothing.

The entire army had disappeared by the time I looked around again, but the ground they'd been on was trampled. I waved to Cwin and patted my throat.

She nodded and waved her hand and I could speak again.

"Was this who attacked your friend?" I wasn't impressed. We'd been outnumbered fifty to one. Or more. My friends were good, but no one was that good. Aside from a few minor cuts, none of us were injured.

"No, this was Fardoragh's defense system. He's compromised or he would have been able to shut it off instead of simply modifying it; they normally wouldn't have given up so easily. However, I wasn't kidding when I said that any of those people could have killed us." Cwin looked into the surrounding trees. "Fardoragh would have made his defense higher than here where his cabin is. Although most of my fellow siramages left their mountaintops years ago, he preferred the solitude." She narrowed her eyes and looked closer at the trees above us. "I don't sense more of my people, only him."

I patted her arm; I knew she was afraid the rest of the siramages had already been captured or killed. "Maybe they haven't gotten here yet."

She clasped my hand and gave me a small smile. "Thank you. Now let's go rescue Fardoragh, find out who did this, and have him get that flinm spell off of you."

Cwin got onto her horse and took the lead, with Padraig and Siabiane right behind her. The rest of us, aside from Foxy, got on our horses as the faeries, constructs, and brownies returned and ran or flew alongside us.

Foxy didn't like riding his horse much, so he led him.

The woods grew thinner and the air grew cooler as we began a sharp ascent.

Cwin halted and raised her fist. She spoke, and the words drifted back to us softly. "Past here, we need to be silent. Everyone. If anything attacks, kill them as quietly as possible. Fardoragh has deeper defenses here." She didn't wait for responses, but slowly moved her horse forward.

Siabiane cast a spell and even the slight sounds of the horses' hooves and jangling from the harnesses and groans from the saddles vanished. The faeries flew lower but were as silent as the rest of us.

The trees thinned out and soon only large rocks and dirt surrounded us. It took away places for people to hide, but I also felt too exposed to being blown off the mountain.

Crusty switched from my hair back to my shoulder, and she leaned into my ear with a whisper so soft I was amazed it came from any faery. "Is okays. Protects." The words vanished and she patted my ear, then settled back on my shoulder.

The silence was almost too much when the sound of arrows cut through it. Alric raised a spell bubble over all of us and the arrows were deflected. I glanced back but he was fighting hard to keep the shield up.

I couldn't see where the arrows came from.

Cwin held up her hand, then motioned for Alric to

drop the spell bubble. "Run!" Her horse ran when the spell bubble fell.

Siabiane's silence spell was gone as we raced after Cwin. No more arrows, but there was the creepiest feeling that we weren't seeing what was really around us.

"Halt! All who enter this realm will die!" The voice was deep, dark, and sinister.

Cwin's laugh was not the result I expected. "Fardoragh! Damn you, drop your shields! *Fa litnam!*"

A pressure briefly surrounded us and I felt even more like I was going to be blown off the mountainside. Then the air around us rippled and the pressure dropped.

"Thank you for the password. I'm sorry I'm not here to greet you in person, but please enjoy your stay." The voice was still deep, but not as threatening.

Before I could ask what kind of spell Fardoragh created, a group of people armed with swords ran out from behind a suspicious grouping of boulders.

"These aren't illusions or part of a spell!" Cwin yelled as she cast a spell at the fighters. That did nothing but cause her to sway in her seat as it slammed back into her. "Don't use magic! They're protected!"

Even if I could use magic, there was no way I would have against people who could bounce it back into a siramage. I slid off my horse and charged forward with my sword and Rhyfel at the ready.

We couldn't use magic, but none of the attackers were using it either. They might not be magic users, but someone put a serious spell on them to magically shield them. I stopped two of them, and Rhyfel was already reaching out for the next when I heard an odd hooting.

A group of elven fighters came around the boulders. The hooting was coming from the feral dwollers they had on leashes.

Normal dwollers were scary, tall, pale, skeletal beings

with a nasty predilection for drinking blood. For the most part, they kept their kind under control, even killing those who had gone feral.

The ten feral dwollers who were fighting to get to us indicated not all the feral ones were under control or dead. I'd been surprised when the members of the Dark who attacked me in Notlianda had three of them—ones who all learned they couldn't fly. The hard way. But ten? Even Rhyfel's arcs seemed subdued when they appeared.

The faeries flew up and Garbage yelled orders to her troops to stay high but be ready to dive. If they were worried about the feral dwollers, they didn't act like it. Of course, the faeries wouldn't be large enough to even be a snack for them.

The elves holding the leashes released the dwollers but made no move to come forward themselves. They wanted to see what their pets could kill before they went after us.

Welsy, Delsy, and the rest of the brownies charged one of the feral dwollers and I winced. I was too far away to help them. The constructs would probably be safe—but the flesh and blood brownies were perfectly sized snacks for the dwollers.

But they held their own. The brownies remained in formation and attacked the feral dwoller before it realized they were a threat. Within moments the dwoller was dead.

The rest of us had a tougher time of it, magic would have helped, but whatever blocked it was still in place.

Foxy grinned and ran into the charging dwollers swinging his great club. I saw at least three of the monsters fly into the air after he hit them, and not get back up.

I ran toward them, but then Crusty began yelling and pulling my hair. The former leash-holding elves were coming forward, using some sneaky magic to distract us from their movements. I couldn't test the magic block myself, but none of my friends had cast spells. They also didn't seem to notice the Dark slowly coming closer.

"The Dark are coming!" I yelled, then ran toward the elves with Rhyfel shooting sparks. My spirit sword almost ended up killing me as it sang when I engaged the lead elf and it pulled me along for the ride. No idea what the song was, but weapons shouldn't sing.

Especially in battle.

I refrained from dropping it, but it was a close thing. I swung out to hit the much taller elf coming for me with a heavy, two-handed sword, and my spirit sword fried him in mid-swing. It was as if the song my sword was singing slammed into the Dark elf and toasted him like a burning twig.

"How?" I didn't have time to find out what happened before a dwoller turned around and charged me.

My sword went silent, but the faeries dropped down to help me take out the dwoller.

My friends were fighting around me when everything slowed down. Or it seemed to. My friends and the people we were fighting began to slip into slow motion—except me and the faeries.

I panicked, thinking that maybe I was casting some spell I didn't know about, but I didn't feel any magic coming from me, intended or not.

Then a minkie popped up in the middle of the frozen tableau. Everyone who could see a minkie saw them as a different shape—so I had no idea what the creatures actually looked like. But to me, they appeared as white weasel-looking animals, about a foot high on their back legs.

This one grinned and came over to me as if it wasn't in the middle of a bloody battle.

CHAPTER THIRTY-NINE

"HELLO." THE MINKIE'S GRIN GREW wider and everyone, including the faeries, froze completely. "You are on the right path. It's good that Cadhia's sword finally recognized you. Took longer than expected though."

My sword trilled part of a song in response.

"Who was Cadhia?" Not, possibly, the first question I should ask, but all of my friends and current enemies were frozen at the moment.

"Cadhia was a powerful elven sorcerer. He was thousands of years old when he fell due to the betrayal of the Dark during the Breaking." The minkie dropped his head. "He was a good friend also." He sighed and looked up. "His spirit sword vanished when he died. They're supposed to be passed on to another, but this one didn't. Once it began to sing and use its own magic, I knew you had fully been accepted as its holder."

Unlike Rhyfel, I didn't sense a consciousness in the sword, but it did feel alive. "Can all of the spirit swords use magic?" I'd never seen Padraig's or Alric's swords use magic, or sing, but it might have looked like magic coming from the two elves.

"No, sadly. This is the only one."

I looked down at Rhyfel and then the sword. "Does it have a name?"

The minkie's smile was back. "Not yet. It will tell you when it is ready or it will allow you to select one. Again, when it is ready. I stopped time to tell you of the importance of your sword. It fell before the first attack of the Dark, the empress is powerful, but the Dark make her so. Your sword will not stop until the Dark are destroyed. You need your magic back to keep it under control."

My sword sang again, but the tone was sour this time.

"You know it's true. And you also know that this isn't the time." The minkie walked around me slowly. "I can block that flinm spell until the siramage can remove it. Once you save him. He's holding on, but these are but a small group of the forces trying to destroy him." He clapped his tiny white paws together and a wave of warmth flowed over me. "This will last one full day. After the warmth is gone, if you're not cured, stop using magic. Keep an eye on her, Crusty Bucket." With a nod, the minkie vanished.

And Crusty fell off my shoulder.

I'd assumed that she'd been frozen like everyone else. She hadn't moved or said anything while the minkie had been here.

She sat on the ground for a moment, then jumped to her feet and flew up to hover in front of my face. "Minkie." She nodded solemnly and flew back to my shoulder.

Pretty much the faeries all forgot they'd seen a minkie the moment it vanished. But Crusty had mentioned seeing them before. And she wasn't surprised about it now.

No one seemed to know what the minkies were, where they came from, or what they were up to. Blocking the threat to my magic was one of the few direct actions one of them had taken. And somehow, I felt what the minkie had done, beyond the warmth. I hadn't noticed the flinms' spell even when I was being impacted by it. But I felt the blockage of it now.

There was a pop and everyone returned to normal speed. My sword sang out and blocked a Dark elf's strike to my head. I sent a push spell and the elf went flying high in the air and off the side of the mountain.

My friends were too busy to notice what I'd done, but Garbage came zipping over.

"Yous noes…wait." She tilted her head, peered at me closely, and narrowed her eyes at whatever she saw. "Yous okay nows. And sword different. We's talks laters." With a serious nod to Crusty, Garbage went back to join the fighting.

The dwollers stayed away from me now, but the Dark elves kept coming. I couldn't be certain, but it felt like my sword was calling to them.

That was another conversation I was going to need to have. I was honored that this sword had selected me, even if it had taken a while to be sure. But I didn't need something leading me into fights to avenge the death of its prior owner. Justified or not.

We fought off two more Dark elves, with the help of my push spell.

Unfortunately, Cwin had seen me fling the last Dark elf off the mountain.

She ran over and grabbed my arms. "Taryn! You can't…what happened?" She picked up on the same thing Garbage had.

"It's a long story. I'm not cured, but good for almost a day. I can explain once we're safe." I gave my best smile in hopes she'd drop it for now.

Cwin gave me another narrow-eyed look but nodded.

Alric and Covey came running over as the rest checked the feral dwollers and members of the Dark to make sure they were dead.

"What happened?" Alric sheathed his spirit sword but

didn't send it away. Mine took that moment to sing a snippet. "Did your sword just sing?" He looked around for any faeries, but Crusty remained quietly sitting on my shoulder.

"That's complicated and I'd prefer to get somewhere safe." I sheathed my sword and it remained silent. I hoped the appearing and disappearing act was done now. Asking my friends about Cadhia was also a wait-until-safe issue.

"They're all dead. Keep going?" Covey was still in berserker mode and her clawed hands kept twitching. She needed more bad people to kill.

Cwin shot me another concerned look, then turned to Covey and nodded. "Yes. Everyone lead your horses, but move out."

Welsy, Delsy, Flower, and their crew jogged up. They were roughed up but intact and saluted us. "Ready for further fighting!"

Siabiane joined us and smiled at the collected brownies. "You have all done extremely well. Let's rescue Cwin's friend." She and Mathilda followed Cwin, with the brownies jogging behind them.

The rest of us followed Cwin, Siabiane, and Mathilda. I knew that the ones attacking Fardoragh hadn't broken through to him yet, thanks to the minkie. But I was sure it wouldn't last.

"You cast spells." Alric walked alongside me, but it wasn't a question.

"Yes, but I was told I could." I kept my voice low. "It was a minkie." I knew I'd have to tell everyone about the minkie, and the situation with my sword, but I didn't want to until we were safe.

Alric's eyes went wide, and he nodded. "You can tell me later." He stepped a bit away as we walked and took his sword out of its sheath. "Do you feel that?"

I started to shake my head, and then my spirit sword

sang quietly, but it sounded angry. "Yes, I do. It's not good." My sword was practically jumping when I took it out. "You need to not do that," I whispered to the sword, but I knew Alric heard me. That he didn't say anything was nice, but I knew it wouldn't last.

Cwin, Mathilda, and Siabiane left their horses and spread out as a cabin came into view. It appeared normal, a thick swirl of smoke coming from a rock chimney, flowers in the windows, and no vicious killers in sight.

Everyone spread out, even the faeries, with Bunky and Irving holding back. Covey and Foxy stayed in the center. I was impressed that neither of them had charged forward. They both looked more than ready to start smashing heads.

"Is this part of Fardoragh's defenses?" Lorcan pitched his voice so low it drifted on a non-existent breeze.

Cwin's scowl was lost as her fur grew longer. "No. It's a trap. They already have him." Her eyes went red and she stomped forward. "Release him and you can have me. I'm the one you want, Tygathis. I know you're here; I can smell it." The last words were little more than a growl.

Alric and Padraig moved forward, but Lorcan shook them off. "No. Let her do this. I feel him too. Tygathis was at the Breaking." Lorcan usually appeared like a kindly grandfather elf—he didn't now. He'd lived through the Breaking and watched his world be destroyed. If his eyes turned red, I wouldn't have been surprised.

Siabiane and Mathilda were ready to join him and looked almost as bloodthirsty as Cwin.

"Who can we fight?" Covey uttered as she glanced around.

The air was heavy and dark, as if we were waiting for a massive storm.

"Come face me!" Cwin was a few feet away from the

porch of the cabin when she yelled loud enough to rattle the structure.

"You can't stand against us. You never could. I expected an army of siramages to come to rescue their friend, but I get you and some useless elves and non-elves." The voice was magically modified, I assumed to spark fear, but I didn't feel it.

Judging by the surrounding faces, no one did. I was annoyed at the condescending tone about elves and non-elves. Considering that Tygathis and his minions were elves, he was bashing his own kind. Plus, I didn't care if he wanted to insult me, but he was rude about my friends.

"Cut it, Tygathis. You're a loser who can't stand up to anyone with real power. Face me and let's be done with it." Cwin was almost glowing with the spells she pulled in and looked ready to blow the cabin down whether or not her friend was in there.

I wasn't the only one who gasped when a bolt of red lightning obliterated the cabin door, slammed into her chest, and she flew to the edge of the mountain cliff.

CHAPTER FORTY

FOXY, ALRIC, AND THE BROWNIES ran after Cwin. I started to, but my sword realized who was inside the cabin and almost ripped itself free of my hand to go after him. The faeries rallied around me, but the way they all smiled at my sword, I figured it wasn't because of me.

"Taryn!" Siabiane yelled as a whirlwind shot out of the gaping hole that was once the front door.

"I have to do this!" My words were ripped away and I wasn't sure if she heard me. More Dark elves, no dwollers this time, maybe they had run out of them, came from behind the cabin. My sword, with excited support from Rhyfel, dragged me, the faeries, and Irving inside the cabin. Bunky remained outside, and the dark cloud coming over to us appeared to be his people. I hoped.

The interior of the cabin was in ruins. A grimarian lay collapsed and bloody in the corner, but I didn't have time to see if he was alive.

A massively tall elf, with an oddly beautiful face, stood at the end of the front room. "What are you? A human warrior? I came for the siramage." His perfect upper lip curled back. "You are nothing." Since I was holding a spirit sword, and a Robukian dagger, and had my power for the moment, I had to think the minkie's spell was blocking my magic from Tygathis.

All he saw was a slender human woman. I grinned and slammed him with my modified push spell.

He stumbled back five feet.

Not a good showing for my spell, but the brief look of terror that crossed his beautiful face was worth it.

"I am more than you know." I raised Rhyfel and he joyfully sent arcs of green into the metal bracings on Tygathis' arms. I ran forward with my sword high.

The moment would have been more impressive if my sword hadn't burst into a war song loud enough that people back in the village below us probably heard. If we survived this, it and I were having a serious conversation about propriety.

I took a swing, but Tygathis called up a deep red sword. It looked like an anti-spirit sword, if I had to call it anything. He skillfully blocked my blow and returned the favor. My sword blocked him and Rhyfel sent an arc into his red blade.

One that was completely swallowed by the red blade with no effect.

That gave me pause, but not my blades. Rhyfel went after any other metal on Tygathis that he could hit and my sword moved so fast I felt like I was barely holding on; forget about fighting back.

The faeries held back after they followed me inside, forming a solid wall of color against the cabin wall where the door had been. Glimpses of black on the other side told me that the chimeras had arrived and were doing the same outside.

I wasn't sure why they wanted to keep the rest of our people out, but the sounds of fighting past the wall of chimeras pointed out they were also trying to keep Tygathis from backup.

Tygathis stumbled backward again and ripped off all of the exposed metal he had on him. His red blade crackled as a thin flame rolled along it.

"Whatever you are, you shouldn't get between me and my prey. I've seen the deaths of thousands of your kind—*human*. You are nothing special." He came back swinging and this time I danced back.

My sword sang again, but it was a song of defiance and blocked the red blade, again at a speed I had no control of.

This time the faeries cheered.

Tygathis looked up as if seeing the brightly colored audience for the first time. I took a few steps back and to the side so I was closer to Fardoragh. I also got a nice view of the faeries. They were cheering, calling Tygathis names, and sticking out their tongues.

Whether it was a new strategy or something on the spot, it threw Tygathis off. He sent a spell at them so powerful that just the edge of it almost dropped me to my knees.

A shield flared around the entire wall of faeries and the spell shot up and through the roof. Which made the faeries laugh harder.

Then their laughter ended and they raised their war sticks.

My sword and Rhyfel calmed down and held back as if honoring another warrior on the field.

Tygathis raised his sword and grinned.

Bad idea.

Garbage waved her war stick in the air and not only did the hundred-plus faeries with her yell and fly forward, but so did a few hundred more who came in behind them. Many were wilds, and clothed in leaves, but they looked fiercer than the ones wearing overalls.

Tygathis flung spells that seemed to slip through the mass of faeries, his red sword managing to hit a few, but they all came back.

My sword remained silent and Rhyfel was crackle free. A deep groan behind me caught my attention.

Fardoragh was stirring, but not sitting up. A glance told me the chimeras were still holding the line out front and the faeries were attacking Tygathis, so I sheathed my weapons and ran to Fardoragh.

"You don't know me, but I'm a friend of Cwin's," at his blank look I dug up her full name and probably completely mispronounced it, "Cwningen Blewog?"

I was close enough and he nodded. His eyes closed, but some of the tension left his face. Or I thought it did. Fur wasn't conducive for interpreting facial expressions.

I didn't want to move Fardoragh, as I had no idea how injured he was. But I could defend him.

The sounds of fighting were louder, might be reinforcements, or they were closer to the cabin. The wall shook as the chimeras zapped whatever was coming too close—the sounds died down a bit.

Tygathis and the faeries were in a slow-motion standoff. From the shock on his face, I guess he'd cast a spell to stop them. All it did was slow them, and him, down. I expected my sword would want to help, but there was no response from it or Rhyfel.

"Move away! I'm coming in!" I thought Cwin was angry before, the new tone in her voice didn't bode well for anyone in front of her, foe or not. The front room grew brighter as the chimeras cleared away from the wall.

Cwin raced in, covered in twigs, plants, and dirt. Her eyes were almost purple with rage as she turned to Fardoragh first, then Tygathis and his slow battle against the faeries.

Even in slow motion, the terror on Tygathis' face when he saw her was a great thing to see.

"Is he alive?" Cwin watched Tygathis as she shouted to me.

"Yes, but seriusly injured." I moved closer to the fallen grimarian and kept my weapons up.

"He'd better stay alive, Tygathis." Cwin flicked her hands and balls of lightning appeared. I'd never seen spells exactly like that, but the way their energy rolled off and filled the room, I knew I never wanted to be on the receiving end of them.

The faeries were gaining speed as they fought through the Dark elf's spell, and the first wave stabbed their war sticks into him.

He screamed in pain but still raised another spell and the faeries in that wave were slammed out the gaping hole that had been the front door. Garbage was in the second wave, and the spell from Tygathis gave her the ability to burst through his slowing spell. She and her wave surrounded him, with the rest of the faeries picking up speed.

"Ladies! Thank you, but this one is mine." Cwin stomped forward as Garbage and the rest flew out of the way. I'd never seen them obey that quickly, but this was certainly the time for it.

I felt Fardoragh trying to speak before I heard him, although I wasn't sure that he wasn't having a seizure.

"…the gothia path…."

I leaned closer to his face. "What?"

"The gothia path. Send him. Has reinforcements who will follow him." His eyes rolled back in his head and he collapsed. He was still breathing, but speaking took a lot out of him.

"He says to use the gothia path." Yelling what the next plan was wasn't the best thing, but there was no other way to tell Cwin.

Cwin didn't turn away from Tygathis but nodded. Interestingly, so did Garbage and the faeries.

I didn't know what this was or what she needed to do, but I felt the hair on the back of my neck rise.

She threw her two lightning spell balls and before they hit, cast another spell that ripped all light from around us, even outside the cabin went black. The faeries chanted in native faery, Cwin's fire sparked, and Tygathis screamed.

I crouched over Fardoragh, keeping my sword and Rhyfel raised as much as possible. A roaring noise that felt like it was trying to shatter my bones tore through everything. I couldn't grab my push spell or think of anything.

Tygathis' scream went higher and sounded as if he was being pulled apart. He also seemed to be rising to the ceiling.

The sound of an explosion and bits of the former cabin roof falling on me, ended in absolute silence.

The world around us regained its light and Fardoragh opened his eyes and smiled.

"Good girl." He collapsed again.

Cwin and the faeries were covered in debris from the exploding roof as she ran over.

"He's still alive, right? Damn you, Fardoragh, don't you dare die on me after that!" She was shaking and her breath was rough. Whatever she'd done to Tygathis, it came at a cost.

CHAPTER FORTY-ONE

I HADN'T NOTICED AT WHAT POINT the fighting outside stopped. The chimeras stayed near the door but not blocking it, as the rest of my friends came in. Well, Lorcan, Mathilda, and Siabiane ran in, all three looking murderous. Padraig, Alric, Covey, and Foxy followed at a distance.

The faeries held their own fast-paced talk, and then the extras vanished, leaving our group of a hundred. I'd wondered before if the inflated number of Notlianda was going to stay and I had my answer—we were now at a level of trouble where we needed a hundred faeries all the time.

That didn't make me feel good.

"Where is Tygathis?" Lorcan asked as he glanced around the room—then stopped where the Dark elf had been—a nice dark circle burned into the wooden floor. "Is he dead?"

Cwin looked over from where she was helping Fardoragh slowly sit up. He still looked awful, but he was finally awake. "Not sure. Fardoragh suggested the gothia path and honestly, it was the safest option. No offense to all of you, but Fardoragh fell against that monster, and if I fell as well, he would have claimed our powers. All of you would have died."

I had no idea what this gothia path was, but the way Tygathis had screamed as he left told me it was bad. Hopefully, whatever it was could hold him if it didn't kill him.

I was still hoping for a painful death.

Lorcan released the spells he'd been holding. Siabiane and Mathilda did as well.

Padraig and Alric remained on the porch but didn't appear to release anything. Foxy and Covey stayed with them.

"We defeated the latest round he had attack us, but there's no guarantee that was all of them. We'll set up camp out here and then set patrols." Padraig nodded to the brownies and the chimeras. Like the extra faeries we'd gained in Notlianda, the twenty or so extra chimeras didn't look ready to leave. The brownies were even more roughed up than before but looked ready to fight again if needed.

Garbage flew over to me but sent the rest of the faeries outside. "Yous all dones good." She nodded to Crusty, Rhyfel, my sword, and then me last. At least she included me. "Now we's guard." With a look around the room, she left. Most likely her patrols wouldn't be part of Padraig's.

"Yous safes." Crusty kissed my cheek and followed Garbage.

"Thank you, all." Fardoragh's voice was still rough, but he was sitting up on his own. "I tried to stop the emergency beacon once I realized it was Tygathis I was facing, but I was too slow. You didn't see anyone else, did you?" He was earnest as he watched Cwin—he meant the other siramages.

"No. We were already on our way here to seek your help and were down in the village of Rialone. Hopefully, I was the only one to see it."

The non-response from the other siramages could be

bad if they saw it and couldn't come. Or were already dead.

"But was he after all the siramages?" I asked. The tension between him and Cwin felt personal.

Cwin had been sure that Tygathis was after her. And that he needed a ruse to get her here instead of attacking her directly. While he'd tortured Fardoragh, Tygathis hadn't killed him.

Fardoragh shook his head. "He was after Cwningen Blewog. Sorry, *Cwin*." He flashed a smile that fell a moment later. "He wanted you alive. And me as well, at least until he captured you. I was a trap for you. Sorry about blasting you away when you tried to come in. I had the energy for one more spell and changed the trapping one that he was aiming at you. A bit harder than I intended."

Cwin shook her head. "That was a good transformation. Took me three spells to get back up here. He's still bitter?" If she was concerned about being the target, she didn't sound it.

"You left him in a diaogn cave for five hundred years, so yes, he's still bitter." Fardoragh shook his head as he used Cwin to get to his feet. "He's gained a lot of power since then. He pretends to be working for the empress, but he's waiting for her to fail."

"That sounds like the Tygathis we knew in the north," Lorcan said as he, Siabiane, and Mathilda came closer. "He came to us as an envoy from the south, a friend. Then he almost destroyed us all by being one of the leaders of the Breaking."

Fardoragh gave a short bow. "I thought some of you were northern elves. Thank you for coming to save me."

Introductions flew around the cabin and Fardoragh nodded as Padraig, Alric, Covey, and Foxy left to set up patrols and a basic camp. "Now, you were coming here for a reason?"

I turned to Cwin.

"It's okay. Even injured, Fardoragh is one of the most powerful beings in the world. He needs to know everything if he's going to be able to help you." The emphasis was heavy on the word 'everything'.

I began with who and what I was. Then explained about the flinms' attack and the spell they'd stuck on me. I added details of the magic blocking spell Padraig had put on me, and Alric's inclusion in it. And the minkie popping up. I didn't mention the sword, mostly because I didn't think it was relevant. It had refrained from singing for a while, so maybe it realized stealth might be a good thing. Hopefully.

Cwin had magically repaired a large lounging chair and settled Fardoragh on it as I spoke. He appeared to be taking mental notes, but didn't comment until I was done.

"The spell they hit you with is tricky and old." He grinned. "But I'd say that you are as well and the people behind this might know that better than you. I can remove the flinm spell, but I must recover first."

My face must have shown my disappointment, I'd enjoyed having access to my magic back.

Fardoragh's laugh was warm and deep. "Don't worry, with luck and assistance, I should be fine before the minkie's spell vanishes. Plus, I'd rather not try to overlap something one of them set in place."

I glanced at Cwin, but she shrugged. To be fair, I'd never directly asked her if she knew about minkies.

"Lorcan, my sister, and I can work on fixing this cabin." Siabiane pointed up to the open space that had been the roof. "Going into a chilling rain with this won't help anyone." She spoke a few words, raised her right hand, and the roof repaired itself. With new wood, judging by the light color.

"Thank you. The impending storm was something

Tygathis set in place. I don't think we should try and stop it," Fardoragh said, 'we', but he still didn't look like a healthy grimarian.

The sky didn't look bad outside, but I wasn't going to argue with wise magic users. Siabiane worked in the front room and kitchen, while Lorcan and Mathilda went after the back of the cabin.

Crusty came zipping through alone and stopped in front of me. "Theres yous are!" She booped my nose, the sign of a bad habit starting, and flew to my shoulder.

"You're the one who left me. Where are the others?" I wasn't sure at what point Crusty had become my babysitter, but I doubted I was going to able to stop it anytime soon.

"Is yes, but stuff and things. You be outsides now." She waved her hands so much at 'stuff and things' that she almost fell off my shoulder.

I steadied her. "We're working on things in here, but I could go help with the tents." I glanced around but Cwin and Fardoragh were in some complicated discussion and the other three were repairing the cabin.

Rhyfel and my sword were calmly remaining in their sheaths, but I knew I was going to have to do some explaining about the sword when I joined the others. I sighed. "I'll be outside if anyone needs me."

Cwin might have nodded to me, or to something Fardoragh said, but I took that as being okay to leave.

Foxy and Covey were fussing with a massive tent that I'd never seen before with some skillful assistance from Welsy, Delsy, Flower, and the rest of the brownies. Padraig, Alric, the faeries, and the chimeras, including Bunky and Irving, were nowhere in sight.

"Where'd this come from?" I grabbed a part of the tent wall that flapped about. It was of very thick material. And it warmed to my touch. I'd never seen anything like it.

"Padraig created it...but he wouldn't say how, even to Alric." Covey sniffed. "I believe it was from one of the books he took from your library. He claimed it was waterproof as well."

I rubbed the fabric again, then dropped it as Foxy finished the last pole and pulled the entire thing up. It looked large enough to house a few Ancients in dragon form, but I didn't recall us using anything like it.

"It's interesting." I stepped inside now that it was completely up. "It's warm in here." I felt the chill once I left the cabin. The sun wasn't down yet, but probably within an hour or so.

But inside it felt warm and toasty, like I was sitting in front of a roaring fire inside the Shimmering Dewdrop. "How is it doing this?"

"Your family didn't use one?" Covey asked as she placed her bedroll into the very center of the tent.

"Not that I recall, but memories are slow coming back. This is amazing." I ducked out of the tent, brought back mine and Alric's bedrolls, and set them near the center. I appreciated when we had privacy, but there wasn't much of that on the road even with separate tents.

Plus, I hoped we wouldn't be here long.

Crusty yelled and jumped off my shoulder and onto my bedroll. "Is yes! Nice."

Faeries seemed impervious to cold—their lack of reaction while coming down that weird snowy ravine into the village of Rialone for example—but she was almost purring now as she rolled around on my bedroll.

"Crusty? Sweetie? Were you cold?" Aside from spell diseases, I didn't believe that faeries could get ill, but she was really enjoying the warmth.

"Noes. Just goods." She flopped back into the bedroll.

I was going to ask more questions but shook my head. Crusty had been changing over the past few years, but she still was difficult to get a solid answer out of.

"Do you know where Derry went?" I loved my original three, but having one to actually speak to was nice.

Crusty let out a huge sigh. "Noes. Has things. Nots heres." She lowered her voice and nodded slowly. "Shes oldest."

"Yes, she is." I wasn't sure what else to say, or do, so I joined Crusty on my bedroll. After taking off my belt with my sword and Rhyfel on it.

Crusty stumbled across the bedroll and heaved Rhyfel partially out of his sheath. "Friends backs!"

Rhyfel didn't send out his arcs, but a light green light flowed over him as he and Crusty chatted. Rather, she spoke in native faery and he hummed and glowed.

The faeries had been the first to determine that Rhyfel was able to communicate—it was good to see the two together.

I patted the hilt of my sword. "Thank you for everything, but until I explain things, could you not sing? And singing in battle is probably not a good idea at any time."

"Are you talking to your sword? Doesn't it usually vanish after a fight?"

I'd misjudged how close Covey and Foxy were to me. Covey asked the question, but Foxy was close enough to have heard it as well. And was giving me his famous, 'Do I need to cut you off' look from his bartending days.

"I don't want it to feel bad with Crusty talking to Rhyfel." I forced a smile but dropped it when Covey shook her head. "Fine, there have been changes going on in the last few hours, but I want everyone to be together before I tell it." It wasn't a long story—the spirit sword belonged to some powerful elf named Cadhia, and now accepted me. Oh, and it sang.

But I had a bad feeling that the questions and

examinations from the magic users were going to be drawn out.

"I want to hear everything, but I can wait." There wasn't much patience to her words, but I'd take what I could get. "Padraig and Alric were setting lookouts around this mountaintop, but should be back soon." Covey dropped to her bedroll.

"I'll be chatting with Amara before we settle in." Foxy nodded to me, and the sword, and left the tent.

"Can it understand us?" Covey's hands twitched as she looked at my sword.

"I have no idea. I found out about its unique status a short time ago." I shrugged. "I don't have any answers."

Covey watched me, the sword, and Crusty and her wild conversation with Rhyfel. With a heavy sigh, she reached into her black bag, pulled out one of the Ancient historical books from my family's cabin, and settled in to read.

CHAPTER FORTY-TWO

I'D DOZED OFF IN THE tent while waiting for the others, having one of those weird, heart-pounding dreams that vanished the moment you woke up. I always ended up being annoyed at those. If there was something to warn me about, then let me remember it.

The flap for the massive tent was open and from the sound outside, my friends had returned.

Even Crusty had left me.

I straightened my clothes and followed the sound. There was a makeshift kitchen on the reconstructed porch and food was being readied.

Alric joined me. "I wanted to wake you, but the others said to let you sleep. And Crusty threatened to boop me if I disturbed you."

"Don't let her start." I looked around but the faeries, including Crusty, were gathered around a pile of food with the brownies. "She keeps booping my nose."

He dropped his arm around my shoulders. "I'll keep that in mind. How are you feeling? Covey said you weren't down for long, but you don't normally nap like that." The concern on his face was touching.

But, in my opinion unwarranted.

"And how many times since you've known me have I had a chance for a nap?" I laughed. "Trust me, I'd nap whenever I could back when I was working as a digger." We reached the food line, took some hearty looking soup and bread—the rain hadn't started but it had grown a lot darker in the time I was out—and joined the rest in Fardoragh's front room. He seemed to be better now, but remained seated.

Everyone was chatting and focusing on the food, so I thought maybe the whole singing sword issue might wait for another day.

Then Lorcan rose to his feet and called for everyone's attention. "I believe we succeeded in today's challenges. Excellent work. There were no signs of more enemies and we have warning spells up. And we have restored Fardoragh's original alarm and defense systems." He turned to me with a grandfatherly smile. "Now, I will let Taryn explain about the singing we heard during the battle."

I should have known. I quickly told everyone about the minkie, my magic coming temporarily back, and my sword. Who liked to sing in fights and once belonged to an elf named Cadhia.

Everyone remained politely interested, yet quiet, until I mentioned the elf's name.

Even Covey's eyes went huge and she shouted questions with the rest. Foxy was the only one looking around in confusion.

Lorcan calmed everyone down, but unlike the others, didn't appear concerned. I'd say he already had a clue as to what my sword was. Or rather who my sword had belonged to—at least once he heard it singing.

"I can get it if people want?" I still wasn't used to the sword sticking around, so I left it and Rhyfel in the tent. The instant the words left my mouth, my sword, minus the sheath, appeared in front of me. I grabbed the hilt before it dropped too far.

"Thanks. Um, do you want to say hello?" At first, I

thought maybe it had stopped singing completely, or it was mad at me for asking it to stop.

It might have been waiting for everyone to quiet down. As soon as they did, it sang. A cheerful, yet eerie wordless tune, that immediately brought tears to the eyes of the elves. But they were smiling.

"In case we held any doubt this was Cadhia's weapon, that resolved it." Mathilda wiped away her tears. "He was a good leader, a fierce fighter, and loved music."

Lorcan nodded. "We wondered what happened to his spirit sword since it never reappeared after he was lost. They are difficult to destroy, but we feared that had happened. It is good to see you, my friend."

"So, do we know why this powerful spirit sword picked a non-elf? No offense, Taryn." Cwin smiled.

"None taken." The sword gave a little trilling sound as if it was trying to speak words. Which almost caused me to drop it.

Padraig held out his hand for the sword and it practically jumped to him. He smiled as he studied it. "This sword chose who it wanted. I didn't recognize it as Cadhia's before, but I do now. However, it is solidly Taryn's now. It needed to be certain this was its new path before committing."

"You got all that from holding it? I hadn't heard or felt anything like that. It really wanted to go after Tygathis though." That had been clear. At some point, I would like to hear about Cadhia, but the sadness on all the elves' faces when they spoke of him made me decide to wait. Even Covey had obviously read about him in her elven studies.

Padraig nodded. "Yes, it takes time, but you'll come to understand it as well."

"Are there other skills the sword has?" The singing had taken me by surprise, but I wasn't sure what benefit it would be in a fight—startling your opponents only went so far, and the ones we'd faced today hadn't seemed impressed—or frightened.

"There were when it belonged to Cadhia." Padraig gave a sad smile as he handed it back to me. "However, as much as this was his sword, and it will likely want to destroy those who killed Cadhia, it is truly yours now. Its song is for you. Have you thought of a name yet?"

I wished it had shown up with the sheath as I felt odd sitting here with it out. "I thought it already had one? The minkie said it would tell me when it was ready." I looked to him and Alric. "Do your swords have names?"

They looked at each other and shrugged.

"Not really?" Alric finally said. "They come when we call and vanish when it's safe. But the higher level of spirit sword carriers have a different relationship. Cadhia was one of them."

Fardoragh waited until the chatter died down then turned to me. "I believe your magic won't be needed tonight, but the time given to you by the minkie will hold through tomorrow morning. I will cast the spell to remove what the flinms did then. But I'd like to get a closer look at you tonight if possible. Then all of you might want to head for your tent. I modified the storm Tygathis brought in, but it will still be powerful. He created it to wipe this mountaintop clean."

I moved over to him. His front room wasn't meant for this many people and it took a bit to work my way over. I was grateful that the faeries, brownies, and chimeras remained outside.

Fardoragh was larger than Cwin but had her energy and focus. I'd been around her long enough to realize that this feeling, more than appearance, was what differentiated the siramages from the grimarian hilstrike mages.

Fardoragh smiled as if he heard the thoughts in my head. "Yes, we are not the same. And many grimarians are good without being siramages. It's the grimarian hilstrike mages and their violent, power-hungry ways that impact how most view us." He raised his hands and motioned for me to take the empty chair next to him. "You might feel an odd sensation. I won't touch you with my hands, but will be searching who and what you are." He paused, so I nodded in acceptance.

He closed his eyes and his hands waved over me. Not unlike what some of my magic using friends had done before. "Nirtha. Zirtha. I should have known they would have been involved. Two of the foulest grimarians I ever missed the chance to kill." He opened his eyes. "Thanks to the faeries for destroying them. Neither were major players, but both were foul." He closed his eyes again.

I hadn't thought of Nirtha or Zirtha in a long time. Two extremely unlamented former landladies who tried to kill me. Part of me wanted to ask if all grimarians exploded when they died, but it seemed rude. Not to mention, it could just be a faery thing.

"There's been unhealthy interest in you, even before it was known what you were. That seems to imply that even though the interest was mostly by a few grimarians, someone was directing their movements. Something to keep in mind as you all move forward. As for you, you are something more. Not simply an Ancient. The spell from the flinms will have to be removed with extreme caution." He started to say something else, then opened his eyes and forced a smile. "It was good I looked, but yes, this can be resolved. Tomorrow." Along with his forced smile, he gave a fake yawn. "Now if you will all forgive me, I am exhausted."

Lorcan led us out with Cwin remaining in the cabin. She nodded to all of us, but there was clearly something of concern going on.

With *me*. Great.

I sighed as thunder cracked over us and rain began as we got into the tent.

"What was that sigh for?" Alric asked as I escorted my sword to his sheath. The faeries, brownies, and chimeras beat us inside. Bunky and Irving hovered at the tent flap as if inspecting everyone. They remained there until Mathilda cast a sealing spell on the tent once we were all inside. Then they flew to a far corner with the rest of the chimeras.

The faeries had also claimed a corner and were popping into a few ale bottles. But not many, and they were more subdued than usual.

The brownies appeared to be planning for the next attack.

"My sigh was for whatever Fardoragh saw and what he's probably discussing with Cwin right now. It was a big thing to realize that I was an Ancient. And what I'd done twenty-five hundred years ago. Then I find out that I can turn into a faery, a Xoti, which might or might not even be real, and who knows what else. This extremely powerful siramage now says I'm 'something else'." I glanced around the tent. My voice had been rising as I went through my litany and now everyone who wasn't a brownie, construct, or faery was staring at me.

Then Garbage noticed and flew over to give me a narrowed-eyed stare. "Whats?"

"Nothing." I turned to the rest of my friends. "Sorry, everyone. It's just been a long, weird few days." I could extend that to a long, weird few years, but I was already whining enough.

"And you're exhausted." Siabiane came over with a cup of tea. "Drink this and relax. We're safe here, but don't worry, we have protection out there."

I took the cup. "Thank you."

Foxy and Covey went to their bedrolls. Garbage gave

me a sharp nod then returned to her faeries. Padraig, Lorcan, Mathilda, and Siabiane went to the remaining unoccupied corner, created chairs, and began planning. Even though they'd already done so. I noticed there was a fifth chair.

"They're waiting for you?" I hugged Alric. "I'll be fine. Just a lot going on, and we still need to make our way to the village of Bailinsea. After we fix me, anyway." I ran my hands through my hair. "I'm going to feel stupid if I'm dragging us over there and I don't have a clue as to why."

Alric kissed me and smiled. "At the least, we can visit those retired pirates you found on the way to save me." His smile faded as the memory he kept bottled up snuck out. He shook his head as he saw my face. "I'm fine. And I'm sure we'll find something critical to be done there." The tone of his voice indicated he was concerned as well, but wasn't going to say anything.

"Thanks. Go talk to the others and see what the next magical plans are." I gave a huge yawn and noticed my cup of tea was empty. "And tell Siabiane she's sneaky, but it worked." I dropped down to my bedroll after shoving Rhyfel and my sword off of it. That she helped my sleep wasn't surprising, and already I felt the knots in my back and shoulder unwind.

Alric kissed the top of my head and joined the magic users. I wished I knew more about why we were going to Bailinsea, aside from that it might play a part in me not causing the end of the world as we knew it. That should seem like enough, but nothing about this was clear.

One would think saving the entire world would have some directions.

CHAPTER FORTY-THREE

I DIDN'T REMEMBER FALLING ASLEEP, BUT the howling around me and the rough shaking of the tent told me that I had. And was now waking up whether I wanted to or not.

Alric was sound asleep next to me, and from the gentle snoring coming from all directions, so were my friends. Nothing moved in the tent—aside from the walls rippling in the wind. The howling didn't seem real and appeared to be racing around outside of the tent in the same direction as the winds. I would have thought that such powerful winds would have been able to tear even this magical, pseudo-Ancient tent down. But while it was rippling and groaning, it remained intact. Mathilda's spell on the flaps kept them tight as well.

Still, none of my friends woke up. I picked up Rhyfel and my sword—the sword gave a subdued song but didn't appear to be reacting to a threat.

Since it wasn't morning yet, as much as I could tell from the darkness in the tent, I went ahead and cast a glow. I didn't even try the shielded one, but none of my friends twitched. I scowled as I stalked around the edge of the tent. The faeries were passed out—someone had given them chocolate, a lot of it, considering the amount that was all over them. Crusty had been my self-imposed guardian, but even she was in a chocolate-covered heap.

The chimeras were all out, with Bunky and Irving alongside them. Constructs didn't sleep but they did go into shut-down mode. And I couldn't get them to come out of it.

Welsy and Delsy were likewise turned off in their corner—but the piles of blankets that I thought were Flower and the rest of his troop were empty. And there was a small tunnel near their spot going under the tent wall to the outside.

I refused to believe we'd been that wrong about the brownies. Which probably meant they picked up on something outside and couldn't get us to respond. Nor get past Mathilda's spell on the tent flaps.

I weighed my options. I couldn't see Siabiane giving her sleepy tea to everyone. There was no reason to do that, or to include herself. Not to mention that the constructs didn't drink tea, and any type of tea would make the faeries hyper.

But someone knew what chocolate would do to them.

I tried waking up Alric—one of the lightest sleepers I knew. But he gave no response aside from a snort.

The faeries might be okay to try to wake, but that would involve regular tea, and then I'd be stuck with them in hyper-mode. It was me, Rhyfel, and my sword. I quickly got my boots and my cloak on and then walked to the tent flap. I'd been listening when Mathilda sealed us in, any of us could open it from the inside.

Yet Flower and his brownies weren't able to get it to open. It looked like the same was true for me. I tried a few lighter spells, but it was tricky messing with a spell you didn't know. I glanced behind me to where the brownies had been sleeping. They fit through their hole fine; it would be tight for me. Mind made up, I detoured over to the faeries and grabbed Garbage, Leaf, and Crusty. I'd rather have them with me and not need them than the other way around. My plan was to find the brownies, then Fardoragh and Cwin. I could get some tea from them if needed to wake up my three faeries.

The girls had been playing some of their weird games before they collapsed and had scribbled on paper lying around them. I grabbed a larger piece and rolled all three of the chocolate-covered messes inside it. Then wrapped them in another large piece of paper and tucked them into my cloak. I waved for the glow to follow me after changing it to the less visible orange and squished my way out of the brownies' tunnel. Rhyfel woke up halfway through and gave supporting green glows for my attempt.

I finally made it, but there were no signs of the brownies. Nor anything, really. The odd howling from before was gone and the wind dropped as soon as I pulled out Rhyfel. Fardoragh's cabin was dark and seemed secure. If I didn't see the brownies out here, I would go there next. I wanted to do a quick pass outside of the tent first. With luck, Flower and crew were nearby and had some amazing reason why everyone else was asleep.

Or at least could give me a slight clue before I woke up two sleeping siramages.

The night was silent and dark. And far more disturbing than it should be. I made it almost completely around the tent, when I heard a low voice grunt, "Halt! Go no further!" It sounded like one of Flower's crew, but the voice seemed to be closer to my height.

I freed Rhyfel and spun. Only to knock down three brownies standing on each other's shoulders behind me.

Flower came running out of a low shrub—the brownies still looked similar to each other, but Flower had taken to wearing an actual flower on his vest.

He snapped to attention but kept his voice low. "We couldn't wake anyone and realized something had gone wrong. We were testing out a new form of patrol, one that should be more impressive."

I refrained from smiling as the three brownies scrambled to their feet and looked ready to try their balancing act again. "I think the strength of brownies is *because* of their size. People underestimate you; you often go unnoticed. Those two things give you an advantage over us taller folks." I believed what I said, but I also knew that we didn't have time for this.

He gave a serious nod. "Well put." He scowled and waved the other three brownies off from their attempt.

"Was there a serious wind and howling out here?"

Flower scowled. "There was, but we couldn't find the cause of either event. They both stopped moments before you came out."

It could have been one of Fardoragh's alarms, but I wasn't sure. That the brownies had searched the mountaintop and found nothing was impressive though. "Have you checked the cabin yet?"

"No, we only came out here fifteen minutes ago. But we didn't find anyone on this mountaintop."

I looked around, wishing that I had better eyesight in my human form, or that we had a clear sky. Even partial moonlight would have helped. Then I flung another orange glow into being and set it hovering over us with the first. "How well can your people see in the dark?"

Flower grinned. "Like felines."

"Good to know. I'm keeping these lights with me then. Can you and two more of your men come with me, with the rest guarding the tent?"

He saluted, barked a few low commands, and two of his men jogged over, with the rest spreading out around the tent.

My cloak kicked me and I checked to see if the faeries

were coming out of it—nope, Garbage was adjusting her legs but remained asleep. The other two girls were curled into tight balls.

Most likely to avoid being kicked in their sleep.

"You brought the faeries? They were quite…sticky." Flower was trying to be polite, but his nose wrinkled. His people were obsessed with doilies. One had to maintain a clean house for that.

"Just three of them. Someone gave them chocolate to knock them out. That's the sticky stuff on them." I nodded toward Fardoragh's cabin. "We need to check Cwin and Fardoragh; if they're not spelled, they can help us wake up the rest." I left out what we were going to do if they were also unconscious. And the question of why the brownies and I woke up. I'm sure there was something important there, but right now I was simply trying to keep from freaking out.

Flower saluted and walked alongside me with two of his fellow brownies flanking us with gardening implements held high. They looked whimsical, but I'd seen what they could do with them.

My orange glows followed us under the porch roof. The cabin was still silent and I hoped Cwin hadn't set any protection spells on the door. I didn't sense anything but that wasn't as helpful as it could be.

I knocked softly at first. Then a bit harder.

"Do you mind?" Flower waved his pick toward the door. "I will use the side of it."

I shrugged; we had to do something.

He tapped the door once, then a second time harder. All of us jumped back when the door crumbled into dust.

I continued moving away from the cabin, but Flower and his two companions ran inside. With a sigh, I pulled out my sword, asked it to refrain from singing this time, and with both weapons raised, I followed the brownies.

It was a good thing the brownies had cat-like eyesight; my glows barely lit anything inside the cabin. The entire place was dark and murky. I called up a few more glows, then switched them to regular instead of the stealth orange. That helped a bit, but not as much as it should have. It was as if the room was swallowing all light.

At this point, someone seeing us because of the glows was a lesser threat than whatever was happening in here. One of the brownies bumped into a side table, and it collapsed into dust just as the door had.

"Whats. Dos?" Garbage called out faintly from inside my cloak pocket. They couldn't have been passed out that long, so I figured the only way I'd be getting them awake was tea. I motioned for Flower and the other two brownies to stay in place, then reached in for the gooey faeries.

Luckily, they remained in the paper I'd wrapped them in and were still groggy.

Garbage tried a glare, but a massive yawn stopped her. "Where be? Why be?" She looked down at herself and the other two. "Whens happens?" She kicked Crusty and Leaf until they opened their eyes. "How?" She held up her tiny chocolate covered fingers.

The faeries loved chocolate and would often reminisce about it. Loudly. I had a hard time believing they'd indulged and forgot about it. "You don't remember eating the chocolate? Or who gave it to you?" The faeries could be difficult, especially Garbage. But this was beyond that.

Before I could stop them, all three swiped a handful of chocolate off their overalls and shoved it into their mouths.

Only years of living with them kept me from ending up with it being spit on me a moment later.

"Ick!"

"Is wrong!"

"Bad! False!"

The three spoke so close together that it was one annoyed and disgusted sentence. Then they used my cloak to wipe the substance off. I grabbed the papers and tore them up. "Use these, please. We need Mathilda and Siabiane to see what it was." Not to mention I didn't want more of it in my cloak.

Garbage grabbed the papers and they cleaned themselves off.

I looked around the cabin. There was still a weird dust fog, one that I couldn't see where it came from, but it seemed to be clearing around me.

Or around my faeries.

"Garbage, are you okay enough to fly over there?" I used Rhyfel to point to the far wall.

She did a final inspection of her clothing but appeared clean to me. "Is yes." She launched off my hand and went to the wall. It was still difficult to see even with my glows, but a clearer path followed her flight and expanded around her when she stopped.

"Us too!" Leaf grabbed a partially clean Crusty and flew them across to another wall.

The air cleared again, both in their path and where they stopped.

"It's still clear around you, too." Flower inspected me and the faeries, and he was right.

"I sometimes turn into a faery. Maybe that was it? I have no idea, but we need to find Cwin and Fardoragh quickly." The frame around the formerly brand-new front door turned to dust. "Before this place collapses and traps us here." This was a passive way to attack two powerful siramages, but then again, whoever did this went after another bunch of serious magic users with sleeping spells. Maybe since the fighting didn't work, someone decided to be sneaky. "Girls, do a quick search of this place, see if Cwin and Fardoragh are here." I was proud of the way I kept the terror out of my voice. Not only was everyone outside unconscious, and the siramages missing, but it wouldn't be long before I was back to my magic-less status. I had no idea what would happen if everyone hadn't recovered by then.

CHAPTER FORTY-FOUR

GARBAGE LED THE OTHER TWO faeries down the hall, then came racing back moments later.

"Outs! Get outs! Noes ones, onlys bads!"

A shadow reached out from the back of the cabin to grab the faeries, but it stopped when they passed me and went out the former doorway. I felt a chill as it moved around me slowly, but nothing worse.

"You…" The voice, or voices, was so low and wispy I barely heard it. But the punch of anger that hit as it circled me was clear.

"What are you?" I kept Rhyfel and my sword up and didn't complain when the sword sang this time. It was as low as the voices, and discordant. But the dark wind circling me backed up.

Flower and two brownies came running up with their weapons raised. "What do we attack?"

Before I was able to respond, the darkness struck the brownies and engulfed them. Rhyfel shot out an arc of green energy into the darkness, and I ran forward, putting together the strongest push spell I could create. I first focused a weaker spell where Rhyfel's green arc was clearing a way through the darkness and tried to exclude hitting the brownies. They were tough, but even they couldn't handle a fall off of the mountain. They needed to be separated before the push spell.

The darkness swirled away as it was shoved up, and released the brownies.

"Get out! Protect the others." I had no idea if this was the same thing that knocked the others out, but I knew I needed to destroy it.

Images of darkness filling the skies when I was a child slammed into my head. Whatever this thing was, it was old and nasty. I didn't see any tiny bugs and hadn't felt like I recognized the things that attacked Alric in the woods, but I wouldn't be surprised if they were related.

"Yes, me," I answered the darkness, then grimaced and sent my full push spell. Rhyfel crackled stronger, and my sword hit new levels of painful discord in its singing.

The swarming darkness screamed and was flung through the roof. It took out enough of the roof that I saw it burst into flame and vanish.

My glows immediately grew brighter and I heard groaning from the kitchen. Cwin and Fardoragh, even more roughed up than before, were slowly helping each other off the floor.

I ran to help as the brownies and faeries—all of them as far as I could tell—came running and flying back in.

"Sleeps! All sleeps!" Penqow shouted as the rest of the faeries came in. She was back to her normal black and white pristine self, and the faeries all appeared soggy. Water worked better than random paper.

Cwin and Fardoragh leaned on each other and the counter to take in the state of the cabin.

"Not on my watch." Cwin recovered quickly and shouted out a few sharp-sounding spells. The interior and exterior of the cabin came back quickly, and lanterns filled the room with more light.

"Are you both okay? Can you wake up everyone else? They're all asleep." I wasn't certain how the faeries woke themselves up but, for the most part, none of us were sure how they did anything.

"I'm no worse than I was, just a bit rougher." Fardoragh dusted himself off. "Whoever was controlling that mass of Nalieghs hit us fast and hard."

Cwin nodded. "We'll get our payback. You make sure the rest of the cabin is solid, and I'll check on our friends in the tent."

Fardoragh nodded and waved to all of us. "I'd like for a few faeries to stay and check out the corners, but the rest of you might be needed in the tent."

I knew a dismissal when I heard it. Garbage sent off ten faeries to Fardoragh and then we left the cabin. Flower and his brownies ran ahead of us, stopping on either side of the still sealed tent flaps.

Cwin waved one hand and the flaps moved away. I sent my glows in before us.

Everyone was still where I'd left them, but the constructs were twitching now. "What kind of spell hit all of us like this? And why did I and the brownies wake up? Not to mention the faeries?" Whatever that substance was, it hadn't been chocolate.

Cwin stalked over to Alric as she nodded. "That's an excellent question. Knocking out the faeries and the constructs is difficult."

I told her about the fake chocolate.

"That's even more interesting. I would like to examine this substance." She sent a soft spell over Alric, but he didn't twitch. Her scowl deepened when she got the same results from everyone else. "There's something simple here, an aspect that I'm missing because of that simplicity." She turned to Flower. "How long until sunrise?"

He tilted his head and pulled on his beard. "Twenty-two minutes, I would gather."

How he knew that, I had no idea. Nor how Cwin

knew he was able to do that. He might be wrong, but the look on Cwin's face said she didn't believe so.

"Help me pull away this tent, the morning sun should perk them up. I know what the spell is now. It's extremely old, more than me or Taryn. It can be catastrophic if it is cast on warriors in battle, but time is of the essence with it—at sunrise it will be weakened." She turned to me and the brownies. "You saved us all, but we will have to determine why you woke up once we recover our friends. That element might be a clue to this attack."

We turned to take down the tent. Since I knew we hadn't been traveling with it, I figured it was completely magical and would go back the same way. Cwin disagreed and said we had to mostly physically take it down.

Luckily, that kind of job was right in the brownies' comfort zone. The faeries tried zipping around, helping in their unique way. So did Cwin and I. But after a few minutes of clearly annoying the brownies, we moved away. And I sent Garbage and the faeries on a recon of the mountain all the way back to where we'd arrived out of the fada path.

The tent was taken down with limited magical assistance around the sleepers and neatly folded when Fardoragh and his borrowed faeries came out. He was still limping, but considering I figured he was dying when I found him the first time, his recovery was amazing.

"They planted spells along the ceiling. But we got them all, and I've added defenses against them to my cabin and this mountain. I haven't felt that magic in a few thousand years." He dropped onto a large rock near us.

I looked at Cwin and she smiled. "Yes, Fardoragh is quite a bit older than us."

"And yet, I don't get the respect!" He grinned, then sighed. "It may be time to finally give up my mountain." He waved a hand toward Cwin as he nodded to me. "The other siramages realized that we needed to rejoin this world in this crisis, but I was too stubborn."

"That's good to hear. I believe the village below you, Rialone, would welcome you with open arms." Cwin's smile faded. "I'm afraid things are only going to get worse."

As they spoke, a faint dawn appeared across from us. Where the sky had been clouded when I first left the tent, it was completely clear now. "That cloud cover was part of the attack?"

"Many creatures thrive on darkness; it gives them strength. I'd say the clouds were part of a failed spell." Fardoragh nodded to Cwin. "Want some help waking them? I don't know that we want to wait for the spell to break on its own. I might need help to free Taryn from the spell the flinms put on her."

Cwin and Fardoragh didn't say they needed my help with waking the others, but when they walked over to them, I followed. It seemed to me like Bunky and the rest of the constructs were moving more.

"Taryn, you still have your minkie granted magic, so I'll have you stand in the middle." Cwin marched to one side of the circle of sleepers. "You'll be the conduit for the spell, your magic will instinctively respond to Fardoragh and myself, so you don't have to do anything."

I was usually great at not doing anything, but I felt like I should do something this time. It must have shown on my face as I walked to the center of the group of sleepers.

Or Cwin was able to read minds now.

"Do nothing magical. Just stand there." She gave me a reassuring nod as Fardoragh took position opposite Cwin. "The constructs will most likely wake first, so call Bunky and Irving to wake up as the morning sun hits them."

I waited until the first rays struck the collected constructs and called out to Bunky and Irving. Cwin and Fardoragh ran a gentle spell through me that felt more like a lullaby for sleep than a call to wake up.

Bunky and Irving woke up, hummed, then flew over to me. "Bunky, do you know what happened?" Welsy and Delsy were starting to wake up along with the extra chimeras as both Irving and Bunky gronked emphatically at me. Unfortunately, I didn't understand Irving and my understanding of Bunky wasn't always great—even when he wasn't being drowned out by his friend.

"Slow down." I looked at Cwin who was waving her hands. She was still speaking her spell but waved toward the cabin behind us. I nodded then turned back to Bunky. "We can talk about this later. For now, can you lead the constructs to Fardoragh's cabin?" I hoped that was what Cwin wanted as she went back to layering her spell.

I understood Bunky's gronk this time and he and Irving zipped over to get the rest of the constructs and leave. I thought we might have a problem with Welsy and Delsy, but a short head shake from Cwin as they approached Siabiane got them to follow Bunky and Irving.

Alric woke up first. He jumped to his feet, spirit sword raised, and looked ready to cut us all down. A few blinks and a sharp shake of his head and he was back to normal.

I never wanted to see that look facing me again. For those brief moments, he saw me and everyone else as an enemy.

"What happened?" he asked as Cwin motioned for him to go to me.

"Long story, just wait," Cwin muttered but Alric joined me and stayed silent.

Padraig also jumped to his feet ready to fight, and I noticed Cwin and Fardoragh changed the spell somewhat.

Soon everyone was standing, most were where they'd been sleeping, looking confused, but silent.

I felt the spell Cwin and Fardoragh had been channeling through me vanish.

"How does everyone feel? Probably hungry?" Fardoragh smiled broadly as he turned for his cabin. "Magic kitchen inside."

No one followed him except Cwin, and everyone looked at me. I shrugged.

"Long story, and he's right, I'm hungry. They'll tell everyone once we're inside." I half-pulled Alric with me toward the cabin.

The rest followed after a few moments.

Bunky, Irving, and the rest of the chimeras flew over from the cabin. Bunky filled me in on their plans. They were going to do a recon of the mountain and make sure the paths were clear.

Before I nodded, they all took off.

Welsy and Delsy ran to Siabiane and stayed with her on the way in.

"Are you okay?" Alric was going to have to drop his arm before we could go inside, but he was concerned.

"I think so. For some weird reason, myself and the brownies woke up on our own. So did the faeries, eventually. Cwin and Fardoragh know far more than me."

He gave me his best, 'you'd better not lie about being okay' look, then dropped behind me as we went inside.

The food was probably great, but I was too hungry to notice. Cwin and Fardoragh were cryptic about the attackers and admitted neither of them was ready to discuss what knocked everyone out. They weren't being secretive, neither were certain yet.

The information about the weird darkness wasn't good.

It was related to those tiny bugs we'd faced on another mountain. Fardoragh called them the Naleigh but didn't clarify more than that. The looks on all of the magic users' faces weren't good.

More old and deadly spells coming back for us.

"I think Taryn and the brownies woke up for different causes." Siabiane was watching Flower and crew with a few glances my way. "I've been looking over the tea I gave her, a common recipe, but she drank it when we'd already been exposed to the Naleigh. The tea altered the spell when it hit her. Which tells me things about who cast it. It was left behind by Tygathis as a trap, before we even came on this mountain." There was no doubt in her voice but she paused and watched Cwin and Fardoragh. "He knew that not only Cwin, but the rest of us, would be coming to see you."

Lorcan scowled. "Tygathis never had foreseeing abilities. Granted, that was over a thousand years ago, but few have been able to do that. He's a powerful magic user, but not that good."

Cwin shrugged. "He had help. And that he left that spell to knock everyone out, and none of us sensed it? He had a *lot* of help."

"Why didn't he set a spell or something to kill us?" I was still weirded out about him knowing we were coming here. And having the foresight to leave a spell behind in case he was unable to cast it. That thought was going to haunt me as well.

"He had a set plan for at least one of us. And I'd say whoever is helping him didn't trust him not to screw it up." Padraig was watching me. Of course. "Knocking powerful magic users out for any length of time isn't easy—especially if you don't intend to kill all of them. If you and the brownies hadn't woken up as you did, we'd all be prisoners, or worse."

CHAPTER FORTY-FIVE

I LOOKED OVER AT SIABIANE, WELSY, Delsy, and Flower's group as they dropped into an animated debate. One that Flower and crew didn't like, from the sound of it.

"Okay, so the sleeping tea helped me, but what helped them? They were up before me." I would deal with the faeries later. Most likely it was simply one of their weird things.

Siabiane looked up. "I think it's an essential part of the brownie makeup. According to Flower, they came inside, went to bed, and woke up a short time later. It just took them a while to be able to move."

I shook my head when they all turned my way. "No lag for me, just asleep, then not, and then I couldn't wake any of you. What helped the faeries? Whatever that goop was, it wasn't chocolate, even though it knocked them out like it was. They hated the taste and wouldn't have eaten it. And they woke up without tea faster than they would have with real chocolate."

Garbage, Leaf, Crusty, and her other sub-commanders were leading groups of faeries through the cabin but were also maintaining a patrol over the entire mountain with Bunky, Irving, and the chimeras.

I'd already handed over the papers they used to wipe

off to Mathilda, Lorcan, and Siabiane. It didn't look like anything to me, but maybe they could find something.

Foxy looked around the room. "I'd say it was something intended to take the faeries out, but it was made by someone who had no idea what chocolate was. Had that with a few ale fakers a few years ago back home. Con mages who never actually drunk ale." He sighed and shook his head.

"Oh yeah! That stuff was horrible." It was so bad I stopped drinking for a few weeks. "What happened to them?"

"I kicked them out of town. Never was sure what they'd wanted. When I found where they were living, they still had the coin I paid them hidden away. Hadn't used any of it." Foxy rubbed his brow. "There's something there, but I can't recall. It was many years ago—before I even met my Amara."

Now it was Alric's turn to frown. "I recall that. I was working for Locksead as Carlton at the time. But I remember one of his mages coming back from the pub and almost dying. He couldn't do any magic once he recovered."

"That's not good." Mathilda was the only other one of the elven magic users who hadn't been inside their enclave at during time. "I'd say they were trying to make something to impact magic users. Or one."

I held up my hands as she turned to me. "Wait a minute! I didn't have magic back then, remember? You didn't even know who or what I was—I certainly didn't."

Fardoragh was listening and watching in silence, but now shook his head. "But someone had a clue as to you being more than you appeared. Nirtha and Zirtha wouldn't have come to your town on their own. They were your landladies? For how long?"

I didn't like the increased attention being tossed my

way. Even Covey and Foxy looked like they were now picking up on things they hadn't noticed before.

"Yes. Nirtha had been my landlady for a year or so. Zirtha only showed up when the faeries killed Nirtha."

Covey and Foxy shook their heads in unison.

"No. You complained about Nirtha for years." Covey turned to Foxy. "About three?" Even though Covey and Foxy hadn't been friends back then, they'd known each other. He nodded.

I sighed. "I guess so?" I was so focused on getting the rent money at the time it felt both longer and shorter.

"And then that syclarion pretending to be your patron." Covey was in full analyst mode. "We assumed these things were separate, but it was a planned attack. Someone had an idea who you were."

"The effect that dragon bane had on you was a tip-off," Alric said. He opened his mouth to say more, but at a sharp look from me, shut it again.

Yeah, I'd attacked him, something I would never be okay with. But it was old news, no one needed to know who didn't know about it already.

"How did anyone, and we're not even sure who, know what I was when I didn't know?" I felt the blood drain out of my face as a few things clicked in my head. "Unless they'd been around twenty-five hundred years ago and knew me from that final battle." Edana, her evil son Nivinal, and the rest of their Paili crew had been winning the last fight until I used my relic staff and ended the war. "The Paili. They're sneaky and evil. The ones who murdered my parents are gone, but they had plenty of time to tell others about me. Are the Paili working with the empress?" I didn't realize how cold I was until Alric pulled me close and held me.

As more memories came back, so did my absolute hatred and fear of the Paili. Recalling what they did to my parents was enough to trigger that.

Fardoragh and Cwin shared a look I didn't think I liked. Thanks to being around Cwin for the past few months, I was better at reading a grimarian's face.

Those looks were bad.

Fardoragh spoke first. "The Paili aren't working with the empress, according to our information. But they have been up to something for the past fifty years. They weren't around much in the thousand years before that. At least not down here."

"Where were they during that time? There were syclarion groups up north before the Breaking a thousand years ago, but no Paili." Lorcan looked to Siabiane, Mathilda, and Padraig, but they all shook their heads.

"I sent my people elsewhere, or else *when,* and I changed the surviving syclarions to genetic throwbacks—so where did the Paili go?" I had hoped that since we only saw small groups down here and up north, they'd mostly died. It appeared I was wrong. "Is there any way we can get them to fight the empress directly? Maybe instigate something? She was fighting her people for a while—it might work?" I didn't want to start any more fights, but if we were able to weaken both sides, I was all for it.

"I think we need to figure out what the Paili are up to, and where they're hiding," Mathilda said. "Remember, they got into Ageora's *tir cudd* without a problem, and even the faeries said the Paili had access."

I'd been counting on my people having been thrown into *tir cudds* when I fought the syclarions twenty-five hundred years ago. The idea that the Paili might be inside them as well made me almost physically ill.

Alric rubbed my arms. "The reason your people were losing that prior battle was due to uneven numbers— your people were scattered all over the world when that attack came. If it's a fair fight, the Ancients will win."

I hadn't said much to anyone about my *tir cudd* theory, but, luckily for me, Alric was smart.

Cwin nodded. "He's right. The siramages were completely solitary back then, even more than in the last hundred years. But had we realized what the Paili were doing, and how uneven the battle was, we would have fought to help you. We felt the spell you released, but weren't able to find you after."

The entire group went silent.

"Whats?" Garbage came zipping in with a hundred or so—our current full contingent—faeries behind her. They were all wearing war feathers and carrying war sticks. She scanned the room and came to hover in front of me. "Yous doings things. *We* needs dos things. Whats. Yous. Dos?" She folded her arms tightly and gave an excellent version of her one-eyed glare.

I didn't want to ruin her moment by laughing, so I covered my mouth with my hand. But she and her girls were what I needed right now. I couldn't do anything about the Paili at the moment, even if they and my people were trapped together. The faeries were a great reminder that there was more in the world than fear and pain.

Maybe *that* was the real reason they existed.

"We're trying to figure out what knocked all of you out and how you got that goop in you and on you." We weren't, but it was a question we needed to resolve. Chocolate or not, that stuff knocked out the faeries— that had to be taken seriously.

"Tricked." Crusty zoomed up and nodded so hard that she rotated in the air. Then laughed and did it a few more times without clarifying the 'trick' issue.

Garbage rolled her eyes at Crusty's antics before turning back to me. "Is yes. Tricked. Noms appeared and smelled like noms. Eats, taste icky, too lates, pass outs. Bad tricks." She didn't reinstate the glare but did tighten her arms. "Nows whats dos?"

Mathilda looked ready to ask questions, but even she shook it off. Examining the weird goop directly would probably yield better answers.

"We're about to heal your friend, Taryn." Fardoragh held up his hand, palm up, and Garbage flew over without a pause. I would only get that fast of a response if I had sugar in my hand.

"Goods." Garbage glanced over to me with a judgment-filled scowl. "Needs works."

"Do you need the rest of us here? I'd like to see if there are further clues before we head out." Padraig stood.

"No, just Cwin should stay. Thank you all for helping me. I can't travel with you now, but I will be working with the other siramages." He smiled at Cwin. "They're all fine, by the way."

Cwin rarely worried, but the relief on her face at his words indicated that she had been.

Alric kissed the top of my head, then followed the rest out.

Garbage shouted orders to her faeries, and all of them except my original three, zipped out of the cabin on some sort of mission.

Better not to ask sometimes.

"We's stays." Garbage, Leaf, and Crusty landed on the table next to Fardoragh's chair and politely watched us.

Fardoragh nodded to them, then motioned for me to scoot my chair closer. "This will feel odd, but unless it actually hurts you, please don't respond or move. The spell those flinms hit you with is unstable at best. We'll have to move carefully." He patted my hand. "Don't worry, there is plenty of time."

I hadn't been worried until he mentioned it. I knew the spell the minkie cast would be gone soon, but I figured that didn't matter for this.

"Why is there a time limit?" I watched both siramages carefully. Cwin hadn't brought up a time limit either.

The three faeries continued watching us as if we were going to do tricks.

"There's not." Cwin winced and then waved off Fardoragh before he corrected her. "There might be. But it wasn't in place before we went down the ice ravine. I know most of us didn't realize the passage of time there, or what happened. But I believe it changed things."

"Wait, what? I know we missed time, which is pretty upsetting, but we missed things that happened? To *me*?" This was adding more levels of bad onto an already massive pile of it.

Crusty had been the only one who indicated she knew about the trip down the ravine taking over eight hours, even though we all thought it was only a few. She flew over and sat on my lap. "Nots goods. But hads to gones."

That was unhelpful even for her.

"Can we discuss the issue after I get my magic fixed?" I refrained from looking at anyone at this point. Denial was my friend.

"I think we need to hear what fully happened. It's necessary to know what else occurred."

"I seriously don't have any memory of anything happening—" My words vanished when Crusty flew up, tapped the left side of my head, and said a few words that I didn't understand. "Minkie say do."

Immediately, I was on that snow-filled ravine as we led our horses down toward the village of Rialone. The area didn't look familiar, but the snow kind of made it look the same as what we'd been going through since we landed on that mountain. My friends were continuing down, but everyone looked forward as if in a trance—including the horses, faeries, brownies, and constructs.

Then three spikey trees stood in front of me. Long dagger-like branches reached for me and bright yellow eyes opened and glared at me.

CHAPTER FORTY-SIX

HOW IN THE HECK DID I face these things before and not remember? I looked around but all of my friends were still unaware, even as they kept moving. Then they and the horses came to a halt. Still staring sightlessly ahead.

The tree people snarled in an unknown language as they blocked the path.

"I don't know what you are, or why. But you need to move. We don't mean you any harm, we're just heading down into that valley." I didn't know if they understood names, but while I was pretty sure that I'd heard my friends mention this town we were going through, I didn't recall it.

The tree monster nearest me yelled and moved slowly closer. They probably had a real name, but even my old memories didn't recognize them. Not even bedtime stories had foes like these. They moved so slowly, that I wondered how they were able to get in a position to hurt us.

Then I looked back to my friends and saw my answer—there was a lot of magic in this ravine, and we were told not to look around us. I wasn't sure why I was aware and not in that stunned state like the rest.

"Is yous! Yays!" Crusty's voice, oddly echoing off the snow and rock, was as shocking as it was welcome.

"Me what, sweetie?" I kept my eyes on the slow-moving tree monsters as I motioned for Crusty to come to me.

"Yous fights. Noes know who, but is yous!" She gave me such a massive grin that I felt like she'd given me a prize.

Which in her head, she might have.

"Why is it a good thing that I get to fight? Do you know what those are?" I pointed to where the other two tree monsters had come alongside their leader.

"Someones hads to. Yous might wins! Thems, noes." She glanced at our friends and shook her head sadly.

Which brought up so many questions that I knew I didn't have the time for. And Crusty probably couldn't answer anyway. But if she was right and I was the only one who might survive this fight, I needed to try. "What are they?" I tried again, not that it mattered since I had no memory of them and the smart magic users were completely out of it right now.

"Is loctinspecklenats. Shoulds be dead. Bads loctinspecklenats!" She waggled her finger at the tree monsters so hard she did a few flips in the air.

That name hurt my brain, but it stirred something from the tree monsters, they sped up.

"Don't say that again!"

"Loctinspecklenats? Why noes?" Crusty was even louder this time, which made things worse. And the monsters moved faster.

"That! Don't say it. You're making them speed up."

"Ohhs. Sorrys noes say, loctin—"

She was close enough to me this time that I was able to grab her and cover her mouth. The tree monsters didn't speed up again. Sadly, they also didn't slow down.

I released Crusty and adjusted my holds on Rhyfel and my sword. I thought I felt an odd warmth in the hilt of my sword, then it faded.

The three tree monsters spread out, ignoring my friends to focus on Crusty and me. Good strategy. Once they killed me, they could take their time with everyone else. I swung out with my sword as a tree arm stabbed toward me and I lopped it off.

They were living beings, so that had to have hurt. I swore when a new limb appeared—this one was thicker and had more stabby branches.

I needed to stop them without creating newer and more powerful weapons.

"Crusty? How do we stop them? Can you do anything?" She wore her overalls, not war feathers, and her war stick wasn't in sight. I might be fighting for my life and those of all of our friends, but she was enjoying the show.

"Is…no." She tapped the side of her head. "Says no in heres. Is watch. Yous do. Alls good."

Someone was speaking to Crusty, and that meant someone powerful knew what was going on, and I was on my own. Not a happy thought.

Crusty flew a little away from me but was silently cheering me on. Then I realized that she was mouthing the word Rhyfel in her chant, not Taryn, or nice lady. I wasn't sure if that was a hint or not, but I'd take it.

I leaned forward with Rhyfel in front of me and we faced the next charge. Again, only the leader moved to attack me, but the other two were ready to block my escape.

I swung out with my sword again, aiming for the trunk this time in hopes that I didn't create new weapons. Rhyfel crackled his green arcs and covered the entire tree monster. I thought the arcs worked best on metal. But these were causing pain to the tree. Good.

My sword hit the trunk, but stuck there. Rhyfel's spell stayed away from my sword but didn't help getting it free. Crusty appeared ready to shout something but covered her mouth with both hands instead.

Then Rhyfel freed himself from my hand, flew, and stabbed the tree monster between the eyes—shooting green arcs the entire way.

My sword's hilt heated up and I was able to pull it free of the trunk. No idea what was going on with it, but I'd take it. I swung higher this time. Rhyfel's arcs of controlled lightning bounced to my sword and it sliced through the tree's head. Or what would be a head.

Rhyfel flew back to me, something I'd only seen once, right before he lost power, and the tree monster leader collapsed. The other two tree monsters froze. I wasn't great at reading tree faces, but these two appeared to have no idea what happened.

"These should not have awakened." The voice behind me sounded like the scary totem from the entrance to this place.

I kept watching the two tree monsters as I tried to glance back to see the speaker. Yup, the totem. It hadn't been very happy about us coming this way, and I wondered if this was a trap.

Crusty came back and landed on my shoulder. Maybe whatever told her to stay out of the fight hadn't counted on this thing.

"Sleep, my friends," the totem's voice was softer now.

"It has…" the rest of the closest tree monster's words were in an extremely unnatural language.

"That is not your duty. Return to sleep. The awakening will come."

The tree monster bowed, retracted his claws, and then he and the third tree pulled the remains of their leader away and vanished into the snow.

The totem turned to Crusty and me. "Forget. Return to sleep."

I gave a massive yawn as I fought his spell. Yet, I walked to my horse and picked up the reins without wanting to. The world grew dim as we moved forward again.

I jumped to my feet as I came out of the trapped memory Fardoragh had released.

"How did that happen without me recalling it? Why me and not Cwin, or the others? I mean, I don't want my friends to have gone through that either—but they're all better magic users and fighters than me." Now that the memory had been released, it was as if I'd always known. That was too creepy.

"Crusty?" I knew she'd been holding a lot of secrets lately, but she was getting too good at keeping them.

"I knows!" She clapped her hands. "I dids!"

Leaf and even Garbage beamed at her in pride.

I tried to clarify things with Crusty and the faeries, then shook my head. Not worth it and I already had a headache. I turned to Fardoragh and Cwin—even though he'd been the one in my head bringing the memory forward, Cwin acted as if she'd seen it all play out as well.

"Do you know why I woke up and no one else, aside from Crusty, did? Why those tree monsters went after me, and what was the term that the one called me?"

Cwin shook her head. "That language was old even before the faeries were born. But as for why you, the more we find out, the more unique you appear. I would say that uniqueness impacted the flinms' spell and is something we need to keep in mind as we go to Bailinsea."

"I agree and this gave me insight into fixing you." Fardoragh motioned to the faeries. "Ladies? Would you take positions on Taryn?"

Crusty claimed my left shoulder, Leaf took the right, and Garbage sat on top of my head. I had no idea what they were going to do, but they were having fun with it as usual.

Cwin smiled and stood in front of me as Fardoragh began chanting a spell that made the hair on my arms stand up. I'd sorted out that spell chanting usually meant something big and heavy, magic-wise. I hoped my magic abilities never reached that level. I used to want to be stronger, but now I was fine with being a mid-level magic user.

A chill slammed up against me and Garbage pulled my hair to keep me from moving.

"Ouch! Stop that!"

"Stays still. Spell mights goes booms." She gave another short tug of my hair then shut up and remained still.

Cwin held up her hands and seemed to be acting as a mirror for the spell. It began behind me with Fardoragh, then swirled around to Cwin and back again.

I doubled over in pain as an invisible fist hit my mid-section. Hard.

"Noes! Stays." Crusty and Leaf echoed each other and Garbage pulled on my hair harder.

Unfortunately, the pain in my stomach was far worse than Garbage's hair pulls and I dropped to the floor in a curled position.

"Fight it! They don't want you to be able to tap into your magic. You have to fight back!" The voice was a perfect blending of Cwin and Fardoragh and felt like it was coming from the cabin itself.

"Can't..." I barely got that word out when another stab of pain hit my gut. I shut my eyes tightly as the world spun around me.

Crusty and Leaf ran off my shoulders and tried to force open my eyes.

"Looks!" Leaf was more insistent and managed to get the eye on her side open.

Bright colors and peaceful waters flowed around me. Not trying to rip out my gut, but trying to soothe.

I opened my other eye. "This isn't bad. Can I—" The words 'get up' were swallowed in another wave of pain. This time the vision changed to what I saw in my non-nightmare, and had been trying to ignore, in Notlianda—the cell I was in as a group of syclarions planned what to do to myself and the other Ancients that they'd found. "NO!" I fought back now. Something inside me said my current reality was in danger, and the nightmare vision was trying to take over.

I wouldn't be the only victim if that happened.

Garbage stopped pulling my hair, and the other two faeries scrambled to jump back onto my shoulders as I forced myself to stand.

My gut still felt like someone was using hot pokers on it, but I was pissed now. My family, my friends, everything I knew was on the line for destruction. The Paili, the Dark, the empress, Tygathis, and more were all trying to destroy my world. They'd won a lot—but not this time.

"I will not let you control my body or mind." That was clear. But the long rattling words that also tumbled out of my mouth after that—in a language that I didn't speak and had a tiny bit of understanding for—rocked the cabin.

Possibly the entire mountain. For a moment or two I sensed everything in the world. And felt a lightning strike as the reason why we had to go to Bailinsea before it was too late. We needed a scroll. If the enemy got it before we did there was no way we would be able to stop them from taking over everything and everyone. And a name—Marluk. Jadiera's former pirate friend. Something I'd sort out later.

"You can't destroy me!" I clenched my fists and let my

anger, fear, and a bunch of other emotions fly free. Then I looked at the stunned faces of Cwin and Fardoragh, nodded once, and collapsed.

CHAPTER FORTY-SEVEN

I'D FOUND MYSELF WAKING UP to being comforted more times in the past month than in the last three years.

Alric was next to me; my odd hyper-awareness faded quickly but I sensed him before he said anything.

I felt Covey and Foxy near me on the other side. Everyone else was hovering on the edges of my sensing and their terror for me was almost palpable.

A low humming began and was picked up by all the faeries. I took a chance and forced open one eye. Yep, it looked like people had been crying. I opened my other eye.

"I'm still alive, right?" I wiggled my fingers and toes— they moved. "All body parts intact?"

"Taryn?!" Alric grabbed me so tightly that I might not be intact anymore. "You're alive!"

"Yes. When was I dead?" Any more words I wanted to say were lost as the flood of faeries, led by my original three, swarmed in and kissed me.

Also Alric, as he wouldn't let me go.

"I don't think you were dead." Fardoragh looked even more exhausted than before, and Cwin didn't look much better.

"She was dead." Covey hovered over me between Alric and the faeries

"No, Fardoragh's right. That spell fought dirty and tried to take everyone else out with grief as it went after Taryn." Cwin gave me a small smile. "Luckily, Taryn is tougher than that."

"How do you feel?" Mathilda also looked ready to grab me if she could have gotten close enough.

"Bruised. Everything feels bruised. Even the bottoms of my feet and the backs of my hands. What happened? Is the flinms' spell gone? Is my magic back?" It appeared to be later in the day outside, but I had no clue as to the time.

I certainly didn't feel like I'd been dead. Annoyed, furious, ready to kill, yes. Dead, no.

"You have it back, the minkie's magic faded a few hours ago." Lorcan leaned on Padraig for support and also appeared to have been crying.

"Hours?" I tried to force my way up against the faeries and Alric's objections. "We need to get on the road. *Now*." I turned to Fardoragh. "You're safe now, right?" When I was seeing everything everywhere, I felt how important the siramages were to whatever was coming.

"I am, only tired. Three more siramages are on their way here. We'll be fine. I take it you gained new information?"

"During my being almost dead?" I shook my head when others were ready to contradict me. I'd deal with whatever happened later. "I now know why we were sent to the village Bailinsea. We have to save them, they can't fall. We have to save Marluk and the diviner's scroll." It was far more eloquent in my head, but it got the point mostly across. I had no clue as to what the diviner's scroll was, but I knew we needed it—and to save the village.

Alric, Covey, and Foxy helped me to my feet but were still frowning. The faeries flew a few feet back but were far more focused on me than I liked.

"We don't have time to plan this out. We were going there already." I grabbed Garbage. "Your queen, Derry, and a lot of your people are in danger." That had been one of the horribly weird feelings that had stomped on me while I was floating around in my head.

"Noes. I'd knows…" Garbage scowled, closed her eyes, and tilted her head. Then her golden eyes flew open. "Is bads! Blocked! Boths!"

"What's this scroll are we after? I've never heard of it. And Bailinsea is a simple fishing village, they're retired pirates, but not heavy magic users. Marluk wasn't a magic user," Mathilda said. She and Padraig were the only elves who'd been on that crossing between the continents. Alric, Siabiane, and Lorcan were captives at the time. We didn't go to Marluk's village as planned, as it had fallen under attack while we were with Jadiera on the *Dangerous Lady*.

I shouldn't know exactly where that place was…but I did now. As if I had a full map in my head that led me right to the village. Sadly, it didn't tell me the name or exact location of the scroll. I got the feeling that Marluk knew.

"I hate to sound like a faery, but it's in my head. That village, and Marluk and his people, are more important than we knew. Then the enemies knew until recently." I paced as more bits popped up. "They were guarding something old." I winced, it wasn't a chest but the things I felt were fading to feelings, not details, all too quickly. "It's a scroll. I know, we have a bunch of them…" I stopped mid-step as a connection hit me. "Oh! There's a bond between one of our scrolls, maybe more than one, and the one in the village."

"But you don't know which scroll or scrolls of ours? Or what this one in Bailinsea does?" Lorcan was being gentle but there was concern on his face as well. At least everyone appeared to be recovered from my almost dying.

"No. Maybe I do? I have a feeling that I'll recognize the one, or ones, that we have when I see them." I let out a long sigh. "Which means they all have to come out of their bags so I can examine them." I had no idea how this would work; I needed to have the scrolls out of those faeries' bags to know which ones were needed. But I also knew we'd been delayed here and needed to get on the road immediately.

And we were going to have to ride to the village.

"I can see about a fada path. It won't take us directly into Bailinsea, but it should help get us through the Lledir mountains." Cwin frowned as I shook my head.

"We can't use the paths." I shrugged at their looks. "Again, no idea how I know that, but we can't. It'll take us a week, at least, but that can't be changed." How I knew that without looking at a map was yet another entry in the long list of concerns about whatever was happening in my head.

Fardoragh watched me intently for a moment, then smiled. "Odd question, but did you by chance swallow a clarit?"

That stopped all of us in our tracks, even Cwin.

"How did you know?" I wasn't going to deny it. I felt the truth in his question—he wasn't guessing; he knew. We had to trust him at this point.

"I realized something I felt when we were chasing the flinms' spell out. I couldn't place it at first, but I can now. I think the clarit is now part of you and is modifying your skills, possibly your very essence. It's not solely doing it, but I have a feeling you won't be able to cough the clarit back up. In any of your forms."

I dropped to a chair. The clarit was a mystical relic that would provide massive amounts of magical power to the user. Once. Then it vanished. I'd swallowed the one we found back in Yosi when I got the bright idea that existing inside a dragon's gullet would keep it safe. Maybe too safe?

"No one ever swallowed one before." Fardoragh raised both hands. "I'm not saying it was wrong. I'm simply surprised that one survived the wars of the past. However, it's part of you now." His eyes went wide. "You don't have the canfydd crown, do you?" The note of terror in his voice was obvious.

"No. We did. But it was taken," Padraig answered before I could. "They didn't get the gems though."

Crusty opened her mouth to yell, but Garbage jumped on her and covered her mouth.

I wasn't worried about Fardoragh knowing, but it was a good policy when it came to Crusty and her stones. Actually, with all the secrets she seemed to have inside that little blue head, it was a good policy overall.

"Good." Fardoragh didn't get to his feet, but he leaned forward in earnest. "Taryn, this is the most important thing I can say to you. Under no circumstance can you put that crown on now. Gems or not. The world literally depends on it." He paused as my brain caught up to Queen Mungoosey's horrible future vision. "I see in your eyes that you know what I mean."

I went to sit before I realized that I was still sitting. I gave a small nod.

He looked at my friends, including the faeries, brownies, and constructs. "None of you can let that crown get on her head. No matter what the cost."

I couldn't look anyone in the eye. In my mind, he was telling my nearest and dearest that they might have to kill me to stop me from destroying the world. In general, I agreed with that sentiment. The horrible feelings from that vision weren't something anyone would be able to live with. But short of me finding a way to put that vision, emotions and all, into their heads, I wasn't sure how I would get them to understand.

I didn't want to destroy the world. But I also didn't want people I loved to have to kill me to stop it.

"We's dos!" Crusty shook off Garbage and flew to me. After a few moments, so did the rest of the faeries.

"You would stop Taryn?" Fardoragh smiled gently like a kindly grandfather. Not like someone discussing my potential demise.

"We's turn her faery. Noes crownie crown fits. Ones of us!" Crusty started the chant, but then the rest picked it up.

The canfydd crown had adjusted large enough to fit my dragon-sized head. It was good to know that it couldn't go small enough for a faery-sized one.

Garbage flew to the top of my head. "Nows?"

"No, no I don't think that's necessary at this point." Mathilda held out her hands, which were now filled with sugar. She turned to me. "If it has to be done, it would need to be permanent. Otherwise, the crown would still call to you. You'd be a faery forever."

I had a bad feeling when the girls said they'd turn me into a faery, it would be permanent. Not sure how I felt about it being confirmed. I guessed that would be better than dying or destroying the entire world. But my life would change drastically. As much as he loved me, I didn't see Alric settling down with a faery wife.

"Noes dos nows!" Leaf shouted around her mouthful of sugar.

"There must be other ways to stop her—if we had to." Covey wouldn't meet my eyes and Foxy looked like he needed to smash something. Possibly Fardoragh, for his implication of having to kill me.

"Ask her. She knows deep inside." Fardoragh was solemn.

I watched my friends process the information—I'd

already told them of my world-destroying vision and they were all bright enough to realize that the canfydd crown was behind it. Only one way to go at this point. "I do. Trust me. Let's not deal with that now. We all know what will happen, and now we won't let it happen. But we do need to get moving." The pull to get to Bailinsea was stronger now that I wasn't in pain or seriously freaking out.

Alric stood in front of me. "Are you sure you're okay?"

"Just keep asking me that." I gave him a quick kiss and marched for the door.

It took a few moments, but everyone followed me out. The sugar-filled faeries were the last. They weren't in sugar collapse yet, but it was better than having them trying to figure out when to turn me into a faery permanently. If they got loopy from too much sugar, we could shove them into the black bags.

Covey almost walked into me when I came to a sudden stop as an idea hit me.

"What's wrong?" She glared around us.

"Nothing. It's what's right. I can turn into a faery, not for good," I waved off her objection before she said anything. "As a faery I can go into all of the bags that have scrolls in them. I know I'll recognize the one we need when I see it. Or ones." I still wasn't sure how many there were, but whether it was the clarit or something else, I knew I'd recognize it or them.

"You realize knowing things without the why or how isn't always safe, right?" She folded her arms and gave me her best annoyed professor glare.

"I know. But we don't have time. Going through those bags, pulling the scrolls out, and fussing with them wouldn't be easy. Not to mention, think of what it might do to the scrolls. What if we're attacked on the way when I had the scrolls out?" That was the perfect argument for my scroll loving friends.

Covey narrowed her eyes, but finally nodded. "You're right. Be careful. I know the faeries, their cats, and puppy all go in and out of those, but you're sort of an odd faery."

That was a good point. "I'll be careful and we can have a way to bring me out if something goes wrong."

"Okay. Pack up and let's tell the others. I don't envy you telling the faeries."

Another good point. But they were currently on sugar benders so hopefully they wouldn't put up a fuss. Especially as long as I promised to stay away from their personal stashes and ale.

CHAPTER FORTY-EIGHT

WE GOT ON THE ROAD extremely fast, especially since Cwin wanted to wait for the three new sir-amage arrivals. Luckily, we didn't have to wait long for the fada path they rode in on to arrive. All three were grimarians, and all nodded to the rest of us then went with Cwin and Fardoragh into the cabin for a meeting.

A few minutes later, Cwin came out and got on her horse.

The faeries had been in too much of a sugar rush to care about me diving into their bags. In fact, Garbage, Leaf, and Crusty handed over a bag collection to Covey, she being the official bag holder for me. Then they all dove into the green and brown bag and went to hang out with the war cats and war puppy. Covey tucked that bag into a separate pocket away from the rest.

I waited until we rode down the other side of the mountain before testing my bag theory. It seemed smart at the time, but now I was having doubts. Even having just watched the faeries fly into a tiny bag without a problem, the concept of me fitting inside one was scary.

What if I somehow changed back while inside there? Logically, I knew that I wouldn't even be in my four-inch-high faery form once inside the bag—that was physically impossible based on the bag size, but there were too many unexplained questions about those bags in my head.

"You said you wanted to wait until we got down off the mountain—we're off and heading for the Withros plain. Then you said you needed the faeries taken care of, and your horse." Alric motioned to my horse neatly tied behind his.

He'd already given me a far too passionate for public kiss, so I couldn't even claim that as a stall.

"You'll be listening for me, right?" I looked past Alric to Mathilda. I would be able to contact her as a faery if something went wrong inside the bags. Or she could call me if they needed me out here.

"Yes, I promise." She smiled. "You'll be fine. We shouldn't remain here too long though, we're fairly exposed."

She was right. There was a thin forest on the edge of this plain, but the area we were currently in was open. I sighed and turned into a faery. Then patted myself down to make sure everything was in place. Covey held the first bag open.

I looked around at my friends, then climbed inside the bag.

I had a fairly good imagination—usually for what might go wrong. But I had no idea what to expect inside the bag.

It looked like the front room of a lovely cottage. Sofas, chairs, low tables. Two unassuming chests along the wall. The faeries weren't able to describe the interiors of the bags before they sugar-crashed, but they had said it varied and could be changed.

I liked this room, but it wasn't one I knew. In my mind, I changed it to my front room in Beccia.

At first, nothing happened. Then the entire place blurred and a decent copy of my old front room appeared.

Everything was my size and the chests were still there. As much as I wanted to see what else I could change it to, the Shimmering Dewdrop pub would be nice, I had no idea how long it would take to go through all of our scrolls.

I walked to the closest chest and swore when I realized what it was. It was the smallest of our chests, at least that I recalled. We'd found it outside Alric's elven enclave.

It belonged to the Dark.

I'd forgotten that one was with us. I didn't think a scroll from the Dark would be one needed to help save the world.

Then a nagging voice, sounding unerringly like Derry, pointed out that ignoring anything wasn't an option. The voice also said to hurry up, she wasn't getting any younger. I tried to reach out to her, but I didn't get a response.

Sighing at the words of wisdom that might have only been from my mind, I dropped to the ground in front of the evil chest. I reached for it but then recalled all the traps the Dark had left behind when we'd found it.

I pulled in any and all protection spells that I recalled and dumped them on myself. Then found that I was unable to move my hands due to the massive protection on them.

With a long sigh, I pulled back the spells until a simple glove-like one on each hand remained.

It was barely visible and my hands and fingers moved like normal.

The urging to open the chest came solely from my brain.

A tingle ran through my fingers as I unlocked the chest and lifted the top. But it faded quickly when the spell from the chest was blocked by the protection spells I had on me.

There were a few books and odd items that I stayed

away from. I didn't know what the scroll or scrolls I was looking for were, but I knew they were scrolls.

Yup, three old, cracked scrolls were there. I touched each one quickly but didn't feel anything. I had a bad feeling I was going to have to look at the scrolls' interiors to tell.

Without releasing any evil spells that might be hiding in them.

Whoever gave me the insight about the scrolls needed to include more instructions. And maybe another level of a protection spell.

I debated crawling out of the bag and asking the others, but I eventually came upon a way to deflect whatever the scrolls tried to pull. A combination of my push spell and a small containment spell that I'd found in my old books. If it worked right, I should be able to see the topic of the scroll but push back the magic.

Hopefully. If it didn't work, I wondered how long it would be before my friends figured out how to get my unconscious or dead body out of here.

Holding my breath, as if that would help, I unrolled the first scroll. Immediately my weird combo spell kicked in. I saw the words but glanced right over them. Nope, this wasn't what I wanted.

I rerolled it and tried the next two. Both also caused my spell to kick in, and also, I didn't react to either of them.

I almost wept when I locked the evil Dark chest back up. Lorcan wanted to keep it and the other magic users didn't fight him too much on it. At this point, I might not have been the only one who'd forgotten it.

I'd be happy to drag it out of this bag, change into a dragon, and fry it to cinders. Sadly, I doubted anyone would let me.

The next chest appeared to be filled with scrolls Lorcan brought with him when he left the enclave this last time. There were a lot—I stopped counting after forty. I'd say none of these had been needed on this trip, but he often stayed up at night reading, so he was stocking up on spells and information from somewhere.

I finally made it to the bottom of the chest. Not a single scroll indicated they were something I needed.

I got up and turned where the entrance had been. To find my Beccia home's hallway that led to the bedrooms.

Leaf said getting out was as simple as getting in. I should have checked with more faeries. I spun around and thought of the room I'd originally been in.

Crisis averted as the bag entrance returned once the room transformed back. I crawled out to find night had fallen and Covey was sitting in front of the fire, staring into it.

"How long was I in there?" Yup, it looked like night had fallen a while ago and dinner was over.

"Oh! Sorry, you scared me." Covey blinked rapidly. "About seven hours, I take it you don't notice the time in there?"

"No. And that should have been something the faeries told me." I looked around, but while Bunky and Irving were sitting on a log nearby, the faeries were missing. "Have they come out yet?" That length of time should have meant the end of their sugar crash a few hours ago. But it had been a while since they'd played with their war cats and war puppy.

"No. I have to say it's been pretty peaceful." She handed me a plate of food. "Didn't know when you'd be back or which form you'd eat in." The plate was human-sized but I remained in faery form and ate almost all of it.

"I wanted to ask the faeries about a few things, including this time issue. But I promised to stay out of the brown and green bag. I'm not tired, so let's try another bag." I was worried about the time difference.

I had to find whatever we needed before we got to Bailinsea.

This bag had a cozy pub, sadly not the Shimmering Dewdrop, but still charming. I didn't change the scene since that bit of panic when the exit vanished in the last bag lingered in my mind. Three chests in this one—and I didn't recall ever seeing any of them before.

When we finished fighting whoever was trying to destroy Bailinsea and take the diviner's scroll, I was going to suggest some scroll organization take place.

Again, nothing in the many old and dusty scrolls called to me. Now I was worried. I'd felt so strongly that I'd recognize the scroll or scrolls that we needed to work with the one in Bailinsea. What if I'd been wrong? Weird random feelings and directions might not be the best way to get through this. Especially if the entire world was at stake.

"You were right about knowing when you find what we need. But if you don't move faster, there won't be anything to save!" That was definitely Derry's voice. Faint, but it was her. *"The shield around the village is failing. There's a spelled dust grounding the faeries and most are unconscious. Move faster!"*

Again, she popped out before I responded. At least this time I knew it was her.

I climbed out of the bag, and the pocket Covey had it in, and was almost flung away. I didn't see any attackers but it was now mid-afternoon and all of my friends were crouching low over their horses as they ran hard. Even Foxy.

"Hang on, Taryn!" Covey yelled as the horses picked up speed and Padraig at the front of the line released a spell. Siabiane yelled from the back of the line and echoed the spell. An opalescent glow covered all of us.

"Do I need to change?" Bunky and Irving were flying low under the protective spells, but I didn't see any other chimeras. They'd shown up quickly when we needed them last time, so, appearances aside, we might not be in big trouble.

But the faeries were still missing.

"I think you should go inside another bag," Alric rode up alongside Covey. His spirit sword was out, but he wasn't casting spells. My horse was happily running behind his.

"Have the faeries come out at all? How long since we left Fardoragh?"

"Not at all and Mathilda keeps calling them. We're three days away from Bailinsea." Alric looked up and swore. "Padraig, they're making holes in the shield!" He gave a nod to Covey and me, then moved his horse up the line and sent support spells.

I was torn. We needed the scroll or scrolls that would work with the one in Bailinsea —provided that we got there before their shield fell. Before hearing about it during our brief water crossing a few months ago, I'd never heard of something large enough to cover an entire village—aside from the massive ones used by the elves to protect themselves after the Breaking.

We still had three days. And I knew my faeries, they would never stay away from whatever was going on right now. Not to mention that Derry's words about the faeries with her collapsing worried me. "I need the green and brown bag!" I had to yell to get Covey's attention. Her eyes narrowed, but she switched the bag in her hand and held up the green and brown one.

I knew Garbage told me not to go there, and they didn't have scrolls there—but something was seriously wrong.

CHAPTER FORTY-NINE

I RAN TO THE BROWN AND green bag and dove in. And found myself surrounded by a fleet of war cats. The war puppy, who was much larger than he'd been, was busy barking at a bright pile further inside.

A pile of passed-out faeries. Covered in a familiar light blue powder. Varlick powder had been spelled to take down the faeries before. Mathilda kept finding ways to combat it, but whoever was using it kept modifying it. I had no idea how anyone could have gotten inside this bag to hit them with it though.

The interior of this bag wasn't a room but a massive field with trees, grass, and running water in the distance. The light was diffused but similar to a slightly overcast day. Food stations, toys, and beds were plentiful.

And more piles of unconscious faeries in the distance.

Until I came up with this idea to search the scrolls from inside the bags, no one had worried about the faeries being attacked inside of one. If I hadn't changed, we might not have ever known what happened to them.

I reached out to pull one of the faeries off the closest pile, then froze. If it was contagious, and what was taking out the faeries with Derry, then I currently fit the bill. Most likely a variation of the varlick powder used to attack my faeries before. One time they'd been able to combat it by holding their breath, but I wasn't sure how long I could hold mine. Originally, cleaning them off had worked.

There was no way I was leaving them like this. They were breathing, but as far as I knew they'd been in this bag unconscious for four days. More or less, if the weird time issue impacted this bag as well.

I stepped back, but a group of cats were right behind me pushing me forward. They were worried about their faery riders, and so was I.

I paced around the pile trying to sort it out. Dragons were tough, but I wasn't sure how we fared against poison spells. Although I hadn't reacted to the varlick powder before, it didn't mean it couldn't happen now. If they really existed, Xoti were impervious to poisons. I'd changed into one of the mythical creatures in my human size a few times, so in my head they were real enough.

My size seemed to be fluid, so maybe if I focused on a mini Xoti I could grab a faery or two to sort out what happened.

Holding my breath, I focused on becoming a tiny Xoti.

And almost got squished when the cats ran forward. I wasn't much taller than their paws.

These bags were too weird. I concentrated on a regular Xoti and ended up about the same height that I'd been as a faery.

The cats moved back and the puppy growled. Once he sniffed me, he also stood back.

I had clawed fingers as a Xoti, so I was gentle as I pulled Garbage off the pile.

She swung one arm around but there wasn't any force to it. She was coated in the light blue dust. I looked at the water feature in the bag, but at my size, it would take too long to drag them all over to it.

I screamed when mini versions of my singing sword and Rhyfel appeared out of nowhere and dropped to the ground.

"How did you do that? What did you do?" Grabbing them wasn't easy with my clawed hands, but I managed to do it. My sword sang or hummed, as it didn't use words.

Rhyfel sent a lighter-than-normal-looking green arc at Garbage and the sword hummed louder. I wanted to help, but as I had no idea what either was doing, I stayed out of it.

The cats ran to Garbage and I was afraid they thought Rhyfel was hurting her, but they began cleaning her frantically. I had no idea if the dust was bad for cats, but they kept at it. Rhyfel and my sword must have changed the dust somehow so that the cats were able to remove it.

Garbage was hidden behind a pile of fierce war cats when I heard her start laughing. "Is tickles!" It was a welcome but unusual sound.

"Garbage! Are you okay?"

She stopped laughing and crawled out of the cat pile. "Yous noes be heres." She glared around as if I was there to take her secrets.

"I had to. You didn't tell me about the time change in these bags. You all have been here for four days, or more, outside. I came in to save you." Rhyfel and my sword pulled me over to the nearest pile of faeries and repeated what they did. They could only work on one faery at a time though.

"Oh, noes!" Garbage ran over to the pile and pulled the faeries out, except Crusty, who the weapons were currently working on.

"Can you heal them?" I was glad that Rhyfel, my sword, and the war cats had a system, but there were over a hundred unconscious faeries in here, and at the rate they were going the battle would be over before we got them all fixed.

"Noes. Nice lady can."

I almost stabbed myself in the side of my head at her vague term. Those Xoti claws were dangerous.

"Which nice lady?" I waved her off before she responded. "Never mind. You're right, we need help. But everyone was riding for their lives when I came in here."

Garbage tilted her head as if listening to something, then shook it. "Nights now. Same day. I fix. Needs gets outs."

She pushed me toward the bag opening.

"Garbage, the weapons can help." The cat brigade was already working on cleaning the nullified dust off of Crusty.

"Goes gets Bunky and Irving. Big mouths." She opened her mouth as wide as it would go and pantomimed eating things.

"I have no idea how to get them in this bag."

"Is her." Garbage nodded to Crusty as she crawled out from the cats.

"Fine. Come on, Crusty." I really hoped that Garbage had been right about fixing the time issue, I still had a lot of bags to go through.

Crusty waddled along behind me, she still seemed a bit groggy as we left the bag. Yup. The sun had set and everyone was chatting around the fire.

"Which day is it now?" I shouted at Covey.

She screamed and tried to smack me until she saw Crusty. I'd forgotten I was still a Xoti.

"Don't do that. It's a few hours after you went in there. Where are the rest of the faeries?"

My friends came closer as I explained the situation and Mathilda handed me a bag of purple powder, thicker than the varlick dust. "I prepared this after the attack at

Fardoragh's. It will work better than water. But it would be best to get them out of the bag."

"Big mouths." Crusty pointed to where Irving and Bunky hovered and they dropped down.

"Garbage says they can go inside the bag, scoop up the faeries, and bring them out here." I shrugged.

Lorcan peered at the constructs and the bag doubtfully.

"Thems follows!" Before anyone responded, Crusty zipped to the two flying constructs, said something in native faery, and turned back to the bag. They followed her inside with ease.

"I guess they're about the same size as the war cats." I changed back to my faery self, as the Xoti felt weird. "I'm going into the next bag."

Alric put his hand out before Covey held up the bag. "You do realize that you haven't slept in four days, right?"

"Four days to you. It's only been a few hours for me. I have to find the scrolls. Derry said the faeries are in danger. Ours clearly were." I was glad to know that Bunky and Irving fit in the bags, but we'd never have known to send them in.

Bunky and Irving came out of the bag, dropped off a pile of faeries each, and then went back inside.

"I agree with Alric," Siabiane said. "We don't have any idea what the time changes are doing to you. And how did you get your dagger?"

"He and my sword popped up. They worked with the cats to help Garbage and Crusty break free of the sleep spell. You don't think I need to stay for that?" I handed Mathilda her bag back.

"No. I'd like you to stay so you don't collapse inside a bag, but I can take care of this now." Mathilda wasn't happy, but was already focusing on the first faeries.

Covey also looked unhappy, but she held up another black bag.

I dove in before anyone changed their minds.

This was my favorite interior so far. Not one I'd ever seen before, but a cozy yet spacious front room with a garden out the front window. I sighed. This would be my dream. If the world would stop trying to explode long enough for Alric and me to have something like this.

Only one chest this time, but it was one I knew. A chest from the Library of Pernasi—in fact, the original one that a mysterious and annoying ghost had given me back up north. I felt a twinge for not thinking about Zaelian or the others for a while, but we had been running a lot as of late.

My hands started tingling as I opened the chest. I was going to take that as a good sign and not an indication that my body did think it had been awake for four days without food and limited sleep.

A feeling hit me that I hadn't gone through with any of the other chests. Zaelian. It was as if…

"Zaelian?" My voice sounded odd in the bag, but it was as if she was here. Yes, she was a ghost, but sometimes she was more visible than others.

"Taryn?" Her voice was faint and confused. "Why are you here? The village is under attack."

"Bailinsea?" Last I'd heard, Ageora and Zaelian had fled to another *tir cudd*—Nasif and Dueble had left Notlianda to join them.

"Yes. We're in a *tir cudd* near it and trying to keep the shield standing. Nasif and Dueble are inside."

"Is Ageora running the shield?"

"Yes, but she can't keep it up. She's too limited by being in the *tir cudd*. We need you!"

I wanted to ask how she was able to speak to me through her chest in a faery bag, but the answer would probably only hurt my head.

"We're trying to get to you. I'm looking for some

scrolls that are supposed to work with one in Bailinsea. Do you know which ones they are?" This was her chest after all.

"There are no scrolls of importance in this village. I would have…wait, what? Why didn't you tell me?" The last part was to someone I didn't hear, but I recognized Zaelian's annoyance. It was almost her permanent vocal setting.

"Ageora says there is a scroll of importance here, the scroll of the diviner. The former pirates built their village over it to guard it decades ago. And yet, somehow, she forgot to mention it to me. *Me*. A Librarian of Pernasi." Only Zaelian could throw that much attitude to a goddess.

"Great. Do you know what I need from your chest?" I wasn't getting between a ghost and a goddess.

"No, because I didn't know about this one." She paused, then came back a bit more settled. "Ageora says you'll know them when you feel them. She's not sure how many you'll find, but they'll all be in my collection."

Great. "Thanks. Any other tips for us coming in?" I unrolled scrolls and gently set them aside when I didn't feel anything from them. It would have saved a lot of time to have started with this bag, had we known.

"Ageora says hurry. Almost all of the faeries have collapsed, and the pirates that Marluk called for help haven't arrived yet." She paused again. "There was some wreckage coming ashore yesterday. Hopefully, that wasn't them."

I hoped so too. Most likely Marluk had called for Jadiera and her ships. "Tell them all we're on our way."

"Hurry…" the word faded to nothing.

"Damn it." I picked up speed looking at the scrolls but made sure to treat them carefully and roll them back up as they had been.

Halfway through, my hands hit a scroll that almost lit up when I touched it. Pulling it out verified that it wasn't my eyes; it was actually softly glowing.

I was glad to find one, but a quick scan left me extremely confused. It was a list of crops from the city of Pernasi a few thousand years ago. I read through it again, but nope, that was it. With a disappointed shrug, I sat it away from the others and went back in.

The chest wasn't small, but it felt like the number of scrolls kept increasing each time I removed one. I finally found a second glowing scroll. As exciting as the first—this one was on sportsball teams fielded by Pernasi and their match outcomes. "Seriously?" No answering ghost this time.

I needed to speed this up. If they glowed when I touched them, I should touch the remaining ones, then grab whichever ones glowed.

Or not. A few quick swings through the chest brought nothing.

Finally, only one thick scroll remained. It glowed when I touched it. This must be the one that made the others make sense. I almost held my breath as I unrolled it.

A giant treatise on the sewage and aqueducts in Pernasi.

I scanned it, but it was a huge scroll and the person writing it had tiny penmanship.

Figuring out why these scrolls were needed wasn't my job. I gently returned the rejected scrolls to the chest, grabbed my three, and ran out of the bag.

So much for Garbage fixing the time issue. It was mid-afternoon now and my friends were fighting a bunch of umbaji—the weird mini-throw-back dwollers might be small, but they were stubborn.

Chapter Fifty

I TUCKED MY HARD-WON SCROLLS INTO one of my black bags, then flew away from Covey and changed.

I was aiming for my human self but went full dragon instead. I tried to change back, but nothing happened. Then a pack of umbaji saw me and charged my direction.

They were fierce, and kind of scary in that they looked like their dwoller cousins, but they weren't nearly as smart. Running toward a massive dragon was a good way to die.

I stomped them into the ground before any of my friends even looked over.

"Taryn!" Alric yelled from across the fight. He was holding off another pack of the little beasts.

It looked like all of my friends were fighting groups of them off, even Flower and his brownies. There were more dead umbaji than live ones at this point. I shook my head—this didn't make sense. Umbaji usually had keepers, often members of the Dark, like the feral dwollers had. But I didn't see anyone with these.

"I'm fine, where are the faeries?" I also didn't see the constructs, but I got distracted by more umbaji coming my way.

"They were right here," Mathilda yelled as she fought

more umbaji off. Then she swore and held up her staff. "Stop fighting!"

All of my friends stopped, aside from Foxy who was having too much fun swinging his club around. He stopped after a few moments.

The umbaji ran through me. I'd felt them under my feet before, but now, nothing.

"Damn it. Garbage, where are you?" I yelled it physically and mentally as all of my friends looked where they'd been fighting the umbaji. Lots of torn-up ground, but no dead bodies. Even the ones from before were gone.

"We's heres!" Garbage and her massive fleet of faeries, looking like far more than the hundred or so we had before, swooped out from a low hill behind us.

That gave me an interesting and disturbing look at the Lledir mountains. They were massive. I wasn't upset at all that I missed going through those. Maybe faery bag travel would become my preferred form from now on.

Bunky, Irving, Welsy, and Delsy followed behind.

"Where were you?" Mathilda shouted out before I could.

"Over theres. Things doing." Garbage appeared confused as she pointed to a few different places beyond the hill they'd flown over.

Alric and Padraig rode to me and I focused on turning back into a human. It took three tries but I made it.

I patted the pocket where my faery bag with the scrolls was. "I don't know how or why these are going to help, but I found three scrolls. Oh! Zaelian reached me and she and Ageora are in a *tir cudd* near Bailinsea. Nasif and Dueble are inside the village but the shields are failing fast." I turned to Cwin as she'd joined us after we met Ageora, but she waved me off.

"Thank you, but I know about your goddess friend. It does explain the shielding on the village, although from what I heard, they had a simpler shield when you passed through before. What isn't clear is why this illusion of the umbaji is here. They slowed us down, but didn't do any damage to us." She held one hand up as if sensing something, then swore. "We need to get to Bailinsea, now."

Alric rode over and I untied my horse from his. "Wait, don't we still have a few days?" I glared toward Garbage but she ignored me.

Finally, she spun around to me and shrugged. "Oopsy! Didn't work. You brokes it!" The last part was a spur-of-the-moment idea.

Lorcan had his hands out, magically searching for anything left behind by the fake umbaji. "We're less than an hour away." He dropped his hands but was furious. "I think everyone needs to be prepared for serious magic use when we get there. If we hadn't realized what was happening here, we'd stay here fighting until we died. Did our ghost say anything else?"

I started to shake my head, then stopped. "She said wrecked ships were floating onshore and that Marluk had called Jadiera for help."

"Noes!" Garbage, Leaf, and Crusty yelled at once and took off before we could stop them.

They'd met Jadiera at some point in the past few years and built a bond. She even had her own group of faeries now.

I understood their concern, but I needed to talk to Jadiera and find out what was happening. I looked around, some of the faeries with us had met Jadiera during our channel crossing last year.

"Do any of you remember Jadiera? The nice pirate lady with a ship?" We were already walking our horses toward a large hill and then Bailinsea.

Penqow zipped forward. She was one of the hardest

faeries to watch move fast—the black and white random patterns on her made me dizzy when she flew.

"I's was!"

I nodded. "Can you reach the faeries with her and find out if everyone is okay?" Before I clarified how to reach out, Penqow vanished. I'd gotten mostly used to faeries popping through solid things, but into and out of thin air was always going to be disturbing.

A moment later Penqow popped back, along with two of Jadiera's faeries. At least I assumed that was why they had a tiny skull and crossbones on their overalls.

They hadn't had those the first time we met.

"Yours." The yellow one handed me a note, nodded to Penqow, and then popped back out. The second one waved, then also left.

"Thank you, Penqow. You didn't happen to see Garbage and the other two?" I opened the letter.

"Theys at ships. Says hi." Penqow nodded, then flew back to the faery mob.

"I wouldn't question it, you know how Garbage is. I assume the note says Jadiera is fine?" Mathilda cut me off before I could complain about Garbage, Leaf, and Crusty.

"Sorry." I scanned the short note. "Yup, they're fine and approaching Bailinsea from the waterway. Ran into some trouble on the way, and half of her ships are trapped in the islands. But she's glad we're coming to help."

"How many ships?" Padraig asked. The number of ships wouldn't matter in a land fight, but the number of crew on each would.

"She says eight ships and about a hundred and fifty fighters." I grinned. "And some heavy magic users."

"Good." Padraig began going up the hill and waved for all of us to pick up speed. "We need to be there, *now.*" A simple word to his horse and it took off and was over the hill.

Mathilda waved her hand. "We have to save Bailinsea!" With her yell, she, Lorcan, and Siabiane rode over the hill.

I rode in the middle of our group, behind Flower and the wildly screaming brownies, but in front of Alric, Covey, Cwin, and Foxy. I was a bit messed up about the timing still, but fortunately I didn't feel like I'd been awake for seven days.

My yell died as I almost brought my horse to a stop at the top of the hill. Bailinsea was in the middle of a wide plain which opened to the sea.

And was surrounded by massive armies of attackers.

The rest of our group had the same reaction I did and pulled to a halt. Mostly.

Covey yelled even louder, stayed on her horse until she reached the plain, then jumped off, and dove into a mob of elves holding a Dark banner. The dagger and circle mark of theirs had been secret once, but it wasn't anymore.

"I don't recommend duplicating her actions." Cwin rode past the rest of us and conferred with Padraig. They weren't running down the hill, but they were moving again.

"Shouldn't we go after her?" Although Covey was making a nice path as she worked her way through the Dark.

None of the other enemy fighters reacted to Covey, or the rest of us and continued marching toward the shielded village. It might have been me, but the faint glow of the shield didn't appear solid. It was fading in and out in spots.

"Covey's holding her own and I have a feeling our eyes are lying to us again. There are more protections on these than the umbaji illusions. I can't break all of it in a single shot, but this will tell us what we need to know," Lorcan spoke a few low words, and a spell slammed into the closest attackers to us. Unlike the umbaji, they didn't all vanish, but where there had been fifty in the group nearest to us, there were now fifteen.

"What kind of spell is this? I felt those umbaji we fought before." I wasn't going to let my friends face this alone, but I kind of wanted more of a plan. And for those fake ones to stop making things look worse than they were.

"Not a good one," Siabiane rode next to me. "Like so many we've been seeing lately, it's old. Extremely so. The spell of the umbaji was a more recent version. This one takes serious magic to use it. There are few who could complete it at this level. If we go down there with that spell in force, none of us will make it out. Covey will keep fighting until she dies if we don't stop the spell." She watched Cwin as her frown deepened.

"A siramage?" I whispered, but I had a feeling Cwin heard me. If Siabiane made the connection of who was able to use this type of spell, Cwin would have as well.

She didn't turn back to us. "I'd say one of my people switched sides." Her voice was steady, but she was sparking spells off her gray fur. "I didn't recognize the spell at first, and I'm still not certain of the caster, but I can destroy it completely. It won't stop any real fighters down there though and we need to be ready to fight our way to Bailinsea once I cast it."

Garbage, Leaf, and Crusty, each leading a flank of faeries, dropped over the fighters. Loud gronking pointed out that Bunky brought in chimera reinforcements. A few hundred of them filled a section of the sky.

"I've never met Jadiera, but I think the pirates have arrived." Alric had his long glass out and aimed toward the water. A mob waving the black pirate flag was coming our way.

"I'll give them a few more moments to catch up to us. But whoever is behind this will know who destroyed their spell the moment I break it." Cwin flexed her fingers and went full grimarian—fluffed-out fur, red eyes, and long teeth. "Don't challenge the real ones unless they block you, the village's shield is about to fall and we need to get there before it does."

A group of ten faeries popped in and startled my horse. All were wearing the skull and crossbones on their overalls. "Lady says thank yous for waiting. Cannons now. Big booms." The little yellow faery grinned and her group joined Garbage's.

"Cannons?" Foxy squinted toward the mob; they were moving a lot faster than I'd expected.

"Are those sails?" I had okay eyesight in my human form, but I wasn't sure what I saw rising over the approaching pirates.

"Yes, they are." Alric laughed. "They have landships. Small, but they're moving quickly. Magic must be filling the sails. And yes, they have cannons."

Covey was still going after more of the Dark, although she'd destroyed all of the banners near her.

Cwin watched Jadiera's people as they approached, then nodded and cast her spell.

The hill we were on shook and darkness filled the sky. Then a wind tried to push us all backward.

Cwin's laugh reminded me far too much of evil grimarian hilstrike mages as she snarled and sent another spell. "I know who you are now! You should have remained dead!"

The darkness exploded and the majority of the enemy fighters vanished.

Then the shield around Bailinsea shattered like a massive broken glass.

CHAPTER FIFTY-ONE

CANNON FIRE FROM THE PIRATE crews jolted me out of my shock, and my horse and I followed the rest of our friends down the hill. The cannons also did some major damage to the remaining enemies around them.

Cwin swore in a dozen languages and sent violent spells at anyone remotely in her way. "That bastard connected his spell to the base of the village shield!"

Jadiera's crew fired more cannons and a few horse riders broke away from the landships releasing spells ahead of them.

Unfortunately, once the shield fell, the enemy no longer cared about us. The only good thing was that few of them were on horseback so we had the advantage of speed.

"*Come find us…tower…right…hurry…*" The voice in my head faded almost too quickly for me to understand the words. It was Derry, but she probably passed out as she spoke.

I brought my horse alongside Mathilda, staying clear of her rapidly swinging staff. "They attacked the faeries in Bailinsea the same way they got ours, with varlick powder. Is it okay for our faeries to go in?" I figured we needed all the fighters we had, but if my faeries might be poisoned again, I would send them away.

Not to mention—if the enemy went to that much effort to sneak a spell through that shield, they feared something the faeries could do.

Mathilda didn't pause as she tossed me two pouches of her new cure. "Good luck! This will work faster than water and leaves them immune to another attack. Our faeries are also immune now. I made sure of that." She grinned and rode after a group of giants running for Bailinsea.

Alric followed her. Bailinsea had a wall and gates, but the enemies had the gates down in moments. My horse didn't need nudging as we ran for the open space.

"Good to see you, Taryn!" Jadiera's voice carried to me, even though her people were still a bit away. Most likely something she had for her ships, and like her cannons, had found a way to bring it along on land.

I waved in the direction of the mob, then I was through the broken gates. I needed to find wherever this diviner's scroll was, but we needed Derry and the rest of the faeries up and running first.

I made a sharp right and went for the first tower up against the outer wall. Two elven guards in full armor appeared unimpressed at my arrival.

I jumped off my horse and pulled out my sword and Rhyfel.

Rhyfel loved enemies in metal.

He gleefully crackled green arcs into both guards, then paused as they twitched. I swore he said something to my sword. My sword gave a reinforcing chirp, and Rhyfel went back to attacking the guards.

I raised my sword closer to my face. "Did you just tell him to go on?"

The sword's answering chirp indicated yes. Soon we'd be having full conversations over tea and biscuits.

The guard on the right fell over unconscious as the arcs of static attacked his metal suit and his body. The second one ripped the armor on his arms off, revealing a Dark tattoo, unsurprisingly, and then charged forward despite Rhyfel's continued attack.

The jolts still caused him to twitch, but he was fighting them.

My sword let loose the most annoying and discordant song I never hoped to hear again.

The Dark elf froze, doubled over, and I thought he was going to collapse. Then he straightened up and charged me with his sword raised to strike. Veins on his face, neck, and arms bulged and he appeared to be in extreme pain.

Good.

I held my sword and beat him back, but it was a near thing. He was taller than me but was as strong as Foxy. A few more matched strikes from each of us and we pulled back. The elf took his helmet off as Rhyfel continued trying to fry him.

He smiled and I heard footsteps running up behind me.

I switched Rhyfel to my sword hand, grabbed my push spell, spun around, and released the magic.

To be fair, I'd been without my magic for a while, and Fardoragh's spell to fix the issue might have bumped things up a bit. But I was almost as surprised as the five members of the Dark as they went flying into the air.

Judging by their fading screams, I began to doubt that.

I turned to face my remaining foe and raised my empty hand.

He debated for a moment, but whatever my sword's song had done to him was still messing him up and he was batting at his ears. With a snarl, he feinted toward me before running further into the village.

Fine by me. I moved Rhyfel back over then ran to the tower door and kicked it open. Which might or might not have been needed, but I had a lot of adrenaline.

There was nothing but junk on the bottom floor so I ran up the curving stairs. To find a few hundred faeries collapsed everywhere, including over each other. Derry was passed out near Queen Mungoosey, and even in sleep still appeared to be protecting her.

I pulled them over and used the powder Mathilda gave me on both. Much easier than having a cat clean them. From the sounds outside, the fight in the village was a rough one.

I now regretted kicking in the door.

Derry recovered first and started swinging her fists without opening her eyes.

"Direidus Saliva! It's me! Taryn!"

"Oh, good." She opened her eyes, grinned, crawled to the queen, and started shaking her.

Luckily the queen was more composed upon waking than Derry had been.

"The shield fell, the city is under attack, we need the scroll, and I have this to wake the rest of the faeries up." I held up the two bags.

"One for each of us," Queen Mungoosey gave me a very feline smile, including a brief slow blink. "Thank you, Taryn. We'll wake them, go take care of the rest. Some people will be extremely unhappy to see us."

I nodded and scrambled back down the stairs. I had no idea where any of my friends, including Nasif and Dueble, were, but my horse was still where I left her. I sheathed my weapons and got back in the saddle.

The boom of two cannons going off gave me direction.

I returned to the main gate and I got to see two of the mysterious landships in person as they raced by. They really did appear to be small, very flat, ships. Ones that each had a massive ship's cannon mounted to the flat deck.

Jadiera spotted me from the lead one and waved. "Did

you save some for us?" Her deep red-brown hair was tied back, but it wasn't going to stay that way for long.

"More than plenty! Good to see you!" I yelled, but she was quickly out of sight. Considering there wasn't an alarmingly strong wind in the area, I was pretty sure magic users were still filling the landships' sails.

I had a feeling that Alric and Padraig would be bugging her for how to build them when this was over.

Sounds of fighting came from further into the village so I turned my horse to follow.

The faeries flew past me, yelling something. Derry dropped down in her war feathers.

"Run! We're holding back what we can, but they planted lathisite on the base of the village walls! They are triggering an explosion!"

I'd never heard of lathisite until recently, one of the towns under attack by the Dark mined it. But the reaction from all of my magic using friends when it had been mentioned wasn't good.

It was a dangerously unstable explosive.

I wanted to help the faeries but knew that even if I changed shape, I wouldn't have a clue what they were planning to do.

A wave of gronking chimeras passed overhead, leaving the walls. They didn't sound happy and appeared to have been sent away.

Mathilda came racing up on her horse. "Where did the faeries go?"

I explained and expected her to send us after them, but she grabbed my arm and shook her head. "The faeries can slow down the destruction, but it's too late for them to stop it. Too complicated to explain now, but faeries can modify lathisite." She didn't release my arm but nudged her horse away from the walls. "It's why the enemy compromised the faeries. Help me get everyone away from the walls."

I nodded and we raced in opposite directions. Luckily, it seemed most of the villagers had moved closer to the center of the village. But I did chase a few out. The fact that no enemy fighters remained out this far wasn't a good sign.

What I couldn't understand was why whoever was behind this still wanted to take down the walls. They were already inside.

Then the largest explosion I ever heard almost knocked my horse over.

CHAPTER FIFTY-TWO

THE SOUND WAS DEAFENING AND I couldn't hear anything even though people and animals were running around and yelling.

Then there was a massive popping sound and I heard everything.

Including a horrific roaring sound and a wave of heat coming from behind me.

I spun my horse, ready to jump free of the saddle and transform into a dragon if needed.

But instead of another fire-breathing monster, I faced an odd orangish-yellow, slow-moving wall that filled the entire width of the village. It was the height of the village walls, and only about a foot closer than they'd been, but whatever it was, it was moving.

The mass of faeries came zipping overhead, looking more fatigued than I'd ever seen them.

Queen Mungoosey, Derry, and Garbage dropped down to me. They were covered in soot but weren't injured that I could tell.

Queen Mungoosey dropped closer to me. "Thank you for saving us. My people and I couldn't stop the spellfire caused by the explosion. We slowed it down, but couldn't keep it from happening." There was more sorrow than I'd ever heard from a faery in her voice.

"You need to rescue the diviner's scroll, find Marluk, then save everyone else."

Derry and Garbage remained silent but nodded solemnly. The entire mass flew toward the center of the village.

There was no fighting now as I continued heading toward the center of the village. The people I saw were villagers without a single enemy facing us. We needed to escape, but I knew we couldn't let the people behind this get the diviner's scroll.

I also had no idea how to find it.

The sound of horses running up behind me caused me to turn and raise my sword. It was Alric and Padraig, both looking roughed up, but no obvious injuries.

The enemy had fighters, but not enough real ones. They'd been counting on their spellfire to do the work. And any of their people who'd survived had fled once the spell hit.

"We need to get the villagers out of here." Alric didn't jump off his horse and run to me, but he looked like it crossed his mind.

"I need to find Marluk and that scroll." I nodded toward the wall of creeping spellfire. "How long do we have?"

Padraig watched it for a moment then turned back. "I've never heard of one moving that slowly. They're a tricky spell and something broke part of it."

"We's dos!" Garbage yelled as a small faery gang of herself, Leaf, Crusty, and ten more zipped over from behind a building. They were still covered in soot but smiling.

Alric smiled back. "The faeries messed up the spellfire? Excellent work, ladies. Do you know where Marluk or the scroll Taryn needs is?"

I figured he was pushing things, but Crusty dropped down and stood on my shoulder. "I knows!"

Garbage beamed as if it was all her doing. "She knows! Goes!"

I'd never had a faery command my horse before, or seen it done, but Crusty raced down from my shoulder, ran to my horse's head, and whispered in her ear.

My horse took off at a full run with Padraig and Alric swearing behind me.

Garbage and her crew escorted us, but it was Crusty's directions that my horse was listening to.

I needed to find the scroll and Marluk, but I wasn't sure what I felt about Crusty, or any faery, taking over my horse.

We made a few sharp turns before reaching a small group of enemy fighters who had circled a sealed building and were trying to get inside. Three dead village guards were piled up against the wall.

The building was only a single story, had no windows, and was extremely bland.

My horse ran right for it.

"Crusty? We need to stop!" I pulled the reins but they had no effect. Crusty waited until we were almost to the enemy fighters, then patted my horse's head.

"Nows."

My horse did stop. But then she spun around and kicked out at the two closest enemies and sent them flying.

"Crusty? What are you doing?" I hung on but had no control over my horse.

"We's needs in!"

Alric and Padraig jumped off their horses and made short work of the remaining enemy guards.

That was something to deal with later.

I jumped off my horse and drew my sword and Rhyfel as Alric blasted the door with a low-level explosion spell.

"Are you sure this is the place?" There were more

than a few ornate buildings that I would have checked first.

Crusty jumped off my horse and sat on my head. "Yes! This way!" She tugged my hair to make me run forward.

Padraig and Alric followed closely.

Then my sword started singing.

"I thought we agreed that singing during a fight wasn't good?"

He gave a chirp and continued singing anyway. Rhyfel's green arcs kept time with him.

"He's knowing where to goes! Ooo! Bads!" Crusty jerked my hair and sent us off to a small room to the right.

Someone was tied to a post. He looked up at our approach—it was Marluk. One eye was closing and he was covered in bruises.

He was gagged as well. Alric, Crusty, and I untied him while Padraig kept watch around us.

I helped Marluk to his feet. "Can you walk?"

"Lady Taryn, I can run if I need to." He took my hands then his eyes grew round. "You! You are the one, and you hold the other three scrolls. Had we only known sooner. Too late now. We must get the scroll." He started to run out of the small room, then stopped. "You have to promise me that you will protect this scroll with your life. *All* of your lives." He nodded to Alric and Padraig.

They both gave short nods.

"I promise?" Crusty jerked my hair at that moment so it came out with a yelp.

"Good. Follow me." Marluk wasn't a young man, he'd retired from a life on the sea a long time ago. But, even beaten up, he was fast.

The small plain building had a secret chamber under it.

Padraig froze as we passed books and relics under protective spells.

Marluk said a word and all of the protections fell. "Take what you can, this place will be destroyed."

Padraig grabbed what he could and Alric helped. The faery bags they had were getting a good workout.

Marluk led me to a thin, long, and narrow black box. "Place your hands on the top. And think of who you are."

I wanted more explanation than that, but we were out of time. I did what he said before Crusty could pull my hair again.

The box opened and a scroll that looked like it had been old before my parents were born appeared.

"You *are* the one. Take the scroll in its box. Do you have somewhere safe to hide it? Like your friends?" Marluk noticed Padraig and Alric using the faery bags.

I grabbed one of my black bags and gently put the box and scroll inside, then tucked the bag away.

"Now we run!" Marluk again defied his age as he sprinted to the main floor then out the door.

Our horses were still there, but no one else was in sight.

"They've gone to the back, come on." Marluk took off running so we led our horses after him.

The village looked hauntingly beautiful, but there was no one in sight.

Finally, we rounded a corner and were met with a wall of archers. "Halt!"

CHAPTER FIFTY-THREE

MARLUK HELD UP HIS HANDS. "You know me, these are my friends."

I saw my friends, including Nasif and Dueble, behind the archers in a mass of people and animals that reached back further than I could see. Most of our friends looked ready to start spell flinging if the archers didn't stand down.

Then a massive wave of faeries and chimeras came swooping down to block the archers.

"You will stand down, valiant defenders." Queen Mungoosey, still flanked by Derry and Garbage, waved to the archers.

They lowered their weapons.

My friends pushed their way forward and hugged the three of us. Jadiera and her crews were there as well and she grabbed Marluk fiercely.

"We must leave," Marluk said. He wasn't hysterical, years as a pirate might have removed that emotion, but he was closer to it now that the adrenaline was leaving his system. "Bailinsea will fall. It has fallen. We're funneling villagers out to our secret cove along the ocean entrance and can get them to safety along the coastline." He watched the slow-rolling, but unstoppable, wall of flame as spellfire swallowed his village.

The faeries slowed it down and saved hundreds of

lives, but they couldn't stop it. I shuddered when I realized how much worse it would have been if they'd not regained consciousness.

Jadiera swore. "I'm sorry. I thought we could save it. Do you have a safe destination? We can come around to that side with our ships and escort yours."

He shook his head. "I'll be sailing with you if you don't mind, I'm the guardian of the diviner's scroll. We have ships for everyone in Bailinsea, including their livestock, and the ships can protect themselves—hopefully they won't need to. They were a last chance option if things went bad. I need your crews and ships to be a distraction, to lead the enemies away. I'm hoping that seeing me and Taryn's group leave through the channel will draw the enemies after your ships."

Jadiera nodded. "Solid thinking." Then turned to the rest of us. "I hope none of you get seasick, beyond Taryn. I'm not sure when or where I can get you back to the mainland, but none of us can remain here."

Marluk moved his people faster than I would have guessed. They would be safe, but this place was gone. Considering the villagers they'd wanted to destroy, along with the artifacts and scrolls, were going to survive, I'd say the enemy failed.

But it was a painful win.

"Just tell us where to go." Padraig glanced at all of us and handed me a few wither sticks that appeared out of nowhere. I shoved them into my cloak pocket glumly. Better than being sick the entire trip, but still not ideal. I had no idea where we were going or how long we'd be on the water.

Nasif had his arm in a sling, but his color was good. "Dueble and I will return to the *tir cudd*. Ageora has some important information on mapping the other *tir cudds* and finding the rest of the deities. We'll be safe there no matter what happens out here." He paused and turned to Marluk, "Your people could come in as well. Then return when the spellfire is gone."

Marluk smiled. "Thank you. But even just having heard of these things, I can tell you my people wouldn't go. We're mostly old sea dogs and our families; we have a lot of superstitions. And seeing Bailinsea once it is gone would be too painful. They will start again far from here. Maybe even to the north." He clasped Nasif's good arm. "Stay safe."

Nasif and Dueble gave all of us quick hugs, then ran down an alley.

Jadiera gave a sharp whistle and the surviving landships moved closer. "Are your horses sound?"

"It appears they held up better than the rest of us. But I'm not sure that they can run to your ships. It's been a hard fight for everyone." Alric had already checked the horses in case we needed to make a run through that spellfire.

"I can help with that. A short fada spell will get us there, and won't draw unwanted attention. Using prolonged magic right now wouldn't be a good idea with that spellfire still running." Cwin tilted her head toward Jadiera. "But I'd need to know where your ships really are."

Jadiera grinned. "Good of you to notice. I have three mages hiding their real location. Shalin, can you show the nice lady?" She waved to a slim half-elf with long blond hair.

He bowed to Cwin and lifted his open palm past her eyes.

"Well done. I know how to get there now." Cwin grinned. "We should move. Your people are okay with the path? The landships will fit."

"Anything is better than that." Jadiera pointed to the slow-moving, but inescapable, wall of spellfire.

Cwin called up the fada path quickly and all of us,

landships, faeries, constructs, brownies, and horses ran for it. The mass of chimeras had left once they were done. Bunky had appeared concerned but said they had other fights. I wanted the brownies to ride, they'd fought hard here and were clearly exhausted, but Flower and his men were too proud and ran alongside the landships.

"Boats! Yays! Have booms!" Garbage led the massive faery fleet into the tunnel. Queen Mungoosey and Derry led a smaller wave of faeries to follow the villagers on their ships after both said goodbye to me. Derry said she'd find us once the other ships were safe.

This fada path was wider than others but extremely solid. And short, the ending was visible the moment I stepped inside.

The eight large ships we dropped in front of at the end of the path appeared fully exposed, but no enemy fighters were in sight. I'd take Jadiera's and Cwin's word for it that they weren't where I thought we'd seen them.

A few magic words from Alric, Lorcan, and Siabiane, and the horses calmly walked up the ramp to the *Dangerous Lady*. They'd spend the voyage in a contented half-daze spell below deck.

Alric brought me to the railing. "You need to stay here. No fighting on the ocean, no magic, nothing." He kissed me. "You're not water-friendly."

Considering that he'd been the one to dive in and save me when I fought with Edana over the ocean, I couldn't argue.

"But this is different. And we made the other crossing fine."

"No." Another quick kiss and he went to join the rest of our magic users.

I popped a wither stick in my mouth the moment the ship pulled away.

Marluk joined me at the railing and watched his village consume itself, but his face was impassive. He turned to me with a sad smile. "You'll be glad to have those sticks, I have a feeling our Jadiera is planning on leading them on a merry chase."

"They taste awful, but better for all of us if I have them." I paused. "Are you okay?" It sounded inane, the man had fought to protect his village and was now watching its demise. But I needed to say something.

He patted my hand. "I will be. What was lost were buildings. The soul of Bailinsea is in its people, and the enemies were trying to destroy that as well as the diviner's scroll. We are at war. And it's not one I intend to let them win." His grin was fierce and chased the sadness from his eyes.

"Agreed. We now have all four of the scrolls, plus a lot of stuff that Padraig and the others were excited about. Hopefully, my friends can sort out what the scrolls mean and why they're important." I nodded to where Mathilda and Padraig were discussing something. The others were below deck.

"The diviner's scroll has finally found its holder. We'd begun to believe that you might not be real, you know. Your friends will be involved, but you will lead the final charge—with the scroll's help." He nodded solemnly.

Before I could ask what he meant, the woman in the crow's nest yelled down.

"Captain! Two enemy ships off the stern. Coming fast!"

I was close enough to the front that I heard Jadiera's swearing. "Faeries! Take your positions on the sails and cover all of our ships."

The eight ships were clumped fairly close but were beginning to spread out as we moved further from shore. Yup, there were two ships, smaller than the ones Jadiera commanded, but they were coming up behind us way too fast not to have been magically enhanced.

"I want us to get to the open ocean before they catch us. Faeries, on my mark, push the sails." Jadiera had a strange horn that sent her voice across to the other ships. Every ship had a group of faeries waiting at the sails.

We seemed to already be moving fairly fast and the spit of land that marked the end of the mainland for the south approached faster than I expected.

"Faeries, mark!" None of them hesitated at Jadiera's yell and all eight ships picked up speed.

"Ten more enemy ships off the port bow, coming from the islands." The woman in the crow's nest kept her voice calm, but within moments even I could see the ships facing us.

Unlike the two chasing us, they were huge.

"Cannon fire!" The yell came from the ship nearest to us and Jadiera increased her swearing. "Everyone except this ship head toward the Jacobian Islands, don't go home until it's been clear for a few days. No debates."

The crew on the ship closest to us looked as confused as I felt. There was more safety in numbers, even if we were outnumbered.

"What do you want me to do, captain?" Shalin watched as the other seven ships changed direction.

Jadiera's smile wasn't friendly as she watched the enemy ships change direction to follow the rest of her crew. "We need them to follow us until we can lose them. Make it work, Shalin, use whatever you need."

Mathilda, Lorcan, Padraig, Cwin, and Alric came closer to the grinning half-elf. I couldn't hear them, but it appeared that their offer of help was accepted.

I chewed harder on my wither stick and hung on to the railing. Marluk went down below to help with the cannons. Covey and Foxy were nearby but appeared to be engrossed in the wild chase.

Copies of the other seven ships appeared around us, including the faeries who were now all pushing our sails.

Then I noticed the actual rest of Jadiera's ships vanished. And we were going faster than I'd ever flown, and appeared to be wildly out of control.

CHAPTER FIFTY-FOUR

W E'D MANAGED TO PASS THE ships facing us without damage due to our speed and spells thrown by Shalin and two fellow magic users on the ship. They also maintained the illusion of all seven other ships. But now twelve ships were chasing us.

The faeries were good, but I was pretty sure this was their maximum speed.

"Vortex dead ahead, captain!"

"Thank you!" The laughter that followed from Jadiera was a bit disturbing. I didn't think there was any way for something with that name to be good. For anyone.

I was trying to hide my panic, but Jadiera turned to me from the helm and grinned.

"It's okay. We couldn't fight them fair, so we're going to cheat." She grabbed a pair of heavy ropes near her and handed me one. "All hands, prepare for the vortex! Secure yourselves and seal below decks!"

That didn't sound good, but even with shaking fingers, I tied the rope around my waist and watched as my friends did as well.

"All magic users, drop the illusion and help us with speed!" Jadiera turned the wheel sharply as the illusion ships vanished and our magic users sent support to the faeries in the masts. Shalin and the other two pirate mages created a mist around us. Not enough for the following ships to lose us, but enough to confuse what they saw.

A whirling dark mouth appeared in the deep water before us. For a moment, I feared Jadiera had been at sea too long.

The ships chasing us slowed down as it came into full view.

"The people you want are here! Come get them!" Jadiera used her horn to call to the enemy ships.

The ships picked up speed again.

My friends were tied into whatever was going on with the sails. I thought I trusted Jadiera; the faeries were rarely wrong about people, but I would blow her off this ship if she was betraying us.

A lot happened at once.

Jadiera yelled for the faeries and mages to stand down from increasing our speed. She turned the helm to circle to the edge of the vortex in the water. It was even more terrifying up close.

"Hold!" She kept one hand up and the faeries and magic users stayed in place but didn't push the ship.

I'd think two hands would be better when facing a gaping pit trying to swallow your ship. But I was never going to become a sailor. Or a pirate.

"Now!" The *Dangerous Lady* groaned as the ship fought the helm as we continued our circle. The first two ships behind us weren't as lucky and were pulled into the gaping swirl of water and destroyed. The next two fought longer, but they were also lost.

The rest radically reversed course. It looked like a few were damaged, but they managed to move clear.

I was about to breathe again when two cannonballs crossed the vortex. One missed our ship by inches, the second one caught us in the side right at the waterline. The vortex spun us away and we careened far from the remaining ships. The magic fog spell clung to them and grew denser as we left.

"All hands, keep us up!"

All of the magic users were pale and clearly exhausted but were doing what they could to keep us from sinking. It might have been a last-ditch random cannon shot, but it was a lucky one. Even I could tell without using magic we were going down fast.

So much for all of my enemies wanting me alive.

"Faeries! Push!" Jadiera yelled and the masts were full of faeries before she finished.

We were moving at a good speed, but we were still sinking.

"What can I do?" I was tired from the battle for Bailinsea, but so were my friends. They hadn't wanted me to do anything on the ship, but we didn't have a choice at this point.

"Do you know any spells to keep a ship afloat?" Jadiera kept fighting the helm. "I know a safe place to hide, but it's going to take longer to get there than we have, even with the faeries."

I started to shake my head, considering that my people hated water, I doubted there was any such spell in the Ancients' magic books. "But I have a push spell. Maybe I can keep the water from the hole?" I took a chomp to grip my wither stick and looked over the side. "Yup, I might be able to."

"Try, we're out of options." Jadiera went back to swearing at the listing ship as she fought the helm.

I focused a low-level, tight version of my push spell at the water near the cannon hole. Water moved out of the way, but not enough. The waves were making it difficult, but I kept at it. Finally, only a small amount of water was getting in. That was the best I could do.

A glance up showed me at least two islands ahead, but only one was close. Too close.

"Stop pushing and brace!" Jadiera yelled a moment before the ship slammed into something under the water.

I almost tumbled over the railing but Alric was fast and grabbed me. Even though I still had the rope tight around my waist, I wasn't going to argue.

Everyone dropped low and hung on to anything heavy they had near them as the ship scraped over hidden reefs. Aside from the faeries who squealed with laughter as the ship jolted to a halt on a wide beach.

"I think we lost them," Marluk said as he came up from below. There were no signs of any ships following us, just a few planks of debris that followed our path. "Don't know that I've been on this island before."

"It definitely wasn't one I was hoping for." Jadiera picked herself up. "It's one of the lost islands, said to be myths, but I recognize that outline." She pointed to a distinctive mountain range in the distance. "Few survivors over the centuries, but this was used as a cautionary tale to young sailors. We need to secure this ship against the tide. It's in bad shape, but it's all we have."

The crew and our people worked to get the ship higher up the beach. My contribution was again a controlled push spell from the back. We were all soggy but the *Dangerous Lady* was far above the tide line when we finished.

"Is there anyone living here?" The island was larger than I thought, but no signs of civilization that I could see.

Marluk shook his head. "No one lives in the lost islands, no one can usually *find* the lost islands. We're on our own."

Cwin shook the seawater off her fur and surveyed the area. "I've lived in worse. And I think it might be good that no one can find us for a bit."

All the magic users, except for Cwin and me, dropped to the sand, and even the faeries appeared tired. Foxy and Covey helped the crew bring out the horses. They were still in their spell-daze and calmly went where they were led. The brownies and constructs came out of the cannon hole.

Bunky and Irving went to the faeries, Welsy and Delsy ran to Siabiane, and Flower and his brownies surveyed the land. "So. Where should we build?"

**The End for now—
the story will continue in
The Mystic's Scepter—
The Lost Ancients: Dragon's Blood Book Five!**

D EAR READER,
I am so grateful for you following the exploits of the faeries and their crew (Garbage is threatening me… so it's their crew…not Taryn's…. or mine…OUCH!)

I hope you're enjoying these stories as much as I love writing them. Part of me thinks I would love to have the faeries with me in real life, the other part is terrified. But they are fun to write and read!

There will be two more books after this one to close out The Lost Ancients: Dragon's Blood series. The next title is The Mystic's Scepter and will be out early 2026. There will be more adventures in this world (Garbage! Stop jabbing me!) but this series will close at 6 books (hmmmm—like the first series ;)).

If you want to keep up on the further adventures of any of my characters, make sure to visit my website and sign up for my mailing list. *http://marieandreas.com/index. html* or scan the QR code below.

I don't send a lot of emails, but it's the best way to follow me.

Another good way is through BookBub. You can sign up for notifications of new releases as well as preorders. *https://www.bookbub.com/authors/marie-andreas*

If you enjoyed this book, please spread the word! Positive reviews are like emotional gold to any writer. And means more than you know.

Thank you again—and keep reading!
Marie

About the Author

Marie is a multi-award-winning fantasy and science fiction author with a serious reading addiction. If she wasn't writing about all the people in her head, she'd be lurking about coffee shops annoying total strangers with her stories. So really, writing is a way of saving the masses. She lives in Southern California and is owned by two very faery-minded cats. She is also a member of SFWA (Science Fiction and Fantasy Writers Association) and Novelists, Inc.

When not saving the masses from coffee shop shenanigans, Marie likes to visit the UK and keeps hoping someone will give her a nice summer home in the Forest of Dean or Conwy, Wales.